The Elite Prodigies Series

Code

Jon Gibson

ISBN

Paperback: 978-1-969120-14-5
Hardcover: 978-1-969120-15-2

About The Book

Long ago, an apocalypse shook Earth to its core. Emerging from the ashes were the Elites: humans whose DNA had been entirely rewritten. With seven supernatural abilities at their disposal, they painstakingly remolded Earth into a Pangaea over time. Now, in the distant future, they sharpen their skills within academies across their supposedly "utopian" nation.

Enter Ethan Crambe, child of one of the nation's leaders. Following his expulsion from his own academy, he's unwillingly transferred to one closer to his father. His sole directive: assimilate and avoid trouble.

Unfortunately, the promise takes a hit when Benjamin Valdez, a second-year student at Ethan's new academy, falls victim to an enigmatic attack.

Thrusted into events against their will, they embark on a quest for answers about the assault. However, unraveling the truth requires putting their lives on the line.

Embark on a journey to a reimagined Earth, where the essence of humanity takes on a new definition.

Table of Contents

Chapter 1:
Warzone

In the Year of 633 P.H.

Benjamin Valdez stumbled forward, coughing for oxygen. Black smoke in the air strangled his lungs. The situation around him was critical.

The rainforest he stood in was on fire, sending everything into a chaotic frenzy. What were once beautiful lush green vines and tropical trees on a starry night were now in violent flames. Sky once bejeweled with stars, was now dropping red-hot flames. The woodland became a trampling ground for blank panthers that mercilessly stomped over the vibrant purple orchids and lobster-claw flowers – tearing through dozens of fellow men and women running among the chaos.

Blue poison frogs launched from behind the stunning flora in the forest. Thousands of Toucans screeched a terrible tale – immediately fleeing into the skies. Armadillos rolled away in fear as squirrel monkeys screamed out in the woods.

The night sky was looming with a bloody hue as flashes of red lightning ran across the 1.2 billion acres of land. Several fights continued to break out by the riverbed, with the bodies of the deceased floating downstream. The air smelled of deep undertones of death and decay. Many Elites resorted to trees to seek shelter, while others hid behind the piles of bodies stacked around them.

Running out of breath, Benjamin slid to cover behind a pile of bodies. His hands shook as he lay behind the corpses of his kind – eyes stinging with drops of salt water dripping from his forehead. His vision was painted red with blood as he lifted his hands to wipe the sweat off. His mouth began retching his breakfast onto the ground no sooner than a second later. It took him a minute to catch his breath. His nerves were shot, and he latched on to a faraway thought of happiness. The miserable boy felt a despicable presence or a lack thereof.

Benjamin struggled to halt his hands from trembling with fear. All he could think was: this forest is a warzone. Adrenaline is better than death. Adrenaline is better than death. Adrenaline is better than death, he muttered under his breath in an attempt to calm his nerves.

Someone was wailing nearby in pain, snapping him from his thoughts. The ground was rumbling in the distance, shaking the forest. Benjamin's breathing became uneven again. He peered over the pile of bodies and saw someone lying on their back, crying. Benjamin crouched down to the ground.

"What do I do? How should I-I—I—?" He was mortified. He couldn't speak or form the words to actualize this experience.

"Please, anyone, help me… I don't wanna die here." The Elite sobbed weakly.

Benjamin placed his hands on his mouth, screaming at the top of his lungs, hoping it might take away some of his fear. He then huffed himself up and ran in the direction of the Elite.

Finally reaching who turned out to be a young boy, he saw the red robes, identifying him as a Brute Class user. Ben crouched down to meet his eyes. "We don't have much time. Can you stand?" he asked.

The boy made an effort to what seemed like shake his head. His face was scarred with burns. "Thank you… helping me. I… am trying… to… escape." The Brute coughed hoarsely, barely managing to get the words out of his mouth.

He leaned on Benjamin's waist as they stood up and stumbled towards cover. As they made their way through the terrain-covered forest, their ears rang with explosions. Ben tried to distract his mind – comparing the sound to corn kernels popping viciously one after another; *Pop, bang. Pop, Bang*; branches falling in every direction.

Like arrows flying from the sky, the branches boomed around the two of them. Benjamin screamed in his head – terrified a branch may land on them as they ran. The boy cried out loud. Every movement around him forced a flinch out of him.

"Keep moving! We don't have time to stop!" Benjamin screamed.

"I'm trying! My leg isn't healing for some reason!" he cried as he hobbled along Benjamin.

Benjamin shuddered. Their bodies recovered supernaturally. If it hadn't healed after all this time, the boy must have been hurt.

A bolt of red lightning cracked down in front of them, raising the hair on the back of his neck. The heat felt like a thousand suns on Benjamin's skin. The light draped a curtain before their eyes as the Brute fell into the dirt and winced in pain.

Benjamin's anxiety shot up like a live wire. "Get up, Brute! We don't have time!" He reached down and grunted as he lifted the Elite back up. They limped further into the tree line, the heat swirling around them.

Benjamin propped him up against an enormous rubber tree. White substance dripped out of the tree onto the boy's shoulder. The gashes in the tree trunk made it look like it was crying.

Closing his eyes as he tried to fill his lungs with some air, the Brute muttered weakly, "I just want to go home." Benjamin said nothing. Medics ran up and down the scene, entering the carnage. Two medics rushed by and took over for Benjamin.

"Don't let these kids die," Ben whispered and ran into the heart of the forest.

It was melancholy for miles and miles. Screams of agony and pain played a distorted symphony. Fiery explosions set destruction to the forest. The skies poured red lightning downwards, violently assaulting the ground.

Ben found himself standing in the center of all of the chaos. On one side, groups of Elites were fighting back against opal-robed individuals. On the other, plenty were fighting each other in droves.

Elites in green robes were tactically in groups of four. They used their elemental abilities as they danced and weaved between trees. Without hesitation, they generously shot flames from their hands to their targets, attacking everyone but their own.

Brilliant colors of ruby red- and white-hot flames combust; they oozed from the tree branches and delicately layered around him, inches away from his bronze skin. Benjamin could feel the heat glazing the epidermis of his arms and face. He tore away with an underlying feeling of disgust and confusion, taking way in a new direction.

These Naturalist Elites crushed the very ground on which they stood, leaving elemental devastation in their wake. They chomped on the dirt like beasts, allowing themselves power.

The ground quaked fiercely, causing many to scream from the fissures that pulled them in. The air felt tight and constricted with more dust than oxygen. The deeper Benjamin went into the forest, the worst the visibility became with fog.

Neon-red lightning struck the night sky and crackled as speed-gifted Elites nearby drew on its electrical charges for power. They zigzagged through the woodland area.

Benjamin peered ahead, his gaze piercing through the gaps of trees and bushes. The jungle enveloped the colossal Citadel nestled in the heart of the forest.

Raising his eyes, he locked onto the dark, looming vortex spiraling atop the Citadel, which absorbed dark blue and white energy in its grip.

"GET DOWN!" someone screamed. Benjamin swiftly dove to the ground as a flaming red fireball whizzed past him, hurdling into a nearby Kapok tree.

The burning tree crackled and spat, unleashing an ear-splitting sound resonating from its ancient roots. The aged wood groaned like worn floorboards, prompting Benjamin to roll away just in time. A wave of fiery air brushed against his back. Dazed, he wiped the soot off his face, his ears still ringing.

A girl rushed up to Benjamin, extending a hand stained with blood. Noticing his gaze, she bashfully wiped her hands on her muddy gray robes.

"Hey, that was insane! Are you okay?" Her green eyes glowed amidst the soot smudging her face.

"What did you say?" Benjamin struggled to hear over the nearby explosions.

"Are you okay?!" she repeated, raising her voice.

"I need to reach that Citadel! But I fear I'll perish before I can even try," Benjamin grunted, pointing through the thick foliage as he sat up.

A monkey screeched by, startling them both. The girl shouted, "We all have a role to play. Keep moving!"

Benjamin realized he had no idea who this girl was. Yet, amidst the chaos, she displayed kindness and smiled. So, when she reached out her hand to help him up, he took it.

As Benjamin struggled to rise, he stumbled and fell back down. Closing his eyes in pain, a blinding, fiery red light flashed before him, followed by a tremendous tremor. When he opened his eyes, the girl had vanished. Only a severed, bloodied hand remained in her place.

He dropped it into the blazing dirt and sat still, processing what had just happened. Benjamin briefly couldn't hear the shouted commands in the nearby distance. Instead, a ringing sound resonated in his ears. Benjamin realized she must have been vaporized.

Regrettably, conflict took center stage, drowning out all serenity and order. Wiping away tears, Benjamin remembered his location. With a grunt, he rose to his feet and sprinted deeper into the forest.

He began a mantra—He cannot die here.

As he surveyed the surroundings, ensuring a safe path to the Citadel, the surrounding Elites began to recognize him. Others tending to the wounded cried out, "Clear the way! He must reach the Tower!" The words rippled through the injured like a wave, and Benjamin realized these people entrusted their lives to him.

Driven by that conviction, Benjamin hastened toward the pivotal point that would determine their collective fate. He touched nearby Elites, replicating their Code, causing his eyes to ignite with a fiery orange.

"Where is everyone else?" He spoke to himself. Pausing for a moment, he scanned his surroundings to orient himself. Worry began to creep in.

Benjamin could replicate the power of a Pulse Class Elite; there were plenty in the vicinity. With that Code, he could locate his comrades.

But Benjamin was well aware of the risks involved. He would rather not risk losing his sight due to a mistake.

In the midst of his distraction, an enemy seized the opportunity and struck him from behind. Benjamin was disoriented, forcing him to employ one of the Codes he had copied.

Suddenly, everything halted. He looked around, perceiving with heightened clarity, realizing he had replicated the power of a Sprite Class Elite. Everything became lucid, accompanied by a ringing in his ear.

No, he understood what was transpiring. It wasn't merely that everything had stopped; he was also processing information faster than it occurred. He had mere seconds to make a choice, with no time to spare.

Raising his hand to the sky, he became a conduit for a crimson bolt of lightning. The surge of red energy coursed through his body. Briefly shutting his eyes, he endured the sheer force of the lightning within him.

Using the speedster ability, red electrical currents burst all around his body as he propelled himself closer to the Citadel. He winced in pain. Being a non-Sprite Class user, moving at such a rapid pace would eventually take a toll on him, even risking his life over time. Yet, he had no choice.

Benjamin dashed and weaved through the sea of Elites, each determined to achieve their objectives. His skin began to burn and peel as he swiftly passed multiple skirmishes.

Time was their enemy, and Benjamin keenly understood this. Sound started to catch up, resembling a tape recorder playing in reverse. Elites gradually resumed their normal speed.

Sliding on the ground, he evaded flames shooting in his direction, rolling seamlessly into a sprint. He yelled at a nearby gray-robed Elite, "Hurry, I need you to launch me toward that building!" The Shifter's eyes turned gray, extending his hand and slashing open a black spatial rift.

Benjamin raced toward the dark portal—a long, black gash in the air that swiftly opened before him. In the same instant, his gray-robed ally began to scream, engulfed in flames from behind. Benjamin squeezed his eyes shut in fear as he leaped through the portal, attempting to drown out the sound of the Elite's agony.

Upon jumping in, the world around him dissolved into nothingness. He encountered a resistant force within the void. If only he had been born a Spatial Class user, he would have been able to perceive everything in his surroundings. Relying solely on his senses, he pushed through the darkness until he emerged from the portal, finding himself in a chamber within the Citadel.

The grandiose room housed a round table adorned with seven chairs. A chilling breeze crept through the dimly lit chamber. Silver and gold accents adorned the walls, while chandeliers with exquisite gemstones and flickering candles swayed, showering dust from above.

Coughing and swatting away the dust, Benjamin stepped over rubble on the floor, crunching shards of glass beneath his feet. Swiftly scanning the chamber, his eyes widened as he sifted through a multitude of documents on the table. "Wait a minute... These are the results from all the—" Suddenly, a massive explosion erupted, demolishing the ceiling above.

Two Elites plummeted from the collapsing debris, crashing onto the table. Benjamin stood frozen, disbelief etched on his face.

"Kira? Liam? Why aren't you at the top? Where is everyone else?" Benjamin fired off rapid questions. Kira stood up, wincing as she brushed off her clothes, her once glittering gray robe now singed.

Liam sat up and whispered to himself, "They're dead. Oh no, they're so dead." His bloodshot eyes darted anxiously. He removed his blood-splattered, glittery red robe and cast it to the ground. "Who's dead?" Benjamin's expression turned grave.

Kira glanced at Liam before returning her focus to Benjamin. "We were betrayed. Nothing is going according to plan, and we must still reach the top with the others."

Benjamin narrowed his eyes. "No, we agreed on this. If something went wrong, we were supposed to decide who would go for it."

The ground shook violently around them. Liam struggled to steady himself, his arms flailing. Benjamin tightly gripped onto a nearby chair for support.

"The others aren't here to make that decision with us! I won't assist you; it's too dangerous a choice," Kira said, her voice filled with disdain. She turned her back on Benjamin, starting to walk away before abruptly halting.

"Kira, listen to me. Just read those documents right there, and you'll understand," Benjamin urged, pointing to the roundtable.

"It has to be me, please. I know we don't always see eye to eye, but you just need to trust me." Benjamin's eyes gleamed with determination as he extended his hand, waiting for her to take it.

Kira stared uncertainly, her hesitation palpable. Benjamin clenched his other fist, awaiting her response. She opened her mouth, but the voice that emerged was not hers.

"Well, well. Of course, you wouldn't die from that kind of fall..." A voice drifted from the hole above them.

The three of them looked up, spotting a man in a black robe and hood peering down at them. He lowered his hand in their direction.

Benjamin immediately glanced back at Kira and Liam. "Move! now!"

A bolt of red lightning struck directly down, propelling the three of them forcefully to the floor. Kira collided with the wall and slumped limply.

Benjamin landed on a bookshelf, wincing in pain as he crawled towards her. Liam scrambled back up from the floor.

Another smaller red lightning strike crashed down to the floor. Emerging from the blinding light were four Elites—three men adorned in opal-clad robes, each carrying a glowing white chain. They encircled their leader while their hooded enemy sneered in defiance.

Liam rushed to the front, positioning himself before Kira's unconscious form. Benjamin checked her pulse and exclaimed, "She's alive."

Liam nodded nervously. "Good. Then I'll hold them off. Take Kira and go help the others!" He charged forward, seizing the first man and crushing his head with his bare hands, ending his life in an instant.

Swiftly leaping backward, Liam clapped his hands with a thunderous force, obliterating the two men rushing toward him into a crimson mist of blood.

The impact of the soundwave sent Benjamin flying away from Kira, causing the wall behind him to crumble. It revealed they were several stories high within the Citadel. Flames raged below, devouring the ground with an inferno. Sweat dripped down Benjamin's face as he felt the scorching heat.

Shaking off the disorientation, Benjamin sat up and noticed blood trickling down from his head. Numerous battles raged below, but he couldn't spare his attention for them. Their lightning-wielding adversary had swiftly evaded Liam's attack, utilizing astonishing speed.

Remaining vigilant, their foe descended upon Liam, who stood ready to counter the assault. Liam raised his arms, his jaw clenched, and his fist poised in front of his face, prepared to fight.

Suddenly, the entire building convulsed violently, freezing everyone in their tracks. A harrowing, vacuum-like wail reverberated from above.

Their enemy gazed up at the ceiling, a malicious smile spreading across their face. Liam turned to Benjamin, fear evident in his eyes. "We're too late!" Benjamin glanced at Kira, then back at Liam.

The Citadel quaked and pulsated as if responding to an unfathomable event unfolding at its zenith. Sinister, dark particles cascaded over the surroundings, and Liam futilely attempted to swat them away.

"No... There is another way," Benjamin said, his voice filled with sorrow, as he cast a final glance at Liam.

"I am deeply sorry, but I have no choice," he murmured, propelling himself toward Kira's lifeless form, his eyes ablaze with an orange glow.

Drawing upon the Code of the girl who had extended her hand in the forest, the room plunged into darkness once more. The battle between Liam and their Adversary came to an abrupt halt. Realizing Benjamin's intentions, both of them screamed in unison, "NO!" as he reached out and touched Kira within the black spatial rift.

Chapter 2:
The Troublemakers

---Present Day: Three years earlier---

Four pairs of boots, each a different color, struck the ground, creating splashes in the puddles. "Ethan, we're leaving!" Liam called out, his faux hawk hair tousled by the wind as he started running. Three teenagers, all seventeen years old, hurried closely behind him, escaping from Sector security. The Guardians, also known as "The Guard," were the law enforcement of each Sector but were currently regarded as nothing more than a nuisance.

A group of five Guardians chased after the group of Elite teens dressed in their distinctive opal robes. They carried glowing white chains around their waists and black canisters filled with various items.

"Hey! Stop running!" shouted the leading Guardian, swinging his chain forward. Ethan Crambe instinctively ducked, narrowly avoiding the chain as it whizzed past his head. "Are they trying to capture or kill us?!" he exclaimed, ducking again to evade another chain aimed at him.

The evening air carried warmth as they made their way through the streets, or rather, the dirt roads and grassy prairies that predominated in Sector 53. The citizens of this Sector had the responsibility of preserving the prairies while providing agricultural support. The architecture reflected their choices, with sleek black and gray skyscrapers, steel warehouses, and brick homes in the prairie style scattered across the land. Sector 53 was not a popular tourist destination or particularly remarkable, but then again, every Sector in Pangea had its unique characteristics.

The teenage boys led the pursuing Guardians straight into a quiet factory plant, deliberately drawing attention to themselves. The gray fog that blanketed Sector 53 concealed its true beauty from those outside, but it was also a double-edged sword. Fortunately for the teens, it made visibility difficult during the nighttime. However, a curfew had been imposed in the Sector half an hour ago, explaining why the Guardians relentlessly pursued them.

"Riley, we're counting on your eyesight here," Liam gasped, their escape having lasted at least ten minutes.

Riley shook his head. He was always the one bailing them out of trouble. In fact, when he first met the three of them years ago, he had helped them escape from Guardians as well, instantly becoming part of their group.

"There's a warehouse straight ahead where we can lose the Guardians," Riley suggested, pushing up his red-framed glasses.

Bruce gave Riley a quizzical look. "Are you still wearing those glasses? We don't even need them!"

"It's about aesthetics, Bruce. Gotta look good both in and out of our Classification tunics," Riley replied, readjusting his glasses. "Besides, I just bought them today." Exhausted, he slowed down a bit, and Bruce matched his pace, with Ethan and Liam trailing closely behind.

"Jeez, I can't see a damn thing," Ethan gasped between breaths.

"Hold on," Riley said, slowing down to match their speed. He touched the back of their heads as they ran, sharing his vision with them. Now all four of them had glowing eyes, emitting a whitish-blue hue, allowing them to see what Riley was seeing.

"Ah! I see it!" Liam exclaimed, leading his friends toward a warehouse up ahead. He charged through the door, and the rest of the group followed as the door crumbled behind them.

As the last two entered, Bruce stopped and turned to look at the concrete ground outside. He slammed his hands onto the ground, transforming it into a quicksand-like substance. His fingers sifted through the ordinary dirt, gathering a handful of it. Bruce then hurried inside while holding the dirt grains, quickly squeezing his fist and swallowing some of it.

Embarrassed, Bruce rushed through the doorway, witnessing the dirt in his hand transform into a fine sandy powder. With a controlled exhale, he blew the same substance toward the entrance.

As if responding to his command, the dirt, and sand formed an encasement, gradually solidifying into a sleek, brown door.

The Guardians relentlessly pounded on the door as Bruce hurried deeper into the warehouse, joining the others who were waiting. Their eyes had returned to their usual colors. Riley was in the middle of speaking as Bruce approached. "I'm still working on it, but I'll master it in no time," Riley said confidently. "Doesn't it gross anyone else out that Naturalists have to ingest or touch the element they use?" Ethan gave Bruce a disgusted look but quickly followed it up with a playful smile. "Ethan, I've told you to stop making jokes about that," Bruce replied, looking away and feeling offended.

Ethan threw his hands up in defense. "Hey, at least I didn't call you a mud eater this time."

Bruce ignored him and focused on the urgent matter at hand. "That door won't hold for long. We need a plan, and we need it fast," he informed the group.

Ethan scratched his head and waited for someone to take charge. Meanwhile, the dirt door began to show signs of cracking under the Guardians' relentless assault. "Riley, arc you ready yet? My Code isn't holding," Bruce said, squeezing his fist and straining to maintain the door's shape.

Finally, Riley spoke up. "There's another exit two doors down, past those crates in the hallway," he said, his chocolate brown eyes glowing with a bright whiteish-blue hue behind his red square-framed glasses.

To the rest of the group, the warehouse appeared as a regular space, but to a Pulse Class like Riley, it was transparent. He could see the entire layout of the building as if he had X-ray vision. His eyes could also detect heat signatures of any nearby individuals. Liam, Ethan, Riley, and Bruce found themselves in a vast factory filled with mechanical appliances, with steel beams and crates lining the walls. The exit door was obstructed by metal poles and a mechanical engine.

"We need to get moving. I can't afford to get caught," Ethan said aloud, voicing the urgency of the situation.

"Don't worry so much, Ethan. We've got this," Liam reassured him, playfully punching him on the arm. Ethan rubbed the spot where Liam had hit him.

"Ethan, Liam, you're up, Brutes," Riley directed, pointing toward a large engine and a pile of metal beams blocking the exit door. Liam sprinted forward and began lifting the engine above his head while Ethan swiftly maneuvered past him to start moving the beams.

"Hurry up, guys," Bruce urged, his focus still on the door. Riley paced next to him, waiting for a clear path.

Ethan cleared the last of the metal poles, and the group rushed toward the door. However, Liam accidentally dropped the engine, much to Riley's dismay. "Damn it, it's heavy!" Liam complained, wiping sweat from his face. He made another attempt to lift the engine. "Guys, I can't hold it anymore!" Bruce yelled in exasperation as the door started to crumble. Yelling could be heard from beyond the door.

Ethan grabbed a nearby crate and rushed toward the entrance. "Ethan, I'm serious. Help me lift this off the damn door!" Liam pleaded, his sea-green eyes begging Ethan for assistance. Ethan was struggling to block the previous doorway with crates.

"Just scatter them, and come on, Ethan. We don't have time for this!" Liam dropped the engine once more. "I've got it. Just give me a second!" Ethan grunted as he pushed another crate into place.

Despite their efforts, one of the Guardians managed to slip through the doorway, successfully striking Ethan with a chain. Ethan cried out in pain and collapsed to the ground. Soon, a white aura began to envelop him.

"Dammit, see? Now they caught up. We're going to get caught," Riley exclaimed, throwing his arms up behind his head in frustration. He shook his head, and his eyes changed back to brown. Liam rushed over to the entrance, pushing one last crate to block most of the Guardian's path.

However, it was too late. The chain already had a grip on Ethan's leg, dragging him forward and forcefully slamming him into the stacked crates, causing them to topple over.

With the crates down, the other Guards unleashed their chains, successfully hitting each of the remaining boys. The impact disabled their Code, leaving them unable to fight back.

The Guardians swiftly gathered them in a row. Bruce glared in Ethan's direction. "Ethan, what the hell were you thinking?" Before Ethan could reply, a Guardian stepped forward and sneered, "You morons are in a world of trouble." He raised his hand, his eyes turning purple as he spoke, "Go to sleep."

The four boys then collapsed, rendered unconscious before Ethan could fully process everything. When they regained consciousness, they found themselves in one of the Guardian headquarters. Ethan sat up and glanced to his left, where Liam and Riley sat silently, already awake but restrained in their chairs.

Looking to his right, he saw Bruce still unconscious. Ethan scanned the drab room with his eyes, noticing a Guardian leaning against the exit door—the one who had put them to sleep.

He had a stern face that meant business as he walked over to a white table in front of the boys. Brushing down his shiny opal robes, he took a seat opposite them. In the center of the table, the Guardian Emblem proudly showed. Clearing his throat, he spoke, "My name is Macon. I was the lead Guardian on your case, but we're not here to talk about me."

He looked at all four of them, his posture rigid and stiff. He kept tapping his finger on the table, and the smell of smoke began to annoy Ethan. Riley let out a brief yawn, earning him a glare. Macon continued, "Let's start with all the rules you broke last night."

His tone was short and clear, conveying his disinterest. However, Ethan couldn't help but feel like the Guardian was dragging his feet. He watched as the man scratched at his scruffy beard.

Ethan sank into his seat, wanting to fold his arms but hindered by the chains around him. "Article 37-3 clearly states that all non-Academy inducted Elites cannot use their Code unsupervised." Ethan rolled his eyes. The Guardian seemed to be going through the motions, reciting textbook knowledge. The Guardian took notice of Ethan.

"You're well aware that you don't have permission to use your Code outside of an academy unless a parent or professor is present to take responsibility," the Guardian stated more as a statement than a question.

"Yes, sir," they replied in unison. Bruce was still asleep, and Ethan wondered if that would be a problem.

"Article 6-12 - All Elites are required to wear their classification tunics or robes when in public... which you clearly are not," the Guardian said with disgust, gesturing at their jeans and shirts.

"The cost of breaking that in a first offense is no credits for two weeks," he added, pausing to observe their reactions to the punishment. Seeing their blank faces, he continued, seemingly annoyed.

"Most importantly, Article 1 states that all citizens of Pangea are required to use their Code to make Pangea better or face execution. Considering you ran from my squad and fought back, why shouldn't I consider this for you four?" Ethan almost passed out at this threat, and Liam's face drained of color. Riley, their quick thinker, spoke up first.

"Sir, we are loyal to Pangea. We were trying to train and better develop our Code because of this loyalty," Riley said, catching the Guardian's attention.

"Our friend here required a lot of Code training," he nodded toward Ethan. "When we started practicing, it was with our parents after school. But he needs special training, so some time had passed, and we kept going without them."

"That doesn't change the fact that you broke curfew," the Guardian argued.

"Sir, respectfully, I'm trying to explain this to you. If you're going to threaten us with execution, we are allowed to defend our actions," Riley responded, successfully grabbing the Guardian's attention. Ethan knew Riley was skilled at convincing lies, as he only shared half-truths. Yes, Ethan needed extra training due to a Code deficiency, but they never informed their parents about their practice sessions.

"It's true, we should have worn our tunics, so you got us on that." Riley was in his element, and the lies flowed easily.

"We would have gone home immediately after seeing you, but your team attacked us without warning."

"You were using your Code during curfew, which is not allowed," He argued back, unaware that he was falling into Riley's trap.

"And you used Psyche manipulation on us without permission, or did they just change that rule tonight?" Macon finally regarded Riley thoughtfully, realizing that they were well-versed in the country's regulations, as stated in the article.

Ethan and Liam exchanged smiles, recognizing Riley's valuable intervention. Amidst the chaos, they had forgotten about this crucial rule, which could potentially dismiss most of the charges against them. "You're accusing me of corruption? Good luck proving that. The Guardians have public favor," Macon retorted.

"Okay, but are you sure you want to harm a Sector Official's kid like that?" Riley questioned, earning a disapproving glance from Ethan, who didn't want his mother involved.

Macon's mask cracked, revealing surprise. "A Sector Official's kid? Our Sector, you mean? Quintella Crambe?" He appeared increasingly concerned. "Hmm, you don't look like a Crambe. Although, I believe they do have a son," he nervously scratched his head. "I'll be right back; I need to verify." He paused and glanced at Bruce. "Don't worry about him; it's just a little Psyche Class mental manipulation. Your friend will wake up soon enough." Macon exited the room, leaving behind a basic black matted interior with a window facing the captives who were chained to their chairs.

Twenty minutes passed before the Guardian returned, wearing an embarrassed expression. "I'm sorry," he muttered, unchaining them from their chairs. "Your parents are on their way." The Guardian left them alone in the interrogation room.

Ethan felt as though his head was splitting. "Don't worry; they'll release us soon enough," he groggily assured the others. The room fell silent. "Why did you try rearranging the boxes when we could have just left, Ethan?" Bruce must have regained consciousness. Riley stretched and then straightened himself up. Ethan twiddled with his necklace. "Bruce, you needed help, and I wanted to prove to myself that I'm becoming stronger. Guys, I'm really sorry for jeopardizing us." The four friends remained silent as they were called out of the room one by one. Ethan lingered in the room long after everyone else had left.

Finally, his mother arrived to fetch him. Quintella appeared flushed with frustration as she gazed at Ethan. "Ethan, let's go. We're going home." His heart sank at the sight of his mother, and his face turned bright red. He could only mumble, "I'm sorry," before rising from the chair and leaving the room.

The buildings housing the Guardians all bore a striking resemblance. Their grand opal-tiled floors shimmered underfoot as they walked. Arched doorways led to various rooms scattered throughout the structure. A bustling crowd of opal-robed Guardians filled the space, intermingled with citizens donning robes of different colors, all seeking guidance from their law enforcement agency.

Ethan and Quintella descended a set of balcony steps toward the lobby. The lobby floor was adorned with the sealed symbol of the Guardians—a radiant white shield crest with chains. The points of the shield proudly displayed all seven of the Code emblems. Ethan stole a quick glance at his mother as they descended. Quintella wore her customary stern expression as she led the way through the crowd, her flowing purple robes trailing behind her. Ethan wondered if she would scold him. Lately, he had been getting into trouble for using his Code outside the permitted hours. His mother usually managed to cover it up before things got out of hand, but this time felt different.

In a hurry, Ethan and his mother exited the station and hastened towards a nearby travel tube at the end of the sidewalk. The tubes, scattered throughout Sector 53, came in a dark seaweed green or fiery red color. Walking close behind Quintella, Ethan approached the green tube. "Ethan, hurry up. I can't be seen here," she urged, grabbing his hand and pressing a red button on the door. Ethan shrank back in embarrassment. "I can keep up without holding your hand, Mom," he muttered.

They stepped into the floating pod within the tube, and the AI speaker chimed in. "Destination, please," it requested. Quintella, straightening her purple robe, spoke up. "Residential city limits, please." The tube then opened into a chamber of air distinct from their pod's current stream, propelling them forward. They ascended above the city, revealing a foreboding view of slick black towering buildings with silver-framed windows. The entire Sector was engulfed in a gray fog, indicating it lacked proper sunlight. And yet, Sector 53 was designated for various agricultural purposes. From above, one could see plots of land stretching for miles. Wearing their respective classification robes and tunics, Elites worked in the fields, utilizing their Code to farm vegetables. Naturalists controlled the water flow, ensuring the plants received adequate irrigation. Brutes cleared the area, lifting logs, rocks, and debris to make way for construction. Numerous Elites strolled along the grassy sidewalks, going about their business. Ethan marveled at the sight from within the soaring pod.

As they reached the city's edge, both of them disembarked at the terminal, and the pod shot back up through the tube. "Ethan, as you know, this will go on your permanent record. Fortunately, I managed to get your friends out of trouble. But for you... it reflects poorly on your father and me," Quintella stated flatly. Ethan turned to face his mother, averting his gaze from the neighborhood ahead.

While Ethan was shocked that his mother couldn't pull strings for him this time, the mention of his father gave him a sour expression. "I don't care what it does to him. He's never here anyway," Quintella glared at Ethan. "I lied for you and your friends,

Ethan! I covered and told them you were with me, but I stepped away for a business call."

Ethan's expression softened. He knew how much his mother valued her position. "So, for once, can you not complain about your father? You made this mess, not him." Ethan shrank a little as they continued walking.

Quintella didn't say anything more on the matter. As they approached their house, Ethan stopped walking. Dozens of boxes were being carried out by AI. Ethan noticed his bedroom dresser being moved. "Why are we all packed up? What's going on?" he questioned. Quintella looked at him blankly. "Ethan, you're moving closer to your father. He's started a new project." Quintella looked at her son with hope. "This is a fresh start for you. If you move Sectors, the record will not follow you upon arrival." While her demeanor turned hopeful, Ethan's sank with dissatisfaction.

"I don't want you to use your influence to help me," Ethan said, tired. His ashy blonde hair fell onto his face as he glanced at the door. His icy blue eyes appeared chilled and resigned. "What am I gonna tell my friends?"

"You made this mess. You'll figure it out," she replied, walking into their house. Ethan wasn't ready to have that conversation with his friends.

Later that evening, Liam, Riley, and Bruce wore somber expressions after hearing the news. The sun was setting, and a light breeze blew as they stood outside Ethan's driveway.

"I should have done a better job mapping our location. I'm sorry, Ethan," Riley apologized, his head bowed. He was tinkering with his communication device as a distraction.

Bruce drained the life from the grass in front of Ethan's yard, his fingers directing energy to a dying tree, restoring its youth. A black patch of grass encircled him. Riley told Bruce to stop while Liam approached and hugged Ethan. "I can't help but feel like it's our fault, Ethan. We never get caught," Liam expressed. Ethan looked at them.

"My Mom said we were using our Code to practice outside the bylaws. And on top of that, getting caught breaking and entering, I was barred from applying to Academies in Sector 53," Ethan explained. "My mom and dad are making me move Sectors because the incident made them look bad."

Riley looked up. "So basically, your parents are paying for our mistakes." The tension in the air grew heavy, and no one said anything.

Ethan grimaced. "My mom says Sector 71 is pretty awesome and advanced, at least." They all stared at Ethan in disbelief. "Sector 71 is awesome! That's the floating architecture Sector! Why are you going there?" they asked.

"My father is the new Sector Official for them. His name was apparently submitted by a landslide for the position. My Mom will remain Sector Official of 53," Ethan explained. The others fell silent.

"They got your dad now, too, huh?" Liam said gloomily.

Ethan looked down at the ground, his eyes filled with determination. "My father has always prioritized work over family. He knew the risks. This is just another example." Liam gave Ethan a sympathetic look and reached out to hold his hand. "When you're chosen to be a Sector Official, it's one of the highest honors." Liam continued, "But when your term is up, they wipe your memory for security purposes. Your parents may not remember you or could die... Are you sure you're okay?" Ethan unlinked his hand from Liam and kicked the ground. "I know that already. Do you really have to ask?" Liam turned red and sheepishly looked away. Bruce spoke up, filling the silence, "We're probably not going to be seeing you for a while."

Finally, Ethan looked back up at them and gave his best smile. "Listen, guys. We've been friends since we were kids. You've always had my back. And I'll always have yours." He made eye contact with each of them. "If one of us ever needs help, we'll all meet up and support each other like we always do. Besides, I know we'll see each other again soon." He finished with a huff of air. The three of them quietly stared at Ethan momentarily, the tension dissipating.

Riley perked up first, flashing his own radiant smile. "You've got yourself a deal."

Bruce whistled. "Wow, Ethan, you're not usually one to give an inspirational speech." Ethan shook his head, giving a nervous smile.

Liam tackled Ethan to the ground and said, "Though, are you sure you want to leave behind all these ass beatings?" His joke was light enough to diffuse any remaining tension, allowing Ethan and his closest friends to laugh, briefly forgetting their worries.

Chapter 3:
Black Robed Strangers

Ethan sat in his new room, lost in his thoughts about that day three months ago. Despite staying in touch with his friends as promised, he felt their absence keenly. The boy had packed up his childhood and moved halfway across the country to be with his father, whom he hadn't seen since he was sworn into office—ironically, also three months ago. As he prepared for the new school year at Unity Prep Academy, Ethan wondered what kind of Elites he would meet and whether he would fit in or make enemies. Ethan tried to find a silver lining, reminding himself that by moving to Sector 71, he had left his past behind and had a fresh start. He placed his clothes down and walked towards the window.

His mother, Quintella, knocked on his door and entered. "Ethan, tomorrow you start your Secondary Training, and I need to make sure you understand what's at stake," Quintella said, her face serious and her eyes gleaming with determination.

She wasted no time getting down to business. "In your Secondary Training, you'll be attending an academic program to fully develop your Code. You have to be accepted into the school program to continue," she explained. Ethan groaned and sat on his bed, finding his mother irritating when she got like this.

"You'll be reviewed by a committee periodically over the next two years to assess where you fit for a career when you graduate," she continued. "I've given you a letter of recommendation so you can take the entrance exam."

Ethan rolled his eyes and walked around his mother, engrossed in his school notes. "It's always the same, Mom. A new year, a new reminder to be the underdog," he muttered. He wondered why he couldn't just live a normal life. His mother interrupted his thoughts, insisting he shouldn't stand out because he was different. Ethan felt sick at the idea of trying to stand out when he had already struggled to fit in.

"Ethan! Are you listening to me?" Quintella barked, her eyes glowing purple. "You're lucky the law is preventing me from using my Code right now."

Ethan sighed, shuffling through his notes. "Seriously, Mom? No one is watching you. What's stopping you? It's not like it doesn't happen," he retorted, side-eyeing her from behind his papers.

"Ethan... that kind of talk could get you killed," Quintella replied, looking terrified. "Rules exist for a reason."

"Don't you ever feel like some rules are meant to be broken?" Ethan shot back, surprising his mother. Her expression seemed distant, lost in thought.

"Besides, how strong would a Code-deficient Brute be?" Ethan's mother didn't respond. She just watched and listened.

"I just wish my Code would have developed better. I'm really a Brute in name only. I'm not going to stand out," he said, putting his papers down with a sigh. He stood up and walked over to his closet. His mother observed him as he pulled out his tunic and laid it over his chair.

Quintella calmed down a bit and hugged Ethan. "I understand, Ethan. You have a chromosome deficiency in your Code. It's not your fault," she reassured him. Ethan rested his head on her shoulder.

"As long as you wear your necklace, you'll be fine," Quintella said. Ethan broke away from the hug and ran his hand across his neck. He walked back over to his desk. "Of course, I keep my primary school notes to remind me. Look."

When Elites are young, their "Code" or genetic coding in their DNA that determines the Elite's classification becomes prominent. The Code remains a dominant gene based on the gender of the parent and child. Thanks so much, Dad!

Ethan, being a male, would receive his father's Code and not his mother's. However, Quintella coiled back and slapped him across the face. "Don't be cute. You think it's funny to be snarky, but one of these days, you'll see not everything is a joke." Her tone was assertive and concerned.

Ethan scoffed, throwing his hands in the air. "Will you give me a break? I never even take it off!" He left his room and headed downstairs with his mother in tow.

Ethan was deeply offended. His right cheek was slightly warm red. Rushing downstairs, he realized there was nowhere he could go to escape a conversation with his mother. So, he turned around, shoving past her back into his room. He locked the door behind him.

Had she been drinking again? She could be so insufferable whenever she drank that red liquid. Ethan understood she had a stressful job, but she only got this out of hand when she drank.

Ethan's parents were Sector Officials, those in charge of ensuring their region in Pangea runs smoothly. Ethan's actions matter to his parents. They had an image to uphold to the public, but he felt as though that should go both ways.

It wasn't a crime to drink. The drinks weren't the same as they had been in the distant past. Far less harmful, but the desired effect is more potent. This is why many tried not to get hooked on the stuff - at least Pangea had no death toll from drinking.

"Ethan, open the door." Rather than reply, he lifted the necklace that was supposed to enhance his strength.

His necklace was a ruby-red diamond-shaped pendant. It had a warm glow to it with a gold chain.

It was not uncommon for Elites to wear enhancement objects to help better control their Code. Some even had objects manufactured to stabilize their Code.

Elites, like the Psyche, use temporal headbands to clear out the many thoughts in their heads.

Elites in the Sprite Class used plasma gloves to conduct electricity through themselves better.

Many in the Brute Class used arm bracers to better control strength, but Ethan had the opposite problem.

Thanks to Pangea's government, they issued the necessary equipment to the public, which allowed free access for everyone.

But like all luxuries in Pangea, anyone could acquire anything, thanks to their Utopian lifestyles. And, of course, there were some Elites that did not want anything.

"I got this, Mom. Trust me." Ethan declared behind the door. With that, the conversation ended. She paused before saying, "Alright, have it your way then." Quintella walked away from the door and left him alone for the rest of the evening. At some point, she would leave to return to Sector 53. Ethan also imagined that if she was drunk, it would have to be a while before then.

For most of the night, Ethan tossed and turned. He could not help but wonder about what his school life would be like. Ethan could not sleep at all, so he decided to take a walk in his neighborhood. Getting dressed, he quickly opened his bedroom door and turned down the hallway.

Quietly tiptoeing down the steps, Ethan could not help but feel grateful; everything was going smoothly. However, he spoke too soon. "Where do you think you're going, Master Ethan?" someone asked, causing Ethan to jump. "I'm taking a walk, Gallium. Don't tell my Mom. I just need to clear my head," Ethan whispered.

Gallium, the house AI, was an interface that controlled most of the day-to-day housework and basic needs. With an upgrade, your interface could be downloaded into your AICI, which housed a multitude of information, from video calls and background information on Elites to movies and music. All simple tasks and the majority of jobs that were once done by people in the distant past now had an AI designated to them. This included retail, customer service, hospitality, and financial careers. Elites were needed to focus their attention on the sustainability of Pangea, as the country was a man-made physical Pangaea itself. With the AI handling these tasks, it freed up hundreds of thousands of Elites to complete other duties.

AICI could also be carried with you. It was a round silver watch-like electronic device that anyone could wear on their wrist. Ethan, of course, had one because his parents knew how much trouble he got into. "Master Ethan, you realize there is a Sector curfew for a reason. Level 1 crime has increased and has not been regulated as well during nighttime," Gallium explained.

"True, but I always have you in my ear, so what do I have to worry about?" Ethan chuckled. "You've been in our family forever, so nothing new to you. Though, I'd appreciate it if, for once, you don't tell my Mom what I'm up to."

A red beam lit up in front of Ethan, and a red hologram of an outline of a man wearing a tuxedo appeared. "I shall stay behind just this once, young Ethan, but please stay away from trouble," Gallium nodded toward the door.

"You're the best, Gallium! I appreciate you," Ethan grinned. With that, he snatched up a bag by the door and strutted outside.

The neighborhood was quite beautiful; it was springtime, and the houses were an array of baby blue and bright yellow lined in rows. Hundreds of buildings floated above ground in the distance. Everyone had a garden with a colorful assortment of flowers and at least one evergreen tree.

The above streets had see-through glass panels with blinking blue arrows that showed the directions for flying vehicles. Evergreen trees scattered around the area. The panels and colorful lights gave life to the street below it. Large tubes with pods scattered and arched around the sky. Thanks to the beaming arrows, the roads were quite bright, but other than that, the stars were the main pieces glowing up in the night sky.

Ethan did not feel it was wise enough to enter within the inner-city limits with his allotted time, but his housing was right on the outskirts of the inner section of the city. He would travel far enough that he could see the skylines up close. There were ads on the holographic screens as he walked by. "Are you tired of getting stuck in your own time loop? Spatial Class friends playing tricks on you? Try The Watcher! A new..." Ethan walked around the streets before pulling out his sketchbook from his bag.

"Sector 71, The luxurious floating sector! Many buildings in Zone 1 and 2 levitate thanks to state-of-the-art technology given by the Psyche Class!" Voices with different slogans and offers chatted at Ethan, canceling the quiet. Ethan hated the advertisements. At the risk of encountering numerous advertisements, Ethan took great pleasure in observing and studying the architecture of the buildings at night. Most of these structures resembled tall glass pillars with cut slabs on top, powered primarily by Sprite Class energy. As a result, the buildings appeared darker during the nighttime but emitted a vibrant, green glow. Ethan believed the city earned its nickname, Emerald City, due to this unique feature, although his mother mentioned it was a moniker from the past that had stuck. Engrossed in his surroundings, Ethan spent considerable time sketching the skylines and jotting down notes. When satisfied with his material, he decided it was time to head home before drawing any unwanted attention.

Meanwhile, in another part of the city, a student had just made perhaps the most significant phone call of her life. Shortly afterward, she found herself being pursued by three mysterious individuals clad in black robes. Determined to reach home, she navigated through an alleyway, urgently panting for breath. Seeking a momentary refuge, she stopped behind a brick wall near a dumpster, attempting to steady her breathing.

While she attempted to catch her breath, the sound of approaching footsteps reached her ears. Frustrated and fearful, she muttered, "Damn it, what do they want from me?" Gathering her strength, she resumed running through the dimly lit alleyway as the wind picked up. The usual green glow that illuminated the streets began to flicker and fade. The sound of footsteps drew closer, accompanied by distant whistling. In a hushed whisper, she pleaded, "Please, give me strength," and continued her desperate sprint.

However, her escape was short-lived as she suddenly felt a powerful tug at her heart, causing her to cry out and lose sensation in her body. She collapsed face-down onto the ground. The approaching footsteps grew nearer, prompting the teen to rise to her feet. As she turned her head to face the assailants, an immense force compelled her back down to her knees.

One of the black hooded figures, the leader, declared, "This one seems to fit the description." He approached, bending down to caress the student's face. His voice carried a raspy quality, and she could discern the stubble on his chin beneath the hood.

"Tell me, lil lady, what's your name?" The man appeared to be in his mid-twenties and continued to stroke her face as though she were a prized possession. Though not afraid, she instinctively understood she was outmatched. Another Elite among them scanned the area, expressing annoyance, "We don't have the luxury of dragging this out."

Hushing the impatient Elite, the leader spoke, "Shhh... Do not rush my methods. The streets are clear, and the curfew is in effect. No one is coming for this one here." He redirected his gaze back to the young woman, whose disheveled plume of curly, honey-blonde hair showcased her nearing nineteen years. Tears streamed down her face, betraying her frantic voice as she defiantly asserted, "Nyla Winthrop. I don't know who you are, but you're making a mistake!"

A gust of wind lifted the man's hood, revealing gashed holes where his eyes should have been. Nyla recoiled in horror as he widened his smile, displaying unnaturally perfect white teeth. Mockingly, he remarked, "Does my face bother you? Gosh, your face bothers me too." His breath felt as hot as an oven.

Nyla, far from foolish, knew one of two outcomes awaited her. Either there was a reason these individuals were hunting her down, or they intended to kill her right then and there. So, she said plainly, "If you're going to kill me, just kill me." The eyeless Elite's left hand began to spark and crackle with red electricity. "It would be my pleasure, Nyla, but it's not up to me." He finally frowned.

With that, Nyla gasped, feeling an even stronger pull on her mind until she ultimately lost consciousness. The second hooded figure hoisted Nyla Winthrop over his shoulder, and the three figures silently disappeared into the night.

Chapter 4:
Unity Prep Academy

Ethan woke up with a start, realizing he had slightly overslept. "Okay! First day, let's do this," he thought aloud. His heart began to race, prompting him to jump out of bed. "Gallium, I need you to start the shower for me." Ethan's room glowed a warm red before fading back to its usual blue, signaling that the AI, Gallium, had acknowledged his request.

Hurriedly, Ethan left his room and rushed down the royal blue hallway toward the bathroom. He showered quickly and stepped out of the water, shaking his hair as he paused to examine himself in the mirror. "Everything needs to be perfect," he mumbled, momentarily fussing with his hair.

Realizing he shouldn't make himself late for school, Ethan abandoned his hair-taming efforts. Many students considered him quite the looker, with his wavy, ash-blonde hair that always seemed to fall onto his face. He had been advised to keep his hair shorter because his icy blue eyes were captivating, resembling a frozen lake. Ethan possessed a boy-next-door image, a melodic voice, and a cheeky smile. His furrowed dark eyebrows and narrow jawline completed his enticing appearance.

Having a toned physique from his Brute Class training, Ethan dropped to the floor and began a series of push-ups. After completing about seventy push-ups, he decided not to overdo it. He stood back up and jumped into the shower. Upon getting out, he briefly admired himself before concluding he wasn't particularly special. Most Brutes had a solid physical build due to their rigorous training from childhood into adulthood, which aimed to strengthen their bones.

Dressed in his red velvet tunic, Ethan adjusted his hair one last time before clasping his arm bracers. Embedded in the bracers were identical pendants resembling the one on his necklace. "I am so glad I don't have to wear those foolish Classification Robes yet," Ethan muttered to no one in particular, rushing to the garage to grab his Hoverbike.

For his fifteenth birthday, his father had sent him a Halo, a hovering bike designed to prevent Ethan from begging for a car when he turned sixteen. Most Elites had the vehicle version of a Halo, as they, too, traversed the floating buildings in Emerald City. Traveling across different Sectors could be lengthy and challenging in the vast country of Pangea, which unified various old lands to create a utopia for everyone's needs. Citizens needed faster means of transportation, so those who didn't own a Hoverbike or Hovervan opted for tube travel, conveniently available in each Sector. However, those fortunate enough to possess Sprite or Spatial Classification had even easier means of travel compared to other Code users.

While Ethan didn't care for his father or his gifts, he gladly accepted the white chromed Hoverbike. With this bike, he could experience the wonders of flying. It resembled a sizeable floating motorcycle with numerous wires and a front holographic control screen displaying the surroundings. The bike featured a quiet, humming cube-shaped engine on its bottom, which was visually appealing and easy to operate. Running primarily on solar energy, which charged through its two sideways inverted wheels, the Hoverbike emitted ghostly blue flames that trailed to the engine. Ethan's bike hummed, ready to go, and he swiftly mounted it, flying towards the flying port.

Air travel proved somewhat challenging due to the multitude of people moving in different directions. Although there were air patrols to ensure smooth traffic, Elites often got carried away with the sensation of freedom above ground.

Ethan bobbed and weaved across the traffic of hundreds of Hoverbikes as he passed travelers. He caught sight of holographic billboards displaying a woman engaged in a historical debate. "Pangea is a utopian dream!" she exclaimed on the screen. "Each Sector's region has a unique design to meet the needs of its people. It could never have worked like that in the past."

Dashing behind glass buildings, Ethan couldn't contain his excitement and yelled out. There couldn't be a better feeling than this, flying on his Hoverbike with no one else around. No parents, no rules—just letting all the other noise fade to black. In these few moments, he was truly free.

As he entered the inner-city limits, Ethan spotted his school, Unity Prep Academy, floating just beyond some shops on the hill. From there, he could see the beautiful Emerald City Lake shimmering in the distance, its blue waters captivating his gaze.

Parking for Hoverbikes was located at the bottom of the hill, near the school gates. The massive staircase, which faded and disappeared when not in use, was an impressive feature. Each step changed color as someone stepped on it, adding to the sense of importance when approaching the school.

Unity Prep Academy stood tall, occupying an area equivalent to three football fields in length and width. Like most buildings in Emerald City, it floated effortlessly with its sleek glass structure. The school boasted a skywalk that divided both sides of the campus, showcasing a remarkable design of pumpkin orange and white with an interior adorned in green.

After parking his Hoverbike, Ethan walked up to the open golden gates and observed other students making their way up the grandiose staircase, accompanied by friends and laughter. Suddenly, a voice emerged from the blues, interrupting his thoughts. "You were not as late as you thought, Master Ethan," Gallium chimed in. Irritated, Ethan huffed and responded, "Gallium, I know your programming allows you to hear what I say through my AICI."

"But I swear I will break this communication device if you don't stop eavesdropping on me," Ethan griped, annoyed by the lack of privacy. He rolled his eyes, realizing there was never any escaping Gallium's surveillance. Silence followed before Gallium spoke again, saying, "As you wish, sir." A beeping noise from the device signaled that Gallium had shifted its attention elsewhere. Ethan sighed, relieved.

Ascending the seemingly never-ending steps to the school felt like an eternity, but eventually, he made it to the top. Ethan was baffled to find that the inside of the school was equally expansive and grand. The entrance lobby featured a captivating gold marble interior with seaweed green accents. At the center of the room, a grandeur golden waterfall fountain shaped like a glittering DNA code replica added to the grandeur.

A circular balcony surrounded the lobby, offering a view of seven staircases leading up to doors adorned with classification symbol emblems. To the far left was a crown emitting a purple hue, with a golden eye in the center, representing the Psyche class—the individuals gifted with psychic abilities. Teachers stood nearby, smiling as they directed students and pointed them toward their respective destinations.

Ethan's attention turned to the massive staircase. To the right of the Psyche door was an arched entrance featuring the emblem of a water droplet. Inside the droplet, a pair of burning hands held a vibrant green tree—a symbol representing the Naturalists, who can control natural elements.

Continuing to the right, another door showcased a bright orange flashing camera, indicating the Sketch class—the individuals capable of memorizing and temporarily utilizing anyone else's Code ability.

Ethan glanced over at the next door and noticed an azure blue heartbeat, a symbol representing the Pulse - Elites who possessed exceptional tracking abilities. Students pushed past Ethan as he directed his gaze towards the arched door adorned with a neon red lightning bolt cutting through a hand, indicating the Sprite Class. These students harnessed electrical currents to enhance their speed and facilitate the conduction of electricity. The second-to-last door at the end showcased a ruby red flame engulfing a heart with a flexed arm at its center, representing the Brute Class—individuals gifted with immense physical strength. Although quantifying their strength was challenging, one Brute possessed the potential to rival an entire army.

Further down the corridor, there stood a door adorned with a gray spiral, encompassing an hourglass featuring a sun and a moon—a symbol of the Spatial Class. This group consisted of two subtypes: Shifters, who manipulated matter, and Tempus, who commanded time at will. Students donning various colored tunics and robes eagerly rushed up the staircase, filled with excitement for the commencement of their new journey. Ethan followed them, his awe growing as they ascended towards the colossal entrance of the Brute Class. As he moved along, students stared at him oddly.

Amidst the hustle and bustle, other Elites dressed in red and blue tunics rushed past Ethan. Out of the corner of his eye, he caught sight of a boy with reddish hair standing near the Brute Class doorway, appearing to mentally prepare himself. The boy noticed Ethan's gaze and offered a harmless smile. Ethan raised his hand and waved back before the boy turned around and walked through the door.

Everyone seemed to be heading toward their respective staircases and entering their designated doors. Some wore expressions of nervousness, while others radiated excitement or determination. Ethan looked up at the reinforced glass roof and observed vehicles soaring above the school.

"Freaking Sector 71," Ethan muttered to himself, reminiscing about his home in Sector 53—a place that was grand but not extravagant. For a fleeting moment, Ethan almost didn't miss home. Almost. As students began whispering and pointing in his direction, he overheard a conversation between two students wearing orange robes passing by.

"Is that the Sector Official's kid?" one of them asked.

"So much for an equal life for all in Pangea," scoffed the other student as they continued on their way.

Ethan felt a pang of embarrassment and slowed down for a moment. Suddenly, someone bumped into him. "Watch where you're going, idiot!" the student snapped, his face turning to horror.

"Oh, shit. I am so sorry! I didn't realize you're a Crambe. Please don't tell anyone what I said," the guy hurriedly apologized before rushing off to his class.

For some reason, this irritated Ethan. He hadn't even said a word to the guy. Deciding it was time to proceed, Ethan walked through the large ruby-red doorway adorned with flames. It felt like a gateway, as he was instantly greeted by a bright blue sky and an open field. Surrounding him and the other students were grassy green plains, mountain walls, and rocks.

Aligned in a row, eight teachers stood in the field. The number of teachers compared to the incoming students seemed disproportionate, making one-on-one training appear impossible. Ethan scanned the field and noticed the committee his mother had mentioned standing some distance behind the teachers, their expressions stoic.

"Welcome to your first day as a Brute in secondary training," announced one of the Elites, stepping forward. "Here, unlike primary training, you have chosen to refine your Code by applying to an academy of your preference." The man surveyed the field, creating an atmosphere of intense pressure.

He continued, "Eventually, you'll join the workforce alongside the rest of us Elites." The speaker, a burly Elite with a caramel complexion, introduced himself as Professor Carson, the head of Brute studies. "These are my associates," he said, gesturing towards the seven other Brute class Professors, "and they will select their students based on your skills." Several students shifted uncomfortably in response.

"As you know, our great country relies on bright minds and the collective efforts of all Elites to thrive. To achieve this, we must understand your strengths and weaknesses to effectively utilize your Code," Professor Carson explained, his voice resounding across the expansive grassy field teeming with aspiring Elites.

"For the next two years, it is our responsibility as your teachers to push the limits of your Code and determine the best career path for each of you," concluded Professor Carson, folding his hands.

Some students smirked or exchanged fist bumps, but Ethan felt his heart sink with fear. He hadn't realized how closely he would be observed by the examiners. "Normally, we would have you compete against a classmate to determine the strongest among you, but our superiors believe it is not a comprehensive method of assessing strength," explained Professor Carson.

"Therefore, we have decided to enlist the assistance of Spatial Classification Type 2: Shifters. They have teleported us to a terrain suitable for today's exam," Professor Carson continued. The aging man with white hair that appeared beyond his years suddenly ripped off his red robe, revealing a chiseled eight-pack and well-defined biceps. Moving with the agility of a much younger man, Professor Carson exuded determination and ease in every motion, as if he had never experienced fatigue in his life.

"We wish to witness your raw potential," he grinned, turning his attention to a boulder behind him. With a display of power, he shattered the boulder and caused the ground to tremble beneath the students. A red-haired Brute near Ethan, the same boy he had seen earlier at the doorway, expressed a mixture of nervousness and excitement. Ethan examined the stocky boy, noting his well-conditioned muscles that surpassed his own.

"If he's worried, then I'm in trouble," Ethan muttered, inching closer to the larger group. Perhaps by blending in, he would go unnoticed. Professor Carson instructed the students to line up against the mountain walls and deliver fist punches to the boulders in front of them. Ethan cursed his luck as sweat began to form on his forehead, his heart racing even faster.

Everyone took their positions and started striking their boulders. Some dented them, while others created holes or shattered pieces. One student even managed to bring down half of the boulder. Professor Carson spun around, clearly impressed. "This is what I want to see! Young Elite, what's your name?" Carson asked, his gaze fixed on the red-headed Elite named Leo.

Praising Leo, Professor Carson continued observing as the rest of the students took turns delivering their punches. Ethan prayed to any higher power that would listen, desperately hoping that nobody would notice his inability to dent his boulder. Suddenly, a teacher spotted Ethan and called for everyone to stop. All eyes turned to him. Professor Carson approached Ethan, scrutinizing him from head to toe.

"Young Elite, who are you?" Carson inquired. "Ethan," he replied. "Well, Ethan, that is no way to address your professor. You can't even make an impact on a rock. Are you holding back from your classmates?" Carson questioned. "No, sir," Ethan replied sharply. "Then punch the damn rock, Ethan!" Carson bellowed.

Ethan frowned at the boulder before him, then glanced up at Professor Carson, who watched him cautiously. While some students paid varying degrees of attention, relieved to have the spotlight off themselves or hoping to witness someone's failure, Ethan reminisced about his years of training with Liam.

***

"Come on, Ethan! As Brutes, it's our duty to demonstrate our strength!" nine-year-old Liam urged, jumping up and down. Ethan, also nine at the time, was covered in sweat as he sparred with Liam.

"I don't understand why you're not getting it. Look," Liam said, walking toward a tree in the playground. They were in Sector 53, with snow falling outside. The dirty snow covered the black dirt roads, and young Elites and their parents were engaged in snowman-building activities. Ethan and Liam found themselves in the playground of the shopping district, surrounded by Elites in various colored tunics, bustling about on their way to different stores.

"Look, you just tighten your stance and punch!" Liam shot his hand out, hitting the barked tree square in the center and ripping a hole through it. Ethan's mother, Quintella, came running up, bags in her hands, her black hair frazzled in the wind. She looked concerned as she approached them.

"Liam, what are you doing? You shouldn't be using your Code for this!" Quintella expressed genuine worry, dropping the bags and lifting Liam up. "Your mother would be furious if I got you taken away from her." Liam simply smiled at her. "I was trying to teach Ethan how to be a better Brute. He doesn't put any effort into his punches." Quintella placed Liam back down and turned her attention to Ethan.

Ethan looked down at the ground and kicked the snow. "It's my fault, I asked Liam to play with me, mommy." Quintella ruffled Ethan's ash blonde hair, clad in purple robes. She pulled them up and leaned down to look at her son. "Ethan, we've discussed this. It's illegal to use your Code outside of training if it doesn't benefit our society." Ethan's icy blue eyes grew somber.

He tugged on Quintella's robe and glanced at Liam. "But Liam can punch a tree. Why can't I punch a tree? Why do I feel so tired compared to him?" His eyes welled up with tears, and he looked on the verge of crying. Quintella shook her head, instructing Liam to pick up the bags. Liam smiled, twirling his hair, and promptly obeyed, retrieving the dropped shopping bags from the ground.

Quintella turned her attention back to Ethan. "Listen to me, dear. You are different from many other Elites. Your father and I faced challenges when you were born." Quintella continued to caress Ethan's face. "Sweetheart, your Code is not as clear as others'. You have a bone deficiency. You'll have to work twice as hard as most and might not achieve as much." Ethan's sadness deepened, and tears formed in his eyes. Quintella reached up and wiped away his tears. "It's okay, Ethan. You have your father and me. You don't need to fight in this life."

Ethan sniffed and straightened his back. "Do you promise I'll get stronger?" Ethan seemed determined, fueled by his mother's words. "Of course, honey. You just need to do your best. That's all. If you do that, any Brute would see your burning heart." Liam ran up to them, hugging Ethan. "Don't worry, Ethan! I'll protect you. If you're ever in trouble, just rely on me!" Quintella chuckled. "And, of course, you have this." She held up the ruby red pendant hanging around Ethan's neck.

***

But you're not here to protect me now, Liam. Ethan thought to himself, touching his ruby necklace. He cocked his arm back and grunted as he swung, punching the rock with all his might. However, the rock showed no signs of damage like his classmates' had. Ethan ended up with split knuckles, and disappointment crushed his heart.

Another professor spoke up, questioning, "How did you receive recommendations for this academy if you can't even punch a rock?" Ethan kept his gaze fixed on the ground, fearing that he might start crying out of frustration if he looked up. "I excelled in academics and fitness. It's not that I can't punch the rock; I simply dislike the physical aspect of the test, sir." His classmates began snickering. "I'm not a fighter," Ethan continued, avoiding eye contact to hide behind his lie.

"To exhibit zero overall raw power in a test, you must have strong recommendations, boy. Who recommended you?" Carson squinted, demanding an answer. "My parents did, sir," Ethan finally looked at him. His classmates burst into laughter. "Silence! No laughing!" One of the female professors scolded the class. "What's your last name, boy? Who are your parents that you could be so mentally weak but highly regarded?" She inquired, and the room fell into a hushed silence.

Ethan dreaded this moment. He could almost anticipate the outcome, the same as before. He sighed, realizing there was no way to avoid answering the question. The entire group waited for him to respond, and he glanced around, feeling trapped. Ethan reached out and touched his red pendant for comfort. "Quintella and Richard Crambe, ma'am," Ethan stated. The room grew deathly quiet, followed by whispers. Some students' eyes widened, while others narrowed at him. Even the professors showed various reactions, ranging from disbelief to awe.

"Your parents are Quintella and Richard Crambe? The top scientists in Pangea? The Sector Officials?" Professor Carson, maintaining his composed demeanor, directed his gaze at Ethan. "Yes, sir," Ethan nodded nonchalantly. Professor Carson shook his head. "Interesting. It would be disrespectful to insult our Sector Official's child." Ethan stared fiercely at the unyielding boulder in front of him. "I hope my weakness doesn't affect your opinion of my exam, sir. I have more to offer than just physical strength and my family name." Ethan locked eyes with Carson.

Carson raised his eyebrows, meeting Ethan's gaze. There was something in Carson's expression that Ethan couldn't decipher. "Very well, continue with your exam," Carson said, stepping back to resume the lesson. Ethan wondered why his mother had worried about him in the first place.

They continued with more exercises, including endurance tests like holding up objects such as Hoverbikes and metal pipes. Ethan, unfortunately, struggled greatly in these tasks. In the physical fitness portion, he managed to secure third place, catching the attention of a few teachers, but also attracting glares from several students. Next came the sparring session, which he also didn't excel in.

Then came the section on the basic knowledge of Brute history. "Can anyone tell me the mantra of the Brute class from start to finish?" one of the teachers asked. "You may paraphrase, but it must stay true to the essence." A girl confidently answered, "We are the strongest and best among all the Classes, and people truly have no idea about our capabilities." She smiled, proud of her response.

The teachers looked at her, but their expressions didn't seem to appreciate the answer. "Anyone else?" another teacher asked. The girl's face turned crimson with embarrassment. "What about you, Crambe? Anything?" Ethan had studied this mantra extensively but hadn't realized he knew it until the words began to flow from his mouth. He took a deep breath and closed his eyes.

"Brutes are considered the most fundamental of the seven classifications. Our Code doesn't offer any special abilities, only variations in strength. Our bones are like metal, enabling some to demolish buildings with a single touch while others struggle to lift seven houses. Brutes resemble our ancestors the most among the Primordials, but none of us are as weak as they were," Ethan spoke, the words pouring out effortlessly.

"We perform the heavy lifting and take on jobs that not only most people cannot do, but wouldn't do. Our opportunities may be limited, but they are rewarding because no one possesses the physical strength that we do. Although our Code has the least variation, we make up the majority of society," Ethan continued passionately. The room fell into a profound silence as everyone listened intently. Ethan opened his eyes, feeling the electric energy in the air, driven by an honest and intense desire to speak further.

"We are the strong, and we are the brave. We embody the tried and true method, for we are the Brutes. 'The Strongest Will Overcome' is our motto," Ethan concluded. Professor Carson's eyes sparkled with delight. "Excellent. I can't recall the last time a student nailed it on their first try." The atmosphere in the room changed. The history of the Brute class resonated deeply within them, preventing society from undervaluing their contributions and identity.

The professors exchanged glances and began conferring with each other. "We will now commence the selection process to identify the most promising students. The remaining students will be redirected to another Academy that suits their needs," one teacher announced. Twenty minutes passed as the professors deliberated, and the students waited anxiously for the results.

Finally, Professor Carson stepped forward, clearing his throat to address the group. "While a potential sixty students will be divided among the eight of us, I will personally select three students to work under my guidance," Carson declared. He paused briefly and added, "Which, I must say, is a great honor. In my heyday, I was known as one of the finest Brutes on the Guard, and there wasn't a criminal I couldn't apprehend," he boasted proudly.

"When I call your name, please step forward to your corresponding teacher," Carson instructed. One of the teachers began calling out names, and several students were chosen. Approximately fifteen students remained, and Ethan's panic began to set in as he realized the likelihood of being selected was slim.

He couldn't believe he would be rejected. Ethan's mind raced, contemplating a graceful exit from the situation. The thought of embarrassment consumed him as he scanned the room for the easiest way out. Just as he was about to make his decision, Professor Carson approached the group.

"The first student I want is Leonitas Evans." Many students pumped their fists in approval. Professor Carson continued, "The second student shall be Felix Hammond." Nods of agreement rippled through the crowd, accompanied by the sound of a boulder denting.

Professor Carson took a momentary pause to ensure his decision was final and then announced, "And last but certainly not least, Ethan Crambe." The students and other professors turned their heads in surprise at the mention of Ethan's name. Swearing and questioning erupted from many, while others shook their heads in disbelief.

Professor Trischel Kara, who had spoken with Ethan earlier, appeared frustrated. She stomped forward, expressing her opinion. "Sir! While we acknowledge his lineage, he hasn't demonstrated sufficient performance to deserve such an honor. He should be redirected to another school!" Her stance was crystal clear.

Professor Carson stood tall and resolute, proclaiming, "My decision is final. That will be all for today's training." Looking at Felix, Leo, and Ethan, he added, "For the next two hours, you are to familiarize yourselves with the school and then report to the stadium for orientation in the afternoon with your class."

Turning towards the remaining students, he concluded, "Those of you who were not selected will be redirected to another school. Please proceed to the main office afterward to receive your new assignments. Thank you for your effort."

Twelve students in the room were left unchosen. Some began to cry, while others tried to puff out their chests and stand tall, despite not being selected. The air grew heavy, and these students seemed to drag their feet as they glanced back at the smug expressions worn by the accepted students. Some nodded in understanding, while others waved goodbye mockingly. Ethan, on the other hand, felt a mix of relief and shock that he had made it in.

With that, Professor Carson left, followed by the committee that had been evaluating the students. The other professors also departed, and Ethan couldn't believe what had just happened. Somehow, he had managed to get into Unity Prep Academy. He couldn't help but wonder if his parents had influenced Professor Carson's decision, and if they had, he would be furious.

Ignoring the glares from his fellow students, Ethan hurried back to the portal, hoping to catch up with the boy named Leo. Just as he was about to go through the portal, Leo approached him. "Hey man, congratulations on being in my group! I hope we get along," Leo said, giving a genuine smile.

Ethan looked at Leo skeptically and made the decision not to trust him. Elites who were overly friendly often had ulterior motives. "It's not your group, and I don't need your pity," Ethan retorted, glaring at Leo. Leo narrowed his eyes in response. "Chill, dude. I was just trying to make conversation. You look like you could use a friend, but whatever," Leo gruffed and walked away through the portal.

Feeling a pang of regret for misjudging Leo and missing a potential chance at friendship, Ethan rushed through the portal, hoping to catch up with him. However, once Ethan arrived on the other side, Leo was nowhere to be found.

Deciding to explore the classroom area first, Ethan walked through the magnificent halls of the large school. Each room had a unique and magnificent design based on the Classification occupying it. One room had glimmering chandeliers and gold-rimmed lining, while another had a white and blue-lined projector that displayed information as the teacher addressed the students seated in stadium-like seating. Ethan passed by other classes like Sketch, where he saw a room with a bright orange wall and blue carpet that flashed and made a camera-like noise, as if a famous Primordial was being greeted on a red carpet.

After over an hour of exploring, Ethan stepped outside to the skyline. The wind blew gently as he looked up at the bright sky and sighed. "It's incredible that this Sector is practically all glass," Ethan mused to himself. As he turned around, he saw Leo approaching. Leo had bright orange hair, freckles, muddy brown eyes, and a well-toned body. Upon closer inspection, Ethan realized that they were the same height.

"You look like one of those animals I learned about in class. What's that furry cat called?" Ethan joked. Leo's eyebrows furrowed in response. "If you're going to insult me, I can leave," Leo replied. Ethan laughed, realizing his mistake. "You take life too seriously, dude. Lighten up," Ethan said, extending his fist towards Leo. After a few seconds of hesitation, Leo shook his head and replied, "I should be saying that to you," giving a cheeky smile as he fist-bumped Ethan in return. To the Brutes, a fist bump was a sign of acknowledging one's strength and, in this case, an apology.

As they stood by the railings of the skyline, looking out towards the city, Ethan asked Leo about the Sector. Leo's face lit up at the question. "Well, as you know, it's one of the abundantly flourishing ones," Leo beamed. Ethan's curiosity was piqued. "Your dad runs this Sector and ensures it thrives on glamorous life and glass," Leo explained.

Ethan stiffened at the mention of his father and looked down at the ground. Leo noticed his reaction and waited for a response, but when none came, he continued. "Right, well, its vibrant colors and floating buildings make it a sight to see," Leo said. Ethan beamed at the remark. "I know! I want to work in architecture. I love the construction of buildings," he shared. Ironically, Ethan knew it would be an uphill battle for him to pursue that career.

"After graduation, I want to work on designing buildings," Ethan said, realizing he was opening up about his personal life to someone he barely knew.

Leo's orange hair blew in the wind as he looked away. "Not to sound like an ass, but the likelihood of that happening is slim. You're too weak to contribute to building a site," Leo continued. "Anyway, we need to go. We're gonna be late." With that, Leo turned and rushed off to the other side of the skyline, disappearing through the door.

Leo may not have intended to offend Ethan, but his words left Ethan feeling embarrassed and blushing dark red. He pushed the comment out of his mind and looked back at the other side of the skyline, becoming flustered as he wanted to see the different classifications of the school.

As the wind and breeze blew past him peacefully, Ethan realized he was running behind schedule. He could see the city all around him, with its vibrant green glow and buildings of various sizes on the ground, some levitating to make room for more business opportunities. There were many evergreen trees in Sector 71 and large electrical glass domes. Citizens zipped and zoomed around buildings, and a historic monument, a romantic tower, shone a brilliant green light, giving power to the heart of the city. Ethan had never known such peace.

As Ethan rushed to the school's stadium, he couldn't help but think about what Leo had said and wonder why Professor Carson had not only allowed him to stay at the school but also picked him to be in his group. His parents might be an afterthought, but a Sector Official cannot influence Secondary Training. Did Carson honestly think he would be a good fit for this school? "Gallium, do you think I got in fairly?" Ethan asked, out of breath.

The red light came on Ethan's Communication Device, and Gallium responded, "Master Ethan, if I'm honest, I find it strange that your parents would even send you to this school. Any school would have trouble accepting your lack of power in your Code for your Classification, but take this as a good thing and prove you earned it."

As Ethan ran back up to the portal, he glanced behind him at the DNA statue, wondering if he had what it takes.

Chapter 5:
A Brilliant Display

Unity Prep Academy's stadium was positioned on the northwest corner of the campus. It boasted a sphere-shaped dome that could accommodate all first- and second-year students if needed.

As they walked up to the impressive stadium, first-year students laughed and chatted while strolling along the walkway. Lined with evergreen trees on both sides, the path led them to a beautiful, lush garden filled with growing vegetables.

Ethan's awe was interrupted when he caught a flash of red hair in the crowd. It would be nice to have someone to sit with, he thought to himself. Racing past some of the students, he ran up behind Leo and playfully punched him in the back.

"Sup, furball. Wanna sit with me for orientation?" Ethan joked. Leo turned, saw him, and smirked.

"Oh, that joke again so soon? You're gonna need new material by the end of the day," Leo playfully rolled his eyes. "Sure, why not? I don't know anyone else."

They walked up to the stadium's front door, squeezing their way past other students. The domed building had columns of neatly placed steps cascading towards the ceiling. Inside, hundreds of students began lining up in rows, conversing with each other. Teachers directed them to their designated locations, and signs along the rows indicated the students' classifications to help guide them.

"Where the heck did all these extra Brutes come from?" Ethan was confused as they found their seats. "There were sixty in our class, but at least two hundred filling these rows!" He gawked.

Leo raised his eyebrows and laughed. He threw his arm over Ethan and gave his head a playful noogie. "They must have taken additional exams while we were exploring the school, you moron!"

Ethan swatted Leo's hands off his hair and began straightening it out. As he was about to speak, the lights suddenly went out, and bright stage lights shot down to the center of the stadium.

In the spotlight stood a man on a podium, wearing a flashy modified version of the purple Psyche classification robes, resembling a circus ringleader. The room hummed with excitement as holographic screens floated across the stadium, displaying his face.

"Good morning, my young elites! My name is Cassius Fairday!" He took a bow in his bright purple robes, holding onto his purple hat. "I am your fun-loving Principal!" The stage burst into colors of red and blue flames, and the stadium erupted into cheers and applause. "Wow, he's a bit eccentric," Leo laughed.

Seven students in different colored robes joined the principal on stage. "Congratulations on making it this far, but this is where the trials truly begin!" Principal Fairday declared, his golden-brown eyes lively and captivating.

"First things first! We must give thanks to our divine protector, Libertas! Watching over us and granting us another day of glorious freedom." The majority of students bowed their heads out of respect, while Ethan rolled his eyes, not buying into the whole religious aspect. Leo, with his head bowed, briefly looked up and elbowed Ethan, signaling him to behave.

"Now, onto business! Your orientation class is a lucky one!" Fairday announced after raising his head. "Each one of you has been chosen to be a bright example of the Academy. Our Academy ranks 20th in best academic Code achievement throughout all of Pangea, whether you're a Pulse Class or a simple Brute." Principal Fairday laughed and bowed. "It is my honor to present to you an extraordinary treat approved by our very own Sector Official Richard Crambe!" Leo raised an eyebrow at Ethan, asking if he knew about it.

"No, I don't pay attention to my father's actions," Ethan replied, sulking. Leo fidgeted with his hands, stealing glances at Ethan. "May I ask why you're always so bristled about anything your father does?"

"No," Ethan said without hesitation.

"Okay, I understand. I'm sorry if that was too personal," Leo said, trying to ease the tension. Ethan looked at Leo briefly before deciding if it was worth answering. Finally, Ethan sighed, "I'll tell you, but keep it to yourself. My parents are very secretive." He brushed his hair from his face, his voice warmer but his glacial eyes still unwelcoming.

Leo gave him a cheeky grin. "Ah, my winning personality has softened you up a bit!"

Ignoring him, Ethan continued, "It's been a year since I've seen my dad. He's never present, probably because he cares more about his latest gifts to Pangea than training his son to be a better Brute." He trailed off, clenching his fists.

Leo fell silent, unsure of how to reply. The principal effectively cut through the heavy conversation, shifting the attention back to him. "These are the best and brightest second-years we have had in a long time! And thanks to Sector Official Crambe, we will have them spar for you!" The crowd erupted with excitement.

"In honor of this year's Class Clash Day, the Academies have been permitted to practice matchups for the event. This is a great way to showcase excellent Code usage outside of studies." The students started chanting, "Fight! Fight! Fight!" Fairday raised a hand to quiet them. "This is all for the betterment of Pangea! Remember, every time we use our Code, it must improve our society!" The dome resonated with the unified cry, "FOR THE BETTERMENT OF PANGEA!"

Soon, the stadium fell into a hush, with all eyes fixed on the principal, awaiting the next development. Fairday finally broke the silence. "Here's your first lesson of the day! What is a Tempus' best ability?" Fairday's question seemed simple to Ethan, who rolled his eyes. Time manipulation, he concluded in his head. All that tension just for a dumb question.

The person being asked the question wasn't visible, as many students shifted in their seats, trying to get a better view. Fairday's eyes glowed purple as voices in the room began to whisper.

Although no one spoke, a flood of internal thoughts filled the stadium, manifesting as physical shapes in the air around them. Students looked around nervously.

"As a Psyche, it is my job to always see the truth," Fairday said to no one in particular. Rewinding the clock a familiar voice spoke clearly above all the rest. Fairday clapped his hands in glee. "Excellent to the Brute, Ethan, for thinking that first."

Ethan's face turned pale as he processed what had just happened. Had the principal heard his thoughts the entire time? And even his smart-ass remark? Snapping out of his stupor, Ethan noticed Leo grinning from ear to ear. "I think the principal just called on you, Ethan." The crowd started whispering Ethan's name and looking around. Ethan spotted Professor Carson in the crowd, giving him an approving nod.

With his chest puffed out, Ethan stood up. Principal Fairday raised his eyebrows, his eyes still displaying a purple pool of curiosity. "For answering my question in such a Psyche style, come see me at the end of the day for a reward." The principal shifted his attention back to the impending cage match, while some students gave Ethan jealous stares, eager to get ahead.

Ethan sat down, his face burning red. Fellow Brutes fist-bumped him while Leo told some girls nearby he was friends with Ethan. "Bring out the first two Elites!" the speaker echoed. The stage began to rise higher, and the rectangular rim around it pixelated into a rectangular box. A glass wall descended in front of the students' seats, separating them from the stage. Two students, a Spatial class student in his gray robe and a Sprite student in her electric yellow robe, remained on the stage.

"In this corner, we have a Spatial class user: Type 1 Temporals. Using their Code, he can bend time to his will... or lose his mind trying!" The principal's mood seemed to have darkened a bit as he began giving commentary for the Code matchups. The Spatial student, wearing a gray robe adorned with navy blue and gold hourglasses, walked forward with a serious look in his eyes while the crowd cheered for him.

"Over here, we have our very talkative Sprite Class! Best known for channeling electricity through their bodies. How exciting!" Fairday clapped his hands in anticipation. The two students took their respective corners as a buzzer went off, signaling the start of the match.

The Temporal took a step forward, and a static blue force field surrounded him within a five-foot radius. The Sprite student sprang into action, her yellow gloves sparking as she shot forward at extreme speed. However, as she entered the force field's radius, she dramatically slowed down, falling into slow motion. Taking advantage of the opportunity, the Spatial student sidestepped and landed a punch in her stomach at normal speed.

Fairday scoffed, "Is that the best a Sprite has to offer?" The crowd, however, didn't care and continued cheering on the fight. The Temporal continued to land blows while the Sprite struggled to move slowly. Suddenly, the blue force field dissipated, giving the Sprite the opening she needed. She raised her left hand, causing everything that utilized electricity to fritz. Lights in the room flickered as streams of red electricity converged towards her.

In a blur of red, she bolted forward, unleashing a blinding flurry of punches on her opponent. Running in circles, she landed blows around the Spatial student until he collapsed on the floor. Finishing the fight with a red electric shockwave that immobilized him, she stood victorious. The defeated student attempted to get up but was restrained by the shockwave's effects.

The stadium erupted with cheers and applause for the Sprite's unexpected victory. However, Fairday sighed, unamused by the outcome. "That was amazing!" another Brute screamed in excitement. Ethan, impressed by the Sprite's speed and turnaround, remarked, "It's amazing how fast she used her speed to turn the tables on that Temporal!"

Ethan glanced back at the stadium and noticed the boy had gotten back up, seemingly ready to fight again. He raised his hand near the Sprite, but she understood his intentions. They shook hands and respectfully stepped down from the stage while the room remained charged with the roar of the students.

"This school is insane! It's crazy what a high-performance school can get away with," someone near Ethan exclaimed. Leo caught up in the excitement of the crowd, exclaimed, "Did you see that?! That was crazy!" Ethan, still captivated by the spectacle, hadn't heard Leo's words.

Several more fights took place before a Naturalist and Sketch student appeared. The principal began the introductions, and Ethan's attention was drawn to a blonde girl with braided ruby-red tipped hair sitting behind him. As she leaned forward, her soft hair brushed against Ethan's skin, sending a chill down his spine. Turning his head, he noticed a glowing blue rose tattoo on her neck.

"Nice tat," he yelled, pointing at her neck. Surprised, she responded, "Huh? Oh, thanks!" Her hazel eyes locked onto his, and he stumbled over his words, "I don't know any Elites that still have those." She gave him a wink, saying, "Technically, you still don't since you don't know me at all." Ethan blushed as her playful remark sank in.

She smirked and leaned closer, "I'm messing with you. Yeah, I got it at an underground scene." Leo's excitement continued to fill Ethan's ear while the girl's intriguing aroma filled the air. Ethan took a deep breath, savoring the captivating scent that he couldn't quite place.

As a rumble and crash emanated from the stage, Ethan and the girl turned their attention back to the match. This cage match had a unique setting, a botanical garden simulation with rocky terrain, trees, and ponds. The Naturalist girl seemed to be consuming dirt from the garden while the Sketch student maneuvered skillfully through the spikes of dirt popping up around him.

Wearing his signature terracotta orange robe, the Sketch student's curly black hair was matted to his face, and his eyes lacked their usual orange glow. "He's not using his code? Wow," the tattooed girl behind Ethan commented, capturing Leo's focused attention. "Super dangerous... That's kind of badass, though," Leo remarked, his eyes narrowing at the unfolding match.

Ethan's excitement grew as he observed someone who knew how to navigate without constantly relying on their Code. He watched with eager anticipation as the Naturalist halted the spike attacks once her opponent drew near. Rushing to a nearby pond, she dipped her fingers in the water, triggering the formation of a water-based armor around her. Punching the ground, she shattered the rocks and transformed the debris into dust by manipulating the dirt.

From the dust, a sand statue emerged, charging toward the Sketch student. The statue swung, knocking him into a nearby pond. The Naturalist strained to control the dirt statue, putting all her concentration into its movement. However, it couldn't maintain its shape, and as it broke apart, a sandstorm began to swirl, spreading throughout the stadium.

The audience leaned forward, captivated by the unfolding sandstorm. As the sand whipped around, Ethan shielded his face, feeling the occasional sting of sharp dirt against his skin. The stadium erupted into a frenzy as everyone yearned to witness the Sketch student's defeat with their own eyes. Confused and unable to see, Ethan yelled, "What's happening?" Leo, cupping his hands like glasses, replied, "I don't see anything!"

Gradually, the sandstorm subsided, revealing the Naturalist lying on the ground, unconscious. Standing over her was a soaking-wet Sketch student waving to the cameras. The stadium fell silent, disbelief washing over Ethan. He had been watching the Sketch student up until the sandstorm, and the student had been far away, beyond attacking range. How had he managed to defeat her and move across the field in the midst of a sandstorm? It seemed impossible.

Ethan surveyed the scene, noticing fallen trees and medics teleporting in with a Spatial Class professor to assist the unconscious student. "Brilliant! Just brilliant! Another perfect display from our second year, Benjamin Valdez!" Fairday announced, applauding the student's victory and the mystery behind his triumph.

The students applauded the outcome of the fight, but many whispered in confusion or awe. The principal stepped forward, addressing the excited crowd, "I know you're all thrilled to explore the full potential of your Codes during your second year at the Academy. However, it's important to remember that our focus is on teaching Code applications, not promoting violence." The room fell into a hushed silence. "Let me reiterate this to avoid any misunderstandings: We don't use our Code for violence. Doing so can result in expulsion. Only professors may approve fights outside of normal studies, as we are responsible for further developing your Code. Don't be the one who gets caught," Fairday warned with a somber tone.

"Thus, I challenge you all this year to learn how to apply your Code to the world. With our abilities, we've reshaped continents, purified oceans, and stabilized volcanoes! How will you use your Code to create a better tomorrow?" The principal's words hung in the air, resonating with the students as they contemplated their potential and the responsibility that came with it. The room buzzed with a renewed sense of purpose and curiosity.

Chapter 6:
Brute Vs. Spatial

Professor Carson stood and watched as his remaining student rushed through the portal in haste. "This is why we have you all explore the Academy, so you're not constantly late and wasting precious time," he remarked. Ethan's eyes cut at Leo and Felix, who somehow beat him back from the stadium. Leo gave an apologetic look, while Felix wore a snarky grin on his face, seemingly pleased with Ethan's lateness.

Instead of offering an excuse, Ethan looked around the large grassy field surrounded by mountainous rocks. "What's going to be our training for today, sir?" he asked, perplexed. He didn't want anything that would cause further suspicion.

"Today, we aren't going to do much of anything. Let's go over what you want from me," Professor Carson stated. All three of his students looked confused.

"Come now! Surely, you have hopes and dreams! Where do you want to work after you finish training? With me as your teacher, you could go anywhere!" Professor Carson exclaimed enthusiastically.

After some thought, Leo decided to speak up, sounding discouraged. "I feel like as a Brute, our only options come down to heavy labor or law enforcement."

"What's wrong with law enforcement?" It was the first time Felix spoke, displaying disdain for Leo's comment. "My family comes from a long line of Guardians, who have proudly served these sectors well," Felix added.

"I'm sure Leo meant no harm, Felix. Calm down," Professor Carson's voice boomed. As he spoke, an urgent notification lit up on his AICI device screen. "It seems this is all the time we have for today. I want you to think about your answers for the next class."

Leo seemed deep in thought about what Felix said, while Felix appeared to be lost in his own world, not paying attention to Professor Carson's words.

"We regroup with the other classes at the end of each week, so for now, go to lunch, and you're dismissed for the day," Professor Carson concluded.

Ethan felt a pang of annoyance and confusion. He couldn't understand why they had been called there just to be sent home for the day. "We don't need to come back to class for the day?" Ethan voiced his question, the other boys mirroring his confusion.

Professor Carson chuckled. "I'm the headteacher in the Brute department. Does that answer your question?" The boys simply nodded their thanks and began making their way back through the portal.

Ethan and Leo walked through the courtyard to the school lunchroom, a spacious building with white checkered floors. The area was furnished with red velvet chairs and sofas. Drink machines and snack bars were lined up in rows at the back. There was someone serving at the sandwich and salad bar, although it seemed more for show than anything.

Elites didn't require food for survival. Their bodies were developed enough that food became more of a luxury habit. Holograms played current news in the four corners of the room while music played from the other side of the cafeteria.

As Ethan searched for a place to sit, Leo called him over. "Ethan, not that way," Leo motioned, beckoning him to follow. "We're over here with the others," Leo added, walking towards the left side of the cafeteria. Groups of Brutes were gathered in the back, sitting on plush sofas near the music machine.

Annoyed at being told where to sit, Ethan asked, "Does it matter where we sit?" He glanced around the room and noticed that plenty of students seemed happy and were laughing.

Leo explained as they grabbed their artificial food in the sandwich line, "Sure, it doesn't really matter where you sit, but the other classes don't consider us on their par. They don't acknowledge us completely." Leo whispered to Ethan, emphasizing their treatment as Brutes.

Ethan piled artificial chicken sandwiches onto his plate, growing frustrated. Leo seemed aware of his frustration and asked,

"Are you used to this treatment at your old schools?" Ethan pondered for a moment. From what he could remember, it wasn't like this in his old Sector. There were ups and downs, but not such blatant hostility. So, Ethan replied, "My old school was all about survival of the fittest; if you were strong, you were in." He started thinking about Liam, who helped him get in shape and kept him on track. The thought made him happy, and he considered giving Liam a call later.

"Yeah, well, my last school was like this. It seems the more the budget, the more entitled the students think they are," Leo grumbled.

Leo pointed towards the center of the room, where some students wore tunics while others wore robes. "Well, we know where the first-year students sit since they have tunics," he remarked, observing the electric blue tunics with red heartbeat lines running through the back.

"Those are the Pulse Class Elites. What about them?" Ethan inquired.

Leo smiled and replied, "They're cool to talk with, but they have this weirdness about them." Ethan laughed and chimed in, "Hey now! One of my best friends, Riley, is in Pulse. They're not that bad." Ethan scanned the room, searching for the purple tunics. "If anything, Psyche is the worst! Just because they can listen to everyone's thoughts, they think they know everything." Ethan laughed even harder.

At this, a few Psyche students looked up at him, confirming his statement. In response, Ethan directed his not-so-kind thoughts toward an onlooking Psyche Elite. In turn, the Elites at that table flipped Ethan off. Both boys burst into laughter.

"Some Academies only care about results. If they have strong graduates, their budget goes up," Leo commented as they made their way back to the table. Ethan faced some resistance as they arrived. Some students whispered and nodded in his direction, while a few made snide remarks.

"Aren't you the guy who practically failed the exams but still made it into Professor Carson's group?" a girl asked. "I heard he bribed the teachers through his parents," added another boy.

"Shut up. It's not like that at all," Ethan muttered in response. They returned to the table, but a few Brutes looked over, scoffed, and left. Ethan glanced down at the synthetic food on his plate.

"Ignore them, Ethan. You know Brutes always follow strength," Leo sighed.

"Well, it doesn't sound like he has any of that. And if your classmates don't think so, maybe you shouldn't be here," a tall redhead with green highlights interjected, holding some historical books in hand. His face expressed his intent to give Ethan a hard time.

Ethan immediately recognized his type. "Lucky for me, it's not up to them. Who are you again?" he asked dismissively, trying to play it cool.

"I'm Skylar. Not that it's any of your business, but I'm in the Spatial Class," Skylar responded, placing his books on the table.

"You mean the Classification that nearly destroyed the country? Yeah, I'm familiar with it," Ethan retorted, inciting jeers and taunts from students who overheard their conversation.

"We don't know what happened that day, as none of us were there," Skylar shot back, attempting to regain control of the conversation.

"And yet, no one really trusts you. So, as you can see, I'm having a hard time understanding why I should care who you are. Spatial Class sucks," Ethan stated, causing students in green, gray, and yellow tunics to gather like flies. Leo retreated further away from Ethan, sensing the growing hostility in the air.

Skylar took a step towards Ethan. "It's funny you mention things that suck," he said, jabbing a finger at Ethan's chest. "I heard an interesting rumor that some kid who displayed bare minimum talent somehow ended up with the top professor of their class." Skylar lightly pushed Ethan, who stood firmly in place.

"Ethan Crambe. The Sector Official's kid is getting special treatment, of course," Skylar taunted, pointing with his thumb and maintaining his glare. Students whispered about him now, slowly converging in the hopes of witnessing a dramatic confrontation.

Ethan despised these types of Elites. "Look, dude, go back to your group and stay the hell out of my business," Ethan pushed Skylar back, asserting his space. Leo hung back, watching them square up to each other.

Ethan took a good look at Skylar, noting that he was about two inches shorter than him, not quite stocky but not skinny either.

His red hair was a mix of green slime and cinnamon, neatly covering his right eye, no doubt intentional. Ethan made a note to himself: he's a tool. Skylar had bright blue eyes and a few freckles on his face, which took away from the glare.

"You Insipids are always causing problems and think you're above the law. Yet, you want the same respect and responsibilities as us," Skylar said, his tone dripping with contempt. "Your presence in this academy will only serve as a distraction from important work."

"What did you call me? Insipid? At least my group of people didn't get wiped out!" Ethan stepped up to Skylar, unable to hold back his anger. "Is that all you can do? Bring up the past? How about you and your cowardly friend over there focus on not being trash?" Skylar spat at his feet.

Leo, who had initially stayed out of the confrontation, couldn't hold back any longer. "Hold up, I was planning on staying out of it since this wasn't my problem," Leo intervened, his fists clenched. The room was brimming with tension as everyone's eyes were on them. Skylar noticed Leo's hands and smiled.

"So, you wanna fight, huh? Alrighty, I'll give you the fight you're looking for," Skylar said, his eyes turning gray. Ethan took a step back just as Skylar's body transformed into a smokey black mist, disappearing before their eyes. Ethan and Leo looked left and right, trying to anticipate Skylar's movements. Suddenly, Ethan was punched in the face, stumbling backward.

Before Ethan could react, Skylar reappeared in front of Leo, delivering a powerful blow to his nose. "He's a freaking Shifter!" Leo groaned. "Of all the Elites to pick a fight with, it just had to be a Shifter," Ethan shook his head, preparing himself for the battle.

Leo picked up a chair, closed his eyes, and took a deep breath, trying to anticipate Skylar's next move. Just as he swung the chair at thin air, Skylar reappeared and followed up with a roundhouse kick, sending Leo flying backward into a table.

Ethan focused on Skylar's jump movements, realizing that Skylar could only move in a generally straight path, and made several jumps to do so. The timing between his jumps was fast and increasingly slow, creating chaos. Ethan deduced that it was a tactic to unsettle his opponents and hide his lack of skill.

The lunchroom erupted with excitement. "A fight on the first day?" someone exclaimed, expressing their delight. "Wait till I tell my buddies who missed this!" Spatial classmates ran around, shouting with enthusiasm. Skylar continued to appear and disappear, shifting closer to Ethan.

There was a shimmer in the air, signaling the timing Ethan needed. Skylar popped up with a kick, but Ethan swiftly moved out of the way, causing Skylar to crash into a lunch table with full force. The room fell into a temporary silence as Skylar tried to recover.

Taking advantage of the moment, Leo regained his bearings and threw two jabs at Skylar's stomach before picking him up and sending him flying across the room. Skylar screamed as he collided with a group of students who broke his fall. Disheveled and panting, Skylar crouched over, hands on his knees.

"Get up, Skylar! They're nothing compared to you in skill," one of his classmates snarled, attempting to rally him. However, Skylar looked sheepish, realizing his defeat. Professor Kara, annoyed by the incident and Ethan's presence in the academy, intervened.

"Enough!" Professor Kara yelled, pushing past students to the center of the brawl. The room gradually quieted down. "What the hell is going on here? Challenges are forbidden without teacher approval unless it's Class Clash Day. Who authorized this fight?" Professor Kara's voice oozed annoyance.

Skylar, breathing heavily, spoke up, "Professor, I was minding my own business when that Brute came up and took my seat." His face turned red with anger. "After telling him he doesn't sit there, he tried swinging at me!" Skylar exclaimed, attempting to manipulate the truth. Ethan prepared himself for the confrontation.

"Liar! He was talking crap about the Brutes and started swinging at me!" Ethan defended himself, refusing to back down. Professor Kara pushed her red glasses up and smiled slightly, knowing that the truth didn't matter to her. "Ethan, you and Skylar are coming with me," she scolded.

Leo, who had remained silent until now, couldn't hold back any longer. "What's the issue here?" Professor Carson appeared behind them. "Sir, I am taking your students to the Principal's office for discipline due to starting a fight," Professor Kara announced.

"He didn't start that fight, Professor," everyone turned around to see a young girl with an olive complexion and electric blue streaks in her black hair. She confidently approached the teachers, exuding an aura of control. It was a wonder Ethan hadn't noticed her before.

"I saw the whole thing. Skylar agitated them. They stood up and told him to leave, but then he shifted and attacked them," the mysterious student revealed, exposing the truth. Skylar began to look sheepish under her gaze.

The girl turned to Professor Carson, ignoring the whispers of "snitch" from the students around her. With one hand on her hip, she wore a gray robe with the signature blue and gold hourglass insignia of the Temporals in the Spatial Class. "Thank you for your candor; I will handle the situation from here. Skylar, you're coming with me," Professor Kara stated, clearly disappointed by the turn of events. She and Skylar left the lunchroom.

Professor Carson addressed the crowd, "Everyone, finish your lunch and get to class!" The students dispersed, returning to their tables or leaving the room. Ethan groaned, realizing the consequences of his actions, while Leo looked mortified. "Are you going to be okay? You know fighting goes against our Code! Why would you do something so stupid?" Leo expressed genuine concern.

"You were in that fight too. You just got lucky you didn't get caught," Ethan retorted, rolling his eyes. Leo stood there awkwardly. "Maybe you let people walk all over you, but I don't," Ethan replied, dismissing Leo. Leo gave him a hurt look and left the lunchroom.

"Your mother will not be pleased, Master Ethan," Gallium reappeared, stating the obvious. "And here I thought maybe you wouldn't notice," Ethan sighed. "Nothing gets past me, young Ethan."

Ethan began making his way to the principal's office. As it was in the main lobby with the DNA statue, it wasn't hard to find. Ethan turned to the right of the lobby, where there was a sign stating 'Main Office.'

Ethan walked into the office timidly. He looked around the basic white room with chairs lined against the wall. There was an AI waiting behind a desk. When she glanced up at him, she sounded annoyed, which fascinated Ethan.

"Yes, that's me," Ethan replied, surprised that she knew. "I'm sorry, how'd you know?"

The AI gave him a blank stare, seemingly deciding whether to reply. "I was told," she finally answered, and Ethan mentally kicked himself for asking such an obvious question.

"Instead of asking me pointless questions, you should be seeing Principal Fairday," the AI curtly remarked. Ethan raised his eyebrows and gave a dirty look as he walked past the desk through the double doors, where the principal sat waiting.

Upon entering, Ethan bowed. "Sir, I can explain what happened."

Fairday looked up from his desk. Though he didn't look angry, there was an unfamiliar edge in his eyes. "Ethan Crambe...to see you again so soon."

Ethan took a deep gulp, his hands starting to sweat. Would Fairday kick him out on his first day? His mother would kill him.

"So let's cut to the chase, shall we, Ethan? Every second we spend on this is a setback to your education," Fairday said, gesturing to the seat in front of his desk.

Ethan took a seat and listened as his principal gave him his full attention. "Do you know why we have actual Elites and not AI teaching you all?" Principal Fairday clasped his hands together.

"I don't know, sir."

"It's because of emotions. That's something an AI can't teach. There are no circumstances or situations to take into consideration with an AI."

Ethan listened as Fairday spoke. It made perfect sense when he put it like that. "Sir, have you never wondered if they have sentience after all they do for us?" Ethan asked, genuinely surprised.

"No, AI was programmed to do the daily labor primordials did so we can focus our attention on keeping Pangea afloat," Fairday explained, his brown eyes fixed on Ethan.

"Question. Would an AI report you for fighting after I just told your class not to this morning, or would it forgive you?" Fairday's face was dead serious.

"It would report me, sir," Ethan replied, feeling his heart sink.

"And yet, this is indeed a circumstance. For starters, you answered my question correctly first at the stadium. I do owe you a reward."

Ethan relaxed ever so slightly. "So this is your reward: I'm going to overlook this, one time. But consider this for a selfish cause."

Ethan raised his eyebrows, surprised by the response.

"To be honest, I've wanted a favor from your father for quite some time," Fairday admitted. Ethan met his gaze.

"You see, something they don't tell you until your second year is that the assignment chosen for you is the assignment you stay with for life, excluding special assignments such as becoming a Sector Official."

Ethan already knew this, but he let the principal speak. Fairday was letting Ethan off the hook, and he certainly didn't want him to change his mind.

"It's not really your concern, but I wish for a different assignment. It's my hope that by doing this, you'll put in a good word for me with your father?" Fairday stood up and extended his hand.

"Thank you, I'll do my best, sir," Ethan said, shaking Fairday's hand. Fairday tightened his grip.

"You'll do one better. You'll get it done," Fairday stated matter-of-factly. "Of course, sir. Consider it handled," Ethan lied, not intending to bring it up.

"You may go. If I catch you in here again, you'll be finding a new academy. Do you understand?" Fairday looked up one last time before returning to his paperwork.

"I understand."

"Good, then consider this our secret," Fairday gestured towards the door.

Ethan walked back out the door and again wondered why his mother even worried about him.

No one gave Ethan a hard time in any of his classes following the cafeteria fight. He left the school for the day when he couldn't find Leo.

As he began to head down the school's steps, he noticed the girl who had stood up for him. Quickly rushing down the steps to catch up to her, Ethan smiled and said, "Hey! Thanks for sticking up for me back there." He walked beside her. "I'm Ethan; I never got your name." He outstretched his hand.

She looked at it as if it could be poison. "Kira. And I did it because I enjoy seeing Skylar knocked down a peg now and then," she said, ignoring his hand.

"Well, I gotta get home now, but I guess I'll see you around?" Ethan asked. She shook her head at him. "I doubt it. We aren't in the same Class, but who knows? Take care," she said, tossing her hair, sauntering over to her Hoverbike, hopping on it, and flying off.

"Wow, she's something else," Ethan stood there dumbfounded. While he felt she came off quite rude, he couldn't help but feel drawn to her mysterious vibe.

Ethan jumped up on his Hoverbike and flew home as well. He always enjoyed the rides on his Hoverbike. He could feel the breeze hitting his skin and the machine's movements taking him faster than he could ever go. As he arrived home, he placed the bike in the garage and headed to the living room. His mom was there, busy in the kitchen with food. Quintella looked frustrated, and her black hair appeared unkempt. "Your father won't be home tonight," Ethan thought to himself, knowing it was the usual. "I heard that. Are we going to talk about what happened today, Ethan?" she asked, her face half-sterned. Ethan sat at the kitchen table, glancing at the red interface in the corner.

"Master Ethan, it was your Principal," Gallium said with an indifferent expression, making him hard to read for once. "Well, then, it wasn't my fault!" Ethan exclaimed, his hands slamming on the table. "I'm always perceived as weak and hated because of you and Dad! When will you just be on my side for once?" Ethan's eyes welled up with tears, frustration evident in his voice.

Quintella surveyed the room, taking a deep breath as she tried to decide what to do. She gazed at her son, her love for him overflowing in her heart. Life hadn't been easy for Ethan – leaving friends behind, always one step behind everyone else. But he never made it easy; he always found a way to get into trouble. Quintella knew he had been a troublemaker for a while. Ethan loved challenging authority, and if he had control over his Code, he would readily use it to his advantage. Sometimes Quintella worried, but most of the time, she wished her husband was home.

The move was meant to make things easier, allowing Ethan and her to see Richard more often. But Richard hadn't been able to visit, leaving Quintella lonely. Raising a seventeen-year-old on her own was one of the hardest things she had to do. Now, here he was, with tears in his eyes because he felt misunderstood. Ethan couldn't see that Quintella understood him completely. Her eyes softened, but her mouth grimaced. Lecturing Ethan wouldn't solve everything; she knew that.

Quintella struggled with how to tell him that her assignment as Sector Official was ending. Who would she pay to keep fixing his necklace? She had always stressed about this day but wasn't quite sure how to address it yet. So, instead of revealing her news, she simply said, "Do better, Ethan." Turning away, she walked upstairs to a spare bedroom, leaving Ethan downstairs in a state of confusion. Surprised by the lack of an argument, he took it as a good sign and told Gallium he was hungry. "Ethan, you know there's no such thing as hunger," Gallium scolded.

"I'm aware. I just meant that when you come home in the evening, the traditional thing to do is sit with your family and eat," Ethan replied, his tone somber. He dragged his feet to the kitchen table in the kitchen quarters and sat down. Gallium's red form pixelated in front of him as the AI walked toward the cylinder-shaped food synthesizer. Gallium gestured toward the machine and asked, "What would you like me to make for you today?" Ethan pondered the question before responding, "I'll try some of that pasta stuff."

"Interesting choice, sir. Would you like to add anything to that?" Gallium inquired. Ethan cocked his head and replied, "Add some meat and extra seasoning to the ingredients. I want to really savor the flavors." Gallium nodded in approval, and the machine began to hum. Moments later, it emitted a ding, signaling the completion of the food. Gallium picked it up and delivered it to Ethan, saying, "Here you are. Is there anything else you require of me?"

"No, Gallium. Thank you for your help. But may I ask you a question?" Ethan said. "Of course," Gallium replied. "Does it bother you working for me?" Ethan asked, his curiosity evident. Gallium paused for a second, seemingly pondering the meaning of the question. "We AI are designed to make life easier for Elites. Simple tasks such as cooking and companionship are easy for us," Gallium explained. Ethan pressed further, "But you are programmed to fulfill every customer service-related task. Does that bother you?" He wondered if Gallium had feelings.

"If you mean taking care of you, Master Ethan, it is my great honor," Gallium replied respectfully. "Do you wish for me to keep you company while you eat?" "No, Gallium. Thank you. You may go," Ethan responded, a hint of disappointment in his voice. "Very well," Gallium acknowledged. As Gallium's form began to break apart, pixelating, Ethan sighed and looked around. The room was quiet.

The walls projected a moving image of the ocean, with colorful green and blue schools of fish swimming through Ethan's living room. A single fish trailed behind the school, struggling to keep up. Ethan averted his gaze, ignoring the parallels.

Feeling more alone than ever, Ethan placed a hand on his cheek as he poked at his meal. Finally, he decided to call Liam. He glanced at the AICI on his wrist and spoke clearly, "Call Liam Stronghold, Sector 53."

The AICI began to emit three rings, and Liam's face appeared with his signature grin. "You know, the only Elites who call this late at night are usually up to no good," Liam teased.

Ethan fell into their familiar banter, laughing freely. "Well, I can't be a troublemaker if I don't cause any trouble."

Liam's tone turned genuine as he said, "I miss stirring up trouble with my best friend."

"If only I hadn't been an idiot, I wouldn't be stuck in this stupid school," Ethan sighed.

Raising his dark eyebrows, Liam looked Ethan up and down with his sea-green eyes. Finally, he asked, "Who was it?"

"Some Spatial Class student with a bad superiority complex. We got into a fight," Ethan replied.

Liam's face darkened. "Ethan, you can't keep getting into so much trouble. You'll get executed, regardless of who your parents are."

"Relax, I didn't get into any real trouble. The principal overlooked it. But I did have a sparring match with my mom about it," Ethan explained.

"I'd love to chat, Ethan, but I have to get up early for muscle conditioning. I'm really sorry," Liam apologized, his face softening.

"No worries, I understand. I need to go over some school notes anyway," Ethan weakly lied.

"See ya, Ethan."

"Bye, Liam." The AICI vanished, and Ethan let his wrist drop to his side. Once again, he was left alone.

Deciding to embark on another adventure to the outskirts of Emerald City and seize the night, Ethan ventured out. The leaves rustled as the usual neon street glow illuminated the ground. He thought observing the buildings and engaging in a light jog would ease his mind. As he ran a few blocks down, an Elite in orange Sketch robes turned the corner and forcefully pushed Ethan, causing him to fall onto his back.

"Hey, what the heck is your problem?!" Ethan grunted, sitting up.

The orange-robed individual kept their hood up, concealing their face. The mysterious figure peered down at Ethan, the silence stretching for what felt like an eternity. Ethan remained on the ground, unsure of how to proceed. He couldn't determine if the person in front of him was hostile or not.

"I don't have anything worth taking. It's not worth it," Ethan spoke up, attempting to diffuse the situation. The hooded Elite seemed to contemplate something.

Finally, the figure turned around and continued down the street in the direction Ethan had come from. "This Sector sucks," Ethan muttered as he brushed himself off and resumed his jog in frustration.

Chapter 7:
An Unprecedented Event

About a mile from Ethan, a disturbing chain of events unfolded. Second-year student Benjamin Valdez was elated. He had been secretly training with his Code at night, and today was the best day he could have had. Winning his match at the first-year orientation was an incredible achievement. When his professor selected him to present for the first years, it was a great honor to elevate his school status. If he kept up with this performance, he might even receive an offer from the Artificial Intelligence Interface Agency, fulfilling his dream of working there and creating AI.

Benjamin had dedicated three months to training, determined to surpass his peers. Finally, he had unlocked a door within himself. His eyes blazed with a bright, warm orange glow. The looks on the students' faces when he overcame his opponent on stage gave him an exhilarating rush. They were eager to know his secret, but it was simple. Benjamin was a prodigy; his Code was more refined than most in Sketch Class.

In secret, Benjamin had discovered his ability to copy and use multiple Codes simultaneously, something no other Sketch had been known to do. This advantage allowed him to defeat his opponent in the sandstorm. He had already copied an extra Code before the match began. As he strutted down the streets, his confidence shone. However, his triumph was accompanied by a tinge of sadness. Despite his extraordinary ability, he couldn't share it with anyone. Revealing his skill could lead to being labeled a freak. He had to keep everything focused on Pangea and not let selfish motives taint his actions.

Approaching his house, Benjamin's smile faltered slightly. Although he had achieved something remarkable, he couldn't share it with his parents. They might be angry or proud, and the uncertainty made him chuckle. He was confident his father would take his side in any discussion. Skipping family dinner to study with his friends was a decision he made, and now he was about a block away from home, eagerly anticipating their reaction.

Suddenly, a strange feeling gripped Benjamin's gut, urging him to quicken his pace. His intuition proved right when a sudden explosion erupted from behind his house. Instinctively, he sprinted at full speed, only to encounter a woman in a black robe rushing out of his home. Reacting swiftly, Benjamin tackled her to the ground, his hands gripping her shoulders and his weight pinning her down.

"What were you doing in my house?" Benjamin demanded, keeping a firm hold on her.

The woman struggled under his grasp, attempting to keep her black hood in place. She grunted, fighting against him. "Get off of me, you brat!" she retorted, her hood slipping slightly.

Unaware of her actions, Benjamin focused on memorizing her face, completely unaware when she employed her Code to manipulate dark green vines that emerged behind him. Gasping in surprise, he was thrown aside by the robust vines. Staggering back up, he turned his attention to his house, standing in the middle of the street with the mysterious woman. At that moment, he wondered if a Guardian would arrive and take his side. He needed to reach the safety of his house.

"I have no idea what you're talking about, but if I find out you've done something to my parents, I swear I'll make you pay!" Benjamin exclaimed vehemently, his anger fueling his words.

"You must have hit your head hard if you're trying to pin this all on us," the woman scoffed, pausing to glance at the house.

Suddenly, a deafening crunch resonated from within the house, and the air grew heavy with pressure.

Benjamin's head began to hurt. It felt as though it might split.

"How are you doing that?" She backed away from him.

"I swear I'm not—Agh!" He clenched his fist as a massive headache came upon him. The black-robed woman ran off down the street.

Benjamin did not give chase. Instead, he turned and ran towards his house. If someone saw him fighting in the street, it could get a lot worse. He dashed through the front door, which was already open.

He sprinted into the living room, which had a massive hole blown through the back of it. Benjamin slid to a complete stop. He almost threw up as he saw a few bodies with black robes lying around the room. It was as if someone had applied massive weight on them; their bodies were crushed. Benjamin walked in horror through the glass crunching on the floor. Family pictures and precious memories lay bare and scattered all around.

He had looked everywhere, and there was no sign of his parents. After going back into the living room, he realized there was one place he hadn't checked.

Benjamin walked through the new gaping hole in the wall that led to the backyard. There, a man in an orange robe stood kneeling over two bodies. He reached down and touched the bodies.

As soon as Benjamin began to approach, the assailant used a Code and shifted like a Spatial Class Elite would. The mysterious Elite disappeared into thin air immediately. Benjamin was too shocked to process it all. He was uncertain if the mysterious Sketch was gone.

After deeming it safe enough, he ran forward at full speed. Benjamin tumbled onto the ground next to the bodies. He had finally found his family. His father and mother were sickly gray in the face, eyes sunken, and a hollowed shell of the people they once were. Both of them were dead.

As his eyes widened, tears fell from Benjamin's face, and he started to choke in disbelief. He gently touched his mother and recoiled. Her body was as light as paper. Tears dropped on her face as Benjamin cradled her in his arms, rocking her back and forth in agony. He didn't have the heart to look at his father.

As he tried to speak, he just made a cackled wailing sound. Placing her back down with care, Benjamin stumbled back into the house.

"Why, who did this?!" He yelled to no one in particular, collapsing on the floor and slamming the ground with his fist.

Benjamin soon felt that feeling in his gut again. He immediately realized he wasn't alone.

Jumping back up, he made the split decision to run. But before leaving, he glanced back at his family one last time.

"I love you." Tears rolled down his face.

Benjamin rushed to the front door, but the outcome was decided in his first moment of hesitation.

As he made his way up to the front door, he felt a heavy pull come upon him. It was like a magnet being pulled to a refrigerator. He couldn't move freely anymore. He had never experienced this Code before.

When Benjamin turned around, a flash of the orange-hooded figure stood there. The person writhed in pain and grabbed their head.

"No, I'll be damned if I die here," whispering in disbelief, he found himself fighting with all his strength to move.

He leaned against the door frame and managed to fling open the door. It felt like the skin on his back was being pulled off. His chest felt as though it had a weighted slab on it.

With his luck, he saw a young-looking blonde guy wearing a red tunic running up the street, so with all of Benjamin's last energy, he screamed, "HELP!"

The painful pull faded slightly before feeling it return in full force, and Benjamin sensed himself pass out.

Chapter 8:
Encounter

Ethan began his jog down from his house to the beginning of the inner-city limits. His hair was matted to his face, and he was breathing heavily. After clearing his head, guilt began creeping in.

He hadn't meant to blow up on his mother, but he was tired. It always seems to be his fault when it comes to his lack of strength. How hard was it to understand he wanted to be included and depended on?

Ethan ran for a while before realizing he could see the neon glow. He stopped running, looked up to the sky, and saw it was getting brighter.

He plopped down near a pine tree and just relaxed.

Suddenly, Gallium's red interface popped up. "Unauthorized personnel in residence." At this, Ethan shot up from the tree.

"I've been blocked from the main server there, and your mother has yet to respond to my alarm."

Ethan bolted up and began sprinting back to the house.

Frantic, what could have happened in the house? Why right now?

After running for fifteen minutes, Ethan was rearing up to his neighborhood when he heard a scream for help.

Ethan turned to the left and saw a male leaning against his door, about to collapse.

Frustrated, Ethan had to decide: check on his house or help a collapsed guy.

He cursed to himself as he stopped running towards his house. Ethan ran up, managing to catch the guy as he hit the ground. He saw that this guy's skin was an unhealthy gray color. "Gallium, call the Guard."

"He's just a teenager," Ethan realized.

"Can you stand? What happened?" Ethan asked. The Elite started to speak, but his eyes rolled back, and he passed out again.

Ethan laid the Elite back down and crept into the dark house. The smell hit Ethan before he saw it. The bodies. He would have thrown up, but he saw a black hooded figure walking around. They made their way to the gaping hole in the living room wall.

It spoke with a female voice, "This is all wrong. You shouldn't be here." She whined. She appeared out of nowhere and was standing near the back door.

Ethan had tears in his eyes and gagged from the smell, "What the heck are you talking about? Did you do this to them?" The black hooded figure clenched her fist and ran out the back of the house.

Ethan ran back outside to the front door and saw the Guardians. They were standing there with a healer working on the mysteriously injured guy on the lawn.

The Guardian member standing over the healer wore the typical uniform—an opal-colored tunic paired with scientific Code-blocking chains. The robe started from the neck down to the floor. The chains were typically found around the waist.

Generally, the Guardians are considered one of the most prestigious work positions in Pangea. Any classification can be accepted in the Guardians through several trials and invitations. Lately, the past ten years have been primarily Brute class recruits, which, in the opinion of some Elites, had lowered the prestigious air about it.

When seeing Ethan's red robes, this Guardian's face would probably be considered in that hateful group. He eyed Ethan up and down, already making assumptions.

The Guardian seemed to be in his mid-twenties, holding the glowing white Breaker Chains that restrict a power if need be. He narrowed his eyes at Ethan and tightened his grip on the chains.

"What were you doing in this house?" His voice was full of skepticism.

"I went to look inside and saw a woman in there. She was wearing a black robe."

The Guardian waved his hand at several other members, directing them to rush inside the house. He pulled one back who ran past him. The Guardian whispered to one of the other Guardians.

"It's them again. It seems like they killed everyone this time."

"What? Why now?" The other Guardian muttered back.

"I don't know, but we oughta bring this to the Chief." They both nodded.

Ethan wasn't sure he should do anything, so he just stood there. Another Guardian came outside and gagged.

"Recruit! Get a hold of yourself!" The second Guardian was furious.

The new Guardian had short-cropped hair and freckles on his face. Everything about him seemed young and inexperienced. His brown eyes were frantically moving.

"I-I've never seen a body before." He managed to spit out.

"Do you even know when the last time we had a murder was before? Years, recruit. It's new to all of us." He had a look of disdain.

The first Guardian that spoke to Ethan finally looked back at him.

"What's your name?"

"Ethan Crambe, sir."

"Ah, you're the Sector Official's kid. Great, more reports I'll have to do." He combed a hand through his hair and ripped some out in stress.

He brushed his disheveled hair back into place. The Guardian looked as if he needed a good night's sleep. There were dark circles under his eyes.

"Why the heck were you in that house? My buddy can't even stand to be there without puking, yet you seem fine." He must be annoyed that he had a lot of work to do.

"So because your buddy can't hold his dinner, that somehow makes me a murderer?"

"How about you just answer the question before I stop asking."

"I was just checking out to see if I could get help, but everyone inside is dead," Ethan paled.

"I'm aware. You need to leave this area; this is now officially a level 4 crime scene." The Guardian gruffed.

"Get someone to check the remaining area around the house for that stupid cult." The Guard spoke to a fellow member nearby, who nodded and rushed off.

Ethan found his choice of words odd. How would the Guardian already be aware everyone was dead? He hadn't even been inside yet to know the situation. And cult? What's this about a cult?

"You're not going to ask me more questions? Isn't that against protocol?" Ethan poked the bear.

"So, you want to be arrested as a suspect? I'd advise leaving before I change my mind." Ethan swallowed his accusation. It wasn't the wisest to pick a fight with a Guardian. He wasn't Riley. The Guardian looked back at the healer.

"How is the boy?"

The healer, wearing the typical green and white crossed medical robes, replied, "This boy needs more medical attention than I can currently give him."

He had a frustrated look on his face. "I shall take him to a facility at once." Several more medical drones and Guard members went past him and entered the house.

The healer stood up. He had a sorrowful look on his face. "I've never seen this skin coloration before."

Ethan was concerned as well. "What are you still doing here? Go. Now." The Guardian yet again spoke to Ethan.

The neighbors started pouring outside from all the commotion, and someone screamed. The bodies were being carried out.

Ethan took the hint and went home. Shoot, something was wrong at the house! Ethan remembered. He immediately started sprinting. As Ethan ran away, the Guardian sighed in relief, losing his grip on the chains.

As Ethan ran down a few streets, he felt frustrated that he could forget his worries for someone he didn't even know. Ethan got up to his front door, and the scanner registered him.

"Mom? Mom, the alarm went off! Are you okay?" Ethan panicked.

Ethan rushed upstairs to his mother's room, where he found her standing there. "Ethan? What's wrong?" Quintella looked startled. "Did something happen?"

Ethan relaxed. "There was an attack down a few streets, and I was worried when the alarm went off."

Quintella smiled at him. "An attack? What are you talking about, silly? I didn't hear any alarm at all."

"Seriously? I'll explain it later. So, nothing is wrong?" Ethan felt foolish. Gallium must have been pranking him.

"Everything is fine, Ethan. Go to bed." She turned back around and continued to pick up some documents from her table.

"I love you, Ethan. And I'm sorry this move has been hard on you. I'll talk with your father about it." She brushed her hair out of her face and gave Ethan a warm smile.

"Okay. I love you too, Mom." Ethan nodded and went back to his room to lie down. He was quite relieved. For the first time, his mom didn't yell at him for sneaking out of the house.

Quintella turned back around after Ethan left. Her smile left with him. Her right-hand man, Glade, who visited moments before Ethan came home, brought her some very disturbing news.

Students in her Sector were going missing by the dozens. If she didn't do something soon, there would be repercussions. And now someone was attacked mere blocks from their home. How was Richard handling this?

She didn't want Gallium to hear of this; otherwise, he had no choice but to record its information. Which is why she cut him from the mainframe briefly.

She sat down in her armchair and thought to herself. Missing students. Why would someone take students? Pangea hasn't had serious crime in decades. The harsh bylaws and rules in place kept most from attempting any trouble. Everything they needed was provided for them. So why now? She could only ponder the question.

Chapter 9:
History Lessons

Ethan returned to school the next day and entered through his respective Brute door like yesterday. Today, the room was just a classroom. It was dome-shaped, with quotes from their history flooding the walls. The words were gold and faded as new quotes took their place.

All of the Professors, including Professor Kara and Carson, were present. Professor Kara stepped forward to the class of sixty students. "Last night, a student of this school, Benjamin Valdez, was attacked, and his family supposedly killed."

The class started in an uproar of shock. Most of the students were demanding answers as to why an Elite was murdered, while others were crying, saying they knew him personally.

"Settle down, please! He's not dead."

"Well, his family is, though," Leo muttered under his breath. Ethan gave him a look. Since their classes were in the same room all day, they sat next to each other.

"He's in a medical facility recovering." Professor Kara raised her hand.

"I only mention this because the Guardians plan to stop by the school and ask questions about anyone apart from school activities that could be tied to criminal violence."

The students were rumbling questions off the walls.

"Do the Guardians know who did it?"

"Should we be worried?"

"Why hasn't the CommuniOne covered this story yet?"

They rapidly fired questions at the professors.

"Quiet down! I urge you all to report any suspicious activities that you may see to the proper authority or AI." Professor Kara stepped back, sitting on top of the desk.

Professor Carson spoke. "Now, while he may belong to the Sketch Class and not the Brute Class, we show solidarity to every one of our own." He looked around the room at the students.

"We are not primordial. We stick together in adversity, and so we will inform you when he can have visitors to show support."

The class resumed, and Ethan couldn't help but wonder what would have happened if he had not arrived to help when he did. Why was Benjamin Valdez attacked?

"Ethan? Do you have the answer?" Carson asked. Leo nudged Ethan.

"I'm sorry, what was the question?" The students snickered. The class had begun without him.

"I said, we're studying history. What are the seven Classifications of Code?" Carson sighed.

"Um, Brute, Psyche, Sketch, Sprite, Naturalist, Spatial, and Pulse," Ethan said. "And which of those have three or more sub-type abilities?" Carson quizzed him.

"Naturalist and Spatial, sir."

"Technically just Naturalists. Spatial now has only two because of the Great War. But that is correct." The class clapped.

"Who can tell me about the Great War?" Carson asked the whole class.

"You, Felix. Speak." He snapped at Felix. Felix fumbled with his papers and straightened out his back.

"The Great War was the internal struggle about one hundred and fifty years ago where the Spatial Class Supernova, Shifters, and Tempus users got into a civil war and fought to the death. This caused all seven powers to fight the Supernova users, exterminating them all." Felix smiled, satisfied.

The class clapped. "Correct. The Supernova users were classified as the strongest of all the Codes for their ability to manipulate Gravity." Ethan was writing down notes as fast as possible. "Why is this important?"

The girl with a blue rose tattoo on her neck raised her hand, "Because right now we're facing a lot of technology advancement issues without them." She beamed her answer. The class clapped again.

"Excellent, Cassidy. Tell me which ones."

"Supernovas were in charge of space explorations, as well as Hoverbike flight development and keeping a balance on our gravitational pulls in the country." She spoke with confidence. Ethan couldn't help but admire her. Leo gave him a wink and nodded in her direction.

"To name a few, to say the least." Carson half-smiled. "You could say they are the world's most hated Code. Why?" He shot the question and pointed at another student.

"Uhh, because they started a civil war that required all the other classifications to stop and kill them, sir." The student sat down after standing. The class gave their usual clap of support.

"Exactly. This led to the rules we have in place for our society now. Elites have a mistrust of the Spatial Class due to this. But as you are all my students, any of you caught showing prejudice will be expelled. Do I make myself clear?" The class gave a resounding yes.

Several more topics went by before Cassidy raised her hand again. "I was curious about the Sketch Class, sir." She asked.

"We rarely speak with them, but thinking about Benjamin Valdez made me wonder a bit." Another of the professors, Garrett, stepped forward and spoke, "That class wasn't until next month, but I guess we can talk about it briefly." He looked around for any objections.

After a moment, he continued, "The Sketch Class uses other Elites' abilities for their gain. After analyzing it, they temporarily steal the ability, and the more they have copied, the longer they can use it. However, using certain abilities comes with physical drawbacks, depending on their Code. They learn to control these drawbacks at the Academy, and they are highly beneficial in supporting all Classes," Professor Garrett explained. Professor Kara nodded in agreement and glanced at the time.

"But enough about that. You should all be proud. Every question answered so far has been correct. A few more, and we'll break for lunch," Professor Garrett said, walking over to the round cylinder device.

The AICI (Artificial Intelligence Central Interface) device showed the maps of Pangea and acted as a communication device for Elites. It allowed them to call and video chat with each other. The AICI also enabled AI assistance for searching or connecting with anyone known through the device. A miniature version of Pangea lit up the room, captivating the students. The landscape was vastly expansive, with mountains, Elite-made lakes, ancient monuments, buildings, deserts, and volcanoes displaying advanced technology and thriving well. The hologram flipped through different sectors, highlighting some of them.

In their Sector was a metallic tower known as the Iron Lady, an ancient power source made of interlocking joists resting on the ground, resembling a pyramid with slightly curved sides. Another sector resembling a tropical jungle featured a Libertas statue, worshipped by thousands of Elites.

Ethan yawned, uninterested in religious matters. Most Elites had a god complex, and those who sought religion were viewed strangely. Ethan couldn't understand why anyone would pray for something they could achieve themselves. He glanced at the map and noted that no two sectors looked the same. The supercontinent of Pangea was a patchwork of continents pushed together like a puzzle. He noticed a red "XXX" marking in the corner of the country, indicating a restricted area.

"How many sectors are there in Pangea? And yes, these questions may be basic, but you'd be surprised how many students get them wrong," Professor Garrett asked, singling out a bored-looking boy who seemed disinterested in the class.

The boy, caught off guard, nervously responded, "I would assume eighty-three sectors? I didn't know there would be a test." Disapproval and silence filled the room.

"You assume wrong. You may leave," Professor Kara said firmly. The boy looked genuinely shocked, not knowing where to go. "What? And go where?" he asked, his carefree facade dropping as he sat up.

"Anywhere but here, my dear. You've been dismissed from the Academy," Professor Kara retorted, and the class grew puzzled. Uncomfortable shuffling in their chairs filled the room.

"Oh, you thought that simply reciting some mottos and showcasing a few demonstrations before the Education Committee was enough to secure your place in one of the most prestigious Academies in Sector 71?" Professor Garrett sneered.

"Welcome to our second test," Professor Kara declared, and the AICI lit up, displaying the sectors on the map in different colors. "Our Academy constantly evaluates its students to ensure we train the best minds and Codes."

A student voiced their surprise, "Wait, if any of us had answered a question incorrectly, we would have been dismissed?"

"Exactly," all the professors replied with a smile. "If you don't even know the basic facts of our history, why do you deserve to be in one of the most prestigious Academies in Sector 71?" Professor Kara scoffed. Laughter erupted among the professors. The boy, embarrassed, slowly collected his things.

"Please hurry up and spare yourself further embarrassment," Kara remarked, looking at the boy one last time. The boy left the room, tears streaming down his face.

Professor Kara locked eyes with Ethan, her smile devilish. "Ethan, how many sectors are in Pangea?" Ethan's narrowed eyes met hers. He knew the answer, thanks to his parents being Sector Officials. If Professor Kara was trying to challenge him, she would have to do better than that.

Confidently, Ethan responded, "Ninety-nine. The one-hundredth sector, marked with the red 'XXX,' is the restricted area." He prepared himself for whatever Professor Kara would throw at him, realizing he was becoming a target.

"And Ethan, how was Pangea formed?" Professor Garrett asked, his disappointment evident.

"Pangea was formed hundreds of years ago when the first Elites, tired of the Primordials' wars, took the best land from the best countries and created a supercontinent. They killed each other off, and now we have a thriving nation. We are no longer Primordial, or humans as they were called. We are Elites, the best of their existence," Ethan explained passionately, standing up to face Professor Kara.

The class seemed in awe, but Professor Kara appeared less thrilled. "Then what was the original name of our Sector?"

"It's a trick question. No one knows for sure, but geologically speaking, after the Battle for the 38 states, it was named the Re-Civilization Project, combining two countries," Ethan refuted.

Professor Kara frowned, and Professor Carson intervened, saying, "That's enough. You've made your point." Kara seemed embarrassed and stepped back.

"Ethan, you're excused for the rest of this session. You have shown enough knowledge in basic history," Professor Carson announced, and the class groaned.

"Stop groaning. Each of you will be dismissed one by one as you answer your questions correctly," the professor added.

As Ethan picked up his things and left the room, he glanced back at Leo, hoping it wouldn't be the last time he saw him. Leo noticed and gave Ethan a wink, mouthed the words, "I got this." Meanwhile, Professor Kara singled out two more Brutes to determine their standing in the school.

During lunch, Ethan sat alone in the Brute area, observing his classmates as they trickled into the lunchroom. His nerves settled when he saw Leo energetically dancing his way over to the table, though his eyes betrayed exhaustion. Ethan's spirits lifted. "Glad to see you're still here."

"Dude, that was epic! You knew every answer they threw at you," Leo exclaimed, jumping with glee. "Professor Kara was pissed."

"Obviously! If I hadn't answered correctly, I wouldn't be here, dumbass!" Ethan laughed wholeheartedly.

"Oh yeah, I guess you're right!" Leo joined in, realizing Ethan's point.

"To be honest, it's all thanks to my mom's history books. I used to get bored when I was younger due to a lack of friends, so I would read them," Ethan explained.

"Dude, that's just sad," Leo laughed even harder, causing Ethan to blush.

"Well, twelve Brutes got sent home after you left. If I stick with you, maybe I won't be one of them," Leo said, wiping his eyes.

Ethan smiled back, "If I'm the only thing standing between you and getting sent home, then you're in trouble." They both made noise, laughing again.

"Hey, I just wanted to say I'm sorry for how I spoke to you yesterday. It was uncalled for," Ethan offered his fist.

Leo fist-bumped him back. "It's all good. I should have taken responsibility for my part."

"Trust me, I'm glad you didn't. I think I'm still here because of special treatment," Ethan admitted. They found a table and sat down.

"Yikes, don't let the others hear that," Leo made a face.

"Are you not going to eat today?" Ethan noticed Leo didn't grab any food.

"Nah, I heard the synthesizer they use here is low-budget," Leo replied.

Ethan chuckled, "The budget is probably sitting in the lobby of the Academy!"

Leo snorted, "Ha! You're probably right."

Soon, more Brute students approached Ethan and fist-bumped him for his display of knowledge. Cassidy, a girl with honey-blonde hair and a blue rose tattoo on her neck, joined them, as did Remy, a guy with a bad haircut. They all discussed the challenges they faced during the questioning.

Ethan then spotted Kira, the girl from yesterday, sitting alone in a corner, engrossed in a book. Intrigued by her eccentric vibe, he excused himself and approached her. "Kira, right? It's me, Ethan, from yesterday," he said, reaching out his hand. However, Kira ignored him, continuing to read her book. Ethan grew irritated by her demeanor.

"What the hell? You don't have to be a bitch. I'm just trying to make conversation with you," Ethan expressed his annoyance.

Kira looked up, finally acknowledging him. "Really? I didn't know I needed someone to talk to me," she said, exaggeratingly looking around before returning her gaze to him.

"I'm doing fine. Did you think we're cool just because I bailed you out yesterday?" she retorted.

"I thought we could talk," he replied, hoping for a chance to explain.

She gave him a sideways glance, shaking her head, and stood up, stepping onto her table.

"Hey, is anyone else enjoying awkward flirting at their table? I've already told this guy I'm not interested," she exclaimed, attracting laughter from the lunchroom.

Ethan's face turned bright red. "I wasn't hitting—" he tried to explain, but he realized the conversation was over before it began.

Kira stepped down from the table, ignoring him completely. She grabbed her book and left, finding a new seat on the other side of the room, engrossed in her reading.

Ethan walked back to his table where Leo, Cassidy, and Remy were laughing hysterically at his failed attempt at conversation.

"Oh Ethan, that was gold. I love this school," Leo said, struggling to contain his laughter. His playful look was accentuated by the freckles around his nose and his gleaming white teeth. He sat back down, throwing his arms behind his head and leaning his chair back, catching the attention of some Brute girls who whispered among themselves.

Ethan plopped down in his seat next to Leo, dropping his head on the table. "I could die of embarrassment right now," he groaned.

"You clearly don't flirt often, dude," Remy remarked, munching on his food.

"Ew, Remy. Are you seriously eating that?" Cassidy squirmed away from him.

"Well, duh! Why else would we be in a cafeteria? It's a tradition," Remy defended himself.

"It's not even real. Have you ever seen any animals around?" Cassidy challenged him.

"Just because we don't have them in our sector doesn't mean they don't exist."

Ethan glanced back at Remy, unsure if he liked him or not. There was something off-putting about him.

"Anyway, back to the point, I was just trying to make conversation with her," Ethan redirected the discussion.

"Sure, buddy," Leo replied dismissively.

Ethan was done with the conversation. Why did he have to explain himself to them anyway?

"Does anyone know what we're doing after lunch?" Ethan changed the subject.

Cassidy checked her AICI. "For the first three months, it's just Code assessment and history lessons. I think we'll get our classification robes at month six."

"Nice! I can't wait to wear my crimson-red robe. Hopefully, I won't trip over it," Leo mumbled to himself.

Ethan wasn't particularly excited about the robes or the loss of individual identity outside. But he looked forward to the increased freedom they would bring—no curfew and no need for a professor to supervise their practice.

Ethan looked back at Leo and Cassidy. Would they help him get stronger? He hadn't told anyone about his Code deficiency.

"Have you heard any strange rumors?" Remy asked the group.

"No, what rumors?" Cassidy inquired.

"Apparently, there have been a bunch of students going missing in Pangea."

"My friend's cousin never came home, and the Guardians said he probably ran away to another sector," Leo shared, wearing a pout on his face.

"The Guardians act like they're above everyone because their word is law," Remy added.

"Let's hope they're just rumors," Cassidy joked, trying to ease her concerns.

"Who knows, maybe?" Remy shrugged.

Cassidy shot him a dirty look.

"I heard a rumor that black-robed Elites hunt you down in the dead of night and take you away," Remy continued, but Cassidy interrupted him.

"Enough of that, Remy. We have enough to worry about without rumors of strange-robed individuals kidnapping students."

Ethan remained silent. He had indeed seen someone in a black robe when he saved Benjamin, but telling them wouldn't help. He was already a social outcast.

Yet, the thought lingered in Ethan's mind. If the rumors were true, something terrible was happening behind the scenes.

Would Benjamin be alright? Why was he attacked? Unfortunately, only Benjamin held the answers to those questions.

Chapter 10:
Where is My Daughter?

Two months had flown by at Unity Prep Academy. Professor Carson was growing concerned about Ethan's lack of progress in his Code. To help him, Carson began teaching Ethan how to apply his Code after school.

Unfortunately, it didn't make much of a difference. Ethan was still as weak as the day he started school, but his understanding of how to apply his Code was excellent.

Sector 71 was starting to feel like home, and Ethan had found a great friend in Leo. They hung out every day after training with Professor Carson. Of course, Ethan couldn't forget about his friends back home.

"Dude, my dad said I can come visit you for the Robe Induction Ceremony! Your Sector is awesome, so we'll have a chance to hang out!" Ethan walked around Emerald City, talking excitedly with Liam on his AICI.

"Finally! I miss you, Liam!" Ethan smiled sincerely. "Although I've made so many friends, so maybe I won't need you anymore."

Liam laughed. "Yeah, right. You mean a new partner in crime! But hey, I want to show you some new moves I learned during late-night training sessions." Ethan looked around to make sure no one overheard.

"I don't want to end up like that Benjamin guy you told me about, so I've been training," Liam reminded Ethan.

Benjamin still hadn't woken up, which initially worried everyone. But with time, he became old news. Physically, there was nothing wrong with him, according to the rumors. His skin regained its color, but his mind seemed to be in distress.

The problem was that no Psyche could enter his mind without permission, and with his family dead, there was no one to grant it. Eventually, people moved on as if he were yesterday's trash.

Ethan spent his afternoon exploring the Sector. He loved how it blended elements of the past and present. Some streets had glass-like material, but ancient text and history were inscribed on the walls.

There were handprints and rainbows on slabs with two white lines running through them, serving as old memorials. The words below the handprints read "peace, love, and respect." Ethan smiled at the message.

Three lethargic-looking children in shirts and jeans sat near the walls, gazing at the sun. Passersby whispered and pointed but hurried along. The children seemed stuck to the wall. Curiosity sparked in Ethan, causing him to walk in their direction.

"They're Futiles, Ethan. Stay away from them!" Liam's voice rang through the AICI.

Ethan paused. "What did you say?"

"We didn't have them before, but I've been seeing them more and more since you left."

Ethan felt puzzled. "Why does that name sound familiar?" He took a step back. A woman shot him a dirty look for approaching the Futiles as she grabbed her child's hand.

"That's what we learned about growing up, but we never saw one in person. They're Tempus users."

Suddenly, everything clicked for Ethan. This was why time travel was forbidden in Pangea. It was impossible to perform; the user's mind would break from the attempt.

"Who let these children attempt it without supervision?" Ethan stood in shock, but Liam remained silent.

"They're just kids," Ethan muttered to himself.

"Ethan, don't do anything stupid," Liam scolded him through the communication device.

A group of Guardians, donning their opal robes, came running and surrounded the three Futiles.

"Get out of the way," one of the Guardians pushed Ethan aside.

Ethan watched with dismay as they hurried past him. The whole street stopped in its tracks. An execution was about to take place.

A lead Guardian stood with his hands behind his back as the three accused Elites were brought to their knees.

"By order of the World Government of Pangea, you are being charged with the crime of attempting time travel, which is a direct violation of our bylaws," the man paused, appearing uncomfortable.

He looked to his fellow Guardians. "I know this is your first Futile, but this must be done."

The other Guardians appeared to be mentally preparing themselves. "Sector 71 also charges you for failure to contribute to society or the welfare of Pangea. The punishment for this is death!" The lead Guardian's voice resonated loudly and clearly to all nearby. The remaining Guardians had wrapped their chains around the arms and legs of the Elites.

"What's happening, Ethan?" Liam broke Ethan's concentration.

"They're executing the Futiles for not being able to contribute to Pangea."

"It's messed up, man. They can hardly speak anymore to defend themselves." Liam expressed his disgust.

"If you can't contribute to society, what place do you have?" Words that had echoed from his father's mouth now escaped Ethan's lips. "You sound like-" Liam began.

Ethan interrupted him. "Don't say it." Liam fell silent, and Ethan chastised himself for uttering those words. He hadn't meant to say them.

The Guardians reached for their waist and opened a cylinder containing ice cubes. They were Naturalists, Ethan realized, as there was always one in a Guardian squad. The Guardians touched the now powerless Elites, and ice began to crystallize around their bodies until they were frozen solid.

The last sight Ethan saw was a tear rolling down his face before freezing. The glaze in their eyes vanished. Whispering could be heard among the audience. Ethan averted his gaze before the ice hit the ground. The Guardians shoved the frozen bodies to the ground, shattering them. Glittery powdered ice scattered in the air around everyone—efficient and swift.

Children screamed, and parents hurriedly ushered them away. No one needed to discuss what they had just witnessed. The powdered residue from the shattered ice dispersed in the air. Ethan assumed the Guardians could feel his glare for what they had done, but their faces were filled with terror, mirroring his own.

Dusting off their robes, the Guardians resumed their duties. Ethan shook his head, his eyes landing on the double-lined slab with rainbow and handprints on the monument. Although historical, the sight now felt tainted. No blood was on the ground, but the situation left a stain. Everyone had left the scene except for Ethan. A slight chill hung in the air.

He took a moment to acknowledge what had happened to the Futiles, unable to ignore thoughts of his own shortcomings. "They had all that power and couldn't even use it properly," he mumbled.

"Ethan? You okay?"

"Yeah, my fault, Liam. Can I call you back?"

"Sure, man. Hit me up later."

Ethan ended the call with Liam, knowing they would see each other in the coming months. Right now, he needed to distance himself from the incident as soon as possible. Rows of grounded buildings replaced the usual levitating ones. Ethan stopped at a nearby cafe, its exterior walls splashed with yellow and green paint. Orange leaves drifted down, gently settling on the ground. The wind tousled Ethan's hair as he opened the cafe door and stepped inside.

The theme of the place was to transport patrons through time, offering the chance to catch up on the news, enjoy a coffee, and socialize with friends. At least, that's what the sign said. Ethan would have to show him around when Liam came for the Robe ceremony.

He walked up to the AI behind the counter. After ordering an interesting, dark-flavored caffeinated drink, he sat down and turned his attention to the news, effectively boxing away the horrors of what he had just witnessed.

A father appeared on the colorfully blueish-white hologram, pleading for his daughter's return. Intrigued, Ethan listened intently. The man on the screen had a five o'clock shadow and dark rings under his eyes, looking disheveled.

"She would never run away! Something terrible must have happened to her, and the Guardians aren't doing enough to find her!" The man was visibly distraught. "There have been those strange people popping up around town. I've seen them!" He pointed an accusatory finger at the AI reporter.

"If no one is doing anything to help, I'll contact our Sector Official for assistance," he stated matter-of-factly.

The AI reporter seemed shaken by the brazen comment. "Sir, you aren't supposed to contact our Sector Officials unless it's an emergency."

The man grew even more furious. "How dare you?! Are you saying my daughter Nyla isn't an emergency?"

The AI reporter seemed to reset its expression, swiftly moving on as if Mr. Winthrop had never been there. "Well, that seems to be all the time we have today. If anyone has any information on the whereabouts of Mr. Winthrop's daughter Nyla, please leave a message with any nearby AI or Guardian," the AI concluded.

Ethan pondered why the name sounded familiar. How many schools were grappling with this nightmare?

The AI that ran the store pixelated next to Ethan's table. "Your beverage of choice, sir," the AI said, wearing a similar outfit to Gallium's. Ethan briefly shifted his attention away from the news and noticed the name tag reading "BZ-12."

"Do you have a name?" Ethan inquired.

"BZ-12, sir," the AI replied.

"No, like a real name. My AI has chosen to be called Gallium," Ethan found the AI fascinating. Did they possess free will? Did they have a choice? If so, Ethan wished they could trade places.

"Arturo, sir. But my name isn't as important as yours," Arturo bowed. Ethan waved his hand dismissively. "No need to bow. I'm not like most Elites; we're equals, got that?" Retrieving some credits from his pocket, he handed them to the AI. "Here's your tip. You matter too, okay?"

Placing the credits in Arturo's artificial hand, Ethan felt sentimental. Arturo displayed an expression of deep gratitude, praising him to the highest order. Though Gallium remained silent during the interaction, Ethan knew he had heard. It was partly intended for him.

"—Absolutely! Sectors 28, 71, 42, 53, 7, and 10 have experienced an unprecedented kidnapping rate among their young Elites in Academies." Upon hearing Sector 71 mentioned, Ethan shifted his attention back to the news. His mom's Sector was involved, it seemed.

"The offices of the Sector Officials have yet to comment. Please avoid going out alone at night if possible."

The third AI reporter continued, "In recent news, the Valdez family funeral was planned for today, and their only surviving child, Benjamin Valdez, remains unconscious. There are no leads on the attackers, but the Guardians suspect foul play at this time."

"We must not panic, but given the unprecedented situation, the Guardians have declared a Level 2 Alert."

"Weird. The Guardian at the house said it was a Level 4 issue," Ethan noted aloud.

As the news continued, Ethan imagined what it must be like for Benjamin when he woke up. He contemplated the idea of visiting him in the hospital.

"Terrible, isn't it? Crime is on the rise, and no one is taking it seriously," a frizzy-haired woman in her mid-thirties, wearing Pulse Class azure blue robes, commented as she appeared at Ethan's table without invitation.

"Yeah, I guess," Ethan mumbled, feeling his interest wane. The conversation did not captivate him.

The woman chuckled. "Secondary student, I assume? You should pay more attention to the news. You never know when it could become relevant to you," she said, glancing at her AICI. "Well, I must be going. Take care of yourself...?" She trailed off, prompting Ethan for his name.

"Ethan. My name is Ethan," he blurted, realizing her question.

"Well, take care of yourself, Ethan. It can be a dangerous place out there," the woman said, leaving a tip on the table before departing.

Ethan realized he needed to go as well. As Ethan walked through the door, he crashed right into Skylar.

Chapter 11:
Olympic Valley Hospital

Ethan crashed into Skylar, whose face darkened at the sight of him. "You!" Skylar said, glaring. "I swear, if we didn't have a bylaw against unnecessary conflict in the city, I would crush you right here!" Skylar's anger was evident.

"Skylar, you lost fair and square. Get over it. I have never done anything to you that you didn't ask for," Ethan retorted, dishing out his response.

"I'm not Skylar. I'm his brother, Austin," came the unexpected reply.

Ethan gawked for a brief second as Austin looked identical to Skylar. "You should stop lying, Skylar. It's not a good look for you." Ethan was skeptical; twins were rarer than they used to be.

"My name is Austin. Skylar is my twin. I was there at the cafeteria, so I know what you did." Ethan observed Austin, noticing he didn't have the slime-green hair covering his eye. Instead, his hair was a reddish brown.

"Skylar, what did I ever do to you? You attacked me first!" Ethan questioned, his frustration evident.

"I'm not Skylar," Austin repeated, growing increasingly frustrated. "Yeah, okay, dude," Ethan dismissed his explanation.

Austin sighed in exasperation. "Ethan, just know that you have made an enemy out of us. We won't rest until you're expelled from the Academy," Austin declared firmly.

"Good luck with that, Skylar, or whatever your name is," Ethan replied dismissively, beginning to walk away. However, Austin wasn't done.

"You know, for a Brute, you sure can't punch. He told me he couldn't breathe from your friend's punch, but yours... it felt like a child hit him," Austin taunted.

Ethan continued walking away, but Austin couldn't resist taunting him further. "You're weak. You talk a lot of crap and won't back it up. You just keep hiding behind your parents' names. We'll see how that works out for you on Class Clash Day," Austin yelled. Ethan stopped in his tracks and turned around.

"I'm not my parents," Ethan said, a glare in his eyes. "I will never be my parents. Don't pretend to know about my life or me because you don't know a damn thing about me." And with that, Ethan left before Austin could respond.

Ethan spent his afternoon strolling through Emerald City, exploring vibrant and colorful stores. He tried to push his encounter with Skylar's brother out of his mind. Instead, his thoughts kept returning to the incident with Benjamin. Why had he been attacked? How was he doing now? The school hadn't provided any updates since their last communication. Ethan vividly recalled the night he ran, the overwhelming desire to escape it all, his frustrations with the fight and school, and his mother.

"Jeez, she was acting so strange that night," Ethan muttered, smiling wryly. "You're making it sound like she was involved, you idiot."

The once-bright sky began to glow in a deep emerald green as the buildings lit up, signaling the approaching darkness. Ethan realized it was getting late and decided to seek refuge in a nearby café. He settled at a table towards the back, lost in his thoughts. Ethan contemplated reaching out to Riley about the whole situation, but Liam's impending visit loomed in his mind. Given his interest in Criminal Law theory, he knew Riley would be upset if he hadn't invited him along. Moreover, Ethan couldn't quite piece together all the details surrounding the attack.

Driven by curiosity, Ethan called upon Gallium. "Pull up CommuniOne. I need to check something." The screen displayed a list of Elites in Sector 71 as Ethan swiped through the profiles. CommuniOne was a platform where users could digitally connect with Elites they had encountered before. It allowed sharing of moving photos, memories, event postings, and forums—like a virtual graffiti wall on a mainframe server.

"He's definitely not in my year; otherwise, he wouldn't have participated in the assembly fights," Ethan pondered. The algorithm prioritized classifications and related work, hobbies, school, and interests. "Gallium, do you remember which Class the professors mentioned Benjamin Valdez belonged to?" Gallium entered "Sketch Class" and, after numerous faces passed by, Benjamin Valdez's profile finally appeared.

"Stop! That's him," Ethan exclaimed. The picture showed a guy with a dark caramel complexion, curly-haired afro, and gray eyes. He was captured with a joyful smile, standing beside a girl with auburn hair, her hands wrapped around his waist. The images played in a loop, and Ethan scrolled through several virtual videos where fellow Elites offered their good wishes and condolences for his loss. In many of them, a girl named Lisa, featured in his photo, accepted the condolences on his behalf.

"His girlfriend, huh? I might be able to gather information from her. Gallium, initiate contact with her through this platform." Three blue rings appeared and began scanning Ethan, emitting a soft humming noise. After the third hum, a light beam emanated from Ethan's AICI (Artificial Intelligence Communication Interface). Another set of three rings materialized, and the girl, Lisa, appeared on the screen.

Lisa had another guy playfully nuzzling her as she laughed, but when she saw Ethan, she quickly pushed him away and composed herself. "Can I help you with something?" she asked, tossing her hair and straightening up. "Hi, sorry to bother you. My name is Ethan. Um, I was just wondering if maybe you could tell me if Benjamin is okay," Ethan inquired.

Uncomfortably, she moved in front of the screen. "Well, I don't know too many details. We broke up," she revealed, surprising Ethan. "Oh, so he finally woke up!" he blurted out, feeling a sense of relief although uncertain why.

Her face reddened, and she looked down. "No, he hasn't woken up yet. I just couldn't keep worrying like this, and the specialists at the hospital don't have a recovery timeline for a Sketch Class attack," she explained. Then she asked, "What do you have to do with this anyway?"

"I was there. I found him and just wanted to check in, but I have no idea how to get a hold of him. I was going to ask if I could go to the hospital with you, but..." Ethan trailed off, unsure of what to say. He had just discovered that the girlfriend of the guy he saved was cheating on him while he was in a coma.

"Look, I'll send you the coordinates to the hospital if you stop judging me. Also, as a favor, when you see him and he wakes up, can you tell him it's over? I would... but that would be awkward," she requested, her attention drawn back to the other Elite who was growing impatient and kissing her neck. Blushing, she added, "Okay, thanks. Bye!" The call ended abruptly as the three rings disappeared. Soon, a link appeared on Ethan's screen, directing him to Emerald Fields Hospital. He sat there, processing the information he had just received.

A Sketch Class attack. Why would a Sketch Class Elite attack a Sketch student? Maybe this was related to the kidnappings... As Ethan contemplated this, an AI employee approached him in the shop where he was sitting and informed him that they would be closing soon.

"My apologies. Gallium, send a notification to Mom and let her know I'll be home late," Ethan said, walking outside and looking at the coordinates on his screen. "Liam would kill me if I stumbled upon something as crazy as this and didn't seek answers."

Each Sector had unique characteristics, and cities made efforts to stand out. Cities that preserved relics or maintained their architectural history received better funding from the government. Tourist attractions played a crucial role in enticing Elites to transfer to new Sectors, and it was in this aspect that Ethan found joy. He was deeply fascinated with Primordial history, which ignited his love for architecture. For Ethan, this journey felt like a field trip.

He hopped on his Hoverbike and headed towards Olympic Valley, which was approximately thirty minutes away at his bike's speed. Olympic Valley was a large medical center, almost like its own city. It was nestled closer to one of Sector 71's historic forests in Zone 2. Like everything else in Emerald City, it had been modified and reconstructed. The layout was extensive, accommodating a significant population of Nature Class Elites. Ethan knew that Sector 71 was divided into three zones, spanning a vast area of 470,000 sq km, and he had only seen a glimpse of it.

As Ethan approached, the landscape transformed, with trees stretching out for miles. Elites in this area seemed to live more modern lives in tree huts. Houses of various designs could be seen scattered across hundreds of trees, and children swung from vines and climbed the branches. Academies, shops, and offices were cleverly integrated between trees or on available ground space.

To Ethan's surprise, the hospital didn't resemble his expectations. It was nestled inside an immensely overgrown tree near the lake, with vines spreading out and embedding their roots into the water. Solar panels were cleverly integrated into the branches of the tree. A network of sleek silver buildings adorned with heart symbols extended as far as Ethan's eyes could see. The valley below him blossomed with an array of plants and flowers.

Naturalists, wearing their robes, were on hands and knees, carefully picking out herbs and marking them for delivery to the Sectors. Nature Class users, also known as "Naturalists," served as leading specialists in the medical field. They oversaw health issues, and although diseases were no longer a problem, small fights or work accidents were expected and required treatment.

Ethan entered the massive hospital and noticed that it was relatively quiet. Being well-acquainted with hospitals due to the Class training that often left him injured, he approached the receptionist and asked, "Can you point me to Benjamin Valdez's room?"

The AI receptionist glanced at the screen and replied, "Down the hall to the left, room 108."

Ethan began walking and spotted Leo sitting outside one of the terrarium rooms. Leo seemed surprised to see him and stood up. "What are you doing here?" Leo asked, his tone lacking enthusiasm.

Ethan raised an eyebrow and crossed his arms. "I could ask you the same question," he retorted. Leo let out a sigh and explained, "My grandmother is getting a consultation on age reduction..." He didn't sound pleased about it.

Ethan glanced away momentarily and replied, "Oh, well, I came here to visit someone." Leo stretched his neck and shrugged. "Mind if I tag along? This might take a while, and I need something to do."

Ethan nodded and continued down the hall with Leo. The black and white checkered tiles and chrome-colored walls gave the corridor a distinctive look. Wires ran through the walls, and rainbow lights washed over them, transmitting information back and forth.

The quiet walk gave Ethan time to think, and he was grateful for Leo's company. Leo had become one of his favorite aspects of school if he was honest with himself.

"Hey, I know I was an asshole when we first met, but I just wanted to say I'm glad we became friends, Leo," Ethan admitted, looking at Leo with a sheepish expression.

Leo smiled radiantly, scratching his red hair as they walked. "Hey, it's bridge under the water. You're pretty cool once you get past that stick up your ass."

Ethan laughed and teased him, "You know the expression is water under the bridge, right?" As Leo's face turned bright red, Ethan laughed even harder. They approached room 108 on the left and opened the door.

The hospital rooms followed a standard design. Since most of the hospitals were run by Naturalists, they were often located near medicinal herbs. The rooms were walk-in terrariums with green plants scattered around. Visual images of waterfalls adorned the walls, accompanied by matching sounds. The beds resembled garden beds, with nightstands holding flowers in vases to create a soothing atmosphere for visitors and patients.

However, upon entering this particular room, something felt off. Two men stood over Benjamin, who lay in bed. As they noticed Leo and Ethan, the two men exchanged glances. "Excuse us," one of the Elites mumbled, and both hurriedly left the room. Leo looked puzzled and asked, "Who were they?"

"No idea. Maybe relatives?" Leo examined the room and walked around Benjamin's sleeping form. "So, what exactly did you have in mind coming here?" he questioned Ethan.

"I don't know. The truth is, I'm the one who found him. I can't help but wonder what happened to him," Ethan confessed.

Leo's face displayed surprise. "Seriously? Are you okay? Why didn't you tell me?"

"It's not that I don't trust you. I just didn't want to become a rumor in school again," Ethan explained.

"Very fair, dude. It's like no one has anything better to do than spread gossip," Leo replied, folding his arms.

Shortly after, a medical specialist entered the room. At first glance, Ethan thought she seemed rather young. She wore a green and white uniform, with the colors divided down the middle—a typical Healer uniform. The dress had buttons that ran from top to bottom, and her flushed face and black bob haircut didn't make her particularly stand out. However, her sea-green eyes were her redeeming feature.

"Just couldn't stay away, huh, boys?" she frowned. "There have been quite a few Elites attempting to sneak a peek at the boy who survived a slaughter."

"I'm the one who saved him, ma'am," Ethan stated. The specialist wore a surprised expression but remained silent.

Ethan approached Benjamin's bed, where the boy appeared peacefully asleep. "Any idea when he's going to wake up?" he asked.

Leo stepped up beside Ethan to get a better look. "So, this is Benjamin... Can't believe anyone could or would get attacked like that."

Clearing her throat, the specialist responded, "It could be seconds or months from now. There is no reliable timeline for awakening. He has all he needs to wake up... he just hasn't." Ethan continued to gaze at Benjamin, feeling the urge to shake him awake. There were so many unanswered questions he desperately wanted to ask.

Looking back at the specialist, Ethan asked, "Can you tell us why he was attacked?" The specialist shrugged. "From what I hear, it's related to those crazy conspiracy kidnappings, but this doesn't fit the usual pattern."

"The usual pattern? What do you mean?" Ethan pressed further.

She explained, "I'm saying there's never been a murder involved in these cases before, let alone any trace of the students after the kidnapping." Her gaze turned nervous. "But please don't tell anyone I said that! It's just a rumor among the staff."

Leo craned his neck again. "It's probably because he fought back or something." Leo checked his hologram and walked toward the door. "I need to go check on my grandmother, but I'll be right back." Leo exited the room, and the door closed.

Awkwardly standing in the room with the specialist, Ethan felt increasingly uncomfortable. She remained silent but continued to stare at him. Without Leo present, Ethan made no attempt to engage in further conversation.

The specialist continued to scrutinize Ethan before speaking up. "You shouldn't be here, Ethan." Ethan looked up, feeling a sense of familiarity with those words. Why did they sound so familiar?

Nevertheless, she continued, "You were the last known person in the house. If the Guard suspects you of foul play, you could get into serious trouble." Genuine concern showed in her expression.

Ethan hesitated for a moment, recalling what she had said. "You shouldn't be here." That line bothered him. He had heard it before.

With that thought in mind, he said, "Come to think of it, I've never told you my name." The specialist began to respond when Benjamin suddenly opened his eyes. He immediately turned his head towards them and let out a piercing scream.

Chapter 12:
Unrobed

Benjamin awoke in a sudden upsurge of fear and panic, shocking both Ethan and the female specialist out of their conversation. "Get the hell away from me!" His eyes were frantic, and he appeared even more exhausted than when he was asleep. He tried to throw himself out of bed but collapsed. Ethan stood frozen in shock while the specialist sprang into action.

She lunged at Ethan, swinging her fist at his face, catching him off-guard. Ethan tumbled into the nightstand next to the bed, hitting his head. Dizzy and disoriented, Ethan took a moment to process what had just happened. Where had he seen her before? He replayed the scene in his head.

During that brief moment, the woman began strangling Benjamin while he was on the floor, his face turning from red to purple as he struggled for breath. Ethan regained consciousness as the woman removed one hand from Benjamin and waved her hand, causing vines to erupt from the floor and throw Ethan against the back wall. Benjamin grabbed the specialist's hand, and his eyes flashed bright orange. He unleashed a radiant orange light throughout the room, and the vines seized the woman, hurling her against the wall and freeing Benjamin.

Coughing intensely for air, Benjamin pulled himself up, his eyes flashing once again. He forcefully pulled the woman back toward him and struck her with all his might, knocking her to the ground. His eyes burned with ferocity as he straddled her. "I remember you. You were outside my house!" he screamed. Despite the pain, she kicked out at him, yelling, and managed to flip him over. Everything was happening too quickly for Ethan. He was still trapped in a bed of vines that seemed to drain the air from the room, crushing him.

Just as Ethan's vision started to fade, Leo burst through the door. Leo quickly assessed the situation, lifted the woman, and threw her through the building's wall. She rolled outside, clutching her arm. The vines restraining Ethan withered away, and he collapsed to the floor, gasping for air.

Their assailant stumbled for a moment before fleeing into the night. Leo wasted no time and chased after her. "Hey, get back here!" Ethan tried to shout, but Leo was already long gone.

A doctor and a Guardian entered the room. "What the hell is happening in here?!" the guard member dressed in opal attire exclaimed. Ethan, trying to make sense of it all, spoke first. "One of your staff members just tried to kill me and this guy here!" he exclaimed, pointing at Benjamin, who was rubbing his neck in pain.

"My friend went after her! They were heading toward the lake!" Ethan leaned against the wall frame for support, feeling pathetic and frustrated with himself. He scolded himself for his weakness. While Leo threw that woman through a wall and pursued her, he struggled just to stand.

Benjamin had regained enough strength to sit up while the Doctor examined him. The guard member spoke into an AICI device, "We have suspicious activity at Olympic Valley Hospital. Send backup." The guard member looked at Ethan. "I'm going to have to detain you for questioning. Don't go anywhere, understand?" Ethan felt frustrated. "My friend is out there with a criminal! Do your job and send help!" The Guard looked annoyed. "I have a squad in that area that will investigate," he replied, but Ethan couldn't shake off his bad feeling.

The woman sprinted away from the hospital with all her might, gasping for breath as she reached a tree line near the lake. Pausing next to a tree and turning around, she found herself tackled to the ground by Leo.

"You're not going anywhere!" he growled, mounting her. However, as he began delivering blows to the mysterious woman, he suddenly found breathing difficult. He paused, feeling as if his lungs were being crushed.

"You were getting beaten by him? Come on now, sis," a hooded figure strolled up to them while Leo remained immobilized on his knees.

She giggled, "You still have a lot to learn, my little sister." The woman, who appeared to be a fake hospital staffer, rose to her feet. "Thanks, but I could have taken him down a second later if you hadn't interfered," she grumbled.

"You just sabotaged the entire operation we spent a week planning!" Two men in differently colored robes emerged from the pine trees in the area—one in a red robe and the other in gray.

Leo, unable to move, recognized them as the Elites who had been standing over Benjamin in the hospital room earlier.

"Rayvena, you claimed this girl was the real deal, but all she did was fail to eliminate the target twice," the enraged man berated her.

Rayvenna had never seen him so furious before. "That's why I sent her to rectify her mistake."

"Mistake? We lost seven loyal brothers and sisters due to that stunt at the Valdez'!" he continued, seething with anger. The man in his mid-twenties was burning with anger.

Rayvenna, the hooded woman, stepped forward and slapped the first man across the face. "Where are your robes, Titus? Are you trying to be recognized?" She glanced disapprovingly at his red robes. Titus had a steely glint in his eyes.

"Do you think we can stroll into a hospital wearing dark hooded tunics without arousing suspicion? We had to assess his room first, and it was her job to kill the kid!" he retorted, rolling his eyes.

The younger woman looked irritated. "Titus, YOU were the one spooked by some children entering the room." Then, she turned her gaze to Leo, who was wide-eyed. "We have to kill him. He's seen our faces."

Rayvena stepped forward. "No... I have a better idea. Let's take him with us instead. We failed to acquire another Sketch student, but a Brute strong enough to overpower you will do just fine for the tests." Rayvena snapped her fingers, and Leo slumped forward.

"Wait, what about Ethan? He saw my face!" the younger woman whined.

Rayvena pondered for a moment. "You're right, sis. We can't allow that." She snapped her fingers, and the woman collapsed to the ground. Rayvena sighed and glanced at Titus. "Titus, it seems you were right. She wasn't ready."

Rayvena bent down and gently caressed the woman's face. "Sorry, Maya. Looks like you'll have to be the scapegoat for now..." She gestured toward her companions. Titus seized Maya by the arm and tied her to one of the trees.

Rayvena disdainfully regarded Maya one last time. "Sister... All this talk of sisterhood and brotherhood is rubbish. They want us to feel like family, but I know who my real family is." She twirled her purple locks before adding, "But I suppose she's serving her purpose, so let her take the blame. She'll know what to do when questioned." The quieter Elite said, "I'm ready for us to depart." Rayvena nodded. "Well done, Pike. I need to return to my actual sister, anyway."

The other Elite raised his hand while Titus hoisted Leo over his shoulders. A black portal sliced open, revealing a glimpse of a laboratory within. The three stepped through the virtual doorway, bringing along the unconscious Leo.

Chapter 13:
The Laboratory

Ethan cooperated with the Guardians during his questioning, trying to remain as calm as possible. However, his primary concern was how long it was taking them to locate Leo. Meanwhile, Benjamin had just completed his examination with the Doctor, who concluded that, pending paperwork and checkups, he would be cleared to leave the hospital.

As Benjamin sat on the bed, he observed Ethan. He noticed the frantic gaze in Ethan's icy blue eyes and the way he clenched his fist when Leo's absence was mentioned. Ethan appeared to be a passionate individual, perhaps even an Elite. His wavy blonde hair often fell across his face, and a persistent scowl seemed etched upon his features. While he possessed a decent build, he didn't quite resemble a typical Brute; he appeared more akin to the Naturalist or Psyche Class.

Finally, Benjamin broke the silence and asked a question, locking eyes with Ethan. Benjamin believed genuine understanding could be attained by studying someone's expressions directly. Ethan wore a somber expression as he inquired, "What do you last remember?" Benjamin's face brightened as he contemplated the gravity of the situation, remaining silent for a considerable time.

"Is my family dead?" Benjamin's face turned ghostly pale. "I couldn't protect them and don't even know why we were attacked." Ethan listened attentively.

"I was out practicing my Code with my friends for exams, preparing for graduation!" Benjamin's frustration was evident. "When I returned home, they were all dead." He paused, his eyes distant, far from the hospital room. "My mother... She appeared lifeless, devoid of all vitality. They were blown from the kitchen table to the backyard." His eyes had a distant look as if he had traveled to another place, far from the hospital.

"I told them to eat without me because I thought it was pointless," Benjamin began laughing. "You understand, right? I mean, come on! We don't even need to consume food! Why waste precious time eating for the sake of some outdated tradition?" His laughter trailed off.

Ethan simply looked at him, expressing his heartfelt condolences. Benjamin seemed broken, sitting crumpled on the bed in the hospital.

"...And those other bodies... There were people dressed in black hooded robes, crushed," Benjamin continued.

"What do you mean?" Ethan asked, his curiosity piqued.

Rubbing his eyes, Benjamin replied, "I don't know. Everything was happening so fast, and a Sketch in an orange robe was present."

"Do you think someone is targeting you?" Ethan began to pace, wondering if there was a connection between the attack and recent news.

"All I know is that once I leave this hospital, I'm going to find whoever did this and make them pay," Benjamin declared with determination.

"Don't you think we should leave this to the Guard?" Ethan was taken aback by Benjamin's choice of words.

"Would you? I don't think you're the type to check on people without reason. You wanted to witness the spectacle, am I right?" Benjamin's comment unintentionally sounded harsh.

"I wanted to understand why you were attacked. I just can't shake the feeling that this isn't over," Ethan paced anxiously in the room.

"This is a lot to handle right now, man. Can we discuss this later?" Benjamin's voice cracked under the weight of his words.

Ethan's heart sank as he realized his insensitivity. After all, Benjamin had just lost his family. He ran a hand through his own hair and sighed, remorseful. "I'm sorry. I didn't mean to impose my thoughts on you. And my condolences to you as well."

A knock interrupted their conversation, and both Benjamin and Ethan turned their attention to the Guardian entering the room.

"We found no trace of the Elite you mentioned, Leo, but we have a suspect in custody. We will begin questioning her as soon as she regains consciousness," the Guardian informed them, glancing at Ethan once again.

Ethan's heart sank. Leo was missing.

"Do you have a parent I should call? Your father or someone?" Benjamin observed as Ethan tensed up. "No, there's no need to call anyone. I'll be heading home soon," Ethan replied.

Ethan looked at Benjamin and stretched out his hand. "I'm the guy who found you when you were attacked. My name is Ethan Crambe. I know it's not my place, but I really want to help you find out why you were attacked."

Benjamin held back tears and introduced himself as Benjamin Valdez, preferring to be called Ben. "I appreciate your offer, but I don't have a place to go because of the accident," he explained.

Ethan appeared determined. "That's why you're coming to stay with me until you get back on your feet."

Ben shook his head, surprised by Ethan's willingness to go out of his way to help. "Why would you go to such lengths for someone you don't even know? Now that I think about it, I'm sure my girlfriend will let me stay at her place." Ben's remark was more matter-of-fact than a question.

But Ethan still shook his head. "She's moved on and is with someone else, dude. I'm really sorry," he responded. Ben slumped back onto the bed and requested, "I need a minute alone. Could you please leave?"

Ethan got up and left the room, closing the door slowly behind him. He walked down the hall until he approached a woman in her thirties who was engaged in an argument with the Guardians. Her gestures were animated.

"What do you mean you can't find my grandson? He was right here when I was with the Doctor, and now he's missing?" She turned and noticed Ethan.

She was a rather unattractive woman, as if she had undergone one too many surgeries that made her look plastic and doll-like. This must be the reason for Leo's distress. "Darling, are you friends with my grandson Leonitas?" she asked.

Ethan nodded and replied, "He's missing, ma'am, and it doesn't seem like they're doing everything they can to find him."

Upon hearing this, she let out a shrill cry. "You all better find my child, or else your heads will be on the news!" The Guard glared at Ethan angrily but eventually walked away without saying anything other than, "Yes, ma'am."

Leo's grandmother turned slowly toward Ethan, her eyes filled with curiosity and sadness. "Hopefully, they find him, ma'am," Ethan said. "Call me Karla, child," she responded, examining him from head to toe. "Come sit with me and calm my nerves." The two took seats in the waiting room.

"Tell me, what's it like being in the same class as Leonitas?" Ethan contemplated the question.

"He's a great guy. He works hard, is passionate about his work, and he's always kind, at least to me. He seems to have a strong sense of purpose and fights for what he believes in," Ethan replied. Karla smiled wryly.

"His father died in an accident when he was young, and his mother didn't want the full responsibility, so I helped. Eventually, she decided I was better suited to shoulder her burden and left the Sector without ever contacting me again." Ethan found it difficult to maintain eye contact.

Karla must have noticed because she looked down at the floor. "I'm sure you probably think I'm repulsive with my face like this. Leonitas never liked it," she confessed, appearing troubled.

"But I had the surgeries to stay with Leonitas longer. He's like a son to me, and I don't want him to be all alone," Ethan felt a pang of sympathy for a woman who would disfigure her face to ensure someone else wouldn't feel lonely, even though it would make her lonesome in the process.

"I'm sure he appreciates you, ma'am. Leo is a good guy, and he's resilient. I'm sure he's okay," Ethan reassured her. Karla's expression grew even sadder. "He's going to have to be... the doctors say they can't reverse my aging anymore without causing harm. You see, my second surgery was botched, and now my fourth one is complicated."

She continued, "You can make a person look young as much as you want, but you can never reverse the soul. Deep down, it knows when it's time." Karla took hold of Ethan's hands, which surprisingly felt soft.

"If they find my boy, I want you to look after him. I know I don't know you, but you seem like the honest type," she pleaded, appearing tired.

"You're the only one expressing concern right now, which means you're truly a friend," she added. Ethan met her gaze.

"And if they don't find him?" Ethan locked eyes with her.

Her brown eyes seemed to burn with determination. "Then make whoever took him away from me pay." With that, she got up and slowly walked back into her room.

***

Leo woke up in a brightly lit white room. The entire space was furnished with plush velvet white, devoid of any beds, mirrors, or other Elites. He checked himself for bruises and surveyed the room, patiently waiting for someone to arrive.

Someone had to come. The Elites who had taken him promised a plan and the opportunity to find out what it was. Initially, he had attempted to throw a punch out of impatience, but the room seemed to absorb the impact, leaving him with the realization that he was outmatched. So, he waited, feeling like days had passed before someone finally entered.

It was Titus, the Elite from before. "Do I need to restrain you, or are you one of the smart ones?" Leo simply stared at him and stood up. "Good, this will make things much easier," Titus remarked as he walked towards the door, with Leo following behind.

From Leo's perspective, having seen countless old movies and TV shows through holograms, he understood that irrational and reckless behavior led to a swift demise. If only he had listened to Ethan from the beginning, he wouldn't have found himself in this predicament. If he behaved and played along, he might obtain the answers he desperately sought.

The surroundings appeared plush and harmless. Leo couldn't fathom where they were keeping him. They soon entered another room where another Elite was waiting. "I've brought you another one, Doc. Try not to rough him up too much," Titus announced.

The Doctor raised his hand, signaling for silence, and retrieved a surgical-like object. On a table lay a dark-skinned girl writhing in pain. The Doctor injected a fluid into the thing and inserted it into her rib cage. The girl's agonized screams were muffled by a gag.

As the green fluid flowed into her, she pleaded in anguish as best she could. Titus pushed Leo forward and strapped him into a chair next to her. "You can't hurt me with that. Brute's skin doesn't bruise easily," Leo exclaimed. The Doctor turned away from the girl and replied, "I know, genius. I won't repeat the same experiences for anyone." He then probed the injection site with his finger, causing the girl to wail in pain. Leo screamed, "Stop it! What's wrong with you!?"

The Doctor raised an eyebrow at Leo and withdrew his finger. "Interesting. The injection site was weakened," he remarked. Leo silently urged the girl not to show any signs of distress, reminding her that she was an Elite and needed to demonstrate strength. Titus proceeded to gag Leo with a cloth, rendering him unable to speak, but his eyes conveyed the same intensity.

The girl caught his glance, and they locked eyes. She nodded with determination. The door swung open, and another doctor entered. Leo realized that the restraints were designed to withstand a Brute's strength.

"Alrighty, time to begin with you next. I truly hope you meant what you said earlier. I was watching and observing. Maybe you will yield the results we need," the Doctor declared. He picked up a

12" blade and began cutting into Leo's right arm. Leo grunted as the blade struggled to break through his skin. After some resistance, it finally gave way.

"Good skin, but there are always alternative ways to administer the fluid," the Doctor said, reaching for a contraption to be inserted into Leo's eye. Panic welled up within Leo. "What are you doing?" he pleaded, his voice filled with fear.

The Doctor approached the tray of blades, where a syringe filled with green fluid awaited. Another doctor joined them through the main doors, donning gloves and preparing to make incisions on the girl again. After enduring the pain for a while, she screamed out once more, begging them to stop.

"Stop! You're hurting her, please!" Leo strained against his restraints.

"I would advise you to hold still," the Doctor warned, closing in on Leo. Eventually, Leo's hope that the girl would pass out from the agony faded, and he, too, let out a howl of torment as the Doctor injected the green syringe into his right eye.

Chapter 14:
The Bearer of Bad News

Ethan returned to the room where Ben was waiting and found him ready to go. "Okay, I'll go with you. But only because I need to finish school," Ethan stated, showing a sense of resolution. "I need help finding out who killed my family. I don't know if the Guard will uncover anything..." He appeared worried.

"I don't want to involve you and your family, though. Are you sure it's alright to have me over? You should at least ask your parents," Ethan hesitated, realizing he needed to consult his mother. "Gallium, is my mom home?" he asked. Gallium appeared in his red holographic image and replied, "She has been home all day. She hasn't gone to work for days." Ethan found that concerning and wondered if it was the wrong time for her. "Is my Hoverbike here yet?" he inquired. Gallium assured him, "I already have it on the way." Ethan turned to Ben and said, "It's time to go." Together, they made their way to the front of the hospital.

The night emanated its usual glow as Ethan's hair blew around. A hovering light shone upon them, and the Hoverbike descended, landing gracefully. Ethan hopped onto the white Hoverbike, with Ben taking a position behind him, wrapping his arms around Ethan's waist. With a swift launch, the Hoverbike soared into the sky. The evening was serene, with only a few other Hoverbikes.

Ethan skillfully maneuvered the Hoverbike, darting through the night air, gliding from one building to another until they left the city limits. Ascending even higher, Ethan began performing tricks, filling the air with laughter and a sense of liberation. Observing Ethan, Ben realized that this was a rare opportunity for him to truly be free. Being in the Sketch Classification, Ben could analyze an Elite and determine the best approach in dealing with them, second only to the Pulse Class.

The Sketch Class had careers available in various fields, and Ben aspired to work for CommuniOne, where he could log all database information on Elites. His perceptual skills would be a valuable asset. Out of curiosity, Ben started to raise his hand toward Ethan's back, but they arrived in front of Ethan's yard, interrupting his movement. They dismounted the Hoverbike, and as Ethan scanned himself at the house, the door opened, revealing his mother in the living room.

"Mom, I'm home," Ethan called out and then turned to point at Ben. "This is my friend Ben. He was the one on the news the other night. Can he stay here? He needs a place to stay." Quintella, leaning on the counter with her hands on her head, seemed distracted. "Huh? Oh, welcome home, Ethan," she responded, not fully attentive. Ben stepped inside and introduced himself, "Hello, Sector Official Quintella Crambe. I'm Benjamin Valdez." He bowed slightly and scratched the back of his head. Quintella regarded Ben with what Ethan could only interpret as a look of pity. "You're asking if he can stay? That's fine, but it can't be a permanent arrangement," she replied, resigning herself to the situation. "I'm very sorry about what happened to your family. I'll help you for now, but we'll need to find you a more permanent solution." Ben appeared relieved. "Thank you. I promise I won't be a bother to you." Elaine nodded and added, "Ethan, we need to talk tomorrow after school." Ethan raised an eyebrow but agreed, "Okay, Mom. I understand."

Before the night concluded, Ben settled into Ethan's room. "Hey, I'm going to shower and then head to bed," Ben told Ethan before going to the bathroom. Once inside, he turned on the hot water and began to reflect on his next steps. Why had his family been targeted? He needed to complete this year to secure a career at CommuniOne. He noticed no cuts or bruises as he examined his body, confirming it was a clear Sketch Class attack. But why? What did his family possess that would lead to their deaths?

After exiting the shower, Ben returned to the room to find Ethan asleep. The room was adorned in a dark royal blue color, with green dots resembling stars twinkling across the walls. The open window allowed the soft moonlight and starlight to gently illuminate Ethan. Driven by curiosity, Ben decided to sketch him.

Ben's eyes illuminated in a bright orange hue as he approached Ethan's bed and gazed down at him. What does it feel like to be a Brute? he wondered. Reaching out, he intended to touch Ethan, but as he did, he noticed the necklace around Ethan's neck shimmer—a beautiful ruby-red pendant. Suddenly, Ben felt a surge of sickness and an instinctual urge not to touch it.

Ben felt a sense of unease, but he decided to proceed and get it over with since he was already there. He reached down again and touched Ethan's hand, but this time, he experienced a sudden burning sensation, causing him to retract his hand in pain. "What the hell was that?" Ben exclaimed. It actually hurt him. If only he were of Pulse Class, he could examine Ethan's body to determine the cause.

Perplexed, Ben closed the window and returned to bed, but restlessness prevented him from falling asleep. He eventually gave in to his restlessness and made his way downstairs to the kitchen. Startled, he jumped when he saw the house AI, Gallium, beaming behind him. "Can't sleep, Benjamin?" Gallium inquired. "You already know my name?" Ben asked, taken aback. "I researched your profile for Master Ethan. I must say you are lucky to be alive," Gallium explained. Ben was curious, "Ethan researched me? Why?" Gallium shifted its beam elsewhere in the room. "To ensure your well-being," the AI responded without further explanation. Ben decided to return to the room and berated himself for getting involved with Ethan. After all, Ethan was his junior, and he shouldn't have entangled him in his troubles.

Ben's eyes illuminated once again as he touched Ethan; this time, there was no burning sensation. He must have imagined it. Now, he wanted to test the strength of a Brute. Ben went outside and attempted to kick a tree but recoiled in pain. Maybe punching would work? He hit the tree, only to yell out in agony. "That didn't work either? Damn it, that hurts!" he exclaimed, frustrated. Returning inside, he lay back on the bed, concluding that Ethan must be incredibly weak, although he had nothing to compare it to.

The following morning, Ethan soared through the air traffic with exhilaration. His infectious energy radiated as he enjoyed these moments to the fullest. Ben, holding on tightly to the back of the Hoverbike while gripping onto Ethan, felt queasy. "Oh, crap, I think I'm going to be sick!" Ben shouted. "You better hold it, dude! There's only room for good times with my baby girl!" Ethan yelled back.

They descended to the parking lot of the Academy, where they walked together towards the gate, drawing the attention of other Elites. "That's the guy who found Benjamin and then got that Brute guy kidnapped," someone whispered. "Yeah, I heard he knows a guy who knows the kidnappers and sold the Brute dude out," another voice added. "Katlyn said she broke up with him because she caught them together." Ethan glanced at Ben, who appeared angry and flushed. "Come on, Ethan," he urged.

Approaching the DNA fountain, Ethan and Ben planned to part ways temporarily. "I'm in the Sketch Class, final year. So, I'll be doing committee evaluations and career tests. I'll meet you at the house when I'm done," Ben informed Ethan, glancing around. "Seems like my ex has spread some nasty rumors." With that, Ben left for his class.

Ethan proceeded towards the classroom with flaming red doors and took his seat. Flames adorned the walls, a fitting touch for a Brute-themed day. Rolling his eyes, he sat down. Cassidy, an Elite with a rose tattoo, sat next to him. "Hey, so I hear you were with Leo when he disappeared. Any updates from the Guard?" Cassidy inquired. Ethan shook his head, feeling frustrated. "Nothing. The Guard is useless. They didn't know what to do until I told them to investigate," Ethan replied. Cassidy blushed and reassured him, "Well, I know the rumors aren't true, Ethan, so don't worry."

Professor Daley entered the room, greeted by the enthusiastic cheers of the students. "Okay, students, today we will be discussing Class Clash Day," he announced, capturing their attention. "Class Clash Day will be upon us in the upcoming month."

Excitement filled the air as the class erupted with cheers and applause. Ethan, however, couldn't participate in the event since Elites had to be enrolled in or graduate from an Academy.

Nonetheless, he was determined to listen attentively to the rules. "I will now go over the rules to avoid any confusion," Professor Daley continued.

"It has been decided that our Academy will represent the Sector this year. The event will be featured live across Sector 71!" The class buzzed with conversations, and Ethan wondered if this would pose a challenge for him. The information sparked great interest among the students.

Impatient with the growing chatter, Professor Daley interjected, "Please wait until I finish! Based on the number of potential contestants in the Academy, we have opted for a team battle, followed by one final all-out royal showdown."

A holographic diagram materialized, displaying the festival area and colosseum-like structures. "Many of you will be paired with classmates from different classifications, so make sure to study all seven classes."

The rest of the class became consumed by discussions about the upcoming event. Students chatted in the halls, lunchroom, and even bathrooms, contemplating potential matchups within the Academy. "I'd hate to go up against a Naturalist!" one student exclaimed. Another responded, "Oh, I know! I wouldn't want to get burned or frozen by them!" A voice interjected, "Come on, we're not allowed to harm anyone. Medics will be on standby with first aid stations."

This assurance brought some relief to Ethan. As he walked among the chatting Elites, he absorbed snippets of information. This event presented the perfect opportunity for him to go all out.

On his way out of the school, Ethan spotted Kira with her Hoverbike. Excitedly, he called out to her, "Hey, Kira! Kira, wait up!" She turned around, sweeping her hair away from her face. "Hello again. To what do I owe this honor?" Kira asked, rolling her eyes.

Ethan carefully considered his next words and then said something entirely unexpected, "Would you like to go on a date sometime?" His face flushed, and he hurriedly added, "I know we're from different classifications, but my parents are from different classifications, too, and they're married." Stumbling over his words, he added, "Not that I'm suggesting we have to get married or anything!"

Kira raised her hand to interrupt him. "Listen, I won't deny that you have this cute and mysterious thing going on, but I'm full on charity work." Ethan was taken aback by her response. "I can't handle being around a Brute who can't even punch a boulder," Ethan looked down, unable to make eye contact with Kira. The situation was too embarrassing for him to respond, and several students passing by laughed at his expense.

After a brief moment, Kira had a change of heart, realizing she had truly hurt his feelings. "If you want, though, how about we go to a cafe or something and see where it goes?" she suggested, softening her tone.

Ethan looked back at her, grateful she had spared him further embarrassment. However, he immediately remembered that his mother had wanted him home that day. "Could we possibly reschedule for tomorrow?" he asked sheepishly.

Kira's wall went back up. "You asked me on a date without being prepared to take me out if I said yes? Not a good look, Brute," she retorted, tossing her hair as she got on her Hoverbike.

"If you're serious about talking with me, you're gonna need to get your priorities straight first," Kira stated firmly before starting her Hoverbike and flying off. All Ethan could do was scratch his head in confusion.

Despite the disrespect he had received, Ethan wasn't ready to give up just yet. He was so close to going on a date. Determined, he hopped on his Hoverbike and began his journey home, eagerly anticipating the arrival of his mother.

Ethan, please have a seat. We need to talk," she gestured towards a chair. Wondering what this conversation was about, Ethan complied. "As you know, son, I'm the Sector Official of 53," she began. Ethan was wondering where this was leading. "But three Elites have been nominated for the next Sector Official. Once they officially choose someone, I will have to take the memory wipe." Quintella looked directly into Ethan's eyes, observing his reaction.

A wave of sickness washed over Ethan like the air had been forcefully expelled from his lungs. He had believed they had more time. "How much time do we have?" he asked, his voice filled with anxiety. Quintella looked down and replied, "It could happen within the next four months." The weight of the situation seemed to suffocate them both.

The thought of losing his mother was unbearable for Ethan. She was all he had left. "There must be some kind of mistake," Ethan suggested, clinging to hope. "Maybe they'll change their mind. The government can be unpredictable."

Quintella abruptly jumped up, placing her hand over Ethan's mouth. "Don't speak like that ever again. We don't make mistakes, Ethan," she admonished firmly. Feeling a surge of frustration, Ethan stood up. "There has to be something we can do! Can we petition them?" he implored. Quintella rose from her seat as well. "Glade personally came to inform me. Once the process starts, it progresses rapidly," she explained. Ethan paced back and forth, his mind racing. "That alarm that went off in the house last week was his visit. I didn't know how to tell you then, but I'm telling you now," Quintella revealed.

Ethan couldn't help but wonder why she hadn't said anything on the night Ben was attacked. "What will you remember after the wipe?" Ethan asked, his tone resigned. Quintella let out a sigh. "It could be everything or fragmented memories from the past three years. It's hard to predict until I wake up, and they continue from there," she replied wearily. Ethan's anger surged within him. "You could die if they keep trying to extract information from your mind!" he yelled, consumed by his emotions.

Ben walked into the house and immediately sensed the heavy atmosphere. "Am I interrupting something?" he asked, his voice filled with apprehension. The silence grew thicker as they silently stared at each other. "I was just heading to my room," Ben said, breaking the silence. In a rush of emotions, Ethan stormed upstairs, tears streaming down his face. He would soon have to confront the harsh reality that he only had approximately four months left with his mother.

Chapter 15:
The Road to Clash Day

Professor Carson threw Ethan across the field, causing him to land on his back. As Ethan struggled to catch his breath, Carson dusted himself off and delivered a booming command, "Keep your stance firm, but your body lose!" Determined to give his best, Ethan rose to his feet and charged back into the sparring session. However, he couldn't find his usual rhythm ever since receiving the news about his mother.

Meanwhile, Felix lazily sat on a boulder, observing the training session. His gaze wandered across the expansive green prairie, where the wind blew gently until Carson swung his fists. Ethan noticed the movement and attempted to evade it, but he was clipped by the hit, causing him to grunt in pain.

"May I try, sir? Ethan could use a break," Felix mockingly suggested, finally getting up from the rock. As the second student selected for this group, he still had something to prove, though he considered himself superior to Ethan or Leo.

Professor Carson nodded in agreement as Ethan got back on his feet. As Ethan nursed his arm, he watched Carson and Felix engage in their own intense training. Punches and jabs were exchanged between the two. Felix darted around the training ground, launching an uppercut at Carson, who deflected the attack and swiftly turned to face Felix.

With his long black hair blowing freely in his face, Felix appeared perfectly composed. His dark green eyes narrowed as he focused on his teacher. Taking a moment to collect himself, he assumed a six-foot-apart stance, raising his arms to protect his face. Carson, now dusted off and composed, confidently approached Felix, and the two squared off in the field, face to face.

It had been three weeks, and despite their efforts, they hadn't yet improved enough to hold their own in the upcoming Class Clash Day event. Professor Carson stepped forward and swung at Felix.

Swiftly, Felix rolled away to his right and retaliated with a jab at Carson's rib cage. Surprisingly, the professor shifted his body to evade the strike. Although momentarily caught off-guard, Felix pressed on with his attack.

Instead of hitting Carson's rib cage, Felix's punch landed directly on his stomach. Felix looked at his hand in surprise, opening and closing his palms. However, before he could fully process the situation, Carson seized the opportunity and grabbed Felix, effortlessly tossing him into the air.

"Hmm, good follow-through, although... you're still holding back!" Carson grabbed Felix by the tunic, ignoring his screams as he threw him skyward. The professor relaxed his stance slightly, folding his arms across his chest.

"Do you know why we can infuse so much energy into our movements?" Carson asked, his bare feet firmly planted on the rough, rocky terrain. His expression betrayed a hint of boredom.

As Felix came hurtling back down from the air, Carson unfolded his arms and gently caught Felix's leg, setting him down. "Sir, I mean the utmost respect when I say this," Felix began, but his sentence trailed off as he suddenly paused. His fair complexion turned sickly as he spun around and retched.

"We can endure far more hits than the other six Classifications. Our muscles lack the pain receptors that the others have!" Carson retrieved the answer from his own memories as if delving into his past. "Our body's bone structure is like steel! So, fight as if your life depends on it!" he declared, looking at them with determination.

Felix glanced at Ethan, then back at Carson. "I don't know what that feels like! I have never experienced fear in my lifetime," he confessed. Carson dismissed Felix's words with a disdainful look. "You were just thrown into the air without any guarantee that I would catch you. Stop pretending." Felix averted his gaze, looking down at his feet. "I apologize, sir. I'm not accustomed to feeling afraid. None of us are. Why would we?"

At this point, Ethan, who had been pondering the sparring match, looked up. "What about our classmate Leo? He's missing!"

Felix appeared taken aback. "No, that's not what I meant. I..." Ethan interrupted him and pressed further, "Then what are you saying? There's nothing to be afraid of?" Determined, Ethan stood up and approached Felix.

Felix squared his shoulders, locking eyes with Ethan. "We were classmates in a prestigious academy," Felix said, maintaining an intense stare. "Leo was your friend, not mine. You spent months hanging out with him, so you can blame yourself for not protecting him."

Ethan's anger flared up. "He's not dead! He's just missing. And if the Guard do their job for once, they'd find him." Felix looked infuriated and pushed Ethan. "How dare you?! My family has been serving in the Guard for generations! We protect the Sectors with honor and integrity. We even possess chains that temporarily neutralize a Classification's Code through advanced science!" Felix spat out his words.

Ethan rolled his eyes at Felix. "Give me a break, Felix. You haven't even been given a career placement yet. You're using a lot of 'we' when you should be saying 'them.'"

At this, Felix punched Ethan in the face, knocking him down. "Whoops," he said sarcastically. Instinctively, Ethan touched his necklace and stood up. Professor Carson stood nearby, watching them bicker like a cat watching a mouse.

Ethan ran towards Felix and swung his left fist towards Felix's face, but then feigned and jabbed Felix's stomach with his right fist. Felix laughed, "You hit like a Primordial. Being a Brute just doesn't suit you." Felix retaliated and punched Ethan in the stomach. Ethan gasped and fell to the ground, with Felix kneeling down beside him.

"You have no stamina, and your Code is weak. You have no right to speak for Leo," Felix taunted, cocking his head at him. "I know I'm weak. I hate that I'm so weak. But it's the hand I was dealt," Ethan complained to Felix, appearing resigned.

"Do you always have an excuse for your shortcomings?" Felix gave him a hand, but Ethan rejected it. Professor Carson spoke up, "So that's it, Ethan?" Carson shook his head. "Felix here says you're weak, that your friend going missing is somehow your fault... and you just accept that?" Carson looked disappointed, mixed with something else.

"He's wrong, sir. I believe Leo is alive. He charged directly after the enemy. Leo's far stronger than me," Ethan stood back up. He took a step back from Felix. "I may be weak, Felix, but I'm smarter than you. You hide behind your family name." Felix appeared scared of taking a real hit, something Ethan couldn't say. He wanted to feel every punch, every throw. He had lived quite a lively life so far.

Ethan knew fear. He had to lie every day to ensure no one found out his secret. He thought it over to himself. Ethan was not about to be outdone by anyone. He took a deep breath and ran at Professor Carson at full speed.

Mid-run, Ethan observed Carson's body tensing for the impact. Instead of directly hitting him, he saw an opening underneath. Ethan slid on the ground at the last minute, passing under and behind Carson's planted feet.

Felix understood what was happening and decided to take his shot as well. He threw all his force into his legs and launched himself into the air. Ethan threw a punch at Carson's back while Felix crashed down in front of their teacher with a kick. Carson responded swiftly, grabbing Felix's leg with one hand and blocking Ethan's punch with the other. Carson then swung Felix into Ethan, causing the two students to collide and collapse to the ground.

Professor Carson dusted himself off one final time and looked at his defeated students. They had flushed faces. Felix had his elbow on Ethan's stomach, but Ethan groaned as he sat up. "We have Clash Day once a year so that Elites can showcase their skills. It also keeps everyone in line from fighting constantly," Carson explained, offering them a hand. Felix took his hand and got up, only to be punched back down by Carson.

"Don't take your eyes off your opponent! If you can't discern their objective, use caution!" Carson grabbed Felix by the shirt and threw him across the rocky terrain, causing Felix to hit the wall and groan. Ethan was still on one knee, looking directly into Carson's eyes.

"How do you stay so healthy, sir?" Ethan asked. "Through ancient Primordial training regimens that we've perfected," Carson replied. "We took what they started—" Before Carson could finish his sentence, Ethan threw another punch, but the professor grabbed him and threw him into the air.

Ethan screamed as he reached the peak of his launch, where time seemed to slow down. Ethan began to panic, feeling suspended in the air. "Don't you think you're going a bit hard on them?" a woman in her early thirties walked toward them on the field. She had dark bronze hair tied back and wore a grey robe with a blue and gold hourglass insignia.

"Ah, Alice. Is it time for the joint training already?" Carson laughed. Alice smiled gallantly, and time returned to normal speed. Ethan started falling at a regular rate and screamed out. "Hey, Ethan, try again," Alice said, extending her hand. There was a flash, and Ethan again found himself on one knee in front of Professor Carson.

"Through ancient training regimens from Primordial that we perfected," Carson repeated. Ethan felt confused. The professor continued, "We took what they started and compiled—" Ethan was thrown off again but kicked out at Carson's legs this time. The professor evaded Ethan's right leg, lifted his leg out of the way, and launched Ethan into the air.

Ethan screamed as he rushed toward the ceiling, and once again, time seemed to slow down as he paused mid-air. He had a strange sense of familiarity. "Are you a Tempus?" Ethan asked. In a flash, Ethan was back on one knee.

"Professor, something feels wrong," Ethan interrupted. Carson looked at him and asked, "What feels wrong about this situation, Ethan?" Ethan looked around, realizing something had gone wrong when he swung. He couldn't remember what happened but knew he had already tried it.

The sensation of déjà vu was too strong. Professor Carson stared at Ethan expectantly, waiting for his response. After much thought, Ethan looked back at his teacher and spoke. "We can't win this, can we? That's the point you're trying to make. We're trapped in a time loop."

"Exactly. Now that you can sense the sensation," Alice chimed in, appearing beside them. "Carson wanted to show you that some situations are beyond your control." Ethan still looked confused. "I intervened in your fight because I knew you wouldn't remember me doing so," she explained, wearing a perplexed expression as she walked around, lost in her thoughts.

When Alice finished her contemplation, she looked at Ethan with folded hands. "Only a Tempus can see what happens in the past. I just wanted to see why you chose that method of attack," Alice clarified. "But for a Brute like yourself, it's a wonder you could feel the sensation of a time loop."

Felix sulked, embarrassment burning on his face. His normally slicked-back black hair was disheveled. "I don't accept this loss. There's always a way!" he huffed, stretching his arms in frustration.

Carson finally spoke up. "Professor Alice here is a Spatial Class user, specifically a Type 2: Tempus," he said with a smirk. "Since Spatial is always teleporting the class so much, we figured we might as well bring them along." Ethan sat down on the grassy field. "Tempus... the time controllers? They have the ability to distort time within their radius," he mused.

Soon, two students emerged through a portal. One wore a gray and royal blue robe, while the other wore a tunic. As they approached, their confident demeanor was palpable.

The boy, with short green curly hair and steel grey eyes, caught Ethan's attention. Surprisingly well-built for someone who wasn't a Brute, Ethan noted.

The girl, Kira, was someone Ethan recognized. Her distinctive stride and hair were unforgettable. Ethan blurted out, bewildered, "Kira? What are you doing here?" The boy rolled his eyes, and Kira stated the obvious. "I'm here to help you train."

Felix smirked while Ethan's face turned cherry red. Alice cleared her throat. "Kira Saunders is our most promising second-year," she introduced, gesturing towards her. Kira stepped forward and introduced herself. "My goal is to train you and gain insight to help me in the upcoming matches on CC Day," she stated before stepping back. The other student, Zion Mayfield, stepped forward. "I'm Zion Mayfield, a first-year Tempus who will also be assisting," he said with formality, rubbing Ethan the wrong way. Ethan realized that Zion had briefly glanced at him before looking away.

With introductions out of the way, the two Tempus students took a defensive stance. Professor Carson chuckled and stepped forward. "Come now, I haven't even explained the best part! You four will be paired together for the Tournament!"

This statement caused the students to halt. Felix reacted first, making his point clear. "I'm not working with them. Why would I?" he scoffed.

Professor Alice turned her head quizzically. "Is it because you're insecure about your Code? If you feel inferior, we can have you ready before then."

Felix gawked. "I'm confident in my ability!" He paused, took a deep breath, and then apologized for yelling. "My apologies, Professor. I just have concerns about how useful you could be in a battle," Felix explained.

"Because they can only see what happens, not intervene," Ethan's thoughts started to align. He couldn't comprehend Felix's stubbornness. With Tempus, they could go back and correct their mistakes in a fight!

Kira stepped forward towards Felix. "Shall we spar and see?" Felix raised an eyebrow but accepted. "You say Tempus can't fight. I assume it's because we can witness the past but can't change it, correct?" Kira asked, tying her hair into a bun.

"My problem lies in the fact that you weirdos become brain-dead from going back in time. You're unreliable," Felix retorted. "And I'm about to show you why you're overrated."

Alice stepped forward. "Remember, competition is good, but try to learn something from each other."

Felix decided to start strong. He threw out both his arms and pushed down on his calves, cracking the ground under pressure.

Ethan watched with half-hearted interest, still going over his own failures in his head. When did Professor Alice come near them? Something still didn't add up. Ethan looked at Professor Alice, who was now fully engrossed in Felix and Kira's spar.

"Hey, Professor Alice. I wasn't aware you were watching us train earlier," Ethan mentioned, his eyes fixed on her.

Professor Alice paused her attention from Felix and spoke to Ethan. Her crinkled eyes examined him as she explained, "We Tempus are strange Elites, Ethan. If you're asking why I slowed you down while you were fighting Professor Carson, it was because I simply wanted you to see that no amount of physical force will always be enough." Ethan glanced back at Felix, contemplating the significance of Alice's words.

Professor Carson interjected with his own perspective. "I wanted to surprise you with the training," he said with a smile, patting Ethan on the back. "I even told Alice to step in if it looked like I was about to lose. So be proud, Ethan. Alice must have believed you were about to get the upper hand."

"Ah, Brutes. They never listen," Professor Alice chuckled, rubbing her eyes.

"Sure we do! If anything, Sprite never listens. Always talking a thousand words a minute," Professor Carson replied with a laugh.

Ethan's mind was already racing, trying to find ways to improve his techniques. He needed to explore options beyond physical force. But how? As someone who relied on physical strength, how else could he fight? And how did he know Alice was there?

There was a loud crackling noise, but Ethan was too deep in thought to notice Felix running around the field. Felix was circling Kira like a shark, preparing for his attack. He propelled himself into the air and shot his foot straight down, resembling a meteor re-entering the atmosphere. However, he encountered unexpected resistance.

To Felix, it felt as though he had broken the sound barrier, but to everyone else, Felix's descent appeared slower than that of a snail. Sensing the danger, Kira quickly backed up and moved out of the way, allowing Felix to regain normal speed as she released her ability. Felix's foot slammed into the ground with a resounding boom, leaving a deep hole behind.

"We've been going at this for eight minutes, and you have yet to lay a hand on me," Kira mockingly taunted, reveling in her superior defense.

Ethan finally looked up from his thoughts, realizing he had missed most of the fight. "Oh, damn it," he exclaimed, frustrated with himself for not paying attention.

"What happened? I missed the back end of that fight!" Ethan anxiously looked around, searching for someone to fill him in on what he had missed.

Professor Alice laughed, thoroughly amused by the situation. "Just my point being proven," she remarked, emphasizing how Kira's skills and agility had outmatched Felix's attempts to strike her.

Chapter 16:
The Underground Rave

Ethan returned home from the Academy feeling worn out from training with the Spatial students. He thought of hanging out with Ben, who he hadn't seen since finishing his training. Ethan wondered where Ben had gone, considering he had told Ethan to meet him after school. The fact that Ben didn't see him slightly irritated Ethan.

Ben walked into their shared room and flopped onto the spare bed in the royal blue room. He lay on his back as he teased Ethan. "You know, I'm surprised you picked a blue room," Ben chuckled. "Brutes are always going on and on about how glorious red is and all." Ethan, who was now lying in his bed, simply rolled over and looked at him. He didn't feel like cracking jokes at the moment.

"Where the heck were you? I didn't see you before heading home," Ethan complained.

Ben placed his arm over his face and continued to stare at the ceiling. "I know. I just needed to sort some stuff out," he replied without elaborating further.

Ethan felt a twinge of frustration. This guy had already been attacked once, but he had the gall to wander off without telling anyone. Ethan forced the thought from his mind. Boundaries. Besides, Ben needed fun, not problems. After all, he had just lost his parents.

"Hey, do you want to do something tonight? We could use some stress relief," Ethan suggested. Ben lifted his arm and looked at Ethan, piquing his interest.

"Sure, what did you have in mind?" Ben asked.

"Oh, no. You get to choose. As long as we make it back home at a reasonable time."

"How about we go to The Shopping Plaza? We can buy some new tech or something," Ben suggested with a smirk.

"Never heard of it. I'm new here, remember?" Ethan got out of bed and placed his AICI outside the room, then closed the door. "Sorry, Gallium likes to listen in on me." He sat back down on his bed. "I take it we're doing something we're not supposed to do."

Ben winked at him. "You bet your ass we are, dude. It's a guy's night out. Put on some regular clothes so we don't look like students."

"Hellllo? I'm a first-year student. I don't have normal clothes tailored to my classification yet. Just these wack tunics," Ethan held up his red tunics. "Besides, not that I care, but I also have a curfew."

"Has that ever stopped you before?"

"I really don't want to have to put my tunic back on," Ethan groaned.

Ben smirked at him. "Oh, come on, Ethan, lighten up! Your induction is months away, then you can be miserable wearing robes in public like the rest of us," he laughed.

Ethan shook his head. What was funny about a lack of individuality? At least academy-inducted Elites could wear regular clothes under their robes. Giving up, Ethan started changing into fresh classification clothes.

"You're just lucky I love technology," Ethan said, punching Ben in the arm.

Ben gave him a cheesy smile. "And to think you were born a Brute. You should go work for the CommuniOne. You can help better develop the AICI with me."

"Don't push your luck, Sketch. I'm not that much of a loser," Ethan joked, throwing an arm over Ben's shoulder as they laughed.

Ethan bid his mother goodnight as she left to return to Sector 53 later that evening. After waiting several hours to make sure she was gone, Ethan grabbed his comms and followed Ben outside the house. They ran to where Ethan's Hoverbike was parked.

"Hey, could I fly it tonight?" Ben asked, admiring the bike. "These are some pretty cool specs."

Ethan huffed his chest. "Yeah, it's a no from me."

Ben just laughed, but Ethan was a proud father. "I just bought the new upgrade! It has an X2 processing system that allows it to come to my location." Ethan was expecting a huge deal to be made about this.

Ben raised his eyebrows and scratched his head in confusion. "Wow. I have no idea what you just said," he admitted. Ethan shook his head, feeling the need for more friends from the Pulse Class. "This is why I need more Pulse Class friends. They appreciate technology more than Sketches."

Ethan focused on checking the systems of his Hoverbike while Ben stood beside him, observing. "That's because fine details are what Sketch Class is all about," Ben remarked.

"We're known for running the AI systems... What are Brutes known for again?" Ben replied, playfully teasing Ethan.

Taking the bait, Ethan continued, "Ha, very funny. I'll remember that when my Brute friends become Guardians."

"Alright, enough banter. Are we going to stand around all night, or are we leaving?" Ben questioned, eager to get going.

"Just finished. This place better not be lame," Ethan complained.

"Trust me, Ethan. You'll love where we're heading," Ben assured him, patting the seat of the Hoverbike. They both hopped on, ready to embark on their adventure.

The night sky shimmered with a lively emerald hue as stars twinkled above them. Ethan yelled out into the air as they soared through the night, the wind blowing his ashy hair across his face.

"What if a Guard sees us up here?!" Ben shouted, concerned about the potential consequences.

"I may have swiped my mom's Sector pass that allows her to travel outside curfew!" Ethan confessed, turning to face Ben and making a sharp right turn, narrowly avoiding a glass building. Ben's anxiety was mirrored on the building's glass surface.

Ben choked out a noise of disbelief. "What?! That's for Sector Officials! We could face trial for that!" He looked around nervously, aware that being caught out past curfew could cause trouble for Ethan's father.

"You really think I'll get into trouble with my dad being the Sector Official of Area 71?" Ethan rolled his eyes, confident in his family's influence and status. However, Ben had no idea of the true extent of the boy's parents' power and influence.

"I think you're in a better position to tell me more about that. If we get into trouble, you will get out of it easily! But what about me?" Ethan swung left, dipped downward, and then pulled up to maintain balance.

Growing increasingly uneasy, Ben struggled to see clearly with Ethan in front of him and the wind roaring in his ears. "Come on, don't act as if you're not under my protection now. My mom would surely help you out," Ethan reassured him after a moment of thought. They continued soaring past emerald glass structures, marveling at the architectural designs that kept the buildings afloat.

"Do you see those beams underneath the floating structures?" Ethan pointed briefly to the enormous land under the plaza, which appeared to have been lifted from the ground. Several glowing metal rings were fitted inside.

"Yeah, what about them?" Ben asked, curious.

"Did you know that it's only possible because of Psyche and Spatial Class technology?" Ethan shared his knowledge, proud of the technical advancements made possible by their abilities.

As they soared higher, the wind grew stronger, forcing them to yell over the noise. Ben squinted at the plaza below.

"No, but I'm sure you're going to tell me anyway," Ben responded sarcastically.

"I'll ignore that. I just find it amazing! The practical applications for our abilities are incredible. That's why I want to study architecture," Ethan explained enthusiastically. The bike spun slightly to the right.

"Keep your hands on the handlebars!" Ben gasped, concerned for their safety.

"Relax!" Ethan reassured him.

They descended rapidly from the sky, causing Ben's heart to race, before leveling out and landing on the ground. Ben let out a sigh of relief as they jumped off the Hoverbike. Since Ben knew the area better, he took the lead while Ethan followed closely behind.

Approaching the entrance, the glass door automatically granted them passage, impressing Ethan with its advanced technology. It was clear that a high-class place like this would have magnificent technology and a robust security system, making theft nearly impossible.

"I've always wanted those shoes with the ability to fasten steps," Ethan remarked, eyeing a pair of black shoes with white soles. He turned to Ben and asked, "What's the price?"

"It's right there," Ben replied, pointing to the price tag. "Do you think it's expensive?"

"It's hard to say. We never really have to pay for anything, so I don't have anything to compare it to," Ethan admitted.

"Why do we even have price tags? We can just submit a request for all this," Ethan groaned.

Ben's face soured. "Ugh, come on, Ethan!"

"What?" Ethan stopped looking at the clothes, puzzled.

"You're always wound up. Can't you just relax and have fun?" Ben whined.

"Sure, we can get anything we need from the government, but non-essential requests can take months," Ben explained, scratching the back of his neck as they moved further into the store.

"They do it to make us feel like we have something to work for. It's all about mindset. After we graduate, all we have to look forward to is sustaining Pangea," Ben shared, his tone turning somewhat pessimistic.

"Well, that's a dark take. Everyone has something they can contribute to Pangea," Ethan countered, trying to maintain a positive outlook. He scanned the area, taking in the expensive shoes, clothes, and showcased devices.

"What are we looking for?" Ethan asked, heading towards a display showcasing headset devices.

"I brought you here to have a look. Perhaps you might need something nice for yourself," Ben suggested, glancing at Ethan.

"Eh, I barely have time to not wear that annoying red tunic. Why would I bother with regular clothes?" Ethan replied dismissively.

Ben raised his hands in surrender. "Yeah, and you'll have more options when you're done with your induction ceremony. That's in like two months for you."

Ethan glanced at the clothes on the walls and tables, realizing it was getting late. Soon, Guardians would be searching for teens who stayed out past curfew.

"Ethan, you need to get back home soon. Your mother would not approve," Gallium's voice echoed in the room, causing Ethan to flinch. He had thought he left the AI device at home. How did Gallium follow them down here?

"How did you know I am here, Gallium?" Ethan and Ben stared at each other.

Gallium must have found his way into the plaza. Ethan reminded himself that he had taken the AI off his wrist. Ethan reached into his pants pocket and felt something. His heart dropped. It was his AICI, meaning Gallium was in his pocket the whole time. He must have placed him there out of habit.

"You idiot!" Ben burst into laughter. Ethan could not believe he had Gallium on him all this time. He could've sworn he had left the AI back at home.

"I think we should head back home. Your mom might wake up anytime soon to check on us," Ethan knew what Ben said was true. Quintella would be mad at him if she found out they were out late at night.

"Gallium, does she know we are out?"

"No. She has no idea about your little secret." Ethan looked at Ben, who cocked his head to the side. "Okay, good." Ethan clicked a button on the side of the cylinder device. The three holographic beams shut down, silencing Gallium.

"Is that a good idea?" Ben raised his eyebrow at him.

"No, but I did tell Gallium once that if he even listened in on my conversation again, I'd break him." Ethan shrugged his shoulders as he put the AICI back in his pocket.

"I guess he should consider himself lucky. Anyway, I don't want your mom finding out so we can visit again some other time." Ethan nodded in agreement.

The boys headed for the parking lot to get on the Hoverbike and head home. Voices echoed in the parking lot. Ben stopped walking forward, blocking Ethan from taking another step. "What?" Ethan asked impatiently.

"Shhh... I think someone is in trouble." Ben traced the voice, and Ethan followed behind him. Their ears perked up as they listened to find out where the voice came from. Someone was being screamed at.

At a dark corner of the information center in the parking lot, two men were harassing an old lady. She appeared to be distraught.

"Give us the code to your credits, and we will let you go," one of the men ordered. The old lady resisted and fought back. The man who asked for the Code slapped her, causing her to take a step back. "We will kill you if you do not give us what we need." He pulled out a glittering dagger.

"I don't understand. We don't even need credits. Why do you want mine?" she begged the question.

"We can't join this group without more of it! There's a membership fee to wear a black robe," one of the men replied.

"Hold it right there." The man paused at the strange voice behind him. "Let her go, and I won't report this to the Guard." The men looked at Ben and immediately burst into laughter.

"You should do as he said now while you still have the chance to get away," Ethan joined his voice.

The men glanced at each other. One with red glowing hair spoke up, "This is no place for kids. You boys should run along." He turned to the woman on the floor, sobbing. "They are not going to save you! Now, the Code." He yelled at her, holding out his hand.

"Let her go." Ben made a fist. This won't end with speaking nicely. The men were out to get what they wanted, and it seemed no one was there to stop them. But he would not let anyone get away this time. Ben was tired of Elites thinking they could do whatever they wanted. Who do they think they are to take a life? His eyes glowed orange.

The man in purple robes with a glittering dagger chuckled. "I see you came prepared." He threw the dagger at Ben. Ben moved away, but the dagger flew right back, nicking his arm. The man could control where the dagger goes. He caught it in the air. Ben held his bleeding arm.

Ethan rushed towards the man with glowing hair and dealt him a punch. The man with glowing hair caught his hands in the air and threw him aside. Ethan came crashing into the walls of the parking lot.

As Ben rushed towards the purple-robed man with the dagger, the man threw the dagger at him. Ben ducked. He quickly swung around, immediately grabbing the dagger midair with one hand. He then turned back around in the same motion, propelling forward.

Ben punched him, crashing the robed enemy into the walls behind. He then swung his other fist around to throw the dagger. The man with glowing hair blocked it, but Ben sent in a kick that pushed that man to the ground as well.

Ethan crawled to the lady to help her up. He needed to bring her to safety. Ben would handle the men to create a distraction while he took the lady away. Two figures appeared in the parking lot and began running toward them. "Hey! What's going on over there?!" There was a glimmer of white chains, and a rattling could be heard.

The men spotted the figures and took to their heels. Ben ran after them, but they went faster. He was tired and couldn't catch up. The two Guardians zoomed past him as he slowed down. They took over from where Ben had stopped, running as their chains dangled around their bodies. With the two guards on the chase, Ben took a deep breath. He looked at his arm. It was just a little cut. He ran back to Ethan and the old lady.

"Are you okay?" he asked no one in particular.

"She needs to get home," Ethan said, with a pitying look on his face. Ben nodded. They needed to help her get home. They needed to do that fast if they were planning to have fun before Quintella returned to find out they had been gone for a long time.

"The guards went after them. What did they want from you?" Ben inquired.

The old lady was no longer sobbing. She had not lost her credits, thanks to them. "I'm so sorry! I would have helped, but I'm afraid of getting caught using my Code. You realize they could execute you if they had a good excuse," she wiped her eyes.

"It's fine! Let's get you home," Ethan said, wrapping his arm around her waist. He helped her walk to where she pointed, to where her vehicle was parked.

The old lady started to calm down when they reached her Halo. "Why did you help me even though you could've gotten into trouble? That was honestly reckless," she scolded the boys.

Ben gave her a look of bewilderment. Were they seriously getting lectured after saving her?

"Because a Primordial probably wouldn't have helped you. They would have kept walking, hoping someone else would help," Ethan was silent as they reached their destination.

"And we shouldn't be like them, right?"

"Your academy must have taught you well," she concluded.

"Speaking of which, we could get in trouble for helping, so could you please keep this to yourself?" Ben requested.

"You're students?" she looked surprised, as if she was seeing them for the first time.

Ethan opened her Hoverbike's door when an Opal-robed Guardian approached them.

"Hey! I saw you with that woman when my squad ran by. I have some questions for you." Ben and Ethan froze in their tracks. Ethan began to sweat. He had assumed the Guardians had pursued the men.

Grover, as his name read on his robe, was a young-looking guy with a cut on the side of his face. He pushed his auburn hair out of the way as he approached. His disapproving expression seemed permanent.

"What business do you have here? This one here looks like a student," Grover walked up and eyed Ethan.

"Sir, we were helping this woman get away from those men. If we hadn't shown up when we did, she could have been hurt," Ben had a growl in his throat.

Grover put a slight hand on the metal chains hanging at his waist. The woman saw this and spoke up.

"You would strike these children down for helping me? Is that what they teach at the Guardian Academy?" She was appalled.

Standing a bit straighter, Grover swiped the boys' hands away as they tried to help her. Grover's eyes widened. "No, ma'am! I would never! I just... I didn't... I mean!"

Ethan looked around. It was getting late. His mother probably wasn't even home, realistically. He knew she had to go from Sector 53 to Sector 71 often. They might have more time than Gallium was telling them. But that didn't mean they could afford to get caught. "Ben, we need to leave," Ethan whispered. "I'm getting a bad feeling."

Ben squeezed Ethan's arm as the Guardian gathered his composure. "I, unfortunately, have to arrest you for Code usage without a parent or proper teacher present to take responsibility."

At this, the woman began to argue. "So these gentlemen help me from a crime, and they're being arrested for it?!" She dropped her red bag and walked up towards Grover, frustrated. The Guardian placed his hand on his chains again. Ben, seeing an opportunity, whispered, "Run!"

Both boys raced down the street, leaving the scene behind. Ethan looked back and saw the lady wink at him before continuing to argue with the Guardian, holding him up from following. The large-scale buildings provided them with cover as they weaved behind stores and gift shops in a shopping district. Vehicles hummed and zoomed above them. Ethan could feel the force of the Guardian Hoverbike models passing by. They both ducked down an alley. Fear began to rise as his back pressed against the wall. What if one of those Hoverbikes was looking for them? Ethan did his best to push the thought from his mind.

"This way! I see an empty street where we can probably lose them," Ben breathlessly spoke, running ahead through the briefly silent street. Ethan ran with ease behind him, looking over his shoulder. The sky began to pour rain down from above, but the rain had a dark tint of color to it. Ben zipped up his orange Sketch robe closer, giving Ethan an apologetic look. Unfortunately, Ethan had no such protection. His tunic did nothing to shield his hair from the rain, and his dark red pants were starting to get cold.

Ethan cupped his hands over his eyes and looked through the pouring rain, some of it even getting in his mouth. He grimaced as it tasted like battery acid. Ben gave Ethan a side-eye. "This is the first time it's rained since I've been here! Do the Naturalists not purify the water here at night?" He yelled out above the noise.

Ben raised his hood a bit more. "It's harmless here. You probably think it's bad like in the other sectors."

Ethan wiped the water from his face and breathed easier. The area seemed very quiet as they turned the corner onto a more secluded street. "The climate doesn't allow the rain to burn your skin here. Don't freak out." Ethan relaxed a bit. "And yes, the Naturalist class does use their Code to purify all water in the sector." Ben continued. His face became puzzled. "I don't know why they didn't today."

Ben turned, focusing his attention on a gray building with flashing neon lights. "I think that building is open. We should go check it out." He pointed. The boys walked towards the building and found that the rusty-looking door didn't feel rusty. The building also had no windows, so one could only assume what was inside.

Ben put his hand on the doorknob but made no move to open the door. Why was there a building operating this late at night? Would they get in trouble for being there? Ethan stared at Ben before pushing him aside.

"It's raining out here! Let's go already," Ethan said, effectively ending Ben's suspicions of the place.

They immediately encountered a staircase inside the building that shot several levels down below. Ethan gave Ben a cheeky smile. "Well, this should be interesting."

"It's not too late to just go home. I'm sure we lost those Guardians," Ben suggested.

Ethan began descending the staircase. "Nah, I'm good. After all, you said we need a night out. Let's see where this goes."

As they continued down several flights of steps, a drum-like noise filled the staircase. Both boys glanced at each other but didn't say a word. The sound grew louder, and electronic music could be heard as they approached another door. "Is this what I think it is?" Ben spoke out loud. Ethan pushed the door open.

What they had essentially walked into was an underground rave. Multicolored strobe lights beamed down from the ceiling, and both of them stood in awe at the change in scenery. The enormous metallic black club had emerald green lines glowing bright and dark, creating a Rubik's cube design across the floor and walls. Around 120 young adults packed the room, dancing and drinking colorful drinks to their heart's content. Purple, red, and blue bubbles floated around the room, and Ethan realized they were the Naturalists. They were taking beverages from glasses and holding the substances in midair, turning them into bubble-like shapes.

"This is amazing! What is this?" Ben took off his robe, noticing that none of the teens seemed to be wearing their required uniforms either. Many had glow sticks and a colorful assortment of clothing.

Ethan laughed as he began to walk forward. "And here I was hoping you could tell me!"

"Do you have a tattoo?" a young woman with neon pink hair asked Ethan.

"Huh? No, why?" Ben walked up beside him.

"Because you need a tattoo to be down here," she said matter-of-factly.

"We didn't know anything about needing a tattoo," Ethan groaned as he rubbed his neck.

The girl seemed to annoy him. "Well, without a tattoo, you can't come down. I'm sorry, it's the rules." She folded her arms.

"What? That's so stupid! Why would you need an outdated thing like that to be in here?" Ben looked around and confirmed that many had tattoos somewhere on their bodies.

"My friends here are being modest. They just don't want you to know their tattoos are on their butts," a girl Ethan recognized said, laughing.

Both of them turned around to see Cassidy behind them. The woman at the entry door just shook her head. "You must be pretty special if Cassidy here is willing to lie for you. She's a hardcore raver." She walked back to the door, leaving them alone.

Ethan and Ben sighed in relief. "We owe you, Cassidy. Thanks." She smiled. Ethan noticed she was wearing a black and red fishnet outfit.

"Relax, no one here cares if you're in uniform or not. We're here to just have a good time." She took Ethan by the hand, and they made their way through the crowd. Ethan gawked in awe at how many people were dancing on the floor. Bursts of air came from the floor, matching the beat of the music. The crowd cheered in excitement. Ethan and Ben followed Cassidy to a table. She slapped her hands down on the table. "I need two Fiery Dragons for these two newbies."

An AI behind the table nodded and started pouring an orange-red concoction into two glasses. Ben looked concerned. "What is that?" Ethan was repulsed, but for a different reason. He had seen that drink before.

"It's a drink that allows you to safely experience the feeling of being drunk without the nasty drawbacks of alcohol," she explained, wearing a smile. Ethan, however, did not share her enthusiasm.

"No thanks. I've seen what that drink can do," Ethan shook his head. "My mother used to drink it all the time. It might make you happy but distorts your perception of reality."

Three drinks were swiftly prepared and placed in front of them. Ben stared at his glass with a horrified expression before turning to Cassidy. "Will I forget what happened to my parents?" he whispered, his voice barely audible. Ethan and Cassidy exchanged somber glances as the music switched to an electronic afrobeat tune.

"Yes, Ben. It's possible. I'm sorry. I can't imagine what you must be feeling," Cassidy responded, her voice devoid of cheer. Ethan placed a comforting hand on Ben's shoulder. "We can leave if you want," he offered. However, Ben disregarded the suggestion and downed the drink in one gulp. "No. I need this. I don't know who did that or why, but I just need to forget for one night." He closed his eyes, allowing the music to wash over him.

Ethan contemplated his own situation. Leo was likely hurt or scared somewhere, and here he was, indulging in a night of reckless decisions. What could he do to help Leo? Ethan felt helpless, just one person without a clue about what to do. And so, he picked up his drink and downed it, convincing himself that one night of poor choices wouldn't change anything.

"Well, alrighty then!" Cassidy exclaimed, laughing as she drank her own drink. "I guess we'll let the night take us away." She retook hold of Ethan's hand and spun him around. Ethan forced a nervous smile. "So, how long does it take to be—" but he couldn't finish his sentence because he spotted someone he never expected to see. He let go of Cassidy's hand and hurried toward the dance floor.

"Kira?! Is that you over there?!" Ethan ran toward a girl with shockingly blue hair who was dancing in the crowd. Kira looked surprised to see him. "Ethan? What are you doing here?" she asked.

"You remember my name?" Ethan beamed a smile.

"I got a lot of crap from my classmates for standing up for you," she groaned, twirling in her dance. She stopped and stared at Ethan. She placed her hands around his waist and said, "I actually wanted to apologize to you for my rudeness when you tried to shake my hand." It was clear that she had been drinking.

Ethan was elated that this girl was finally giving him attention, but he couldn't help but wonder why. She hadn't cared before. Yet, in that moment, it didn't matter to Ethan anymore. Warmth filled his body, and his head swam as he cracked a smile.

"No, it's okay. You didn't have to put yourself out there like that. Brutes are social pariahs to some," Ethan replied as everyone danced to a new Afrobeat song.

"No, it was rude of me to talk to a Sector Official's child like that," Kira muttered.

Ethan's smile shattered. "Are you only talking to me because of that?" he asked, his disappointment evident.

"Are you drunk right now?" She pivoted his question. Ethan wasn't sure. The strobe lights beamed a rainbow of dazzling red, blue, and green. Ethan didn't really care. All he cared about was talking to this girl right now. "Don't dodge the question. Are you only talking to me because I'm a Sector Officials kid?" He threw back.

"No, but it does make it easier to talk to a Brute knowing you're in good social standing." Ethan was disappointed in her reply. "I just mean, I'm a Spatial Class student. You think you have it hard? Try being the cause of a major civil war that killed thousands." She added.

The music pulsed, and they continued dancing to the beat.

Ethan wanted to escape his thoughts. His body warmed, and he grabbed Kira's waist as they swayed to the music. Her blue hair brushed against his neck.

"A bold move, Crambe." She chuckled to herself.

He brought his mouth closer to her ear and whispered, "What, you don't like to dance?"

"A Tempus and a Brute together? What will everyone think?" she giggled.

"Who cares about that, Kira? Just for once, let's leave our classifications at the door and have fun," Ethan said, losing himself in the rhythm.

"I care," Kira replied. She slid down his chest, placing a hand on his back, and turned to face him.

They danced together, but it was also dancing around each other, trying to avoid ruining the moment.

"You can't seriously tell me you feel prejudice from something that happened a hundred and fifty years ago," Ethan said, pulling her close as they shuffled in a silly circle.

Kira pulled away, finally breaking their tangled dance.

"You can't seriously tell me you actually got into our Academy fairly," she said blandly, causing Ethan to stop dancing. He was taken aback by her comment.

"I'm kidding, but I've never seen a Brute who needed an enhancement necklace," she continued, reaching out to touch his necklace. Ethan reacted quickly, firmly grabbing her wrist. "Don't touch things that don't belong to you," he warned.

"So, just how weak are you really?" she locked eyes with his icy blue gaze.

"Ethan! Bro, I've missed you so much!" Ben suddenly appeared, wrapping an arm around Ethan, his drunkenness evident. "Ben, great to see you, man," Ethan greeted him, giving him a half hug. "Let's go shake it on the floor."

"See ya later, Kira," Ethan said, pulling Ben away, eager to leave the conversation. They left Kira behind on the dance floor.

"No, bro, you already have someone waiting for you," Ben protested, refusing to budge.

"What? Who?" Ethan couldn't even imagine.

"Cassidy, dumbass! She lied to get you into the rave, got us these killer drinks, and you ditched her to talk to a chick who clearly is making you mad instead of happy right now!" Ben shook Ethan's shoulders exasperatedly.

"Okay, okay, you're right," Ethan conceded, beginning to walk away and realizing it was a bit harder than he remembered. He spotted Cassidy dancing by herself.

"Cassidy, would you like to dance?" Ethan extended his hand. However, Cassidy shook her head. "Honestly, I'd rather make out with you," she said, placing a hand on his cheek.

Ethan's eyes widened with surprise. It wasn't the response he was expecting. She had already placed a hand on his cheek. "You have really beautiful eyes," she complimented, her drink taking hold of her. Her smile caused him to smile back, even though he didn't quite know why. He blushed.

He reveled in the feeling of happiness and wasted no time leaning in to kiss her. In that moment, he felt the full force of his drink. Ethan passionately kissed Cassidy as they slowly backed up against a wall near the dance floor. He fumbled with where to put his hands, unsure but eager to touch her.

Cassidy forcefully guided his hands to her hips, snaking her arms around his lower back as they stumbled toward the wall. Ethan noticed a sweet taste on her lips, similar to his last drink.

As they continued kissing, they finally reached the wall. Ethan paused to catch his breath, gazing deeply into Cassidy's eyes. He lightly brushed his hand along her neck. "I've always loved this tattoo," he murmured, tracing the blue rose.

"Would you rather talk or make out?" Cassidy asked, her eyes filled with hunger.

"Right, of course. Sorry," Ethan's face turned bright red. He leaned in to kiss her again, but suddenly, the power in the building blinked out. The crowd began to boo about the lights, momentarily breaking Ethan's trance. He looked around, trying to make out his surroundings.

"Where's Ben?" he asked, his voice tinged with worry.

"I don't know. I'm sure he's on the dance floor," Cassidy impatiently replied, fumbling with Ethan's hands. However, he pulled away from her.

"I really want this, but I need to go check on Ben," he explained, hitching in his breath as she ran her hands down his stomach. "Are you sure you want to leave right now?"

She smiled, an intoxicating aura of sexual tension filling the air. Cassidy smelled like honeydew, and Ethan's head was buzzing. "I'm just getting a bad feeling. Ben recently got out of the hospital, and I shouldn't have left him alone."

"He's not your responsibility," her smile faded.

"You're right, but he is a friend," Ethan retorted, growing increasingly nervous as the room remained pitch black.

"You barely know him. He could be full of baggage," Cassidy remarked, ceasing her caresses.

"I barely know you either," Ethan replied, not bothering to hide his annoyance.

"Well, you won't know me at all if you keep talking like that."

The lights suddenly came back on, revealing dozens of hooded figures in black robes standing among the crowd, surrounding everyone. Ethan and Cassidy paused, unsure of what was happening.

"We are Libertas." One of the hooded figures declared. "We are here to liberate you from this broken society and oppressive system. Know that your sacrifices will help further and save Pangea from its impending doom." They all pulled out glowing white chains, a sight that was familiar to everyone.

Mass panic immediately erupted as teenagers pushed and shoved toward the two exits. Many were being engulfed in the white glow, disabling their Code. The Libertas members began grabbing the captured teens, using their Shifter abilities to disappear with them.

Dozens of Elites stumbled and fell over each other. "We need to leave! Now!" Cassidy pulled at Ethan's arm, urging him to go.

"I'm not leaving without Ben!" Ethan shrugged off her grip, determined to find his friend.

"Fine, I wish you good luck," Cassidy said, turning away from him and pushing through the crowd.

The space between the Elites was too packed for anyone to use their Codes, especially since most were still afraid to do so without permission. The Libertas group knew they had the advantage. Dozens of teens were being grabbed simultaneously.

Ethan spotted Kira in the crowd and called out to her, "Kira! Come on, I'm looking for Ben. We have to go!" His voice drowned in the chaos of the strobe lights, now bathed in a continuous red hue. Every few seconds, the room bled red, accompanied by the disappearance of a teenager.

"I saw him over there!" Kira pointed toward another room. They forcefully made their way past others attempting the same escape. As they ran, Kira noticed a Libertas member raising their chain at Ethan.

"Ethan, look out!" She quickly moved him out of harm's way, causing the hooded figure to pause and drop their chains before turning away. In the brief encounter, a glimpse of purple hair escaped the hood, catching Kira's attention.

Taking mental note of it, Ethan and Kira finally reached Ben, who was pushing through the crowd with fury in his eyes. "Ben, let's go!" Ethan exclaimed.

"These are the people who attacked me at my home!" Ben shouted, his anger palpable.

"What, you want us to go over there and strike up a conversation? Don't be stupid!" Kira yelled back. "Let's go, or I swear, I'll just leave without you!" She continued forcefully making her way through the chaos.

"Ben, please. I swear, Kira and I will help you get answers. I also want to know what happened to Leo," Ethan pleaded, grabbing both of Ben's arms. Ben paused, willing to hear him out.

"But if you do this and they take you, we lose. They've tried to take you twice now, but you're the only one we know who got away," Ethan reasoned. Suddenly, someone pushed past Ethan, knocking him down. Ben leaned down to help him back up.

"What if we're missing our only chance, Ethan! We only get one chance. We can't go back in time and change it," Ben said, looking at Kira.

"Do you seriously have time to take a jab at Tempus's Code issues right now?" Kira shouted over the deafening screams surrounding them.

Ben scoffed at her. "I have a better idea if we're trying to leave since you're so useless." His eyes glowed orange as he touched someone in the crowd, his hand setting on fire. "Nope, Naturalist," he declared. He touched another Elite, causing him to experience a painful headache as everyone's thoughts flooded his mind.

Help me!

Someone call the Guardians!

I don't wanna die!

I should just fight them!

Thoughts of anguish and anger flooded Ben's head, the pressure making him feel like his skull was cracking. Copying a Psyche's Code would require far more training. He reached out and touched another Elite, his hands disappearing momentarily. Ben finally found a Spatial Class, a Shifter.

"Quick, come to me!" he yelled to Kira and Ethan. Both of them ran and grabbed his hands as they blinked out of the room.

Suddenly, they found themselves in Ben's destroyed home, looking just as Ethan remembered it. "Why are we here?" Ethan asked, puzzled.

"Because Shifters teleport best towards things they've generally touched or seen. They need to know the dimensions of where they are going so they don't get trapped in a wall or something," Kira explained.

"That was a smart move, getting us out of there like that," Ethan said, taking a deep breath.

"Who the hell were those people?" Ethan questioned.

"They called themselves Libertas. Shouldn't we call the Guard or something?" Ben asked, addressing no one in particular.

"No. We were at a party outside of curfew, without our government-ordered robes, and drinking," Ethan responded, immediately realizing that involving the Guard was not an option.

"Are you serious? All those Elites were kidnapped! My parents were killed by them!" Ben yelled, his anger seething.

"I'm sorry for what happened to you, Ben. But we say nothing," Kira supported Ethan's stance.

Ben glared at Ethan as he paced back and forth, lost in thought. Ethan tried his best to dispel Ben's thoughts.

"You're right. It's probably up to us to look into this, but we're just students, Ben. What the heck can we honestly do without help?" Ethan questioned, hoping to dampen Ben's expectations.

"I'll consider helping to look into it. Something about tonight doesn't sit right with me. But we leave the Guard out of it," Kira spoke up, offering her support. Ethan's heart sank at her words.

"But for now, let's drop it. None of us talk about this night to anyone else besides us. I'm tired, and we really need to get home before we get caught," Ethan pleaded, hoping to quell any further discussions.

Both Kira and Ben nodded in understanding, agreeing to keep their encounter a secret. However, the unspoken truth hung heavy in the air—they were all terrified. Because who knows, the next time, they may not be able to escape.

Chapter 17:
Test Subject 339

The air in the room blended with the harsh smell of undiluted chemicals emanating from a shelf on the right-hand side of the lab. Several beakers and flasks stood on the shelf, holding colorful reagents. Despite the terrible smell that engulfed the air, Leo scanned the area in search of the doctor.

Soon enough, he spotted the doctor, but just as quickly, he disappeared again. Where could he have gone? Leo questioned himself. He looked to his left and found the girl they had tested earlier, now fast asleep, as if the doctor had injected her with a dosage to keep her subdued.

Leo attempted to move, only to realize he was bound by chains to the bed. His hands were also restrained, and he wondered where they had brought him. His AICI must have fallen off during the chase, or perhaps they had also taken it from him. If he still had his AICI, it would be easier to escape from these people.

Observing the doctor, Leo noticed him holding a pipette containing a volume of reddish liquid. He watched as the man poured the liquid into another container, causing smoke to evolve from the flask and forcing the man to step back. Once the smoke dissipated, he approached again, waving his head and writing on a piece of paper.

It appeared that the experiment didn't go as expected. The abductors must have been searching for something for a long time now. What could they possibly want from him and the girl? Leo questioned himself. These were the people who had been after Benjamin. Leo groaned, regretting his impulsive decision to chase after that woman. She had led him into a trap. How could he have been so foolish and oblivious not to see it coming? He sighed, weighed down by his own naivety.

Gazing at the sleeping girl on his left, he realized she had never told him her name. How had they managed to bring her here in the first place? Could it be that she possessed something they wanted as well? He had witnessed the doctor extracting her blood too. Something was definitely off about this place. However, his restricted movements prevented him from investigating further. The chains binding his legs and the belt crossing over his belly allowed only minimal space for him to maneuver. He could barely move anything other than his head.

"Hey...! Psst...!" Leo attempted to catch the girl's attention, hoping his assumption about her being asleep was incorrect. "Hey...! Can you hear me?" he whispered urgently. The bed emitted soft whines as Leo vigorously adjusted his body, trying to free himself.

The doctor turned his head fiendishly to the left and moved closer to examine Leo. This caused Leo to flinch. The man drew near, inspecting him closely. "Hmm!" Leo's eyes widened as the man scanned his face, widening his eyes with both thumbs.

The doctor then walked over to a desk and began writing in a book, just as he had done before. Leo observed his actions closely, contemplating whether his body had reacted faster to the substance they injected or if it had a different effect on the girl, causing her to sleep.

Brutes' bodies often reacted differently to stimuli. Leo possessed a strong code and a sensitive system. The doctor approached the girl, checking for her pulse. Observing the man nod and walk away from her, Leo concluded that she was still breathing. However, he couldn't make sense of why he had awakened before her when they had tested her first.

Suddenly, a female voice echoed, and the lab door automatically slid open to allow Rayvena to enter. She held her AICI in her hand, with Titus trailing behind her, appearing bored.

"What, did you find her?" Rayvena questioned someone on her AICI screen. "I think we've taken her as planned," a male voice replied. Leo strained to catch every word spoken.

"Sounds good. I bet she hasn't said anything to them. We don't want this leading back to us. See what you can find out about the address. We'll need to get her out before she has a chance to speak up."

"Trust me, she won't say a word."

Rayvena nodded and tapped on her screen. She then turned to Titus, asking, "Do we have the results?" Titus promptly approached the doctor to inquire about the test results.

Rayvena slowly walked towards Leo, her eyes fixed on him. She didn't need to use her Code to sense that he wasn't just a scared brat.

"It came out positive. He has a strong code, something we could make good use of. But..." The doctor cleared his throat. "It didn't react as expected. We still need more Brutes." Rayvena narrowed her eyes at him, clearly displeased.

He gulped nervously. "I think I can fix it. But that means you can't kill him yet, of course." The doctor proceeded to the table where he had placed various samples, attempting to rectify the situation. Rayvena's gaze shifted fiendishly to Leo, who stared back at her with fury in his eyes. She despised his audacity. Who was he to display nerves of steel in this dire situation? She knew all too well how that often turned out.

Rayvena walked over to the girl. "What about test subject 339 here?" She lifted the girl's hair, revealing her face. She turned her attention to the lab technician, who paused upon being addressed.

"Negative," he responded.

Rayvena sighed in frustration. She brushed the girl's hair away with a single finger to get a clearer view of her face. It was such a waste.

They had to eliminate her before the Guardians intensified their search. And she wouldn't leave the same way she came in.

"Titus, you take care of this one. Get rid of her as soon as possible. Dead or alive, she's your responsibility now." Rayvena stared at the girl for a moment.

Then, looking up at Titus, she commanded, "Make sure you do it discreetly. Not a single soul must know that we had any involvement in this." She glared at Leo, sensing that he would undoubtedly cause trouble.

This boy was with Benjamin Valdez, though, so maybe he had some use. Perhaps he could tell her more about Benjamin Valdez.

"You know, I can see through you and know what's on your mind right now. Sorry to say," she lied. Only a foolish Psyche would try that. "You hold the answer to our prayers."

Leo shook his head as she tried to touch his hair.

"Don't be scared. You will leave here if you cooperate with us."

Leo glared at her. This was the same woman who glued him to the ground back there in the woods. Now she talked about cooperation.

"Good, then you should be able to see me flipping you off right now. You would just be wasting your time on me."

Rayvena's fiendish smile faded away, but she quickly flashed it back at the boy. "I wasn't expecting you would tell me without a fight. I came prepared, boy." She ran her nails across Leo's chest, causing him to panic. "You see, you have no idea why we want your friend so badly. Think about what would become of you and your grandma if you fail to give me what I want." Leo's expression soured on the spot.

Rayvena smiled slightly, knowing she chipped his armor. Who was she to threaten his family? "You stuck-up bitch! Don't you dare go anywhere near her," shouted Leo.

Rayvena's laughter echoed in the lab. Leo struggled to free himself, but the chains and the belt across his chest grew tighter. The more he wriggled, the tighter they became. Realizing the strap across his chest gradually took his breath away, he stopped and relaxed.

Rayvena grew calm. "We already have eyes on her as we speak. When I am ready to get my answers, I will come for them." She tossed her purple-streaked hair and walked away.

Leo clenched his jaws angrily. He would tear her apart if something happened to his grandmother. The Brute made a fist. His Code was useless. The chains on him were the same as those of the Guardians. They restricted him from using his Code to save himself.

"Damn it!" he cursed.

Titus walked up to the unconscious girl, ready to take her away. Leo lunged as far as his restraints let him. "You want me to talk? You let her live! Otherwise, I will tell you nothing." His eyes were determined. Rayvena turned around, looking at him for several moments.

"Titus, leave her for now. Let's just see first if his info is as good as he says." Leo stopped straining against the chains.

"It is. I swear." Titus backed up and joined Rayvena. Both Rayvena and Titus gave him one last pitiful look before they stormed out of the lab. The door automatically shut behind them.

Leo caught the expression of relief on the lab tech and doctor's faces. Perhaps it was not their will to be here working. It felt as if the doctor was being used and not actually part of their group. Well, then again, who would want to partner with such a pretentious woman?

He glared at the door, hoping she was still there to see how much he already hated her.

The lab technician quietly went to the girl to check on her again. Leo thought it wise to speak to the man. Maybe he might be able to convince him to do the right thing after all.

"They are using you," he began. A little rational heart-to-heart would help get the man to his senses. "You know you don't have to work for them if it is not your will." Both the lab technician and doctor ignored Leo and checked the girl's pulse.

"What did they offer you? Tell me, and I'll double it." Leo barely had the money to pay for Grandma's treatment. How was he going to double the man's pay?

He shoved the thought aside and went on, "Name your price, just let us go, and I will get you the money."

The man glanced at Leo, then back at the girl. The lab technician had her hands in his, trying to feel her reflexes. He needed to study her to better understand why the substance he injected them with had a different reaction to her.

He walked back to the table as Leo's voice echoed in his ear. The boy had no idea what he was talking about. The boy had no idea why he had to do this terrible job. If only he knew what had happened to him, he would realize they all needed saving.

It didn't really matter. Getting out of the lab wasn't so easy, not with Rayvena on watch. She would kill them before they made it across that door. Rayvena seemed to have one of the strongest aptitudes he had ever seen in Psyche. Strong enough to call her a prodigy, even.

"What? Are you going to help us or not?"

"Quiet, boy." The lab technician knew they were not alone. Rayvena had ears all around the lab. She would come for him if he said anything meaningful to Leo.

"Do the right thing!" Leo gave up, realizing that was his limit to convince the man to do the right thing.

A slight cough beside him caught his attention. She was awake now. Leo turned to her. The man must have done something to awaken her. "Hey...?" She could barely move a muscle.

Her eyes glowed, and the light in them died out at the same speed they shone. She coughed again, trying to move her legs. Leo saw her struggle and said, "You should relax. You can't get out of it. I tried, but it was useless." She turned to look at the boy beside her.

"What happened to me?" she asked. The substance still had a grip on her.

"I don't know. But I think we're definitely screwed." They were going to get rid of her soon. Leo grimaced. The lab technician walked back up to her.

He examined her the same way he had examined Leo when he found the boy was awake. He nodded and walked away. Leo watched carefully to understand why he always did that and what he kept writing down. He turned to the girl. "We need to get out of here as soon as we can." Leo's eyes met the girl's gaze.

Benjamin Valdez was a target. They wanted him dead back at the hospital. Why did it seem like all this nonsense was planned in such great lengths? Leo closed his eyes. He didn't tell Grandma where he was going. Who knew if she was doing okay or getting worse by the day? She must be sick with worry about his sudden disappearance.

Ethan! Would he be able to keep an eye on his grandmother? No, that was a selfish ask from him. His grandmother wasn't his responsibility. Was Ethan even worried about him right now? Leo mused. Damn Rayvena. She better not lay a hand on his grandmother. He clenched his jaw and made a fist. Because ultimately, that was all he could do.

Chapter 18:
A Troubled Mind

Horns of hoverbikes and vehicles echoed around Sector 53, shattering the peacefulness of the moment nature had to offer. Amidst the noise and discomfort that permeated the area, she couldn't help but watch the sun gradually retire. The beautiful city held precious memories for her.

Quintella sat in her office chair and looked out the window behind her. She was on the second floor of her mahogany office. Troubled about her future, she poured herself a drink and contemplated.

At first glance, Sector 53 appeared as a vast prairie. Its primary function was to supply food sources to other sectors. Since most animals in Pangea were dead or endangered, many migrated there. Food was not a requirement for Elites, as they did not need it to survive.

However, having learned from the past, traditions were necessary to maintain peace and sanity. Most things in Pangea were freely distributed by the government to the Sector Officials to provide for their people. Food had become a pleasure. If you wanted it, you had to work for it.

The region's green mustard grass stretched as far as the eye could see. It was more natural than anything—tall enough to touch your knees, yet soft enough to sleep in. Most of the land had been farmed by the Elites, but dull gray rectangular homes and buildings sporadically dotted the landscape.

Quintella observed as Elites got on their hands and knees, planting different vegetables and fruits. Naturalists came by and touched the soil, allowing the food to flourish faster. Other adults, dressed in green Naturalist robes, carried the produce away in baskets. Children laughed and played in the grass, oblivious to the labor of the adults around them.

For a moment, Quintella stared at the city from the window, tightly gripping her glass of favorite concoction. The glass was already half empty. She glanced at the drink, then at the stool where a bottle of lava-red substance sat.

Ethan would be mad at her if he found out she had been drinking. She didn't need the drink to stay alive. But sometimes, it seemed to be the only escape from one's misery. Besides, drinks were made differently now than in the past, with the same goal but fewer negative drawbacks. Quintella tried to rationalize with herself, telling herself it was safe because her sector produced it.

Her job was stressing her out. She sighed. Nothing bothered her more than the realization that everything would be taken away from her one day. It was reason enough to grab a glass and have a drink. Turning in her chair, she poured another glass from a decanter.

First, they would start by wiping her memory. Memories of her good old days would vanish suddenly. She might not even remember who Ethan was anymore. She shook her head in disappointment.

Why did it have to be this way? She had served as a Sector Official for many years, knowing the rules like the back of her hand. She had never once gone against the rules or done something that could tarnish her good name. Unlike Richard, who prioritized his position and status over family, she always put Ethan first, considering that any wrongdoing on her part might affect him in the future.

Quintella's brows furrowed. How could she fix this so that she could retain her memory? The thought drove her from the window to sit on the mahogany-colored couch. She placed the glass on the stool. Richard wouldn't help her this time. He would want to follow the rules as always.

Perhaps she could find a better alternative to fix the situation at hand. For the first time in decades, Quintella grew scared for the future. Running away would only endanger her further. Taking such a drastic decision would prompt the government to stop at nothing until they found her and wiped out every cherished memory. She crossed one leg over the other and supported her chin with a hand.

Years ago, working as a Sector Official had felt like a blessing. They held special authority and knowledge that others in the country didn't possess. Their task was to socially and economically advance their region and improve the lives of those around them. It was a position of great respect, and only a Sector Official could converse with fellow government leaders. Moreover, it provided a break from their permanent job, although their role was meant to be collaborative rather than authoritative.

Right now, it seemed like the worst idea. Quintella wished she could see the future like Tempus. Over the years, she had allowed herself to be blinded by rank and status. Sector 53 had been under her control for many years, and someone must be preparing to replace her soon. They wouldn't cherish or protect Ethan as she did. It could be any of the people running against her, those who wanted her out of office by any means. She realized she had forgotten about Richard, who held a higher rank and could protect Ethan. Despite their strained relationship, Quintella knew in her heart that Richard loved their son.

"Does Richard love Ethan?" someone spoke out.

Quintella was startled, accidentally spilling her drink. "Oh, now look what you've done! Who is it?" She reached down to pick up her glass.

When she stood back up, she was face to face with an exact replica of herself.

"No, I got rid of you," Quintella stumbled backward, horrified.

Her other self stepped forward. "Oh honey, I'm always by your side." She gave a sweet and gentle smile, caressing Quintella's cheek.

Quintella's hand fumbled with the decanter of liquor. Her shaky hands poured more red liquid into her glass.

"Hun, you've already had so much to drink. Maybe you need something stronger?" Her other self gestured to the cabinet, where a cerulean blue decanter sat.

"No, I won't let you get inside my head!" Quintella held her head in her hands.

Her other self just laughed. "Are you kidding me? I'm already in it!"

She strolled toward Quintella and comfortably sat on her desk.

"You know how this goes, hun. It's just the price you pay for being a Psyche."

Quintella backed against the wall.

"Please, leave me alone! Please." Quintella shut her eyes, tears falling down her face. She slid to the floor, her body trembling in fear.

"You're not real." Her voice was cracking.

When she opened her eyes, the other Quintella's fist slammed into her face, and her head hit the wall.

"Am I real now, bitch?" Her tone turned hostile.

"I told you, don't ignore me. I'm the only one you have." The sinister Quintella placed her hands behind her back as she circled her host.

Quintella looked up at her dark doppelgänger and stood up. "You're not real!" She closed her eyes again.

"I am! Don't shut me out!" Her other self quickly grabbed Quintella's arm.

Quintella was met with silence for a while before she opened her eyes. The other one was gone. She sighed in relief as she poured another glass to drink.

She spoke aloud. "Gallium, has anyone been in here lately?"

Gallium materialized in the room. "No, ma'am, just you. Also, it seems like you've been talking to yourself again."

"I see. That's quite unfortunate. I thought the drinks were working."

The sun was almost down. Quintella glanced at her AICI. "Gallium, where is Ethan now?"

The AI didn't respond immediately. Quintella adjusted, wondering why Gallium didn't answer. Perhaps something had gone wrong with the AI. She cleared her throat and spoke again, carefully enunciating each word. "Gallium, where is Ethan Crambe?"

"Ethan is on his way home with Benjamin Valdez," Gallium's voice echoed.

"Where? And do I have any outstanding activities?"

Gallium quickly scanned through Quintella's schedule. As he searched, he answered part of her question. "It appears to be an underground building, ma'am."

"An underground building?" Quintella lowered her hand, her mind racing. Could he be at a club? Ethan had gotten into plenty of trouble before, but partying in secret seemed unlikely.

Gallium interrupted her thoughts. "You have the entire evening to yourself." Quintella nodded, biting her lip. "But only after you see your guest. He's on his way to you now." Her eyes narrowed as she cocked her head to a corner. She hadn't scheduled an appointment with anyone for the day.

Quintella uncrossed her legs. "And who might that be?" Her voice conveyed curiosity and confusion.

"Glade."

Quintella stood and went to the closet. If Glade was on his way to see her, she needed to appear presentable. He couldn't see her in a shirt and jeans. She could guess the purpose of his visit. She threw on the robe hanging behind her chair.

Glade had her best interests at heart. Maybe he would have a better opinion on the decision she had to make. "How far is he from here?" she asked, slipping into an official dress.

"One block, two minutes, and thirty-five seconds away."

Quintella smirked at an empty wall as though she could see the person whose voice echoed in the room. Gallium always provided accurate details, which assured Quintella that Glade truly wasn't far from the property.

She hurriedly dumped the lava-red substance from the bar in her office into the sink and checked her breath for traces of alcohol. "Shit!" She rushed to her personal bathroom, immediately washing out the taste in her mouth.

"He is here," Gallium announced.

The bright light of a space vehicle flashed through the window as the driver pulled up in front of the building. The engine died instantly without a moan. A gentleman with a well-carved haircut stepped out of the vehicle and walked toward the entrance. Gallium had already arrived at the door before the man took the first step of the staircase in front of the door. The AI scanned for weapons and let the man enter the office.

Scanning the room with his glittering eyes, the man exclaimed, "There you are!"

Quintella greeted him with a smile, descending the stairs and walking across the living room to offer him a handshake.

"Please," she gestured for him to have a seat. He tied his cobalt blue hair behind his back, and Quintella noticed a few strains lingering on his face.

Glade adjusted his gray robes as he took a seat. His matching gray eyes searched her face. "You okay? You seem a bit rattled," he asked, concerned.

Quintella steadied herself on the wall inconspicuously. "It's nothing. I'm fine." She slowly walked and sat behind her desk.

"You're not thinking about your retirement, are you?" Glade's sultry voice sounded musical.

Quintella sighed softly, nodding her head sadly.

"You don't need to worry that much. I will find a way to retain your cherished memories. But it won't be easy. This plan could cost you your life if we're not careful." He took her hand, and she left it there for a moment before pulling away.

Taking a deep breath, Quintella continued, "I don't have a choice but to try anyway. This is hard for me right now. It feels like my world is coming to an end."

Glade frowned, understanding the pain and stress she was experiencing from contemplating the memory wipe. "What would you suggest? Perhaps you have a better alternative to fix your problem," he inquired.

Quintella grew silent for a moment, contemplating her options. After a brief pause, she spoke up. "What about extracting my memories before the process? After the wipe is done, my memories could be reinserted."

Glade's eyes widened in surprise. She must have given this idea deep thought before voicing it out. He had never considered this approach before.

"You might have a point. We shouldn't worry if there's a way out of this. As far as I know, no one has ever done that before, at least not since I started here," Glade responded. Quintella would be the first if she managed to pull it off.

He continued, "Do you know what?" Quintella arched a brow, intrigued. "I will get back to you on this. I need to find out if we can arrange for memory extraction somewhere far from here. That way, the secret will remain between you and me," he suggested, though he appeared worried about the idea. They might not find a way out, but they had to try.

Quintella rose sadly. She had ignored this possibility for too long, and now it stung like a bee. Glade was right—they needed to keep the secret between them; not even Richard or Ethan could know about it. They would have to play along with a plan to make it look like the memory wipe had been successful.

But how long could she stick to the plan? Two years? That was a long time. Ethan might grow tired of her and want to be with Richard. She smirked at her thought, knowing that it would never happen. But still. If his mother didn't try, who would protect Ethan? She was the only thing standing in the way of the truth.

Glade's attention had been consumed by thoughts of the consequences that would follow once they achieved their goal.

She spoke again. "Do whatever you think is best for me. I don't care about the cost, even if we have to swim in the ocean. I just want my life in check." Glade nodded, slowly shifting his gaze to an empty wall.

Gallium remained ghost-quiet as if he didn't exist in the building. It was a secret, and no one should tell Ethan or anyone else about it.

Quickly, the AI scanned the AICI database for possible negative effects of memory loss and reviewed all the reports on previous Sector Officials.

"Is Richard aware of your decision?" Glade asked. Quintella turned to him, narrowing her eyes.

"Richard?" Glade nodded.

She had no plans to tell Richard anything about her plans. He was better off out of the picture, as involving him would only complicate matters. She shook her head, forcing a pained smile. "Do you think it's a good idea?"

Quintella pondered whether she might be making a mistake by excluding Richard from the situation. She didn't want to burden him with this dishonorable issue. He would undoubtedly prioritize Pangea's policy over her selfish interests.

Glade took a deep breath and sighed. "I think we have to let him know about this. You can't keep him in the dark for long. He will find out someday." He cocked his head, hoping Quintella was comprehending all that he said rather than just staring at him.

"Leave that to me, Glade," she said, adjusting her purple robe to cover her chest properly. She knew Richard wouldn't buy the idea; she understood him like a chameleon knows its colors. Glade smiled.

Quintella may not have understood his reasoning for suggesting they involve Richard in all of this. As the Sector Official of 71, Richard Crambe had the power to influence her desires both negatively and positively.

Seeing her growing uneasiness, Glade spoke up, "I have something to tell you."

Quintella swung around, curious to hear what the gentleman had to say. Perhaps he had a better and more trustworthy idea.

Quintella's AICI suddenly rang, and three blue holographic rings appeared, interrupting their conversation. She looked at the screen and saw Richard Crambe, the very person they had been discussing.

"Hey Q, I'll be home for breakfast in two weeks. We need to talk about some things," Richard spoke indifferently and stoically.

What could he want to talk about? Before she could respond, the screen blanked out, returning to its usual background. She glanced at Glade, who stared curiously at her. Together, they turned to silently gaze at the beautiful city.

Chapter 19:
Ethan's Necklace

Two weeks had passed since the rave incident, yet Ethan, Kira, and Ben continued to keep their heads down and attend the Academy as usual. Surprisingly, there had been no news about the matter yet.

The golden hallways of Unity Prep remained crowded and bustling with students moving from Class to Class. Colorful robes shimmered as students hurried with purpose. However, an underlying tension filled the air.

Groups of first-year students in tunics huddled together, engrossed in conversations about the mysterious happenings in Pangea, particularly in Sector 71. Ethan's sudden appearance in the hallway caught their attention, and they started whispering and pointing fingers at him as if he were some kind of anomaly. Ethan slowed down, eventually coming to a halt.

Ben, walking ahead of Ethan, noticed the stares and also stopped. He looked around, realizing that many people were indeed staring at them. Ben waited for Ethan to catch up so they could walk together. Ethan hurriedly joined Ben, wiping the sweat off his hands onto his tunic.

As the two continued toward their classrooms, the murmuring among the students grew, accompanied by disdainful glances directed at Ethan. Ignoring the first set of people at the entrance, Ethan couldn't ignore the second set, whose piercing gazes indicated that something had gone wrong. He glanced at Ben, who pretended to focus on their destination.

"You're seeing this too, right?" Ethan asked, seeking confirmation. Ben remained silent. "Why is everyone looking at us?" Ethan voiced his confusion. The hallway seemed endless, and he wiped the sweat on his tunic once again.

"I think they're looking at you. You have a stain on your tunic," Ben replied. Ethan examined his tunic but found nothing that warranted such attention. It had been his tunic since he first started school, nothing new or out of the ordinary. Why the strange looks?

He pondered, but his thoughts were interrupted as someone suddenly joined them. "Cassidy?" Ethan was taken aback.

"I always knew you were an asshole, Ethan Crambe, but I never thought you'd be a killer," she said, slightly recoiling from him. Ben looked at Ethan and shrugged.

Ethan couldn't comprehend what she was accusing him of. "I don't understand what you're talking about."

"It's all over the school that you had something to do with Leo's disappearance. And some are also saying you were a troublemaker in your previous sector," Cassidy explained. Ethan's jaw dropped, his eyes widening in shock.

"That's not true," Ben interjected. He knew what had really happened at the hospital. Leo had chased after a woman and never returned. The Guardians had promised to handle the situation, but they hadn't provided any information about Leo's whereabouts. "He had nothing to do with it, so watch your mouth," Ben snapped.

Cassidy flinched. "Watch it, Ben. I can always put you back in the hospital," she threatened, glaring at him. "I wasn't the one spreading the rumors."

"I don't see anyone else making baseless accusations," Ben confronted her, getting in her face.

Cassidy scoffed. "I'm over this," she said, then proceeded to walk away. However, she stopped and glanced back at Ethan. "After you stood me up at the rave and didn't even apologize, you think I owe you an explanation? Fat chance in hell." Ethan smacked Ben in the back of the head.

Obtaining information from Cassidy didn't require harsh words or aggression. Someone had fabricated this rumor and pinned it on him to tarnish his reputation. Whoever was behind it, he was determined to find out. Ethan hurried to catch up with Cassidy, who annoyingly walked away from them. Ben paused to straighten his shimmering orange robe, realizing he shouldn't have lost his composure. He ran after Ethan and Cassidy, doing his best to avoid bumping into students moving in the opposite direction.

"Cassidy?" Ethan caught up to her in the main lobby, where the DNA sculpture stood.

The girl turned around on the spot. "What, Crambe?"

Ethan slowed down as he closed the distance. "He didn't mean it that way," Cassidy frowned.

"Look, I'm sorry I didn't leave with you after what happened," Ethan apologized. Cassidy looked scared and pulled him around a corner to speak more freely.

"Sheesh, can you not bring that up here? I don't want to remember that."

"Hey, you brought up the rave, not me," he reminded her.

"Just get to the point, Ethan," she huffed impatiently. "I'm going to be late for class."

"We have the same Class. I need to know who said those things about me," Ethan pleaded with her.

Cassidy sighed. "I won't blame you for choosing to help your friend. I'm mad because it's clear that I like you, and you aren't reciprocating."

Ethan's eyes widened. He wasn't good at picking up on these things. Ben had mentioned it at the rave, but he hadn't paid attention.

"I'm not saying I'm not interested in you, Cassidy, but I'm not in a position to talk or date anyone right now," he tried to explain.

"So you're not interested in anyone else right now? It's just because you're unavailable?" Cassidy began to calm down.

"Exactly. There's no one else, trust me," Ethan lied. He didn't want to complicate things.

Cassidy relaxed. "Okay, I'm sorry for overreacting," she said, smoothing down her red tunic. Ben finally found them and joined the conversation. Other students shuffled past them in the halls.

"All I know is that Ben's ex told people that you visited him at the hospital. She found it weird because you don't even know him. That's why you look guilty, dude," Cassidy explained while Ethan gawked at this appalling information.

"Everyone is accusing me because I was kind enough to check in on him?"

"That and you DID find him. But honestly, I think-" Cassidy's AICI started to vibrate. Ethan's AICI vibrated too. The hallway began to fill with ringing as everyone checked their tech.

"Hello, fellow Elites," a strange voice echoed from the speaker. Everyone held their AICIs in their hands, listening to the mysterious transmission. "We are Libertas." Ben slowly walked toward Ethan and Cassidy, his eyes fixed on the screen of his AICI. "For many years now, the government of Pangea has lied to us. We are not free Elites but slaves to the government. Today, I urge Elites all over the world to stand up and take back their freedom. We have the power to change the world and unleash our true potential."

"The government is aware of our powers and how we can shape this world for the better. No longer should we be slaves. Say no to restrictive orders. Join us today to discover your true identity. The Creator has sent us here for a purpose, but the government restricts us from utilizing our powers for our own interests and benefits."

"If you desire freedom, the freedom to shape your own world, we are here to guide you and fight alongside you. We are the Libertas Society. We stand for justice, freedom, and truth."

Everyone's AICI screen went blank and displayed a short video with the caption "truth." The video showed clips of teenagers and young adults fleeing for their lives in a building. Ethan and Ben glanced at each other while Cassidy gasped. The hallway filled with students watching the screens of their AICIs, some flinching at the brutality depicted. It showed the attack at the underground rave, the same incident they were involved in, but fortunately not captured on video.

"What the heck is going on?" Cassidy asked, her AICI going blank again and returning to its normal display. Ethan shrugged. He had no idea.

"This isn't good," Ben remarked. Some students were already reacting to the video, their attention shifting away from Ethan and focusing on the message. Fearful, they began to leave the school premises in pairs.

Cassidy shook her head. "I knew this day would come." Ethan glanced at her as if she had three heads. She rolled her eyes. "It was a joke."

"Ben, where are you going?" Ethan inquired.

"I'll meet you at home, Ethan. I need to find out what's going on," Ben replied before vanishing into the departing crowd.

"Come on!" Cassidy pulled Ethan by the wrists. "We need to find Professor Carson now." They both disappeared around a bend in the hallway.

***

"What do you mean you have no idea? This is a terrible situation," Carson yelled at someone on the other side of his AICI. "It has to be traceable, damn it!" The caller provided no valuable information about the transmitted message that had reached everyone.

"We are doing everything we can to fix this. Sector Officials are already on it," the receiver assured him.

Carson waved his hand in disappointment. Did this mean the city wasn't safe anymore, despite the presence of Guardians throughout? He hung up and placed the AICI on the table.

The door opened, and Cassidy and Ethan rushed in as if a beast was chasing them. Carson raised a brow; his eyes tailed the two figures as they walked up to him with curious expressions lingering on their faces. Cassidy was about to speak when Carson interjected, "I know why you're here, Cassidy." He walked out from behind the desk towards the kids. "The world is changing now, and the rules might start to change too." The professor's eyes shifted between Cassidy and a curious Ethan. "They are not to be trusted. You mustn't listen to what they are saying."

"Professor," Cassidy interrupted, "a lot of students are leaving the school early. What should we do now?" Rumors were spreading about students going missing, and with Ben and several others in their area confirming it, fear began to grip the student body. No one wanted to disappear. The best they could do was go home while they still had the chance until it was safe to return.

"Go home. Principal Fairday is canceling classes for the day to improve security here for the safety of all our students."

"Why should we run when we have the power to protect ourselves? It's not in our nature as Elites to flee," Ethan retorted. The boy had little combat experience but stood there talking about defense.

Carson glanced at Cassidy, but neither she nor Ethan noticed the look on his face.

Carson's brows furrowed. "Stop worrying about things beyond your control, and go home, Ethan. Be at school as early as possible. We have a lot of training to do." He turned and walked back to his desk. Cassidy's gaze met Ethan's, and she tilted her head and pouted.

Carson picked up a book from the desk. The sound of a closed door made him raise his eyes to an empty room. They were gone now. He took a deep breath, removed his glasses, and cleaned the lenses.

Cassidy left with a silver-haired girl from her Sprite class. Ben was nowhere to be found. It was likely he had gone home. Ethan walked, consumed by thoughts of why he had to go home. Today had been a wasted day. Ethan berated himself, wishing he had stayed home or gone somewhere peaceful to clear his mind.

But Ethan didn't feel like going home just yet. After all, there was no urgent reason to. His father wasn't home, and his mother had to commute between Sectors. As he hid in the Academy's library, brushing up on Code applications, Ethan emerged from his secluded spot when darkness fell.

In the school parking hall, among many vehicles, only one hoverbike remained. Only a few students had stayed behind to gain knowledge or further their training. Ethan climbed onto the hoverbike. His mother might have some information about this Libertas group. Being a Sector Official, she would be aware of everything happening in the country.

Should he call her now and ask, or wait until he got home? He sighed, realizing she probably wouldn't provide him with the answers he sought, even if he asked.

As Ethan attempted to start the engine, someone knocked him off the hoverbike. He rolled onto his face, regained his balance, and stood up disoriented. Scanning the area, he found no one else present with him.

As he turned to look behind, a punch crashed him to the ground again. Then a voice came behind him, "I heard you were looking for me." Ethan raised his face to the figure standing over him. "Well, I'm here now, Brute," Skylar said with a fiendish smile on his face. Ethan stood and dusted his red tunic.

"You said that stuff about me? Why?"

Skylar snickered. "I was right about you, Crambe." Ethan clenched his jaw. He hated the fact that Skylar had the guts to attack him after accusing him wrongly.

"I looked you up and asked students from your old Academy," Skylar sneered. He rushed forward, attempting to land a punch, but Skylar swiftly shifted and delivered a kick. Ethan stumbled and fell.

"You should stay down, Crambe. No one is here to save you now. Don't be hard on yourself," Skylar taunted while Ethan glared back at him. Determined, Ethan rose and waited for Skylar to approach. Then, he rushed forward, intending to pull Skylar off the ground and crash him onto one of the vehicles.

Skylar shifted, causing Ethan to collide with the vehicle, shattering its glass. Swiftly, Skylar shifted in front of Ethan, pinning him against the vehicle and delivering a series of forceful punches. His hands vanished with each swing, making it difficult for Ethan to anticipate the hits. Finally, Skylar grabbed Ethan by the neck and slammed him onto the ground, eliciting a groan from Ethan.

Kneeling down, Skylar locked eyes with Ethan, one knee pressing against his stomach and one arm on his throat. "Kara was right about you. You don't deserve to be an Elite. People like you should be slaves. You have no ability that qualifies you to be an Elite," Skylar jeered. Standing up, he released Ethan and kicked him in the belly.

Moaning in pain, Ethan clutched his stomach, blood oozing from the corner of his mouth. "Show me what you've got, Crambe. Or is the Sector Official's kid all talk?" Ethan rose from the ground, wiping his lips with the back of his palm. His eyes widened as he noticed the blood. Skylar was truly trying to harm him.

"Okay, Skylar! I've had enough of your bullshit," Ethan exclaimed, charging toward Skylar, only to be struck and sent back to the ground. Skylar casually approached him while Ethan struggled to catch his breath. Skylar then stomped on Ethan's chest and snatched his necklace.

"Why wear an enhancement necklace when there's nothing to enhance?" Skylar laughed, mocking Ethan. He increased the pressure on Ethan's chest. Gasping for air, Ethan threatened, "Give that back, or I swear I'll crush you!" He writhed, but Skylar pressed harder, leaving Ethan with no leverage. He had never felt so weak.

Skylar continued to laugh, exerting more force on Ethan's chest. "Good thinking, Ethan!" Skylar tossed the necklace on the ground and crushed it, shattering the crystal stone. A spark fizzled out. Rage engulfed Ethan as he clenched his fist and slammed it into the ground, causing the earth to fracture and create a dent. The ground trembled momentarily, leaving Skylar gasping for air as he fell backward.

Ethan's eyes widened with surprise, unsure of what had just happened. Was his strength finally manifesting? A small smile crept onto his face as he realized the possibility, but the moment quickly passed. Ethan's gaze shifted to the shattered crystal stone. He now needed his necklace more than ever.

"Hey, get away from him!" a voice echoed through the parking hall. Skylar got up and shifted away at the sight of Benjamin, who approached them with lightning speed. Ethan sat up, his hands trembling as he frantically tried to gather the pieces of his ruby stone. Tears of anger welled up in his eyes.

Kneeling down beside Ethan, Benjamin briefly wore a look of horror on his face. "Damn it! I was too late..." Benjamin ran his hands through his hair while Ethan panicked, trying to salvage the fragments of his pendant.

"Your necklace...it's broken. I'm so sorry I came too late, Ethan." He looked genuinely saddened. "Damn, it seems you messed up your arm bracer too." He stood back up.

"Damn it! Now, what do I do..." Benjamin spoke to himself. He began pacing back and forth. He placed his hands behind his head in frustration. He was stressed out.

"You don't understand! I needed that necklace! Without it, I'm nothing. That's all I had," Ethan uttered, his voice choked with emotion.

He stared at his hands, gripping the necklace tightly. Squeezing his eyes shut, Ethan sobbed and let the broken pieces of the pendant fall from his grasp. Defeated, his shoulders slumped as he laid bare his pain before Benjamin.

Kneeling beside Ethan, Benjamin tried to console him. "It's not all you have, Ethan. Your strength doesn't come from that, or have you forgotten your motto?" Ethan looked up at Benjamin, meeting his gaze for the first time.

"The strongest will overcome. But your strength lies in resilience and dedication. That's why the other classes despise you. They'll never understand that. You possess something that most Elites lack: heart," Benjamin explained, his words gradually calming Ethan's breathing.

"I understand that our society can be elitist, but you can't let them break you. Your strength lies in your ability to rise again and again, no matter how much the others secretly hate your Class. The Brutes are the backbone of our country, Ethan," Benjamin affirmed, placing his hands on Ethan's shoulders.

Locking eyes with Benjamin, Ethan's determination flickered. "Anyone can do that. I'm tired of feeling weak. And I'll be damned if people think I'm the reason Leo went missing."

Saddened, Benjamin's eyes dropped, his gaze turning somber as he spoke. "What is it about Leo anyway?"

Ethan, still sniffling, rubbed his eyes to see Benjamin more clearly. "What do you mean?" Confusion clouded his thoughts as he sensed something off about Benjamin's demeanor.

"You're exhausting yourself searching for this guy, but why? Why does he mean so much to you?" Benjamin pressed, his tone passionate.

"He wasn't even supposed to be there, Ben! I can't just abandon him and leave it to fate when I know I have the power to help!" Ethan yelled in frustration.

"But you don't," Benjamin countered, causing Ethan to sharply pull away. "You have no way of knowing where he is. And what will you do if you find him, huh? Bust him out?" He fired back, his words sharp.

"Ben, why are you even here? I thought you went home," Ethan said, weariness seeping into his voice.

"Well, I was actually looking for you. I was... worried," Benjamin confessed, his tone tinged with hesitation. He seemed to have something on his mind.

"Is there something you want to tell me?" Ethan asked curiously, mixed with a hint of concern.

"No, no, nothing like that. I'm just worried about you, man," Benjamin replied, deciding to give Ethan a comforting hug.

In that moment, Ethan was overwhelmed by a flurry of visions. A vivid scene unfolded in his mind as if he were physically experiencing it. Elites ran in panic, screaming, right where he stood outside the vision—back at the Academy. The ground cracked, explosions rocked the distance, and Ethan instinctively stepped back from the fractures. Some Elites fell to their deaths, and a sharp pain seared through his head, causing Ethan to stumble backward in shock.

Suddenly, the earth quaked, and the world spun around him. He found himself bound and chained on a stage in a colosseum, surrounded by a sea of furious spectators. A woman with frizzy blonde hair dressed in opal robes stood before him—strangely familiar. The vision burned with a red hue, blinding Ethan. The stadium echoed with jeers and hateful screams, but he couldn't decipher their words. Rain fell upon the Colosseum, only to stop in midair and float back up.

Ethan's body felt electric, and the vision erupted into flames. Before him, a jungle emerged, and a statue of a woman holding a torch turned its head, locking eyes with him. As Benjamin shook him, the vision abruptly ended, and Ethan found himself back at the Academy's gate, drenched in sweat and gasping for breath. Everything appeared normal, and Ethan looked back at Benjamin, still trying to comprehend what had just transpired.

Unable to find the right words, Ethan's eyes rolled back, and he collapsed. Benjamin stood motionless for a few minutes before letting out a scream toward the sky. He stomped his feet in anger, his frustration palpable. Finally, he fell to the ground, striking it with his fist.

"I should have acted sooner," he whispered, glancing over at Ethan. Straightening his orange robe, he sighed, "This whole thing is turning out to be a terrible idea."

As Benjamin stared at Ethan lying on the ground, he wondered, "Why is it always you who causes trouble for everyone?" He knew Ethan couldn't hear him. "My head is pounding now. I wonder, what vision did you see?" He lifted Ethan's body onto his shoulder. "If I remember correctly, I'm supposed to go to Kira's house next..."

With Ethan's unconscious form draped over his shoulder, Benjamin descended the Academy's steps, his mind filled with uncertainty.

Chapter 20:
Are We Friends Yet?

The complex language used in the Spatial Class textbooks often threw Kira off balance when studying the theories behind kinetic energy. Flipping to the next page, she tried to embrace the laws of gravitational fall, but they remained elusive. Staring at the book all day wouldn't help, as she lacked interest in studying at the moment. Kira closed the textbook and slid it to a corner, replacing it with her own books on her lap. With the first book set aside, she retrieved a notebook and placed it in front of her.

"Kira, can you please check the lights?" her mother yelled from the living room downstairs.

Since her father's passing, it had become Kira's responsibility to handle all electrical appliances in the house. As a future mechanical engineer, she could fix the lights and even repair her mother's vehicle. Her role in the family was crucial, and it gave her a sense of purpose when she walked the streets of Pangea.

"I'll fix the lights in a minute, Mom!" she replied.

Kira's mother preferred not to deal with anything too technical, as it reminded her too much of her late husband. Understanding this, Kira assured her that she would attend to the lights and all technical things.

Even though they could have relied on AI assistance, Kira wanted the practice. Her sister, often away from home, had little knowledge of what needed fixing. It was understandable, considering the impact their father's death had on her. Kira put her school bag down, opened the notebook, and smiled upon seeing the assignment questions from their last class. She could answer these questions effortlessly instead of wasting time struggling with Physics. Groaning, she picked up a pen and began writing the correct answers.

Her father had been a great teacher, as well as a skilled Tempus. He used to tell her stories of his days as a top student in Sector 71.

Kira's ultimate goal was to make him proud and match his intellect. With a smile, she moved on to the third question, which involved balancing a chemical equation—a reaction between NSO_4 and CO_2. She quickly jotted down the question on a separate sheet and solved it, double-checking her work before transferring it to her assignment book.

The next question seemed familiar; she had come across it in class, possibly as an open question posed by one of the professors. Ethan, her training partner, had answered it correctly. She had initially underestimated him as a Brute, but now she recognized his intelligence. Kira swiftly wrote down the answer and turned to the next page.

Thoughts of Ethan interrupted her, and she paused with the pen between her teeth. They had grown closer over the past week, and she found him quite impressive. It had been unfair of her to judge him initially. Only after encountering him outside, following the rave, did she realize his decency.

Several days earlier, Ben felt restless in the room as Ethan sat working on paperwork. Boredom engulfed Ben, who sought an escape from schoolwork and stress. "Are you done?" he asked Ethan, striking his fingers against the table.

Ethan shook his head, indicating he was not finished.

"Come on, you're taking ages. We might miss the show if we arrive late," Ben complained. Ethan, determined to complete the task, asked Ben to stop distracting him. Folding his hands, Ben resolved not to interfere.

"I'm almost done. You should get the bike ready and make sure everything is in order before we leave," Ethan instructed, not taking his eyes off the paper.

Ben rose to do as he was told. Ethan finished writing, he quickly packed his books and hurried to the garage, where Ben awaited him.

"Get on. You're flying it today," Ethan said, smiling at Ben.

Without hesitation, Ben hopped on the hoverbike and brought it to life. Ethan jumped on the back, and they zoomed off into the bustling streets.

Holding tightly to Ben, Ethan yelled, "Where are we going now?"

Ben yelled back, "I'll show you when we get there," as he headed toward a tunnel—a shortcut into the underground that bypassed Guardians and traffic.

They emerged from the tunnel within seconds and seamlessly merged with other hoverbikes and hover-vans darting to their destinations. Ben made a sharp turn that made Ethan's heart skip a beat. Holding on tightly, he trusted Ben's driving skills. Ben accelerated toward bright lights in the distance.

"You're doing great!" Ethan exclaimed amid the loud cheers and excitement.

"I know!" Ben replied with excitement and enthusiasm, proud of his riding skills.

They arrived beside a red hoverbike, and Ethan's eyes widened. The arena in the large open tunnel had a race track with floating seats for spectators to watch safely above the action. The dark green stadium displayed the Elites' Classifications, indicating that only members of their own class mingled there.

The symbols representing each Code's Classification were etched into the ground of the racetrack, captivating Ethan with its architectural beauty. He pondered who had come up with the idea to build it in this location. A smile formed on his lips as he observed the thrilling hoverbike race unfolding in the arena. The sounds of whistles and trumpets echoed loudly, prompting the Brute to cover his ears momentarily.

Ben pulled up next to a person dressed in a blue and white robe and asked, "Hey, who's leading the race?" The man pointed towards a white and gold Hoverbike adorned with red thunder markings on its tail. "Kira!" The name slipped out of his mouth unintentionally. "Where...?" Ethan inquired, pushing Ben aside to get a better view of the leading rider. "Where...?" he repeated. Ben gestured towards the white halo with red thunder markings on its tail. Ethan's eyes widened as he witnessed her surpassing the halo in front and racing towards the finish line. A black Hoverbike pursued her relentlessly, refusing to relinquish the trophy.

"Go, Kira, go!" Ethan cheered.

Kira adjusted some controls and crossed the finish line, mere seconds away from relinquishing the trophy if not for her calculated maneuver. Her consistent success had earned her respect and some winnings from bets.

"How do I get in on the race?" Ethan exclaimed with excitement.

The individuals in blue and white robes gave him curious looks. Ben, feeling embarrassed in his orange terracotta robes, shrank.

"You just need to sign up over there," the man pointed towards a sign-up board.

"Are you sure you want to do this?" Ben interjected, stepping in front of Ethan. He wasn't sure if Ethan had any racing experience, and the last thing they needed was an accident.

"Have you seen my riding? You already know I'm a threat!" Ethan raised his eyebrows at Ben and pushed past him, leaving Ben to smile and shake his head.

"I knew he would love it here." Ben found a seat to watch the race.

Ethan quickly registered for the next race and brought his hoverbike in. A Naturalist Class individual inspected the bike and confirmed it was in good condition. As the racers gathered behind the finish line, Ethan pulled up alongside Kira. Unaware of his presence, she revved her hoverbike, causing it to emit a high-pitched sound among the other bikes. Kira glanced to her left and froze upon seeing Ethan, failing to take off at the sound of the whistle. Ethan shot forward, zooming past several other hoverbikes ahead of him. Cheers from the crowd jolted Kira back to reality, and she accelerated, chasing a hoverbike in seventh position while Ethan battled to overtake the rider in fourth position.

Kira pressed a green button on her bike, giving herself a boost. She maneuvered her hoverbike close enough to the Elite in seventh place, causing them to swerve out of the way. Kira's bike brushed against the sixth-place rider, causing them to wobble and collide with Ethan's hoverbike. As Ethan fought to regain control, Kira overtook him, winking and teasing him as she passed. Unwilling to be outdone, Ethan pushed harder. He skillfully maneuvered his bike over two more bikes and slammed on the brakes, narrowly avoiding a collision with another vehicle in front of him. In a matter of moments, he had reached third place, halfway across the track. If anyone intended to take the lead, now was the time.

Both Ethan and Kira flew on opposite sides of the rider in the first place, exchanging a look of understanding as they closed in, boxing in the other rider. The Elite pulled back to avoid a collision, allowing both Ethan and Kira to surge ahead. They outmaneuvered the young rider who had held the first position on the track. Ethan laughed joyfully as they raced neck and neck. Kira's eyes narrowed as she steeled herself for victory. Ethan's bike inched slightly ahead as they approached the finish line, with the other hoverbikes closing the distance behind them. The audience erupted in shouts and cheers as they neared the end of the track.

***

A cheerful smile adorned Kira's face as she penned down the answer to the last question. Ethan had managed to impress her in the race, securing the second position. Initially, she had doubted her own chances of success, considering the delayed start she had. However, her bike's specialized racing boosters gave her an advantage that Ethan lacked.

There was something about Ethan that brought a smile to her face, even though she couldn't quite understand why. It was a peculiar feeling, and she couldn't deceive herself about it. Such emotions always carried some underlying significance. Shoving the thought aside, she neatly arranged her books on the desk and reached for her AICI to listen to music. Just then, her mother called out to her from downstairs, requesting her to check the door.

Hurrying down the stairs, Kira wondered if it was her sister at the door. Passing through the living room where her disheveled mother sat on the couch, she couldn't help but notice her mother's perpetual state of neglect. She wasn't even sure if her mother had showered that day with her unkempt hair and slightly stained clothes. Her mother merely did the bare minimum to avoid the wrath of the Guardians.

Kira paused, "Mom, did you ask the AI to do laundry?"

Her mother just continued to blandly stare at nothing in particular. Kira sighed her disappointment and sadness deepening.

She empathized with her mother's struggles, but she also longed for the care and support that she herself needed. With her father gone and her sister's absence, her mother was merely a shell of her former self—a broken heart, if she had to describe it. Kira had taken it upon herself to fill the void left by her mother's inadequacy. She couldn't bear the thought of losing both her parents.

However, her mother's dismissive response, shaking her head in denial, only fueled a quiet rage building within Kira. Another knock at the door interrupted her thoughts, and she turned around to make her way back to the front door.

Twisting the doorknob and pulling it towards herself, Kira raised an eyebrow at the sight of two figures standing in front of her door. Benjamin Valdez was carrying Ethan Crambe.

"What are you guys doing here?" she whispered furiously as she gently shut the door behind her. Leading them to a secluded corner around the house, she inquired of Ben, "What happened to him?" as he laid Ethan against the house.

The yard surrounding Kira's house was bordered by a fence, casting a shadow that provided them some cover. The moonlight bathed them just right, giving them the freedom to speak discreetly while waiting for Ethan to regain consciousness.

"Somebody attacked him in the parking lot," Ben informed Kira.

She lifted Ethan's face to examine his minor injury. Fortunately, Ethan wasn't severely hurt, with only a cut on his lip. Besides, her house wasn't a suitable place for medical care. "Why didn't you take him to the hospital to get checked?" she questioned.

Benjamin hadn't seen the face of the attacker, which frustrated him even more, especially since Ethan was still unconscious and unable to disclose the shifter's identity. However, Ben didn't have the luxury of time to wait around and deal with this situation. He had more pressing concerns now that Ethan's necklace was broken. "We need your help," Ben stated, his voice tinged with urgency.

Asking for help from someone outside his Classification felt like a blow to his ego, but he was doing it because Ethan trusted Kira. Ben himself was overwhelmed by a massive headache, leaving him impatient and with little time to spare. Moreover, they hadn't received any information from the Guardians since Leo went missing. It seemed that nobody was talking about it, and like other missing cases, it had been swept under the rug.

Kira nearly turned back towards her front door, thinking that Ben must be joking. "What do you mean you need my help?" she queried, well aware of Ben's capabilities and not expecting someone of Ethan's status to seek assistance from her.

"Are we not friends yet, Kira?" Ben looked at her with genuine disappointment.

"You and I? Not quite," Kira retorted.

"Then, if not for me, do it for Ethan. You spend plenty of time with him these days," Ben responded, his words causing a hint of surprise to flicker in Kira's eyes.

"How did you know about that? Have you been following us or something?" Kira folded her arms, a touch of suspicion coloring her tone.

"Do you think I have nothing better to do than watch you two hang out? Please, don't flatter yourself, Kira," Benjamin retorted, taken aback.

Benjamin massaged his temples, feeling the strain. "Look, we need to find Leo. We can't handle this on our own."

Kira scoffed, feeling detached from the situation. She barely knew Leo and saw no reason to get involved in this matter. "Clearly, things are spiraling out of control. Students are attacking him just because they think he had something to do with it!"

Gazing at Ethan, she wondered why he was going to such great lengths to save Leo. Perhaps it was all part of a plan or some silly prank to draw her in. "I don't think I should be involved in this. The Guardians will do their job..."

"The Guardians aren't doing anything," Ethan's voice rang out as he woke up, his tone revealing his deep concern. This wasn't a mere prank; they were dead serious. Standing up to face them, he made his intentions clear.

Kira's gaze darted from Ethan to Ben and back to Ethan again. "Many students now believe that because I'm weak, I helped this cult take Leo for power."

"Are you serious? Ethan, you can't listen to that nonsense," Benjamin expressed his anger.

"None of them were there. I was. I know the truth," Ethan asserted.

"The Guards have no information about Leo since his disappearance," Ethan continued, wiping the blood from his lips.

"But I do know that if we find him, it'll prove my innocence to everyone," he added, breaking the silence. "And we'll probably be hailed as heroes for saving hundreds of Elites."

Benjamin filled the void, stating their intention clearly. "We're not suggesting barging in and fighting the bad guys. We're merely suggesting that we locate their whereabouts and provide the information to the Guardians."

Kira fell silent, her mind grappling with the situation. Benjamin's gaze locked with hers, and she blinked, briefly glancing at Ethan. The Brute had a point. With over three hundred cases of missing Elites and no action being taken, she couldn't deny the urgency. She had seen news reports about a missing girl she knew, Nyla, and there was no sense of urgency from the Guardians, who seemed to have no leads on the kidnappers. "Okay, wait here," Kira said, leaving the boys, entering the house, and shutting the door behind her.

"Where are you going, Kira?" a voice came from inside the house. Her mother walked out and gripped her arm.

"I'll be back as soon as I can, Mom," Kira gently reassured her, placing her hand on her mother's. "I made some new friends, and we're going out to study."

"Just be careful, Kira, please. I can't afford to lose anyone else," her mother whispered. Kira gave her a hug and looked into her eyes. "I will, Mom, I promise."

Kira planted a kiss on her mother's cheek and rushed to her room. She quickly gathered a few things she might need, glancing down the hall as she closed her bedroom door. Her sister's room remained closed, and the lights were off—once again, she wasn't home.

Brushing aside her paranoid concerns, Kira descended the small staircase in front of the house to meet the boys. She wore a gray hood over her gray hourglass-streaked robe. Ethan still tasted blood on his lips, and his tunic was in disarray. The shame of being dirty didn't bother him as much. The guys followed closely behind Kira.

"If we're gonna locate him, we need to check his last known location," she stated, turning to Ethan. "Where and when did you last see him?" Ethan scratched his head, struggling to recall the details.

The last time he had seen Leo was at the hospital. All he remembered was urging Leo not to pursue the woman, but Leo hadn't listened. Leo might not have gone missing if he had given up the chase. However, Ethan preferred not to dwell on that thought.

"What, you can't remember his last location?" Kira frowned, disappointed.

"The hospital! That was where we last saw Leo," Ethan replied. Kira knew that finding Leo wouldn't be easy, and the guards were of no use. She pouted and took the lead. "You can transport us back in time, so we can trace his steps," she added, glancing at Benjamin, who seemed clueless about the intensity of what he was suggesting.

Going back in time to witness an event she had never seen before would be excruciatingly painful. Benjamin must be out of his mind to suggest it. Kira looked away, opting not to engage in that conversation. "You have no idea what you're talking about. Time travel is impossible. It would kill me," she explained to Benjamin.

He finally replied, "You can let me copy your Code if you're too scared to do it." Kira's annoyance was palpable as she approached him. "How about you try thinking of something you can do without being a copycat?" she retorted, knowing that copying Codes and using them against opponents was a specialty of the Sketch Class. She despised it because it made defeating them nearly impossible, and their versatility gave them an advantage in career placement.

Yet, Benjamin seemed different from the typical Sketch student she had encountered. She couldn't quite figure him out, which made her view him with suspicion. If it were up to her, he wouldn't be joining them on this search. Sighing, she continued walking ahead.

"Hey, do you have a problem with her?" Ethan prodded Benjamin.

"Oh, no! I know why she's mad at me. It's nothing. She'll come around," Benjamin smirked, crossing his hand over Ethan's shoulder. "We should check that cut later. I don't want your mom blaming me for not watching your back."

Kira maintained her pace, paying no attention to their conversation. After all, her objective was to help them find a lead on their friend, and then she could return home. "We're still miles away from the hospital," Ethan complained.

"Come on, we should use the tubes," Benjamin agreed.

Kira quickened her steps to catch up with Ethan, a smile forming on her lips. "That would be too conspicuous. Your friend here has the solution," she said, tapping Ethan on the shoulder and nodding toward Benjamin. She spoke without looking at Benjamin, well aware of the suggestion she was making.

Benjamin furrowed his brows, understanding her implication and feeling unappreciated. What she was proposing was physically and mentally draining for him.

"He could transport us to the hospital in an instant if he wanted," Ethan realized what Kira meant. "Unless he's too incompetent to pull it off."

Upon hearing this, Benjamin cracked his knuckles and swiftly made his way into a nearby crowd. He refused to give Kira the satisfaction of being right about him. He just needed to be sure. Meanwhile, Kira smiled, having achieved what she wanted.

Kira and Ethan walked briskly to close the distance. Elites adorned in their glittering robes hurried past them, each heading to their respective destinations. Benjamin bypassed the tubes, noting that they were currently out of order. They wouldn't have been able to use them anyway. Having witnessed it, Benjamin realized that Kira was once again correct. He possessed the power to spare them the tiresome journey to the hospital, as Ethan's hoverbike couldn't carry all three of them.

Benjamin surveyed the people walking in the opposite direction, searching for someone with an hourglass insignia on their robe. Spotting one, he increased his pace and intentionally bumped into the individual. His eyes briefly flickered orange.

"Oh, sorry!" Benjamin apologized to the Shifter, who gave him an annoyed look before continuing on his way. Benjamin hurried back towards Ethan. "I copied his Code. Now, what was Kira saying?" he said, smiling at his own cleverness. Ethan had been scanning the area and spotted Benjamin running to catch up. Kira smirked, and Benjamin's smile widened.

As they took another step forward, Benjamin grabbed Kira's hand and Ethan's hand. "Wait, let me open the rift first." They swiftly entered an alleyway, shielded from prying eyes. Benjamin held out his hand, slashing through the air, creating a dark rift. However, in the process, he grazed his left hand, causing him pain as his skin slowly regenerated.

"It's a good thing our bodies heal rapidly," Kira commented, feeling a twinge of guilt as she was the one who had suggested this plan.

"Ben, are you okay?" Ethan asked, concern evident in his voice.

"I'm fine. Spatial Class Codes are just really challenging to master. I've been practicing, though," Benjamin assured them, wearing a strained smile.

As they stepped through the rift, they found themselves on the other side, surrounded by unfamiliar surroundings. "Did you do it correctly?" Ethan asked. Almost immediately after posing the question, he turned around and saw the hospital just a short distance away. Ethan mentally berated himself for not considering this option earlier. Meanwhile, Kira glanced at Benjamin, who had a satisfied expression. She responded by rolling her eyes at him.

"We need to know what you saw. That's the only way we can trace Leo," Kira said to Ethan, coming closer and taking his hand. "Think about what happened there. Try to remember everything you saw." Ethan closed his eyes and concentrated, recalling the events of that day. "Do you give me permission to use my Code on you?"

"I do," Ethan replied, opening his icy blue eyes. Kira's eyes glowed gray. Benjamin stepped back, observing the two of them. Their eyes shimmered, reflecting each other's light. Ben watched in awe as the beams of light merged to form a single, bright ray.

Suddenly, the surroundings were engulfed in a radiant light, encapsulating them like a Rubik's cube.

"Wait, I thought you said you have to witness the scene to do this?" Benjamin said accusingly.

"I said I can't physically take us to the past. Ugh, did you learn nothing in class? We can't interact with them." Kira gritted through her teeth as she concentrated.

Ethan, Kira, and Benjamin found themselves standing in the hospital room, reliving Ethan's memories. Benjamin made note of the faces of the strange men they encountered while Kira focused on the woman who seemed to know Ethan.

After gathering the information they needed, Kira released Ethan's hand, and the glow in their eyes faded simultaneously. "I don't see any leads in your memories," she stated, pausing for a moment. "And who was the woman?" Her curiosity piqued.

"The woman at the hospital seemed to know Ethan," Kira said, looking at him with suspicion.

"What?" Ethan was taken aback by her distrustful gaze. "We thought she was there to help until she attacked Ben. I had to do something." Kira made a mental note of this revelation but decided to set it aside for now. She didn't witness Ethan's actions in the hospital room, and he couldn't defend Ben or Leo. Kira pushed the thought to the back of her mind.

Glancing between Benjamin and Ethan, Kira declared, "Well, we can head home for the day."

Benjamin shook his head. "I'll shift both of you home, but I have something else I need to do."

"At this hour?" Kira questioned, expressing her surprise.

"Okay, no worries, Ben," Ethan reassured him with a sincere smile. Benjamin completely ignored Kira and playfully slapped Ethan on the back. Kira scoffed, "You're a dickhead, you know that, right?"

Benjamin winced in pain, clutching his head. "Are you okay?" Ethan placed a hand on Benjamin's shoulder, concerned.

"I'm fine. It's just a headache," Benjamin brushed off the concern, swatting Ethan away.

Kira observed Benjamin from a distance, unable to resist a nagging thought. Perhaps Ben was hiding something from them. Why else would people want him dead? She planned to confront him, but she doubted she would receive a truthful answer. Until she could unravel the truth, she refused to trust him.

Chapter 21:
Digging up Dirt

The sound of spoons clashing against plates echoed in the dining room. Richard Crambe had kept his word and come home for breakfast, as he had mentioned over the AICI. Dining together was meant to symbolize unity, peace, and love. But did those elements, once cherished by Primordials, still exist in this family?

Quintella glanced at Ethan, who had barely touched his food, and at Richard, whose plate was almost empty. Richard picked up a glass of water, placed it to his lips, and then returned it to the table, wiping his mouth with a napkin. "This was awesome," he declared with a satisfied smile on his handsome face. "Hey, are you okay?" Richard asked Ethan. Ethan lifted his eyes to meet Richard's gaze and nodded.

Turning to Quintella, Richard asked, "I have a feeling this process isn't going to be easy for you. Have you planned for retirement?" Quintella looked at him from the corner of her eyes. Would he oppose her plans if she disclosed them? She glanced at Ethan, who seemed disinterested in their conversation.

"I don't have any plans at the moment," she replied sadly. "What do you suggest I do? After all, you are the great scientist of Sector 71," she added with a hint of sarcasm. Richard smiled, refusing to engage in her provocation.

Clearing his throat, Richard continued, "I thought you would have some plans by now. Honestly, I haven't given it much thought, and I can't suggest anything at the moment." Quintella looked down at her synthetic food. Richard hadn't given it any thought, indeed. Why would he when his job took precedence over her? She thought to herself, "The rule stands. You knew this day would come. I feel sorry for you; I will eventually face the same uncertainty when I leave the office." Richard's face crumbled.

Ethan remained silent. Quintella had informed him about her retirement plans. He glanced at the adults as they conversed about their respective challenges. What did he care if his father's memories were wiped? Besides, Richard was rarely home to fulfill his responsibilities as a father. Ethan shifted his gaze back to his plate, managing to eat only half of his food.

Benjamin observed Ethan closely, noticing the sadness etched on his face. He sent Ethan a text message on his AICI, "Dude, you look like shit. Are you okay?" Ethan checked his holographic chat screen and responded, "I feel like getting out of here. This conversation doesn't interest me in any way." Ethan pushed the send icon, and Ben's AICI beeped. Ben looked at Ethan and nodded, understanding that Ethan was going through a lot. He wished these were his parents engaged in conversation. He missed his own family.

Ethan caught a glimpse of the sorrowful expression on Ben's face. He typed a message on his AICI and sent it. "Hey, why don't we leave them to their conversation and step out for a while?" Ben read the message, cocked his head in agreement, and followed Ethan's lead. They collected the dishes and made their way towards the back exit to leave the house unnoticed.

"Hey, Mom, Dad, we're going to leave early to study at the academy," Ethan called out, but his parents didn't even acknowledge him as they continued arguing.

"I don't think that's a good idea, Ethan," Gallium's voice resonated. Ethan glanced at Gallium, perplexed by the AI's objection. "Gallium, I want you to shut up for once. I don't need this right now," Ethan muttered, looking around as if expecting a response from the AI.

Gallium complied with the command, and Ethan and Ben quietly circled the building to reach the garage. They hopped onto Ethan's Hoverbike and swiftly flew off into the distance. It would be some time before his parents realized he was no longer at home.

"And just what are you insinuating, Richard? Ethan doesn't need to comprehend the situation here. He's just a kid. This is undoubtedly difficult for him," Quintella expressed her concern for the boy's well-being.

Richard noticed the look on Ethan's face the day Quintella had informed him about her retirement and the subsequent memory wipe. Ethan had been moody and hadn't enjoyed his meal in peace. Richard also couldn't help but notice that same look on Ethan's face whenever he was at home.

"You are underestimating his capabilities, Ella. You need to let him see his responsibility as a Brute. I receive reports from the school about Ethan. It would be best to have him transferred to a new sector," Quintella exclaimed, springing to her feet. Richard had no idea how difficult it was for Ethan to leave Sector 53, and now he was planning to have him transferred again because of some gossip about their son.

"I won't let that happen, Richard. You have no idea..." Quintella began, but Richard interrupted her.

"I am his father, Ella. I know what is best for my son," Richard asserted. Quintella froze, feeling the weight of his words. "Listen, you are going to need a lot of space after your memory is wiped. I don't want him causing trouble."

She scoffed, unable to contain her frustration. Ethan had never been a burden to her. She had been there for him every step of the way, and not once had she complained to Richard about Ethan causing her pain.

"I will need him by my side when that day comes. You are barely home, Richard! And how do you intend to care for me, huh?" Richard remained silent, his eyes darting around the room. Quintella sighed, her voice tinged with disappointment. "Of course, you have no intention of leaving your job for me."

Richard pushed his chair back, trying to find the right words. "Don't say that. I love you and Ethan. Everything I do, I do it for both of you," he said, reaching out to touch her beautiful face. Looking into her eyes, he continued, "I will be here for you. And for our son."

Quintella gently removed his hands from her face. "Tell that to Ethan," she said, picking up the neglected wine glasses. "At this point, he feels more like my child than yours." With the glasses in her hand, she added, "He needs you to be his father more than being a Sector Official." Quintella turned and walked away, leaving Richard alone in the room.

"You really want to go there? Because we both know what child you mothered," Richard snapped, his composure slipping away.

Quintella turned around, giving him a look of disgust. "You're such an asshole, Richard."

Richard took a deep breath, realizing he had let his emotions get the better of him. He placed his hands gently on the table, feeling the weight of his guilt. He had overstepped his bounds. He considered himself a father to many, prioritizing the needs of Pangea over his own family. And yet, he had somehow failed in his responsibility as a father to his own child.

He bowed his head in shame. Quintella was right. He had been depriving Ethan of the love and guidance a father should provide. But it was difficult. They rarely had time to talk or bond. Every conversation seemed to end in an argument. Ethan couldn't understand the importance of the work Richard did. Richard couldn't fathom why Ethan didn't see how crucial he was to Pangea's progress. The advancements made with Richard's help wouldn't have been possible without him. Ethan had been lucky, with his parents being Sector Officials, which gave him a better chance at a non-laborious position where he could contribute to Pangea in a different way. But he always seemed to get into trouble.

The sound of clashing plates being washed in the sink snapped Richard out of his reverie. He looked around, feeling an odd silence in the air. Where were Ethan and the friend Quintella had introduced? The last time he saw them was when they took the dishes. Where had they gone? He couldn't recall when Ethan had left.

The hallway was crowded as usual when Ethan walked through it. Ben had already left for morning class after they arrived at school. The talk of the day among the second-year students was the Libertas group. It had been a hot topic since the announcement went online. Ethan continued down the hallway and took a left turn that led to his classroom.

Professor Carson's voice echoed in the room. Ethan knew Carson would comment on his tardiness. He had no valid excuse for not being in class before the professor arrived. Summoning his courage, he pushed the door open and walked into the class. Carson turned to see who had entered and shook his head disapprovingly. "You're late, Crambe!" he admonished. Ethan paused, his eyes meeting Carson's gaze. "Would it be wrong for me to send you out of my class right now?" Ethan remained silent, scanning the classroom. "Take your seat. We have very little time to waste today." Ethan walked to his seat as instructed.

"Today, we will discuss how our Codes can benefit the country," Professor Carson announced, beginning the lecture. "Brutes are known for their strength. But how does that strength typically apply?"

Cassidy raised her hand and spoke up, "Building. We can contribute greatly to construction."

"Correct, Cassidy. And what about Sprites?" Professor Carson continued.

Clearing his throat, another student, Felix, responded, "Sprites ensure the power in all the buildings in the country keeps running by channeling electricity through their bodies."

"Thank you, Felix. Now, Garrett, stop dozing off over there! What are the benefits of Spatial Class?" Carson called out, noticing a Brute student drifting off at his desk.

Startled, Garrett snapped to attention. "Sorry, sir. Spatial Class Type One, Tempest. They can slow down or halt the progression rate of earthquakes or other natural disasters by manipulating time."

"Very good, Garrett. Keep going," Carson encouraged.

Garrett sighed. "Type Two Shifters control matter and are essential for instant transportation of products and goods across the country."

"Excellent. Ethan, tell us about Pulse Class," Carson commanded.

"Pulse Class can track down anyone who tries to escape work or run away. They possess exceptional hunting abilities," Ethan responded, thinking about Riley. Would he end up doing that after Academy training?

"Naturalists manipulate elements to shape the land. They were the ones who physically formed Pangea's terrain. They have control over water, fire and earth," another student answered.

"Good, that's enough for now. We'll discuss the rest later," Carson concluded, moving on to a different topic that didn't interest Ethan.

After class, Ethan went to Professor Carson's office to find out why he had been summoned. He knocked and entered when instructed by Carson. "Come in, Ethan," Carson said, adjusting his glasses. Ethan walked in and took a seat as directed.

"Tell me about your time in Sector 53," the professor requested, folding his hands and leaning forward to listen.

"Sir, may I ask what this is all about?" Ethan hesitated, not wanting to revisit his experience in Sector 53.

Carson smiled, leaning even closer. "Yes, you may ask, but I won't answer," he replied cryptically.

Ethan wondered for a moment what this could be about. "It was a good experience, sir. I didn't want to leave at first."

Carson groaned. "Then why did you leave Sector 53?" There was a hint of concern in his eyes.

"We moved here, and my parents thought it was best for me to enroll in Sector 71," Ethan replied, trying to adjust to the uncomfortable conversation.

"Ethan, I asked you to tell me about it because I received a report that you were in trouble in Sector 53," Carson revealed, causing Ethan's eyes to widen in surprise. He had left out that part, and it seemed the professor wanted to hear about it.

Realizing the implication, Ethan bowed his head, feeling a wave of disappointment wash over him. "Does that mean my actions in Sector 53 will affect me here in Sector 71?" he asked, hoping for a different answer.

Carson cleared his throat. "Listen, Ethan. Each sector has its own rules and regulations, and once a rule is broken, the offender is punished accordingly." Ethan stared at the professor, struggling to process the news. Did his mother not resolve the issue in Sector 53 before they left?

"Your mother is quite clever," Carson commented, seemingly aware of more than he let on. "I don't expect you to agree with this decision. You're excused from the upcoming class clash, but consider yourself eligible for the next one."

Ethan's heart sank. "But sir—"

"You may leave now," Carson interrupted, picking up his pen and turning his attention back to his work.

Feeling furious, Ethan rose from his seat and stormed out of the office. Someone must have told Professor Carson about what happened in Sector 53.

Could it be Professor Kara who found out about this? But why? She couldn't be after him that bad. And what would she be digging around to achieve when she already knows she can't get him out of the academy at this point?

Someone must have been digging things about him and he was going to eventually find out who.

Chapter 22:
A Bad Egg

A pair of shoes with sharp tips clicked against the hard floor of the school's hallway as they hastened toward Carson's office. The woman wearing them despised being the sole advocate for Ethan Crambe's dismissal from the academy. It made her appear wicked among her fellow professors. Storming through the hallway, she wore a sour expression and rebuffed any greetings from passing Elites. Some of them were accustomed to her attitude and didn't take it personally. A few students she had snubbed whispered and exchanged rumors about her in a corner. "She is evil," one of them said to the other. Indifferent to their opinions, she paid no heed.

The professor burst into Carson's office, forcefully dropping a file on his desk. Her displeasure was evident, but Carson disregarded her look and focused on the file she had brought.

Ripping open the seal, Carson extracted a fine piece of paper. "What is this?" he asked, puzzled by why she had delivered the document to his desk.

"You should read it, Professor, and see what's inside. It landed on my desk this morning," she replied, her eyes narrowed. Carson opened the folded paper and perused its contents.

A line in the document mentioned photos enclosed in the file. With the woman's eyes fixed on him, Carson retrieved the photos. Adjusting his glasses, he glanced at the first one and involuntarily flinched. The subsequent photos revealed the same scene—they depicted one Elite attacking another.

Carson raised his gaze to the woman. "This is Ethan Crambe. How did you obtain these photos?" He examined them again, ensuring that the assailant was indeed Ethan Crambe. He didn't want to pass judgment without being certain about what he saw.

"He is the troublemaker we are harboring in Sector 71. I told you he wasn't suitable for this academy, but you doubted my opinion, and now this!" Carson was taken aback. The evidence seemed sufficient to expel Crambe from the school without hearing his side of the story.

"Kara, we must handle this matter with care. I don't see much here. All I see is Ethan charging toward a figure. Why aren't the victims' faces captured? Whom was Ethan charging at in the parking lot?" Kara's eyes darted around the elegant office, searching for words to defend her claim.

"Professor Carson, it was dark. Ethan Crambe must have orchestrated this, and we should thank the witness who left the file on my desk." Carson attempted to read her mind, but she had closed him out. He couldn't access her thoughts.

"Did you open this file?" he asked.

"Yes, of course! If I hadn't opened it, how would I have known its contents?"

Carson remained silent. He sensed she was lying. She hadn't opened the file because he had broken the seal himself. Perhaps she had tampered with it; the seal would have been weak and easy to rip. He gently placed the document back into the file and slid it toward Kara. "I will handle this," he said. Kara smirked.

"He needs to leave. He is causing too much trouble, just as he did in Sector 53. We don't nurture troublemakers here." Carson raised an eyebrow. How did she know about Ethan's misconduct in Sector 53? He detected a knowing look on her face that intrigued him.

"We need to address this matter and resolve it once and for all," she declared, concealing her anger. The professor might perceive this as a personal vendetta she held against the student, so she spoke as though she had the best interests of the other Elites and the academy at heart.

Carson shrugged, pushing his lips forward and narrowing his eyes. Kara despised Ethan. He could sense her deep-rooted hatred towards him.

Kara was willing to go to great lengths to ensure Ethan's dismissal from the academy. Her darting eyes betrayed her anger and resentment, though she revealed nothing.

"Ethan is my student, Kara. It is my responsibility to take this matter to the administration. Nevertheless, thank you for bringing it to my attention," Carson said, offering a forced smile.

Kara stormed out of the office, shoving past Ethan and Benjamin, who happened to be at the door. The boys exchanged bewildered glances, rubbing their shoulders where Kara had pushed them.

Carson's voice echoed in the room, inviting them in. The boys entered and closed the door behind them. Carson quickly retrieved the file Kara had left on the table and placed it in his drawer. He would conduct a thorough investigation before saying anything to Ethan. If the evidence proved Ethan's guilt, Carson would ensure that he never set foot in Sector 71 or any other sector again.

"Is everything all right, Professor Carson?" Ethan asked, concerned by the tension in the room.

Carson nodded, still wearing a forced smile. He couldn't stand Kara and her animosity towards Ethan. "So, how can I help you boys?"

Ethan and Ben exchanged hesitant glances. Carson noticed their unease but remained silent, waiting for them to speak their minds.

After a nudge from Ben, Ethan took the lead. "Sir, it's been a while since Leo went missing. No one has mentioned anything about him. What should we do about Leo, sir?" Ethan hoped that Professor Carson, having served as a High Guardian for Sector 71, would offer some insight.

Carson adjusted his glasses. "I think it's best to let the Guardians handle the situation. It's dangerous out there with the recent kidnappings. We don't want more students going missing." His response reflected the reality of the danger posed by the Libertas group, and Ethan and Ben realized they would have to rely on themselves to find Leo.

Chapter 23:
Run

In the lab, silence reigned. Leo scanned the room, but there was no sign of anyone else present. The doctors had left some time ago and had yet to return. It had been over forty-five minutes, and his attempts to free himself from the chains proved futile. His wrists now bore cuts and marks, but he refused to give up. He had to find a way out before the witch returned for him.

"What are you doing?" the girl beside Leo asked.

"What does it look like? I'm trying to escape," Leo replied, frustration evident in his voice.

"You don't know your way around here. How do you plan on getting out?" the girl pointed out, her tone filled with skepticism.

Ignoring her doubt, Leo continued to twist his wrist in an attempt to slip out of the cuff. However, the more he struggled, the tighter the cuff seemed to become. He grimaced as the cuts on his wrist stung. "You should try freeing yourself," he suggested, eyeing the girl.

She scoffed. "Yes, of course! Why didn't I think of that?" Her sarcastic remark frustrated Leo, as he genuinely wanted to find a way out while she seemed uninterested in helping.

"You might as well give up. Those chains are impossible to break. They're made from a combination of three codes," she explained, looking down at the glowing restraints. "No matter what you do, you're only making them stronger by donating your powers to the chains."

Leo glanced back at the shimmering chains, starting to understand their nature. "So, I can't break free from them, no matter what I do?"

The girl nodded. "That's right. I've tried everything, but it's all in vain. These chains are designed for guards, and I don't think I need to explain their features to you," she replied, her eyes filled with resignation. "Brutes never listen."

Taking a deep breath, Leo calmed himself. "How do you know all this?" he asked, curious about the girl's knowledge. He realized that while he had only recently arrived, she had been in this place for much longer.

A sad expression crossed her face. "I don't know. All I can remember is a sharp pain in my head. Then, when I opened my eyes, I was here," she replied, a sense of longing in her voice. "By the way, my name is Nyla. What's yours?"

Leo managed a small smile. "I'm Leo."

"Nyla, we need to find a way out of here. I have a feeling things are about to get dangerous," Leo suggested, feeling a sense of urgency. Nyla nodded in agreement, having her own concerns about their grim fate. She overheard Rayvena talking about getting rid of her, and the fact that the lab technician hadn't carried out the task as instructed puzzled her.

Leo made another attempt to free himself from the cuff, but it proved fruitless. "What else do you remember?" he asked, hoping to gather more information.

She looked at him sadly. "Nothing else. I just want to go home, but I can't get out of these chains," she replied, closing her eyes in disappointment.

Leo took a deep breath, thinking about his grandmother. She must be worried sick, and he couldn't bear the thought of leaving her alone. He wondered why no Guard or anyone had come for him. It seemed as though time had stood still, and he needed to find a way out as soon as possible.

For a moment, silence enveloped them as they contemplated their predicament. Nyla broke the silence, changing the topic. "So, how did you end up here?"

Leo licked his lips before responding, "I messed up. I chased after an enemy who tried to kill someone I knew from school. They captured me, and that Psyche, Rayvena, brought me here." Bitterness tainted his voice as he regretted not heeding Ethan's advice.

"They must be looking for me." He was not sure about that. He hoped that Ethan and Ben would come for him if the guards failed to find him before things turned worse. He wondered where the doctor had gone.

"Who are you talking about?" Nyla asked, curious about Leo's question.

"The doctor. He was supposed to get rid of you. Why isn't he here to do it?" Leo's words startled Nyla, who thought Leo might want her dead. She groaned and clenched her teeth, realizing he was just joking.

"Come on, you should be dead by now. Since you're not leaving, maybe your death would draw the Guardians' attention, and they'll save me. Not a bad idea, right?" Leo burst into laughter, relishing the horrified expression on Nyla's face.

"I'm kidding," Leo assured her, noticing her growing wariness.

"That's a funny way to show it," Nyla responded bitterly.

"So, I guess dark humor isn't your thing," Leo commented.

"It's a no from me," she said, disappointed by his inappropriate joke.

Leo suddenly strained against his restraints, alerting Nyla. He could hear voices and footsteps approaching the laboratory.

The door swung open, revealing Titus and Rayvena, accompanied by the doctor. Titus appeared somber, while Rayvena seemed troubled. The doctor wore a perpetual look of fear. Leo and Nyla braced themselves, resigned to their fate.

Nyla's legs trembled despite her best efforts. Perhaps this would be the end for her. They would probably dispose of her now.

"Well, well, well," Rayvena approached Leo, a sly smile on her face. "It seems your friends have abandoned you. No one is coming for you anymore." Leo furrowed his brows, skeptical of her words. Rayvena ran her fingers through his hair, attempting to manipulate him.

"You can join us and be free from all of this. Free to use your code without restrictions. Free to do whatever you want, whenever you want," Leo remained silent, shaking his head to push her hands away. Rayvena laughed, asking him to make a choice.

Rayvena knew she could not gain his allegiance by using her Code to extract the information she needed. She hoped to convince him to join their cause, believing that Leo could assist them in capturing students and identifying other worthy Elites for the Libertas group. Rayvena smiled and sat on the bed where Leo lay.

"What do you want to know about Ben?" Leo asked. Rayvena's smile widened as she glanced at Titus, who reciprocated the expression.

"That Elite owes us. He was promised as a sacrifice, yet he's causing us more headaches than results," Rayvena revealed. Leo glared at Titus, disgusted by his actions.

"You killed his family. Shouldn't that be enough to satisfy what he owes you?" Rayvena frowned, annoyed by Leo's comment. She hated this game of manipulation they were playing, as it made her feel weak and foolish.

"We didn't harm his family. You seem to have incorrect information. You don't know what you're talking about, which is why you're here now," Rayvena circled around Leo, her gaze fixed on him.

"He won't be coming for you, and he won't let your friend Ethan come either, I'm sure," she continued. "The truth is, you have no idea what Ben is capable of. Maybe if you had been concerned about yourself, you wouldn't be here right now." Their eyes locked, tension filling the air.

For a moment, Leo contemplated Rayvena's words. She was right—the Guardians should have saved him by now. They had neglected him, leaving him to die. However, rules existed for a reason. Leo was certain that their actions were far from lawful. How could their cause be better than the government's? The Sector Officials provided free housing, food, and transportation. Those who sought an extravagant lifestyle needed to gain status. Leo was content with the system, even if it meant he couldn't freely use his Code. He nodded. "What do you need to know about Ben?"

Rayvena's smile grew wider. She could see that Leo was willing to talk. Leonitas was now ready to join their group. "Everything necessary to bring him down," she said gleefully.

"Fine," Leo glanced at them both, ready to share the information.

Rayvena eagerly awaited his words, but he remained silent, staring at them. "What? I can't talk while I'm in chains. I want to be free like you," Nyla's eyes widened.

"What are you doing?" she cautioned Leo. "She's lying to you, Leo. You can't trust her." Rayvena glared at the doctor, who promptly intervened.

Titus removed Leo's chains, both on his wrists and legs. The belt around his belly loosened, and Leo got up, rubbing his wrists gently. They still hurt, but he paid no attention to Nyla's warning. The doctor placed tape over Nyla's mouth, muffling her protests. All that could be heard was her voiceless ranting. Leo glared at her, and she waved her head regretfully, frowning at him.

"So, where do we find him?" Rayvena redirected Leo's attention to their agreement.

Leo's glare intensified. He punched Rayvena in the face, sending her flying into a wall. He swiftly turned his attention to Titus, landing two punches on his face. "We need to run!" he yelled at Nyla, taking a step to help her. He broke her chains and grabbed her hand.

The two of them pushed open the door and sprinted down a long, white corridor.

"Do you know where the exit is?" Nyla gasped for breath.

"No, but it can't be that hard to find," Leo reassured her, squeezing her hand tighter. "We'll get through this," he assured her.

No matter how hard they ran, the endless white plush hallway seemed to stretch on forever. Leo began to slow down when he noticed the same pictures on the walls. He turned his head, taking in his surroundings and looking at Nyla.

"Why can't we get out of here?" Leo's panic rose. They might not get another opportunity like this again.

"We just need to keep running, Leo! Come on!" Nyla urgently tugged at him.

They ran for a few more minutes until they encountered locked white padded rooms with students screaming behind the glass.

"Please, let us out!" Leo averted his gaze, hastening through the halls. They couldn't afford to get caught now.

"Shouldn't we help them?" Nyla's concern was evident.

"Leave them. Once we escape, we can get help. We're useless if we're caught," Leo replied, his focus on finding an exit.

Nyla nodded as they continued moving. Desperate pleas echoed from each door as imprisoned students begged Leo and Nyla for assistance. Yet, Leo refused to divert his attention from finding a way out until he saw it himself.

A ringing sound filled Leo's ears, drowning out everything else.

Snap out of it!

"Did you say something?" Leo turned to Nyla, confused.

She shook her head. "You're overthinking it, Leo. Just focus on what's in front of you."

They slowed down around a corner in the hallway, and Leo cautiously peered his head out.

"I think this hallway is clear, too," he said, relieved. But something felt off—it seemed too easy.

Please, Leo! Listen to my voice! The ringing in his ears returned, intensifying. He covered his ears with his hands.

"This isn't real, is it?" Leo whispered, the ringing vibrating the walls around him.

"What are you talking about? Of course it is," Nyla responded, sounding offended.

"Do you really think all of this is just some dream or something? Are you serious?" Leo's voice wavered as they came to a complete stop.

"Nyla, who is the most important person to me?" Leo asked calmly.

"Your mother, duh. You said your father died," Nyla replied, puzzled by the sudden change in conversation.

Leo stared blankly, wasting no time in punching Nyla directly into the white walls surrounding them. The impact crushed her body with ease, causing blood to spill down the wall from what had been Nyla.

"If this were real, you'd remember that I told you my grandmother was my whole world," Leo declared.

He then took his head and repeatedly slammed it against the wall until he started losing consciousness.

Leo opened his eyes and realized he was still standing in front of Rayvena. Nyla was still tied up—everything had been an illusion created by Rayvena, who stood before him, laughing.

"Brutes are so stupid! I can't believe you actually fell for that," Rayvena taunted. Leo's world spun as he crashed into a wall at her command.

Nyla kicked at the lab technician, attempting to move closer and help Leo, but Titus grabbed her and forcefully slammed her to the ground, rendering her unconscious. He then hoisted her onto his shoulder and carried her back to the bed, securing her with chains once more.

"I was trying to give you the benefit of the doubt, but you ruined it," Rayvena scolded, gradually releasing her control over Leo. Leo gasped for breath, his eyes widening as he clutched his chest. Rayvena had nearly suffocated him.

"You couldn't have escaped even if you wanted to. But I think I should just kill you to be sure," Rayvena threatened. However, the loud ring of Rayvena's AICI interrupted her, preventing her from carrying out her plan. Rayvena released her Code, and Leo collapsed to the floor, coughing and gasping for air.

Rayvena retrieved her AICI from her pocket, glancing at the screen. She gestured for Titus to take Leo back. Titus approached Leo and punched him, rendering him unconscious.

"What have you been up to, Rayvena?" the caller on the other end of the line inquired.

"He said nothing and tried to escape," Rayvena wiped the blood from her lips, caused by Leo's attack.

"You need to make him talk. We need that boy, and we will have him. Do you understand? I could have easily handled this myself, but I must remain in the shadows... something your group isn't doing very well," the caller instructed before hanging up abruptly.

Rayvena turned and glared at the boy who broke her lips. She should have killed him when she had the chance. Now, she had to extract the information she needed before she could finally take his life.

"Let me know when he wakes up. Also, take away their beds as punishment. They can sleep on the floor from now on," Rayvena ordered, her tone resolute.

The doctor nodded in compliance as Rayvena stormed out of the room. Titus followed suit, closing the door behind him.

Chapter 24:
Sweet Sisters

Everything Glade said was true. Getting a Sector Official to avoid a brain wipe was suicide. The World Government would hunt them down like dogs. The rules cannot be broken, as Richard had said. Nothing seemed to be the way it was meant to be. Everything went south in her eyes. Perhaps she had drowned herself in the thought of her fate. Quintella patrolled her office with these thoughts running through her mind. Maybe they left to a distant place to have her memory copied and stored until she needed it, and then they never got to afterward. What would be her fate?

A knock at the door poked her back to reality. She called the knocker to come in. The door opened, and a lady walked into the office. She wore a pretty smile the moment she saw Quintella standing next to the office desk. Quintella reciprocated with a smile, and they hugged tightly. "Where have you been all this time?" Quintella asked. The lady with blue eyes, ruby lips, and hair that flowed to her waist smiled.

"I have been around. I heard you were in town and decided to see you today." Quintella smiled.

"I know I never told you I had moved here. How did you find out, Bella?"

"I ran into Richard at the mall. He told me."

Quintella smiled. *That loud mouth! What else could he have told her?* She questioned herself.

Quintella wasn't good with friends, especially those from college when she was in Sector 47. They never liked her because she always came top of the class. Bella happened to be her senior back then.

"Please sit!" Quintella gestured and walked to take her seat. "To what do I owe this visit?" she asked. People like Bella never run during the day for nothing; they are always after something beneficial to them.

"I have no idea if this would sound silly." Bella cleared her throat and pulled out from the chair a little. Quintella, staring at the woman, leaned forward. "I need your help." *Well, there she goes.* Quintella smiled. She was right that Bella's visit wasn't just to check on a friend but to ask for help.

"Tell me what it is, Bella."

"I want my son in Sector 53." Bella believed Quintella had answers to her prayers.

Quintella smiled. "Is that all you want?"

Bella thought for a while. "Yes!"

Sector 53 has good security to protect her son. With the rate at which kids went missing, putting one's child in a well-secured environment was the best option. Bella wasn't the first parent to come asking for the transfer of their kids to Sector 53. Quintella has received several visitors before Bella. She looked at the lady and nodded. "Are you sure your son can cope with the sector?"

Bella pouted with a brow arched. "Yes, Ma'am. He has good records in Sector 65. I want him in a safe place close to home. You must have heard of the missing kids from sectors all over the world. Every parent now wants their kid to study close to home so we can keep an eye on them." Quintella nodded in agreement.

"Okay. I will help you through the processes, but your son must prove worthy to be in Sector 53. I cannot influence the result. You know the law, don't you?" Quintella asked, smiling. Bella nodded.

Quintella processed the necessary documents and backed them up with an official letter. She handed it to Bella, who gladly took it with a song of thanks. She then left Quintella to her worries.

As Bella left, Glade walked in. Quintella's expression went sour again. She had no idea what news he came with and what he found out about the brain transfer. Glade's look wasn't bright either.

"Hey, what did you find?" She asked.

Glade waved his head. "No one is willing to take the risk. They are too scared," he said somberly.

"What are you saying, Glade? Who are they scared of?" She whispered.

Glade raised his eyes to her, "The government." Quintella grew silent. *So, there is nothing that can be done about this?* She asked herself, staring at Glade. It felt as if the world should fall apart. She felt like screaming it all out, but that would attract attention to her office. So, she may be out of options, she gulped.

"Is there no other way to fix this?" She asked. Glade looked at her. Desperation shone in her eyes. She would do anything to keep her memories. He had never seen a sector officer who had as much guts as Quintella to defy the government. She knew this was not optional and was against the law, yet she wouldn't give up on it.

"When you leave this seat, who takes over your office?" He asked. Quintella said nothing. Glade had no business with her office. But why would he want to know that?

"I have no idea. This position is by appointment. I can't tell who takes over from me." She deliberately forgot Glade ever asked that since he knew how the system worked.

Quintella walked over to her cabinet and poured herself a small amount of Fiery Dragon. She licked her lips as she watched the orange-red concoction ooze into her glass. As she took her first sip, she ignored the sad stare Glade was giving her. She didn't care anymore. Because she was running out of time.

***

Kira loved her peace and quiet. She loved spending time with her mother even more. When there was free time, she and her mother would watch primordials pretending to be someone else on the holographic screens.

But today, Kira didn't pay attention to the TV show she and her mother watched. She tried to cope with the noise but had no choice but to sit in the living room with her Mom. Her mother wouldn't turn down the volume. "Kira, just go upstairs if you aren't comfortable with the noise," she groaned.

But Kira didn't. She tapped her AICI screen repeatedly while having a conversation with her friend. Annoyed, she glared at the screen displaying the primordials. She couldn't stand the fact that her Mom wouldn't turn down the volume. If she wasn't using her Mom's wireless connection downstairs, she would have retreated to her room.

The sound of a creaking door caught Kira and her Mom's attention. Rayvena walked into the house and quietly shut the bedroom door behind her. She said nothing to anyone as she headed for her room. Rayvena had been acting strangely for days now. Kira logged off from social media and followed her, tracing her steps until Rayvena vanished down the corridor. Rayvena's behavior was concerning, and Kira wanted to check on her.

"I don't think it's a good idea to kill her yet. We might need her for something else. Killing her might draw the guards' attention to our activities here. Think about it!" Titus said over the AICI.

"We have to get rid of her, Titus. I do not want things going south."

"We need to carry out a second test on her to see if we can clone her DNA."

"I will ask..." She paused.

"I will call you soon." She hung up and then closed the AICI. "Who's there? I want to be alone." She assumed it was her Mom at the door. Well, stepmom, anyway. Her actual mother had passed away.

Her stepmom always came around to talk to her about being herself. Since their father's death, she felt more like a mom to her than ever before, but she still seemed to be struggling with her own grief.

To some extent, Rayvena understood that the sadness in her stepmom's heart had not fully healed. Her dad didn't deserve to be killed like a street dog. The world government never gave him a chance to defend himself. They eliminated him without finding the truth. And somehow, Rayvena felt responsible for what had happened to her father.

Perhaps if she hadn't helped him with his research, he'd be alive today. Now, she would have to bear the knowledge of his research's results alone.

Tears collected in Rayvena's eyes; she wiped them just as she swung open the door to her room. "I said..." She gulped those words as her eyes caught Kira's little figure stepping into the room.

"Hey." Kira walked in gently as if she knew her sister was in a bad mood. She sat on the bed and folded her legs. "You haven't been home for days now. What's going on with you?" She quizzed. Rayvena looked away. Kira would never understand what she had to do to keep her father's dream of freedom going.

Their father had always believed Elites were not meant to be scared or hide under the shadows of the law. He believed in the freedom to use the Code in procreation and scientific advancement.

"You can talk to me. I am your baby sister. Please, tell me." Rayvena looked at her. She was too young to understand the way the world works. How would Kira react if she told her she had a hand in the missing students? She blinked.

Stammering, she spoke, "I...I... " She couldn't trust herself to say the words.

"You know, I do worry for us. I miss Dad. I miss our family together." Sadness clouded Rayvena's expression.

"You don't need to feel that way. I miss him, too. But we have Mom here, and she needs us."

Rayvena waved her head. Kira had no idea her mother cried every night for her husband. She looked at her sister; Kira had no experience with life. Life is painful. They had power but did not have the right to use their Code in defense of the people they loved because of some government rule. Only a fool would trust this government and adhere to its stupid rules.

"Kira, you have a lot to learn about life. Mother is..." She paused, looking down at the shiny floor, "No one is happy about Dad's death. I will not let them get away with it, Kira. I will do everything in my power to justify our father's death." Kira stared at her sister with a heavy heart. She ensured Rayvena didn't see how much pain was in her heart.

"You are my big sister. I don't want to lose you too," She hugged Rayvena. "We need you now more than ever. I miss our family together." Kira's voice revealed her pain and worries.

Rayvena held Kira's little hands wrapped around her shoulders. Her kid sister must never find out about her deeds. Not even their Mom can know. She wanted to do this and keep her family out of it. The government will pay for what they did to their father.

"It's okay. I will be fine out there. Tell me about your day." Rayvena changed the topic. She might just tell Kira about her secret if she let the girl keep poking her emotions.

Besides, Kira is a little close to some interesting friends; She might know something about Benjamin. "Have you made new friends?" She inquired.

Kira smiled. Thoughts of Ethan crawled into her mind and poked a smile on her face. Rayvena saw that look. She smiled. Her kid sister has feelings for someone. "I have made a few nice friends. They are really good." Rayvena pouted with arched brows. "Though bad stuff has been happening in school." She hugged her big sister again, resting her head on Rayvena's shoulders.

Rayvena sensed Kira's fear. Bad stuff is happening in her school! She smiled. Her little sister shouldn't be scared. "So, what are your friends called? And do you trust that they are good people?"

Kira nodded with a lavished smile. "Ethan Crambe," She said with her cheeks turning red. "You must know him. He is the son of Sector Official Crambe?" Rayvena puzzled pretentiously. She knew the Crambes even more than Kira could imagine. She said nothing but listened to her little sister speak highly of the Brute she was friends with.

"He has an annoying friend, Benjamin Valdez. We train together. I will say while he is quite annoying, I like him for his courage and focus." Rayvena's eyes popped. Kira is friends with Benjamin Valdez! She coughed. "I haven't made any other new friends." Kira paused for a moment.

Silence engulfed the room. Rayvena thought about how Kira was friends with the Elite she had been tracking for months.

"Ooh, I forgot to mention one. Leo." Kira grew sad. "He has been missing for weeks now. I worry for him. Leo is Ethan's friend, and a lot of our classmates think Ethan had a hand in Leo's disappearance. Ethan can't hurt anyone. He's not as strong as his Code should be." For once, she accepted Ethan's weakness. It made no sense to her how the Brute lacked the potential of his Code. Lucky for him, Libertas didn't want weak Elites. Besides, they couldn't go after a Sector Official's kid right now, anyway. The amount of press would be too high. Ethan Crambe and the other Sector Officials' children had nothing to worry about for now.

Rayvena glanced at her kid sister. She had no idea that she directly played a role in all of her new friends' lives.

That's a shame. Rayvena had been the cause of her sister's worries. Kira didn't need to be involved in Rayvena's mess. Once she got the information she needed, she'd leave Kira out of this completely.

She sighed and hugged Kira ever so tightly. Rayvena had no choice but to chase after her father's dreams of freedom for both of them.

Chapter 25:
Mastermind

"You sound as though you have no idea how it felt when we first got into Sector 53. Nobody liked us," Liam said over the AICI. Ethan had him on a video call. He needed to share with Liam all he had been through.

"It was different. At least they didn't like me because they had no idea about my identity. But here, I feel they influence everything about me. Everyone is hateful because I'm a Sector Official's kid. I barely get enough special treatment to be treated this way." Ethan hated the fact that his parents always had a hand in what happened in sectors.

"Don't be such a spoiled brat." Ethan raised his brows at the statement. He was surprised to hear that from Liam, of all people.

"You should be happy you have parents who have the power to fix your problems and remove you from harm without you seeing any blowback," Liam snapped.

Ethan processed what Liam said. He was right. There were lots of kids out there seeking to be in his place. They desired parents who had the power to shape their future and protect them from the government's harsh decisions. Sadness wiped that smile on his face as he recalled he would soon lose a parent.

"What's that look for?" Liam asked, seeing Ethan's mood had changed. Ethan had not told him about the brain wipe his Mom was to undergo in a few months. He wished Liam could just be there with him.

"I have something to tell you, Liam. But just wait till you get here because I can't say it over the AICI." *I hope things don't get worse before I see you again.* Ethan thought to himself. He still was unsure what had happened to him in front of the Academy when Skylar attacked him.

He chose not to bring it up, and Ben didn't seem to be mentioning it at all, either. Although Ben had been acting strange every now and then.

"There you go again, sounding mysterious and scared. I thought we had grown past this fear. Have you forgotten all we learned together, Ethan Crambe?" Liam hated to see his Brute friend sound so down; he had encouraged Ethan to be brave. Liam influenced the best parts of Ethan; he gave Ethan the courage to strive.

"Liam, you know I rarely say this, but this time I am actually scared." He bowed sadly.

"Scared of what? Come on, Ethan, are you hiding things from me now? We're best friends! You should share your troubles with me. You know I care about you." Ethan kept his eyes on the AICI.

He should tell Liam about it already. Perhaps Liam might have a better suggestion on what he should do about these strange things happening to him.

"Remember, a problem shared is a problem solved." Liam's words came softly to his ears. The words triggered a memory that Ethan had pushed aside. Liam gave Ethan a sincere look. "Talk to me, Ethan."

Ethan almost cracked. He wanted to tell Liam. He really did. But Ethan was still not even sure what was happening; he kept it to himself. *Once Gallium hears it on the AICI, it's recorded. Best not to record this kind of conversation.* "Don't worry, I shall tell you upon your arrival here," Ethan assured.

The door opened, and Ben walked in with a headset, nodding to the music playing from his AICI music cloud system.

Oblivious of Ethan's conversation over his AICI, Ben sat on the bed and nodded and sang the lyrics of a song he loved listening to the most. Ethan's AICI caught Ben in the room.

"Who's that guy?" Liam asked. Ethan turned to look at Ben, who had no idea the screen caught him or that Ethan's attention had moved to him.

"This is my friend. Let me introduce you." Ethan held up the device, letting its camera focus on Ben, who looked up and saw someone staring and waving at him on the screen.

"Ben, this is my best friend, Liam." He made a hand gesture toward the screen. "Liam, this is Ben, a final-year student in the Academy. He's living with me right now." Ben waved back at the stranger.

"Hey, Ben, could you do me a favor?" Liam asked. Ben nodded. "Sure." Liam smiled. "Watch over that idiot for me, and I'll get you a drink when I come to visit. Nice meeting you, Ben."

Ben gave a cheeky smile, "Nice to meet you too, Liam." Ethan took the camera off Ben's face and went on with his conversation with Liam.

"Oh, I forgot to tell you! I have a girlfriend now. Maybe next time I am with her, I will introduce you."

"You have a girlfriend now?" Ethan's eyes widened. Liam gave a cheeky smile. He nodded his head. They were not good at talking to girls back there in Sector 53. Well, Liam had the right moves, but he was too scared to approach anyone directly. As for Ethan, he never thought about it until he came across Kira.

"Well, I am hoping to get one soon." He said. He looked behind to ensure Ben wasn't paying attention to their conversation. "Her name is Kira. I do like her, but I haven't told her yet." Liam smiled cheekily.

"Maybe I should talk to her upon my arrival. I am sure she likes you. You're such a cool and nice guy, Ethan. Every girl should just fall at your feet and plead for your love," Liam said mockingly, clasping his hands together. He laughed as Ethan rolled his eyes.

"Yeah, you're probably the last Elite who needs to do that." Ethan chuckled at the image of it. "I will talk to her myself." Ethan looked at the time and realized his Mom would soon be back. His eyes caught the brace on his wrist. She has no idea the stone on his brace is broken. Strangely, since his necklace broke, it hadn't done anything out of the ordinary to him. He expected because of that one incident, more problems to follow. After all, his mother once told him without that necklace, he would never be a strong Brute. He had never taken it off before. But his mother hadn't noticed it was missing since she had a lot going on in her head. He sighed and looked back at Liam, "I have to go now. We will talk some other time." Liam nodded. "Take care, man." Liam waved, and Ethan ended the video call.

Liam has a girlfriend now. Ethan thought to himself. He looked at a photo he had in a frame on the wall. It was of him and Liam making goofy faces at each other by a tree. "Time sure does move fast, huh, Ben." Ethan reminisced.

Ben took his headphones off and looked at Ethan. "What did ya say?" He asked. Ethan flopped down on his bed. "I said time sure does move fast."

"Time is like a river," Ben said. "Isn't that what those Tempus always say? You can go forward or try to go back. You can slow it down or try to stop it, but the river flows on with or without you."

Ethan gawked at Ben. "Who taught you that?" He got up and grabbed workout clothes. "Kira said it once, I think." Ethan just gazed at him and said, "Interesting. Well, come on, we need to train for the tournament."

"I don't really think your training is going to get that much different than before if we're being honest here." Ben laughed. He threw his arm around Ethan.

"Ben, what are you talking about? You obviously know I finally got my Code to work. You were there." Ethan looked over at Ben.

Ben halted as well. "What are you talking about, Ethan?" Ben had a look of suspicion and disbelief on his face. Ethan unslung Ben's arm.

"The Academy? I was attacked, and you showed up and scared that Elite off. You took me to Kira's house, remember?" Ethan smacked his lips. He hated having to explain himself.

Ben gave him a puzzled look. "Ethan, we never did that."

"Very funny, Ben, it's just us. We can talk about it." Ethan leaned back and relaxed.

Ben groaned in frustration. He placed his thumb on the temple of his forehead. "Ethan, I seriously have no idea what you're talking about."

Ethan was quiet for a moment. "You're a dickhead, you know that?" He then left their bedroom to walk off ahead without Ben. He was clearly annoyed with Ben.

Ben scratched the back of his head. "What the heck did I do?" Ben said, following behind Ethan.

***

Professor Kara hated the fact Ethan Crambe remained a student of their Academy. Her plan to pull the boy down with the photos she had presented to Professor Carson had failed. The administration countered her claim, and Richard Crambe dismissed the evidence before it even arrived on his table.

Kara beat her lips. As long as the Crambes remained Sector Officials, she would never get back at Ethan. She would never get the brat out of her way, and she hated it passionately. Back on the first day of school, she thought she'd have to search for days, watching and scouting for students who shared the same ideology as she did. But there was no need; she found one– the very one she had once threatened to report to the administration: the Spatial twin Skylar.

Skylar hated Ethan just as she did. Skylar would probably kill the kid if given a chance to use his Code. Students were far easier to convince. After all, first-year students in Academies and grades below used their Code the least of all in Pangea. So when any opportunity to use it came up, they always agreed. She nodded to her evil thoughts.

The only way to get rid of Ethan from the school was through Skylar. She must succeed with her plans; she needed Skylar to ruin Ethan's reputation. She had also found another who shared the same ideology: His twin.

The photos of Ethan and Skylar in the parking lot attack were all taken by Austin. They had all planned it, and she had masterminded the entire scene. If Benjamin Valdez had not interfered, Ethan would have been expelled, and her problems would have been over by now. She scowled.

She stood by the window for a moment, staring at kids walking to their classes while others hung around having conversations. Ethan needed to leave the Academy. She wouldn't have a Crambe come into the Academy without meeting the qualification criteria. Professor Kara should have the Crambes reported. But how would she go about that when Carson had the boy's back and would cover up messes for him? Kara wrung her hands in thought.

Perhaps they had bought Carson over with a promise of something interesting that had blinded him from the truth. If that were the case, then she would be fighting an entire army of shadows. Carson had more ranking, and she might lose her job if she pressed on this matter. Losing her job meant no reassignments unless she was selected for a special assignment. So, there was no way on earth she was going to get executed because of him.

The Crambes might turn against her and kick her out of the Sector. She frowned, realizing the doom that would befall her if she took up Ethan's case alone. She walked to her desk and sat on it. There had to be a better way of getting rid of the brat. Wait! There was a better way.

Turning Ethan's enemies into her allies was the best step she had ever taken so far. With Austin and Skylar in her palm, the boy was likely to leave the school dead. And while she didn't want to kill Ethan, his weakness and privilege were disgusting. Was that not what Elites worked so hard to prevent? Privilege and status were Primordial benefits. In Pangea, everything was supposed to be fair, or so she grew up learning. So why was she witnessing favoritism right before her eyes? Kara knew it was up to her if she wanted to see results.

And so Skylar and Austin were easy to control since she had offered to help them graduate early. Kara's smile spread. She knew Skylar had a poor academic record, and Austin's wasn't much better. They were really only good in applied studies and in using their Codes. Well, that had been their saving grace all this time... But what she didn't tell them was that helping her didn't mean she'd guarantee their early graduation from the Academy. And to think, this plan wouldn't be possible if it wasn't for that cafeteria fight.

Four months earlier...

"He started it all. Kira is lying! I swear I didn't start this cafeteria fight!" Skylar tried to defend himself. Kara already knew the truth. "Come on, professor, you have to believe me." He kept trying to convince her to buy his lies.

"Quiet. I already confirmed all that happened there. Ethan Crambe did nothing to you. Unfortunately, I have to report you, which will probably lead to your expulsion... and possible execution." The color drained from Skylar's face.

"Or I can keep this between us. But," Skylar's demeanor stood tall. "You have to do something for me." He gazed at her warily.

"I am sorry I lied. Just let me go." Skylar didn't want to hear her offer. This won't end well. He knew it. From one favor to another, and he would become her puppet. He didn't want anyone controlling his actions and deeds.

Kara frowned. "Okay. I will table your matter to the school and have you expelled. How does that sound?" Skylar's brows furrowed. "I guess you have no idea about the gravity of your offense because if you did, you would be on your knees pleading for your life." Skylar grew silent, his eyes following Kara as she walked around him in her office.

"I don't want any trouble, Professor Kara."

"Shh!" She hushed him. "You are already in trouble. Well, I know about your grades, and I can help you graduate if you work with me." She sat on the desk, crossing her legs beside Skylar.

Skylar didn't dare raise his eyes to look at her. "You know about my poor grades?" He was shocked to hear her talk about his secret. He consistently made a daily effort to seem smarter than everyone else, from the books he carried around to his attitude.

Kara nodded – a fiendish smile on her face. She had already gathered all she needed to poison the boy's mind and cause him to do her will.

"Yes. And I can help you if you help me get rid of Ethan Crambe." Skylar couldn't help but look at her, surprised, and scratched his stubbled face. "Not what you think. I want him out of this Academy," she assured him.

Skylar eased a bit, "But you have the power to do that, just as you have the power to report me and get me expelled." He realized the precarious position he was in and decided to tread carefully.

She frowned at his audacity. Skylar quickly shut his mouth before it got him into more trouble.

Kara took a deep breath, trying to contain her anger. "So you mean to tell me you don't find us Brutes disgusting and deplorable?" The desk started to crack under the pressure of her hands. She was seconds from breaking it. Skylar gulped. "Is that not what you've told Elites in the halls today?" Kara's face darkened towards Skylar, a Spatial Class. "Do I need to remind you of the sizable debt Spatial Class owes Pangea?"

Skylar looked at her a second time, though he couldn't bring himself to meet her gaze. "You and I both know Spatial Class paid the price for our mistakes, Professor."

"Enough. Do we have a deal, or do we have a problem?" Kara pressed, her tone ominous.

He did not have what it takes to run up against a professor like Kara. He would be expelled even before he got a chance to tell anyone what went on in the office. Besides, this was all Ethan's fault, and Skylar resented him for getting him into this mess.

Thinking about it, Skylar saw that this arrangement would favor him. With Kara's help, he could maintain excellent grades, allowing him leverage for a good career choice. Plus, it would get rid of Ethan from the Academy, which was an added bonus. He nodded, making up his mind. "Okay, we have a deal as long as you help my brother too."

Kara nodded, her fiendish smile wrapped around her beauty like a serpent coiling its prey. "Of course, dear Skylar. I have plans for both of you."

Now, nearly five months later, her plans to get rid of Ethan still had yet to see fruition. Lucky for her, she had one last trick up her sleeve. And this time, she would have to be willing to risk it all. The stakes were high, but the rewards would be worth it.

Chapter 26:
Target Lost

"What are we looking for?" Titus asked, breaking the silence that had enveloped the black floating hover van parked close to a mall for hours now. The sun was almost setting, and tension hung heavy in the air. Rayvena, seated on the front passenger's seat, gave him a fiendish gaze.

"Target is in sight now," Maya's voice resounded through the van's speakers. She had been released by the Guardians a few weeks after Leo's disappearance. Despite several investigations, they found no evidence linking her to the incident.

On the night of Leo's disappearance, the interrogation room was an intimidating sight. Crystal balls sparkled on the wall under a bright fluorescent light above the table in front of Maya. She was brought in and cuffed, left waiting for over forty-five minutes without anyone questioning her. It was a tense moment, and she was supposed to tell the lies Rayvena had instructed her to say.

Maya couldn't help but feel bitter about her role in this dangerous endeavor. Rayvena always put her in risky positions while the others had safer roles to play. She had once been in a perilous situation, almost getting caught by the Guardians due to Rayvena's plan. But she knew it wasn't entirely Rayvena's fault. She had willingly followed Rayvena on this quest for liberation, believing her innocent appearance would be an advantage. However, things didn't go as planned, and she was now reminded of the consequences.

The door of the interrogation room opened, and a Guardian walked in. Maya flinched at the sight of him, memories of her previous encounter rushing back. She prepared herself to recall the lies Rayvena had told her to say if asked about her activities in the woods that night. The Guardian dropped a file on the table and stormed out without saying a word to Maya, leaving her with a mix of relief and anxiety.

The door opened again, and a woman in her late twenties entered with two Guardians flanking her. Her long opal robe flowed as she walked, exuding an air of confidence. She took a seat facing Maya, and the guards stood firmly at her sides. The frizzy-haired woman opened the file and scrutinized Maya with suspicion.

"I have nothing to do with this," Maya spoke, trying to defend herself even before being questioned.

The woman raised an eyebrow. "You seem to already know why you are here, don't you?" Her arms crossed, and she fixed her gaze on Maya, making her feel uneasy.

Maya scolded herself internally for blurting out her thoughts. She should have kept quiet, but her anxiety got the best of her. She shook her head in response to the woman's question, feigning innocence. "I have no idea what you are talking about. There must be a mistake. I was on a tree when the Guards took me in. I did nothing wrong. Ask your friends. They found me on a tree." Maya desperately tried to convince the woman of her innocence, hoping to get out of the situation.

The woman turned to one of the guards for confirmation, who nodded in agreement. Maya felt a glimmer of hope, thinking her words had worked.

"Do you see now that I am telling the truth?" Maya leaned back, trying to appear composed. "You should let me go now." She added, offering a sly smile to the woman.

The woman's expression remained stern. She then showed Maya a barely clear photo of some Elites in the woods. Maya squinted to see it properly but acted as if she couldn't.

"Are these not your friends?" The woman inquired, testing Maya's response.

Maya swiftly denied any association with the Elites in the photo. "I have no friends. If I did, they'd be here for me," she declared, maintaining her denial.

The woman seemed to grow tired of questioning. Maya's insistence and the Guardians' report of finding her hung on a tree was causing doubt. Maybe she was just a victim, too. The woman decided to reconsider her approach.

***

Rayvena listened intently to Maya's updates on the target's movements. She knew the importance of patience and planning in their operations. Despite Titus' eagerness, Rayvena understood the need to wait for the right moment. They couldn't afford to attract any unnecessary attention from the Guardians.

"We sit here and wait. Do not be too hasty to get into trouble," Rayvena advised, relying on her knowledge of the Sectors and the behavior of potential Elites. She knew that some of them, believing in their strength, would frequent places they shouldn't be.

Maya's suggestion to drive around and not appear suspicious resonated with Titus, and he quickly put it into action. The hover van maneuvered through the streets to avoid drawing attention to themselves.

"Pike, keep an eye on those two and ensure the doctor isn't messing with things," Rayvena instructed Pike, who was monitoring from the lab. Pike had been instrumental in framing Maya for Leo's disappearance, and Rayvena still remembered the events of that night vividly, including the incident where she slapped him.

The team's meticulous approach and calculated moves were essential to the success of their mission. They needed to be cautious, especially with the bylaws in Sector 71 restricting the use of Code on others without permission. The consequences could be severe if they made any missteps.

As they continued to monitor the target and plan their next move, Rayvena felt a mix of excitement and nervousness. The liberation of Elites and the fight against the government's oppressive rules were challenges she embraced with determination. Rayvena was prepared to risk it all to achieve their goals.

The team was on edge as they realized that Maya had lost the target and was now in a precarious situation herself. Rayvena and Titus rushed to the mall to find Maya lying unconscious on the floor. It was evident that someone had harmed her, and they needed to act quickly before they drew any more attention.

Pike was summoned through a portal to assist in carrying Maya back to the hover vehicle. The situation was dire, and they couldn't risk being caught by mall security or the Guardians. They needed to get Maya to safety and assess the situation.

As they rushed back to the hover vehicle, Rayvena couldn't help but feel frustrated with Maya's failure to keep track of the target. The whole mission had been jeopardized because of her incompetence. Maya's inability to stay focused and alert had cost them valuable time and information.

Pike attended to Maya inside the vehicle while Rayvena and Titus discussed their next steps. They had lost the target, and it was all because of Maya's shortcomings. Rayvena knew they couldn't afford any more mistakes if they wanted to achieve their mission successfully.

"Maya has proven to be a liability," Rayvena said, her voice tinged with frustration. "We can't afford to have her jeopardize the mission any further."

Titus nodded in agreement. "I hate to say it, but I think we need to cut her loose. She's putting us all at risk."

Rayvena knew Titus was right, but it still pained her to think about leaving Maya behind. They had been through a lot together, and Rayvena had hoped Maya would be an asset to their cause. But it was clear now that Maya couldn't handle the pressure and responsibility that came with their mission.

"I'll talk to her," Rayvena said with a heavy sigh. "We'll give her one more chance to prove herself, but if she messes up again, she's out."

Titus nodded again, understanding the gravity of the situation. They couldn't afford to be sentimental; their mission was too critical. They needed to be focused and disciplined if they were going to succeed.

As the hover vehicle sped away, Rayvena couldn't help but feel a sense of urgency and determination. They had lost the target this time, but they wouldn't let that stop them. They had one last trick up their sleeve, and Rayvena was determined to use it to achieve their goals. Maya's fate now rested on her ability to step up and prove herself in the next phase of their mission.

A sudden vibration caught Rayvena's attention as Titus brought the floating vessel to life and took the next turn on his left. Damn! She couldn't pick up the call. What would she tell him now? She asked herself. Of course, he wouldn't want to hear they lost the target a second time. He would get mad at her for sure. The phone rang a second time. Titus glanced at the phone and at Rayvena, who didn't look at him. Finally, Rayvena took the call.

"Why are you avoiding my calls?" The caller questioned. "Tell me you have what I asked for?"

"We lost the target again." She could hear the caller trembling with anger. "I promise we will get her soon."

"This is madness. What do you mean you lost her?" Rayvena's lips trembled from not having the right words to excuse her failure this time. "You need to find her and bring her to the lab." The caller was silent for a while.

"Have you found Benjamin Valdez?" He asked.

"No, sir. We are still working on it. We believe Benjamin is under some kind of protection from a Sector Official. We haven't been able to track him. But I have a feeling he might come to us soon." Rayvena was certain her plans with using Kira would work. The caller said nothing; the silence was deafening.

"Will you listen to yourself? He won't come to you! You go to him and take him in with everything you have. Am I clear?" Turns out he was mad after all.

Rayvena nodded, "Yes, I am on it."

"Now... Which Sector Official is protecting him?"

"The Crambes, sir." Rayvena gave up the information willingly.

"Ah, the scientist. Don't worry. I will handle that." There was something dark and cryptic in the way the caller hung up immediately after saying that.

She glanced at Titus, whose eyes had been on the road, but his ears were certainly in her conversation with the boss. She cleared her throat, which caused Titus to glance at her and back at the road.

"If you ask me, I say she is causing us a lot of trouble. We have to find someone else we can trust with things like this. She is such a mess." He didn't want Maya to cause them more trouble.

"You are right. But how do we find someone to replace her? We can't trust anyone else with this mission. We have to handle things ourselves and see how it goes." Rayvena had this feeling that anyone they brought into the team now might cause more trouble than Maya. At some point, Maya was indispensable.

Titus gunned towards a tall building, and as he drew closer, a dark portal appeared in front of them, and he drove into the wall. That portal led to the lab, and the tall building was just a distraction to watching eyes. He pulled up in front of a small building, and they both alighted from the vehicle. Pike stood by the door, waiting for them to close the distance.

He struck a pose, "What happened back there?" He asked nobody in particular. His eyes darted from Rayvena, who wasn't interested in the talk, to Titus, who wore a long face. "Come on, what happened? Someone talk to me." Rayvena glanced at him and into the building. Titus also neglected to answer his question. "Pike, for once... Will you shut up?" Rayvena tossed her purple hair, and they began their walk toward the lab.

Chapter 27:
Clash Class Day

Principal Fairday sat at his desk, surrounded by files, busy planning the upcoming Class Clash Day. His primary objective was to ensure that all students were placed in competitions according to their abilities. He knew that if he made it an open-ground competition, some students might not participate at all, so he carefully matched students with opponents.

The AICI on Principal Fairday's table lit up, indicating an incoming call. He glanced at the caller ID and saw that it was someone higher than his office. Nervously, he cleared his throat before picking up the call. "Good day, Sector Official Crambe," he greeted with a smile.

"I believe I am on with Principal Fairday, Sector 71?" Sector Official Richard Crambe confirmed.

"Yes, sir, you are on the right call," Fairday replied.

"Perfect! Ethan Crambe, I want him in the Class Clash," Richard Crambe stated. Fairday's eyes widened, knowing that Ethan had an issue in Sector 53 and shouldn't be allowed to participate.

"This... Sir..." Fairday began, trying to express his concerns.

"I know what you are about to say, Principal Fairday. I am not asking this because he is my son but because he deserves a chance to display his ability. Ethan is a good kid. Whatever happened in Sector 53 was a mistake. You know how kids are; we should avoid judging them wrongly. So, please, I want him on the list," Richard explained. Fairday contemplated the request, seeing some sense in Richard's reasoning.

"Consider it done, Sir," Fairday agreed.

"Thank you because I really would hate to have to see you in person," Richard added with a hint of humor.

"Sir, while I have you on the comms, I was wondering if you could possibly help me with a career reassignment?" Fairday's voice sounded hopeful.

"So both of us can get executed? No, thank you. Keep doing what you do best," Richard replied, then hung up. Fairday looked at his list and realized he had almost fixed everyone's placement except Ethan Crambe's. He felt frustrated but knew he couldn't ignore a Sector Official's orders.

Principal Fairday considered the situation. Including Ethan in the Class Clash might indeed help the boy discover his potential, but it also puts Fairday in a difficult position. He had a backup plan, but he didn't want to resort to it. The thought of another day dealing with something he hated was unbearable. He closed his eyes, tapped a pen on his desk, and hoped for the best.

***

"Now!" Ethan yelled as Felix threw him in the air. They were in the middle of practicing for Clash Clash Day. Ethan was over the moon when Principal Fairday told him he could participate again. Felix flexed his muscles as he pushed into the training grounds. As he crouched to his knees, his muscles tightened. Felix grunted upward into the air behind Ethan. Ethan laughed as he pulled his tunic down midair. The feeling of flying was exhilarating. Looking down, he saw Kira and Zion glaring at him. He gave a foxy smile, knowing they could not reach him.

Felix soon caught up to Ethan in the air. Ethan yelped as Felix grabbed him by the back of his tunic, throwing him as hard as possible. He shot straight down towards Kira and Zion. Zion was the first to react. He stepped in front of Kira and held out his hands. His eyes turned gray as a bluish tint force field bubbled around the two of them. Ethan soon came into contact with it. He froze in place slowly as time slowed down for him. Kira smiled, slapping Zion on the back. They were confident they had won.

Ethan grunted as he tried to push forward. Closing his eyes, he exerted his weight on the shield bubble. Kira gasped as Ethan seemingly sliced through the bubble like a fish swimming in its water tank. Connecting his fist with Zion, Ethan punched him square in the face. Zion gasped, stumbling backward. Professor Alice also gasped. "Teddy, did you see that? It can't be!" She took off her glasses in shock.

Professor Carson shook his head. "I didn't see anything. You know only Spatial Class Elites can perceive their own attacks."

"Exactly the problem. Ethan just cut through a Temporals' Temporal Bubble. That's a feat that can only be done with Spatial Class energy."

Carson's eyes widened. "Alice, what are you implying?"

Professor Alice folded her hands together. "I'm not implying anything. I'm just saying if it turns out Ethan is displaying abnormal Code usage, and we didn't say anything, it's our heads."

She knew that a Brute could never pull off such a feat. This was reason enough to bring to the Guardians. But her intention in the question was more curious than playing by the book.

"True. But to bring to light such an accusation and be wrong will cost our heads too." He responded.

"Are you protecting him, Teddy? Is there something I should know?" She turned to face him with suspicion in her eyes. They were old friends. If he was hiding something, she should know.

Professor Carson just watched ahead as Felix came crashing down next, swinging at Kira. She slowed his movements with every swing he struck at her. He couldn't land a hit on her like this. Ethan and Zion were throwing hands at each other as well. With each punch, the other boy met with his own block. Ethan rolled forward and grabbed Zion's leg, knocking him down. Zion's eyes were gray as he froze the area. Ethan backed up and waited. "You still can only hold that up for ten seconds. I can wait."

"Oh yeah? Try me." Zion placed his hands down, lifting himself up. Ethan rushed forward again and swung his right leg at Zion's head. He slowed time down slightly to grab Ethan's leg. Ethan narrowly lost his balance as he was pulled forward. He kicked his other leg into Zion's chest before getting a solid grip. Zion lost his breath as he let go of his leg. Ethan fell to the ground as a result.

Professor Carson smiled like a proud parent at his progress. "For the past few weeks, Ethan has been seemingly normal. Except for his strength. He is much stronger now, sure."

His face furrowed into a dark look. "But the impact of the punches seemed very different from Brute's."

Alice raised her eyebrows. "What do you mean?"

"In the way he now punches, it's as if a heavy force is behind him, not coming from him. If that makes sense."

"No, it doesn't." She said straight away.

Carson sighed a bit. "When a Brute punches Alice, they use their steel-like bones to crush their object. But Ethan has been punching, and the impact came after his punch."

Alice stared intently at Ethan. "So what does it mean?"

"I spoke with Fairday and expressed my concerns; he told me all I needed to know." She relaxed at the mention of the Principal's name.

"Which is?"

"Seeing as he's my student, it's none of your concern."

Alice just shrugged her shoulders. "You Brutes sure can be annoying. I'll stay out of it."

"All of his Code training is done within the safety of his teachers. If there's something wrong, we'll learn it here." He spoke and then turned to face the four students on the training grounds.

"All right, that's enough practice to bring it in!" Carson gave Alice a quiet nod.

The four students ran up to the professors. They were heaving and panting from their fights, but there was a fire in their eyes. They were ready to go.

"When this all starts, remember. Many will watch in our Sector to see how our Academy performs." Carson reminded them.

"Just have fun, and make sure you follow the rules." Professor Alice added. With that, they were free to go for the day. Students had the rest of the day to do what they needed to before the events began.

"Kira, I'm going to go get ready. I'll meet up with you at the opening ceremony." Ethan spoke to her.

"I figured you would be standing with your father for the opening ceremony."

Ethan looked puzzled for a second before a light went off in his head. How could he forget? The Sector Official gives the opening speech. Well, Ethan had no intention of supporting him. "Actually, I'll just meet up with you for the fights. Save me a seat." He turned and left.

Professor Carson had gone back to his office and contemplated. Why had he lied? He never spoke with Principal Fairday. In fact, he talked to Ethan's mother. What she had told him, he promised to never repeat. And yes, the responsibility was to Pangea first. He had called to tell her this was a problem, threatening to report it. But then she finally explained the complexity to him. If what Ethan's mother had said was true, then Ethan could be critical to Pangea. And that alone was enough for him to look the other way. Besides, it was an academic professor's word against a Sector Official anyway.

Professor Carson could only hope his decision would not come back to haunt him.

A few hours later, the Clash Class event kicked off into full swing. It was being hosted at Unity Prep Academy.

The cheering grew louder in the audience as two students showcased their abilities. The first was a second-year Sprite student, and the other was a second-year Naturalist student.

Ethan sneaked up the stadium steps at the Academy. He happily saw he had missed the opening speech that his father gave. He wondered if his father was mad or embarrassed. As Ethan climbed more steps, he saw Ben ushering him over. He sat beside Ben and Kira, who were on the far end, as they watched.

Ethan had no idea how his name got on the list after Carson told him he wouldn't participate in Class Clash weeks ago. For a moment, he had stood in front of the school's notice board, still in awe as to why Ethan Crambe was written in black on the holographic board. One thing was certain about how his name got there; his parents must have done it. When Principal Fairday said he was allowed to participate a week ago, he was suspicious Carson must have told his Mom about it. She obviously got him in the competition. Ethan sat watching the heated fights in front of them, no longer caring about why. With his strength coming in, he no longer had to hide. He still hadn't told his mother yet, but that's because he wanted to wait till he had a handle on it to surprise her.

Ethan clapped along with Ben and Kira, who cheered for the first-year Sprite student who narrowly defeated the first-year Naturalist.

Ben tapped on his shoulder, "Hey, are you okay?"

Ethan nodded.

"How do you feel about this? Do you think you can handle your fight?"

Ethan replied, "Yes, dude, stop stressing me out about it."

Ben tapped Ethan's shoulder again, but Ethan was absorbed in watching and cheering for the fighters. Out of the corner of his eye, he noticed Skylar sitting with his twin, Austin. Their gazes met briefly, and Ethan quickly looked away. He felt uneasy as he observed them chatting and glancing at him, whispering to each other. He knew they never liked him, and their presence made it difficult for him to enjoy the fight. Ethan decided to leave.

"Hey, where are you going?" Kira asked.

"I need some air. I'll be back before you know it," Ethan replied, struggling his way through the cheering crowd. As he walked deeper into the hallway, heading for the academy lobby, a ghostly silence engulfed the area. The cheering from the arena faded away.

Ethan wished Leo were there. He felt the need to share his feelings with someone who could understand, as Kira and Ben might not fully comprehend the situation with Skylar. Ethan took the next bend, leading to the enormous golden DNA statue, and walked around, trying to clear his thoughts. But as he touched the sturdy statue, something strange happened.

"Sudden energy flowed inside of me. What the hell was that?" Ethan exclaimed aloud. Curious, he took another step forward and experienced the same unusual sensation. His body seemed to be adjusting to something unknown. Puzzled, he looked around, thinking someone else might be nearby. However, everyone should have been on the other side of the campus, watching the fights.

"What the hell?" Ethan took another step forward, and a black static-like shimmer surrounded him. Just then, he heard footsteps approaching from down the hall. Worried, he tried to find a place to hide, but before he could do so, he gasped as he began to levitate up to the ceiling.

He found himself floating up towards the ceiling, his shock silenced by covering his mouth with his hand. Meanwhile, Skylar and Austin entered the lobby but found it empty. Confused, they looked around for Ethan, whom they thought they had seen going in that direction.

"I could have sworn I saw him go this way," Skylar said.

The twins searched the balcony area but found no sign of Ethan. They exchanged glances, both surprised at how they had suddenly lost track of him.

"Where could he be now?" Skylar asked, scanning the restroom again.

Austin didn't believe Ethan had left the Academy. If he did, he would have gotten into a lot of trouble, especially considering he hadn't fought in his match yet.

"I can sense he is around here. There's something in my spatial field. I just don't understand where I'm feeling the presence," Austin replied.

"Austin, we have one chance to get rid of him. Otherwise, it's our asses on the line," Skylar pushed his brother.

"Hey, we stick to the plan. We teach him a lesson, and that's all. No killing," Austin insisted. He disliked Ethan, but he couldn't go as far as killing him.

"What use is it then? We should leave him alone if we're going to start something and not end it. What if he reports us, huh?" Skylar retorted.

Austin contemplated the possibility of what Skylar said. He was right. Ethan could report them, and they might get expelled from school, or even worse, considering his father was a Sector Official. Maybe it was best to get rid of Ethan, as Kara had instructed.

"That's probably best, but I have doubts," Austin admitted, needing reassurance.

Skylar narrowed his eyes, his gaze turning gray. He pushed his hair out of his right eye, scanning their surroundings. "You don't feel that?" he asked Austin, who had no idea what he was talking about.

"What? Did you see something?" Austin inquired.

"No, but I can still sense him in our spatial awareness. He's still here," Skylar replied.

Skylar looked up at the high ceiling, which he had never bothered to inspect closely. "There he is!" he exclaimed, spotting Ethan's tunic. Ethan was quietly holding himself up in an open duct space. Now that he no longer needed to be silent, he started moving through the ceiling, trying to make his way to the hallway. He hurried, but unfortunately, Austin shifted up and appeared in front of him, causing Ethan to retreat inside the spacious air duct.

Austin moved closer to him, and Ethan had no choice but to keep backing away.

Ethan looked behind and realized he was almost at the spot through which he had gone into the ceiling. He attempted to push his way through Austin, but Skylar suddenly appeared, grabbing him from behind. Skylar locked his arms around Ethan's throat and shifted them to the roof of the building.

On the rooftop, Skylar delivered a powerful punch to Ethan's stomach. Gasping for breath, Ethan keeled over. Skylar seized him again and shifted back to the lobby, causing Ethan to crash hard onto the restroom floor. Austin promptly joined them.

"I just knew you were pathetic. You're such a coward, Ethan. Is this all the Crambes are good for?" Skylar taunted, gripping Ethan's tunic. He shifted them over to the DNA statue, repeatedly smashing Ethan's head into the solid structure.

Dazed, Ethan's vision started to fade. He struggled to break free from Skylar's hold, yelling out in agony.

"Get off of me!" Ethan desperately clawed at them.

"Kira and Benjamin aren't here to bail you out this time," Skylar hissed while Austin delivered a kick to Ethan's belly. Ethan moaned, clutching his stomach, struggling to catch his breath.

***

The cheering reached a roaring climax. Ben looked around as he cheered but noticed that Ethan had been gone for a while now. Soon, it would be his turn to enter the ring. He knew how eager Ethan was to show everyone what he was made of, so his absence felt off. Ben nudged Kira.

"Hey, have you noticed Ethan has been gone for a while now?"

Kira hadn't noticed Ethan's absence. She thought he had been with them the entire time. "Where did he say he was going to?" she inquired.

"I have no idea," Ben said loudly enough for Kira to hear. The cheering made it difficult for them to communicate clearly. "Maybe I should check on him?" He had a feeling that Ethan might be in trouble.

Kira's hand was waving in the air as she cheered. The intense fight captured her attention, causing her to lose focus on those around her. She had completely forgotten that Ethan had left their group.

"Ben, it's just Ethan being Ethan! Stop worrying and enjoy this match before it's your turn!" She encouraged him, continuing to cheer.

Despite Kira's reassurance, something inside Ben told him that Ethan was indeed in trouble. He couldn't explain the strange feeling, but it was persistent. He had been uneasy for a few minutes now.

What could this mean? He asked himself, trying to dismiss the thoughts and join in the cheering. However, his instinct kept nudging him.

Back in the lobby, Skylar punched Ethan, causing the Brute to stagger backward and hit the wall. Ethan's eyes were already swollen from the repeated blows he had received from Skylar and Austin. Despite the pain, he managed to stand his ground. As Skylar approached again, Ethan launched a punch at his chest with surprising force, sending Skylar tumbling toward the stairwell that led to the classrooms.

In a moment of confusion and rage, Ethan reached up to grab the DNA statue. His hands crushed parts of the statue, shocking both Ethan and Austin. Ethan looked at his hand in bewilderment, not understanding how he had done that. Austin rushed to help Skylar back up, and they both glanced back at Ethan, who seemed to be in a daze, dusting off his gray tunic.

"That actually hurt," Skylar sounded surprised.

Ethan's eyes were still swollen, and his stomach was in knots. He had no idea what had just happened. He couldn't explain how he had unleashed such force in his punch. The whole situation left him feeling disoriented and shaken.

"I think he got lucky. Let's put an end to him right now," Skylar's eyes turned gray as he walked towards Ethan. However, Skylar immediately halted. There was something about Ethan's glowing eyes that revealed a black, ominous force flowing around him.

"Holy shit," Skylar winced in pain, holding his shoulder blade. "My body hurts. Ah, what is this?"

Austin shut his eyes in pain as well. "I feel like I'm being crushed!"

Oblivious to the reason behind Skylar's reaction, Ethan walked closer to the boys, ready to fight them off. However, seeing their fear, Skylar and Austin backed off.

"Screw this, let's just leave," Austin whined.

"But we didn't deal with him!" Skylar grunted.

"Yeah, but we sure as hell didn't sign up for this. Something is terribly wrong with this guy."

"Okay." Skylar looked back at Ethan one last time in disappointment. Ethan was holding himself up against the statue. If they were going to get away, it was right now. Their eyes began to glow gray as they shifted out of the lobby. Ethan could hear them running away from the unusual situation.

Finally, Ethan let out a sigh of relief as he fell unconscious on the floor. Eventually, someone came to his aid. Ethan vaguely remembered being picked up before passing out again.

"Ethan...Ethan...?" A voice called from the background.

When he awoke, he found himself in a hospital. He recognized it from the smell of trees. He opened his eyes to a bright fluorescent light above his head. His vision was blurry, and he could barely see the figures standing around him.

"Are you okay? What happened to you?" The voice that had called him earlier inquired.

Ethan tried to look left and right, but his eyes were still unfocused. His body felt tremendously heavy. He could hear voices but could barely see their faces. From their tone, he knew who was speaking.

"Crambe, what happened to you?" The voice sounded gruff.

"Why does it feel so hard to breathe in here?" Someone familiar mentioned.

Ethan looked in the direction where he felt someone touch his shoulder. He could tell the voice belonged to Professor Carson. Carson asked again, but Ethan couldn't answer.

He blinked to clear his vision, but dots of bright light he alone could see prevented a clearer view of the faces around him. Something wasn't right. He had never experienced this before, nor had he felt such strange energy flowing around his body. *How did I get here?* He questioned himself before speaking out.

"What is wrong with me? What's happening to me, to my sight?"

He heard Ben's voice and felt someone grab his hand, "You will be okay, Ethan. Stay calm. The doctor will be here soon." He imagined it was Kira holding his hand. Ethan kept calm.

The knocking sound of a sharp shoe rushed into his ears. He could hear someone approaching but couldn't tell from where or to where. "Ethan?" It was his mother.

Quintella rushed to him and held his hand. Ethan held her hand tightly too. She looked at Professor Carson and Ben, who didn't catch the look on her face. She could feel the strange energy flowing from the boy's body.

She lowered her voice and whispered to him, "Ethan, what happened to your necklace?"

She had noticed that the stone was no longer there to restrict Ethan's power. That was why she could feel the strange energy flowing from his body. She couldn't see it, but there was pressure in the air. A Brute could never do what Ethan was doing.

"It broke. I'm sorry, Mom." He looked genuinely sad about it.

Just then, a doctor walked into the room.

Professor Carson gave way, and Quintella adjusted slightly for the doctor to check on Ethan. After several checks, the doctor looked at Quintella. He then looked at Ben, who stood by the wall with his hands folded in front of him.

"He is getting better. Brutes are strong. Although he seems to be healing slower than the average Elite, he will be fine." The doctor checked Ethan's eyes and nodded. "What happened to him?" he asked.

Ben stepped away from the wall and spoke up, "I found him on the floor by the DNA statue. I think some students ganged up on him." Quintella's gaze fell on Professor Carson, conveying a message that someone was trying to kill Ethan. Carson shook his head in response, and Quintella furrowed her brows in frustration.

"In a few hours, you can take him home," said the doctor, turning down the pain medication drip attached to Ethan's wrist and leaving the room. Quintella approached Professor Carson, staring into his eyes, and asked, "Can you find who did this to my son?" Carson nodded in agreement.

"Find them fast. They need to be banished from the Sector. When I find the students responsible, they'll be begging for mercy!" Quintella returned to her seat beside Ethan, relieved that the strange pressure in the room had disappeared.

Carson remained silent, unable to believe that Kara, whom he suspected, could do such a thing to Ethan. Though she hated the boy, he couldn't imagine she would resort to this level of violence. He looked at Ben, bowed his head, and left the room.

Ben sat beside Ethan and Kira, who hadn't said a word the whole time but was holding Ethan's hand with care, watching him closely. Quintella looked at him with tears in her eyes, knowing that she would lose her memory soon. Ethan's power was gradually returning, and the risk of the truth about his Code being revealed was becoming more daunting. She feared she might not be able to prevent it.

Chapter 28:
A Lead to Leo

The news of Ethan Crambe's hospitalization on Clash Clash Day spread like wildfire, dominating conversations throughout the school. Opinions were divided; some believed he deserved his fate, while others disapproved of the incident. Some students, who previously had no knowledge of Ethan, suddenly claimed familiarity with him and the events that transpired. Rumors ran wild, leaving the teachers without a clear understanding of the truth. However, Professor Carson remained determined to uncover the real story behind Ethan's hospitalization.

Meanwhile, Fairday received a summons from the administration to meet with Richard Crambe himself. The Sector Official was far from pleased with the situation and pressured Fairday to locate the responsible student or risk losing his position as principal. This threat held weight, as Fairday's contributions to Pangea would cease without a job, essentially sealing his fate. But Fairday wasn't prepared to give up without a fight. Upon leaving Crambe's office, he immediately set to work, determined to find answers.

In a different part of the school, Professor Kara stood by her office window, her quietude disrupted by the chirping birds within. Frustration filled her voice as she addressed the twins, Austin and Skylar, who had just walked in. "I don't want to hear your excuses!" she exclaimed, her face contorted in disgust. She silenced Austin before he could speak, her disappointment evident.

Kara had never instructed the twins to attack Ethan in a restroom. The original plan had been straightforward: provoke a confrontation during the competition and cause him significant harm, all while making it appear accidental. However, the twins had veered off course, undermining their own scheme. Kara regarded them with disdain, knowing that the twins would inevitably become prime suspects with everyone investigating the incident. The cancellation of Clash Clash Day was a direct consequence of their actions, and she was aware that the administration's discovery of the truth would result in severe consequences for them all.

"Who came up with the idea to assault Crambe in the restroom?" Kara demanded, her gaze shifting between Skylar and Austin. The twins exchanged glances before pointing at each other. Kara slammed her fist on the desk in frustration. "Idiots! That's what you are."

"What a pair of imbeciles!" she muttered as she moved to sit behind her desk. The twins stood before her, their expressions sullen. Kara contemplated their predicament; their situation could worsen if someone had witnessed them with Ethan in the restroom. She sighed, then continued, "We need a new plan. We must remove that troublemaker from this Academy. Your methods are of no concern to me; get it done, or you'll face the consequences."

Skylar turned to Austin, seeking guidance. "What's our next move?" he inquired. Kara's frustration flared anew as she narrowed her eyes. She had hoped for a more thoughtful question from Skylar, one that offered solutions rather than adding to her problems.

Just when she was about to speak, a gentle knock came at the door. All three grew silent and listened. A second knock came, and Kara ushered the knocker to come in.

Carson walked into the office to behold the boys standing in a corner. They greeted, and Carson responded with a nod. "You can leave now!" Kara dismissed the boys. Carson sat. He needed no permission to sit since he was higher in rank than Kara, who was oblivious to the purpose of his visit.

Taking her seat, "Is everything all right, Professor Carson?" She drew the chair closer to the desk. Carson looked at her and then around the office.

"I was hoping you'd enlighten me about the situation with Ethan Crambe," he said, his gaze fixed on Kara. Meeting his eyes, she subtly adjusted herself in the seat, sensing the gravity of the conversation.

"Professor, I've emphasized before that boy is nothing but a troublemaker," she replied, shrugging dismissively. "As for his recent troubles, I'm as clueless as anyone else. Did something else go awry with the Crambe situation?" Carson nodded, perceiving the falsehood in her voice. Her discomfort was palpable, a telltale sign of her involvement.

"Ethan was assaulted by an unidentified individual," Carson disclosed, watching Kara's eyes widen slightly. "We have no leads on the assailant's identity. Yet, I had a hunch that you might possess some insight. Considering your apparent aversion to the boy." His gaze held an unspoken message, implying that her secrets wouldn't remain hidden for long.

A faint chuckle escaped Kara's lips. "True, I can't deny my distaste for the kid," she conceded, her voice dripping with insincerity. "But I'm afraid I have no additional information to offer you, Professor Carson. The fate of Ethan Crambe is a mystery to me as well."

Carson's gaze remained unyielding, a knowing glint in his eyes. "Your concern for the boy is touching," he retorted, his tone laced with sarcasm. "Given your track record, it's hard not to wonder if you might be involved somehow."

Kara's features twisted into a semblance of innocence. "Professor, I assure you, I have no interest in causing harm to the boy. Quite the contrary, his presence here only tarnishes the reputation of this Academy." Her words were veiled in cunning, a carefully crafted facade to divert suspicion.

"As you've been reminding me all year," Carson remarked dryly, his patience wearing thin. "But let's not sidetrack ourselves with your opinions on the matter at hand. I came to you seeking information about the incident in the Academy's lobby."

Kara seized the opportunity to steer the conversation toward her agenda. "Ah, the incident," she mused, her voice taking on a contemplative tone. "I'm afraid I haven't the faintest clue about what transpired there, Professor. My focus has been on maintaining the integrity of our Brute lineage."

Carson shook his head, exasperated by her attempts to evade the topic. "Your political commentary is duly noted, Professor Kara. However, I'm here for information, not a discourse on societal dynamics."

Kara pouted, realizing she was losing her grip on the conversation. "Of course, Professor," she acquiesced with a sigh, conceding the point. "I apologize for veering off course. If I come across any relevant information, you'll be the first to know."

As Carson began to depart, Kara's unease intensified. She understood the consequences of her secrets being unearthed, and fear prompted her to formulate a desperate plan. As she watched Carson leave, she wasted no time in activating her AICI and making a call. The screen flickered to life, revealing a woman with unruly hair.

"Hello?" the woman on the other end answered.

Kara cleared her throat, weaving her web of deception with practiced finesse. "I have some information you might find... intriguing."

***

Meanwhile, Ethan scanned the room, finding himself alone. His vision had returned, a fact the doctor had confirmed. Something about the chaotic events in the lobby gnawed at his mind. *Why had everyone fled like that?* It was a question he couldn't shake. Unbeknownst to him, a profound transformation had occurred within his body. He had thrown a punch, sending the shifter sprawling. He took a moment to process the newfound strength and density coursing through him.

The door swung open, and Ben hurried in. The worry etched across Ben's face didn't escape Ethan's notice, prompting a chuckle. Ben blamed himself for not heeding his instincts, which had warned him that Ethan was in trouble. If only he had ignored Kira and followed his heart, Ethan might not have ended up in this situation.

"Relax, buddy. It's not as bad as it looks," Ethan reassured Ben.

"How are you feeling now?" Ben inquired.

"Much better. Where's my mom?" Ethan asked.

"She went to speak with the doctors," Ben replied, his concern palpable. "Who did this to you?" he pressed further.

Ethan averted his gaze, his silence a clear signal. Ben knew that Ethan was determined to shield those who had harmed him. The incident in the parking lot, where he had been attacked, remained a topic Ethan refused to discuss openly.

"Come on, now's not the time to protect anyone. They nearly killed you," Ben urged, frustration edging into his voice. "You need to consider the danger you're putting yourself in by shielding them. If you don't expose them, they'll just come back and hurt you again."

Ethan's resolve held firm, even in the face of Ben's persuasive words. He stared at the machinery connected to his body, aiding his recovery. "I understand that I could report this," he finally spoke, his voice tinged with weariness. "But I can't bear the thought of someone dying because of me. I can handle myself."

Ben let out a derisive snort, attempting to reason with his friend. "Clearly, you can handle yourself. Look where it got you, Ethan. You need a reality check. Not everyone in this Academy is kind-hearted. If they're in the wrong, the best thing you can do is report them to the administration."

Sinking down beside Ethan's bed, Ben continued, "And your parents will take up the case. They'll make sure this never happens to you or any other student. Seriously, Ethan, why are you protecting these people?" A hint of anger crept into his tone.

Ethan let out a sigh, recognizing that Ben wouldn't comprehend his reasons for keeping things to himself, for enduring the pain alone. He wished he could return to Sector 53, where he had a sense of belonging, where his comrades had his back. Sector 71 had brought nothing but suffering and turmoil. He hadn't chosen to be here; he had been uprooted from 53 to 71, all because of his father – a man who had never truly cared for him. Ethan straightened up, glancing around expectantly for his mom and Liam, but he knew Richard Crambe wouldn't make an appearance. He couldn't help but question the kind of father Richard truly was.

His gaze flicked to Ben before he looked away. Ben was oblivious to Ethan's tumultuous family dynamics, seeing only the advantages of having Sector Officials as parents. He couldn't fathom the ache of lacking the parental love every child craved from their father. Ethan tried to push the thoughts aside, but they persisted – his father's apathy was an undeniable truth.

"Hey," a familiar voice called out. Ethan turned his gaze downward to see who it was. "Wow, Ethan, this looks pretty rough," the voice continued sympathetically. He lowered his hand from his face, revealing the speaker – Kira. She had joined Ben at his side.

"How did this happen to him?" Kira turned to Ben, concern etched on her face. Ben offered a helpless shrug, his expression mirroring his lack of answers. Kira frowned, not really expecting a response from him.

Turning her attention back to Ethan, she inquired, "So, how are you feeling now?"

Ethan's face reddened with a mix of embarrassment and discomfort. "I think I'm okay to head home. Actually, I feel a lot stronger now," he fibbed, a forced smile tugging at his lips.

Ben shot Ethan a questioning glance, sensing that something didn't quite add up. Ethan had previously mentioned feeling somewhat better, and now he was suddenly claiming to be strong. Ben suspected Ethan might be trying to dissuade Kira from delving further into his condition. He offered a half-hearted wave, almost apologetically.

Kira's curiosity was piqued. "I think I might have a lead on Leo," she began, diverting the conversation to a more pressing matter. Ethan removed his hand from his face, his interest piqued by Kira's words. She nodded, acknowledging his attention. "I overheard some students talking about increased Guardian activity near a mall," she shared, her voice tinged with urgency.

Ethan's eyebrows furrowed in thought. "So, they think Leo might be in our sector?" he questioned, hoping for more details.

Kira nodded, her tone conveying her certainty. "Exactly. They speculate that the Guardians are focusing their patrols around the multipurpose plaza – it's the largest area, after all."

Ben's skepticism emerged. "How do you know this is accurate? We need to be sure we're not walking into trouble."

Kira responded with a playful jab to Ben's shoulder. "Ben, always doubting my sources! What brilliant leads did you bring to the table?" Her teasing smile irked him slightly.

He glared back at her, unamused. "Are you done?"

Kira's playful demeanor persisted. "For now, maybe, considering you're here to lead us to Leo, Mr. Benjamin Valdez." She punctuated her comment with a light punch to his arm.

Ben feigned exaggerated pain. "Ouch! That actually hurt!" he mock-complained. Kira stuck her tongue out at him. "Oh, please, bite me."

Ethan intervened, steering the conversation back on track. "Alright, enough banter. What's our plan? How do we ensure we find Leo before something terrible happens to him?" The weight of suspicion hung heavily on Ethan, adding urgency to his words.

Kira's expression turned serious. "We need to locate one of these Libertas cult members and tail them. Once we're led to Leo, we let the Guardians take over from there."

Both boys nodded in agreement. To pinpoint Leo's location, they realized they needed to conduct some research on the AICI. Their goal was to identify secure buildings in the vicinity of Sector 71. Ben volunteered to handle the research while Kira focused on arranging transportation.

"You do realize we already have a way to travel with you here, right?" Kira chided Ben playfully.

Ben whined in response. "Give me a break. I'm not a Shifter."

Kira shot him a pointed glare, her patience wearing thin. Ethan observed the exchange with a furrowed brow, wondering if there was more to the tension between Ben and Kira than met the eye.

"What are you staring at?" Ben asked curiously.

"You can't shift if you don't have a Code to shift," Ethan explained, clarifying the situation.

Kira's eyes narrowed as she considered his words. "In that case, we'll need to borrow a hover van."

The door swung open, revealing Quintella entering the room accompanied by a team of doctors. The trio of teenagers quickly stood up in respect. The Naturalist handed Ethan a small pouch containing herbs that would alleviate any lingering nausea or dizziness. As the Pulse Elite conducted his examination, his eyes glowed in a brilliant shade of azure blue, delving into Ethan's internal structure. "His bones appear to be in good health, although they are a bit small for a Brute," he noted.

"I'm aware," Ethan responded with a hint of discomfort, wincing as his mother assisted him in preparing to leave.

Quintella turned her attention to all three of them, her demeanor stern. "I may not know the full extent of the turmoil in this Sector, but I'm telling you now – keep your heads down and steer clear of trouble. Do you understand me?"

"Yes, ma'am," the trio responded in unison, their voices carrying a firm resolve. However, their expressions hinted at a different sentiment, revealing their lack of genuine commitment to abiding by her warning.

As the doctors completed their examinations and the group prepared to depart, an air of tension lingered, underscored by the unspoken determination that pulsed between the young protagonists.

Chapter 29:
Judgment

The multipurpose plaza's expansive mall sprawled across the landscape, its several towering structures hovering just inches above the ground. On weekends, the area buzzed with activity, drawing in crowds of people eager to shop, dine, and find entertainment. The movie theater occupied the uppermost floor, while a bustling eatery was situated one level below. The entire complex teemed with life, accommodating well over a hundred visitors who flowed in and out, filling the air with chatter and excitement.

Kira maneuvered the vehicle onto a side street, parking inconspicuously. Ben's impatience surfaced as he questioned her choice, puzzled by the decision to halt before reaching the mall's entrance. "Why are we stopping here? The mall's right there," he complained, not comprehending why they wouldn't simply drive closer to their destination and secure a parking spot.

Kira responded with a measured tone, her eyes scanning their surroundings. "We're trying to avoid being spotted, Ben. Do you want us to attract unnecessary attention and risk being exposed?" Ben shook his head, a hint of sheepishness in his expression. He exchanged a knowing glance with Ethan, who couldn't help but feel an undercurrent of unease.

"We wait for the right opportunity to make our move," Kira added, leaning against the driver's seat with a calculated air of nonchalance.

Their timing was crucial. A black Hovervan passed by, disappearing behind a corner near the mall. It was Rayvena and her team, continuing their pursuit of the girl they had been tracking for days. As the van vanished from sight, Kira, Ethan, and Ben understood that their moment had arrived. It was time to put their plan into action – infiltrating the mall and gathering intelligence about the building adjacent to it. Their strategy involved observing the building from the mall's rooftop, ensuring a discreet vantage point.

Stepping into the bustling mall, the trio navigated through the crowd, making their way to an elevator. They ascended to the top floor, only to be greeted by the presence of two Guardians stationed near the entrance – one positioned to the far left and the other to the far right. Kira called a huddle, the trio hatching their next move in whispered deliberation.

"I've got an idea," Ben announced, his voice pitched low. Both Kira and Ethan focused their attention on him, waiting for his strategy. Ben proposed a diversion tactic – he would engage the Guardians in a distraction, allowing Kira and Ethan to slip away and head to the roof undetected. Once they were in position, Ben would rejoin them.

"Stay put and wait for my signal," Ben instructed, his eyes conveying determination. With a final nod, he left them behind in the midst of the crowded movie theater. The atmosphere was filled with the energy of the ongoing vampire-themed film, oblivious to the covert operations unfolding behind the scenes.

***

Titus positioned himself near the van, feigning the act of smoking despite having never done so before. His first inhale resulted in a fit of coughs and heaves, but his focus remained steadfast. He had been on lookout duty for nearly fifty minutes. The minutes dragged on as he strained to catch a glimpse of the girl they were pursuing. Though Maya was absent on this mission, Pike was stationed inside the van, ready to assist when needed.

Rayvena exuded confidence, her gaze scanning the bustling mall as she hunted for their elusive target. This time, they hadn't brought Maya along, opting to rely solely on their intelligence and instincts. Pike maintained his vigilance from within the van, their communication channels open and active.

Ben staggered out of the cinema room and into the hallway, where the Guardians stationed at the entrance would easily spot him. Pretending to be disoriented, he stumbled toward the exit, his movements deliberate yet convincing. As he reached the door, he collapsed, strategically blocking the entrance with his prone form.

A surge of chaos ensued as some Elites found themselves unable to access the cinema, a cascade of frustration echoing through the hall.

The Guardians, attuned to the commotion, hastened over to assess the situation. Ethan and Kira, biding their time nearby, seized the moment. Ben's diversion provided them the window they needed to slip away and ascend to the rooftop, unseen and unhindered.

"Move him out of the way!" a voice from the growing crowd demanded. The urgency in the crowd's voice propelled the Guardians to act, forcing them to lift and carry Ben to a more inconspicuous spot. Meanwhile, Ethan and Kira seized the opportunity, advancing toward their intended destination atop the mall.

The covert dance of distractions and maneuvers continued, with each player – Guardians, pursuers, and prey – contributing their part to the high-stakes game that was rapidly escalating.

Back at the van, Titus regretted his decision to smoke. He tapped into his AICI, connecting with Rayvena to gather intel on the situation. "What's the status over there?" he inquired, his voice laced with concern. Rayvena's response was disheartening – she hadn't yet located the target. Titus's confidence wavered as doubts crept in, questioning the accuracy of their information.

"We might need to smoke her out," Titus proposed, taking a puff from the cigarette as he contemplated Rayvena's next move. The irony of his action wasn't lost on him, but his focus was on uncovering the meaning behind Rayvena's cryptic phrase, "smoking her out." Just as the words left his lips, Rayvena's voice crackled through his AICI, informing him of a sighting. The girl was headed toward the bookstore section of the mall.

Concerned for Rayvena's safety, Titus offered assistance. "Do you need backup?" he asked amidst his intermittent coughs, earning a puzzled look from a passing child. Rayvena swiftly dismissed his offer, deeming his conspicuous behavior unsuitable for the task at hand. His exaggerated coughing only served to betray his unfamiliarity with smoking, eliciting awkward glances from those around him.

Unease gnawing at him, Titus resolved to retreat to the safety of the hover van. He needed to avoid attracting undue suspicion while maintaining his covert watch. Meanwhile, Rayvena doggedly pursued their target through the mall, shadowing her in the book section. As she moved in for the capture, the girl inexplicably vanished, leaving Rayvena puzzled and momentarily disoriented.

A subtle presence registered behind her, prompting Rayvena to pivot just in time to unleash a surge of energy – a vibrant purple aura – upon the girl. The force sent the girl crashing into a bookshelf, triggering a domino effect that cascaded through the shelves, setting off chaos within the bookstore.

Witnesses watched in shock as Rayvena engaged her quarry, prompting her to conceal her identity by pulling her hood over her head. The girl, however, was not easily subdued. Rayvena attempted to immobilize her, but the girl defied her hold, retaliating with a burst of lightning from her fingertips. The ensuing blaze and the blaring alarm incited panic, driving everyone in the vicinity into a frenzy to escape the danger.

Amidst the turmoil, the girl managed to slip away, disappearing into the midst of the frantic crowd. Frustration and expletives slipped from Rayvena's lips as she grappled with the reality of her target's escape. She vented her vexation by striking a bookshelf, further fueling the pandemonium around her. With her surroundings ablaze and the situation escalating, Rayvena chose to flee the scene.

Amidst the chaos, Ethan's voice cut through the cacophony, questioning the unfolding spectacle. Kira quickly joined him, the two friends standing together as they observed the chaotic scene playing out before them. Suddenly, a familiar voice pierced the turmoil from behind.

"Hey, the mall's on fire! We need to get out of here!" Ben's urgent call spurred Ethan and Kira into action. Without hesitation, they followed Ben's lead, opting to forego the elevator in favor of the stairs. They hurriedly navigated an exit at the rear of the mall, emerging into the open air. Kira's sharp gaze caught a fleeting sight – a woman slipping into a black hover van. The hint of purple hair beneath the hood caught her attention.

"Rayvena," Kira murmured under her breath, a mixture of surprise and suspicion coloring her tone.

"Who?" Ethan inquired, glancing at Kira for an explanation.

Kira's recognition solidified, her suspicions turning into certainty. "It's Rayvena," she replied, the name carrying weight and significance for her. With a yearning to confirm her suspicions, Kira moved to approach the vehicle, but her attempt was thwarted. The hover van sped away, leaving them surrounded by Guardians who had responded swiftly to the unfolding situation. Artificial Intelligence units swarmed in, their efforts focused on extinguishing the fire.

Ethan and his companions wasted no time. They hastened to their own transportation, urged by the mounting chaos and the encroaching authorities. Kira took the reins, piloting the hover van away from the scene, each second carrying them further from the enigmatic figure who had emerged from the shadows and then vanished just as quickly.

"Rayvena? Do you think she's involved with this cult?" Ethan's concern was reflected in his eyes as he voiced his suspicions. "Maybe. I did see someone with purple hair during the Underground Rave attack. I didn't think much of it back then," Kira replied, her fingers tightening around the steering wheel, torn by conflicting thoughts. "I don't know. It doesn't really seem like something she'd get involved in, but things have changed since our father passed," Kira revealed, her voice tinged with a mix of sorrow and uncertainty.

"Executed?" Ethan's question unveiled his familiarity with Brute mortality, prompting a brief glance from Kira. "How did you know?" she inquired, intrigued by his insight. "Well, we don't suffer from health issues, hunger, or aging like other people do. So, statistically, execution is the most likely cause of death for Brutes," Ethan explained in a matter-of-fact tone. Kira chuckled softly. "You're quite the know-it-all." "Of course, I am—the ultimate know-it-all," Ethan responded with a playful wink. However, their lighthearted exchange was promptly interrupted by Ben's interjection. "Can we save the flirting for another time?" Ben quipped, earning an embarrassed blush from Ethan. Kira's lips curved into a small smile, though she remained contemplative before continuing.

"My father sent his findings to the Sector Official office. He believed that certain Sectors were doomed, destined to collapse within about thirty years or so," Kira disclosed, her gaze distant as she delved into her memories. "He wanted to investigate the underlying causes behind the land's deterioration in those Sectors. His curiosity drove him relentlessly," Ethan voiced his fascination with Kira's father's relentless pursuit of knowledge.

"As a Tempus, much of his time was devoted to understanding his Code. His focus on that aspect led him to neglect his official responsibilities... I'm sure you can see where that led," Kira sighed, the weight of her father's choices evident in her words. "What did he uncover?" Ethan's curiosity deepened, his attention captured by Kira's narrative. "He never shared the specifics with me," Kira admitted bitterly, her frustration evident.

The blue hover van smoothly took a left turn, navigating through the urban landscape until the familiar contours of Ethan's neighborhood came into view. Kira continued, her voice tinged with a mix of regret and resolve. "He was executed for 'non-contribution' to Pangea, a violation of our bylaws."

Ben interjected thoughtfully, adding a layer of complexity to the discussion. "But what if his discoveries could have actually contributed to Pangea?" "That's the crux of it. Why am I helping you search for your friend? Because that cult represents a challenge to the government's authority. Perhaps, along the way, I'll uncover something that can shed light on my father's unjust execution," Kira declared, her eyes ablaze with determination.

"In a year's time, we'll be embroiled in our own assignments. We'll be too immersed in our duties to effect change," Kira continued, pausing as a fleet of vehicles zoomed past before resuming her narration. "But I don't want my sister to face the same fate as my father. I'm holding onto the hope that all of this is just an egregious mistake."

Ethan and Ben absorbed Kira's words, gaining a deeper understanding of her motivations and the underlying bitterness that had shaped her worldview. The glimpse into her past illuminated the source of her jaded demeanor. If circumstances had been different, if they had met her under alternate circumstances, their connection might have been markedly different.

Kira expertly maneuvered her mother's hover van, smoothly guiding it downward before leveling out and parking in front of Ethan's house. "That cult is responsible for my family's demise. Just remember that." Ben's words held a weight of accusation as he glanced at Kira before swiftly exiting the sedan-like hovercraft. Kira bowed her head slightly in acknowledgment as Ethan bid her farewell. As the hover van lifted off and disappeared into the distance, Ethan's mind buzzed with worries. The fire at the mall had erased their leads, leaving them no closer to locating Leo.

In the following days, Ethan, Kira, and Ben maintained a low profile, focusing on their studies at school. Then, one day, Principal Fairday's voice echoed through the speakers, summoning Ethan Crambe while he was in class. Ethan hurried through the corridors, his heart racing until he reached the principal's office. A knock on the door preceded his entrance.

Principal Fairday's melodic voice welcomed him in, and Ethan stepped inside to find a Guardian adorned in opal-clad attire seated before the principal's desk. "Please, Ethan, take a seat," Fairday gestured, indicating the spot beside the Guardian. Ethan regarded her with curiosity, his brow furrowed. "This is Chief Guardian Laura," Fairday introduced, prompting the Chief Guardian to offer a friendly smile.

"Thank you, Principal Fairday. I'd like to have a private conversation with the young man, if you don't mind," Chief Guardian Laura requested. "Of course, Chief Guardian Laura. Feel free to have your conversation. Ethan will be in good hands," Fairday granted his approval. He stood as Laura rose from her seat, signaling for Ethan to follow her.

The two walked in silence through the school's corridors, eventually emerging onto a balcony that overlooked the sprawling cityscape – a place where Ethan had once conversed with Leo. Memories of their conversation tugged at his emotions, a bittersweet pang in his heart.

Laura halted, taking a moment to breathe in the crisp air. The wind played around them as she leaned against the glass railing, casting her gaze over the bustling city below. With uncertainty gnawing at him, Ethan waited for her to begin. Finally, Laura turned to him, placing a reassuring hand on his shoulder. "Days like this can be long and exhausting, don't you think?" Ethan nodded in agreement. "It's a small respite from your classes, a moment of peace and tranquility."

Ethan absorbed her words, taking in the rare moment of solitude away from the academic rigors. Gathering his thoughts, he asked, "So, what did you want to talk to me about, ma'am?" A faint smile played on Laura's lips. "Do you remember me, Ethan?" He took a moment to study her, and recognition dawned. "You're the woman from the café, the one who asked me about the news." Her chuckle was warm. "I'm glad you remembered." Curiosity mingled with his confusion. "But why are we having this conversation? Did I do something wrong?" Laura regarded him intently. "Unfortunately, this is a rather grave matter. Were you present at the hospital on the day Leo went missing?" Ethan nodded, a sense of foreboding settling in his gut. Laura's expression soured. "And did you get a good look at the woman Leo was chasing?" Again, Ethan nodded. "If this is about the rumors circulating in the Academy, I swear I had no part in whatever happened." They observed the bustling activity below, hover bikes and hover vans darting like fireflies. "Have you managed to uncover any leads on Leo's whereabouts?" Ethan's voice carried a mix of anxiety and hope as he addressed Chief Guardian Laura.

"No, although we suspect there might have been some unusual activity at the Multipurpose Plaza's mall," she confided in him.

"I trust my judgment, Ethan. I don't believe you had anything to do with your friend Leonitas' disappearance," she reassured him.

"But it's my duty to investigate any peculiar incidents or threats within my jurisdiction," her tone turned even more serious.

"You always seem to be present when trouble arises. Perhaps it's coincidental, but I don't put much stock in coincidences," she stared at him with an unwavering expression.

"If I discover that you are genuinely implicated in this matter, I won't have any choice but to take appropriate action. Do you understand?" Ethan nodded resolutely.

"However, I wish to discuss a different matter with you. The Elite who assaulted you – was it Skylar Masterson?" Ethan's astonishment was evident.

"What led you to believe that, ma'am?"

"I had some Tempus investigate the scene of the attack. His image appeared in their scans."

Ethan wasn't particularly eager to implicate Skylar, but he was also weary of the ongoing confrontation. "What repercussions will he face?"

"I've received corroboration of this information from another Elite as well. With your statement, I now possess sufficient evidence to render a verdict," her gaze fixed on the skyline. A trace of unease flickered within Ethan.

"Walk with me," she gestured toward the opposite side of the skyline. They retraced their steps indoors, strolling along the hallway.

"Who else is involved?" Ethan's concern began to mount.

An announcement echoed through the Academy's speakers. "All students are requested to assemble at the Academy's stadium on campus." Ethan arched an eyebrow, steering himself in that direction.

"I'll see you there, Ethan," Laura said, proceeding ahead. A stream of students flooded the corridors, converging towards the stadium. Puzzled thoughts swirled in Ethan's mind, pondering the necessity of the Chief Guardian's presence.

"Ethan, are you alright? You seem troubled," Kira inquired, joining him while sporting her customary gray tunic.

"Yeah, I just had a conversation with Chief Guardian Laura," Ethan whispered as they merged into the crowd heading toward the stadium. Passing through a grand archway, they ascended a pathway that led to the stadium and student garden.

"What? Why?" Kira's whispered voice carried an edge of urgency.

"She knows who attacked me. I think she wanted me to confirm it."

"Will you finally disclose the assailant's identity?" Kira nudged him, her voice no longer a whisper.

"Skylar."

"Frankly, I'm not surprised, Ethan. Why didn't you disclose this earlier?"

"Not my approach. I'd rather not burden anyone with my troubles," Ethan's blue eyes held a distant gaze as they moved closer to the imposing stadium.

"But asking a friend for help to locate a missing Elite is more your style?"

"Well, look at that – you said it!" Ethan's grin revealed a set of pearly white teeth.

"Said what?" Kira raised an eyebrow at him.

"You said we're friends! That's the first time!" Ethan laughed heartily.

Kira wore a look of surprise before breaking into her own laughter. "Huh, I guess you're right," her laughter was light and carefree, and Ethan was content knowing he had elicited such a response.

Entering the stadium, AI guided students to their designated sections. "Have you seen Ben?" Ethan inquired.

"No, he's probably already here. My group is over there," she pointed towards the left side of the vast circular arena, where the insignia of the spatial class adorned the seats.

Kira headed left, and Ethan went right toward the Brute's flame heart emblem. He found his place among fellow first and second-year Brute students. Cassidy, a few rows up, spotted Ethan and exchanged a smile and wave.

Some Brute students nearby were playfully roughhousing and causing a commotion in their seats, drawing disapproving glances from students of other classifications. The Psyche Class, adorned in their ostentatious purple and gold attire, observed the display with disdain.

Feeling somewhat isolated without familiar faces around, Ethan scanned his surroundings, taking in the scene.

The Psyche students sat with an air of elegance and grace, engaging in hushed conversations or patiently waiting for the proceedings to unfold.

Ethan's gaze shifted to the Pulse Class students, engrossed in showcasing the latest features of their AICIs or enjoying movies together. Their cheerful camaraderie seemed oblivious to the rest of the crowd.

Thoughts of Riley and his inventive projects crossed Ethan's mind, prompting a pang of longing.

Turning to his right, he observed the Sprite Class students struggling to remain still. Many of them tapped their feet or fiddled with cylinder devices, releasing bursts of red electrical energy.

Principal Fairday materialized in his distinctive midnight purple and gold robe on the rectangular stage below, drawing the attention of the assembly.

"Students, staff, esteemed guests. I wish I could gather you all here for more positive reasons. Unfortunately, that's not the case."

His gaze lowered, and a sense of sadness enveloped him. With a clap of his hands, three figures in opal robes approached him, dragging a protesting student onto the stage. A hush fell over the stadium, and Ethan's heart skipped a beat.

It was Skylar being forcibly brought to the center stage for all to see. Monitors swiveled to capture the unfolding spectacle. As Skylar realized the attention focused on him, a mix of fear and embarrassment crossed his face.

His screams echoed, "You think you can do this to me? Just wait till my parents get here and put a stop to this!" He spat defiantly.

The tension in the stadium was palpable, a heavy cloud hanging over the bewildered audience.

Principal Fairday cleared his throat before addressing the hundreds of students. "This is unfortunate, as it is being broadcast live to the entire sector."

"I didn't DO anything!! Release me!!" Skylar writhed, kicked, and spat at the three Guardians holding him in place.

"Owww, you're hurting me!" Skylar turned his head toward the third Guardian, who was tightening the chains around him.

"Please, stop this!!" Austin stood up in the stadium. The attention of everyone shifted to him. Seeing his resemblance to Skylar, many turned their heads away in discomfort as if watching a train wreck about to happen.

"SIT DOWN." Chief Laura stepped onto the stage, her frizzy blonde hair tied back into a bun and her expression serious. Her authoritative presence compelled Austin to comply.

Her command exuded enough authority to invoke fear throughout the room. Nobody wanted to be in Skylar's position right now, subjected to the scrutiny of multiple Guardians, an occurrence typically reserved for executions.

"We are all here today to witness the execution of Skylar Masterson," Laura declared, striding forward with her hands clasped behind her back. She circled Skylar like a predator, preparing to strike its prey.

Ethan felt sweat forming on his brow. Why was he feeling this way? He shouldn't care about Skylar's fate. Yet, an unsettling guilt gnawed at him.

"You are accused of three things: using your Code without proper authorization as a student, assaulting a fellow student, Ethan Crambe, who is also the child of our Sector Official!" The crowd erupted into boos and taunts directed at Skylar. Such trials often fueled animosity.

"Coward!" "You deserve it!" "You think you're above the law?"

Ethan's heart sank as his name was called out amid the derogatory remarks. He wanted no part in the circumstances leading to this trial.

"And most importantly, failing to contribute productively to Pangea," Laura concluded, her voice resolute.

"You can't prove I did anything!" Skylar's laughter sounded desperate.

At this, Fairday turned to Skylar, lowering himself to eye level. "Do you believe it wise to deceive the Chief Guardian? Because, in fact, we can substantiate our claims." He snapped his fingers, and Professor Kara hesitantly stepped onto the stage, bowing her head.

"It's true. After the boy confessed to me about his actions, I was in disbelief," Kara's gaze held a mixture of pity and regret as she looked at Skylar.

"She's lying! She's a lying bitch!" Skylar hurled insults at her.

"He approached me, claiming that we shared similar goals. He mentioned something about hearing a rumor that I disliked Ethan." She glanced at the Chief Guardian.

"He left me with no choice but to report this unfortunate development. He expressed a desire to harm Ethan, citing his inferiority to the Spatial Class." Stepping back, she recounted the encounter.

Skylar tugged against his restraints, his voice quivering. "It was HER idea! How could you do this?" He pleaded with Kara, his eyes brimming with tears as he hung his head. Rage and terror mingled in his emotions.

"Ethan Crambe. STAND." Laura's authoritative voice commanded attention. Ethan jolted upright, wiping his clammy hands on his red tunic. The eyes of many students and teachers were fixed on him, their scrutiny palpable.

"Yes, ma'am?" An AI moved closer to Ethan, projecting his image onto the stadium screens above.

"Did Skylar attack you before the events of Clash Clash Day began?"

Ethan found himself holding a pivotal moment in his hands. He reviewed his memories of Skylar, none of which warranted saving him.

Without fully realizing it, Ethan responded, "Yes, he did, ma'am." The room erupted into shouts directed at Skylar.

And with that, Skylar's fate was sealed.

Ethan stood in silence, his gaze fixed on the Chief Guardian as she delivered her final judgment. It was evident that her decision had been made long before Ethan even testified.

"I've heard enough. Skylar Masterson, I, Chief Guardian of Sector 71, hereby sentence you to death on behalf of Sector Official Crambe and the World Government of Pangea."

Professor Kara allowed a faint grin to escape her mask as she exited the stage, a satisfied air about her. One less loose end to worry about.

"NO!!" Austin's cry pierced the air, a blood-curdling scream that sent shivers down everyone's spine. His classmates rushed to restrain him, attempting to hush his anguished wails.

"Quiet! Do you want to join him?" Hushed whispers from other students reached Austin's ears, reminding him of the grim reality.

Laura motioned for three Guardians to approach. "Since you are still seventeen, Skylar, I will grant you a painless death."

Skylar's gaze darted around, landing first on Kara, then surprisingly on Ethan. He locked eyes with Ethan, desperation filling his gaze. "You can stop this! Don't let them do this to me!"

"You brought this upon yourself," Ethan's voice trembled, a mix of empathy and firmness in his tone.

Tears streamed down Skylar's face, his green hair falling over one eye as he hung his head. He tugged frantically at the white chains, a futile struggle against his fate. "Please, I'm sorry. I don't want to die!"

The Guardians stepped forward, their hands touching Skylar's body. Ice began to creep over him, encasing his chest, legs, and arms in an icy embrace. The freezing cold advanced, reaching his face until, finally, his entire form was enveloped. A momentary pause hung in the air before Chief Guardian Laura stepped forward, a disheartened shake of her head conveying her disappointment.

"Such a waste of potential," Principal Fairday's voice was tinged with a hint of sadness, his eyes momentarily shimmering with a purple hue. He walked off the stage, leaving the chilling scene behind.

As the ice-coated figure lay on the ground, students turned their heads away, unable to bear the sight. And then, with a decisive kick, Chief Guardian Laura shattered the icy prison, sending shards scattering across the stage.

The stadium was filled with an eerie silence, except for the haunting cries of anguish that echoed through the air, emanating from Austin, who had collapsed into a state of inconsolable torment.

Chapter 30:
The Robe Induction Ceremony

Ethan stood before his bathroom mirror, his gaze fixed on his reflection. Today marked the robe induction ceremony – the day he would finally earn his classification robe. However, a frown tugged at the corners of his mouth.

Today was supposed to be a joyous occasion, a milestone in his life. And yet, the weight of the past six months' horrors cast a shadow over the event. One month had passed since Skylar's execution, and it felt as if everyone had moved on, brushing aside the traumatic event like it was inconsequential.

Austin's absence was understandable. Ethan worried that he might be unfairly blamed for Skylar's death. Though many students had offered reassurances – "it wasn't your fault" or "Skylar was a bad guy" – the accusatory glances and judgmental looks lingered.

Ethan scrutinized his reflection once more. He had become noticeably more muscular over the year. His once-short ash-blonde hair had grown, now cascading past his ears. He leaned on the sink and sighed audibly. "Leo should be here too."

Gallium's voice broke the silence, echoing in the bathroom. "I'm sure he will be found, Master Ethan."

Ethan's body tensed. "Yeah, you're right. Thanks, Gallium."

"Today is a special day; perhaps you should cherish it for both of you."

"For both of us, huh?" Ethan pondered Gallium's words.

"Yeah, you're right, Gallium. Thank you." Ethan's spirits lifted slightly. They needed to find Leo. Leo hadn't turned up dead despite everything, so there was still hope.

A knock on the door interrupted his thoughts. "Dude, are you watching virtual porn again in there?"

Ethan choked, caught off guard. "It was one time! Shut up!"

Ben's voice came through the door, slightly muffled. "I mean, it's all AI simulated, so I get why you enjoy it, but..."

"I'm not watching virtual porn!" Ethan swung the door open, his face flushed in embarrassment. Ben's laughter only made it worse.

"I know, I could hear Gallium. I just wanted to lighten the mood."

Raising an eyebrow, Ethan gave Ben a skeptical look. "By accusing me of having personal time in the bathroom?"

"I was just trying to help, man." Ben shrugged innocently.

Ethan grabbed his towel, wrapping it around himself as he headed to their shared room. Ben sat nonchalantly on his bed, striking up a conversation while Ethan changed.

"Listen, Ethan, you can't blame yourself for what happened with Skylar. And you can't blame yourself for Leo's disappearance."

Pulling a red shirt over his head, Ethan responded, his tone heavy with emotion. "You don't know what it's like to be responsible for someone's death."

Ben's shock was palpable. He seemed taken aback by Ethan's words, shaking his head in disbelief. Clearly annoyed, he decided to let the matter drop.

"Forget it." Ben's curt response hung in the air.

After a tense silence, Ethan felt the need to express his feelings more clearly. He could sense that Ben was offended by his previous statement.

"Leo was in that room because I invited him. Skylar was a jerk, but ultimately, I had the final say."

Ben's eyebrows furrowed as he locked eyes with Ethan. "No, I don't get it. But it's like you're wearing your problems for everyone to see."

Ethan's frustration grew. "I'm just saying, Ben, this is a lot to deal with. It's not easy to pretend like everything is normal."

As Ethan finished speaking, he slammed his dresser shut, searching for a pair of red socks. He didn't need to search for long; Gallium had taken care of his laundry.

He sat down on the edge of his bed to put on his socks, Ben waiting patiently for him to finish.

"You need to try, Ethan. Otherwise, this guilt will consume you."

Now fully dressed in his signature red tunic, Ethan knew there was one thing he could look forward to.

A few hours after Skylar's execution, Liam's call interrupted Ethan's thoughts. The AICI rang twice before Ethan picked up. Liam's voice was a comforting presence on the other end as he inquired about how Ethan was holding up. Liam mentioned he would be visiting Sector 71.

Ethan agreed to let Liam stay at his place and ensured everything was prepared for his guest. However, with the robe induction ceremony just hours away, Ethan knew that everyone would be attending the occasion. Liam had promised to meet him there, and that gave Ethan something to look forward to. The robe induction day held significant importance for every Elite – a day when they were accepted into the community as adults, marking the beginning of their second and final year at the Academy, dedicated to tailoring their Code for their chosen careers.

In each sector, a specific time was set aside for the induction of students. Ethan awaited this day, knowing it would bring a sense of freedom. He had discussed the ceremony with Ben, who had experienced it several times before.

"You should make sure you look your best today. All eyes will be on you. Your parents will be there, and they'll expect you to be at your finest," Ben advised, understanding the significance of the occasion.

Ethan considered it briefly. "I suppose you're right, but I'm not sure if it's necessary. My friend, Liam – the one I mentioned before," Ethan clarified, recalling their previous conversation.

Ben beat his finger against his chin, pretending not to remember him.

"The one you spoke with on my AICI," Ethan explained. Ben nodded. "What about him?"

He already knew about the visit but wanted Ethan to feel he could spill the news. It clearly meant a lot to him that Liam came.

"He will be coming here for the induction ceremony. I have already made space for him." Ethan rambled on.

"That's cool, then. So, we're all set for the ceremony. And about what happened a few days ago – are we ever going to talk about it?" Ben's question struck a chord with Ethan.

He stood for a moment, his gaze shifting towards a reading table beside Ben, adorned with a computer and a stack of books. Deep in thought, Ethan grappled with his emotions. While part of him yearned to discuss the recent events, he also felt the weight of keeping things from his mother. She already had so much on her plate, and he didn't want to burden her with his personal issues.

Aware of the significance of discussing matters of this nature, Ethan grappled with conflicting thoughts. His entire life, he had been told by his mother that he belonged to the Brute Class. Yet, the events of the past few days had shaken that belief. Questions swirled in his mind – *what had truly happened, and why had his mother kept it from him?* The constant hovering and surveillance now seemed to take on a different meaning. Could his mother be hiding something significant?

Despite the urge to seek answers, Ethan's internal struggle intensified. He was aware that Quintella was scheduled for a memory wipe, rendering any conversation about recent events futile. He doubted she would reveal the truth even if he asked.

Ethan scratched his head, a gesture of uncertainty. "I don't think we need to delve into this right now, Ben. It's complicated, and I don't have all the answers at the moment. But I promise I'll figure it out soon."

Sitting on his bed, Ethan's conflicted emotions churned within him. Ben continued to watch him, seemingly eager to press for more information, but Ethan remained silent.

Ben's voice broke the silence, filled with sincerity. "Listen, Ethan, I might not be part of your family, but you know you can count on me. You can talk to me about anything."

Ethan looked at him, appreciating the sentiment. "Because I really do depend on you. It might not be obvious, but with my family gone, you're practically all I've got left. You've been there for me, and I'm grateful."

Gratitude and conflict warred within Ethan. Ben wasn't family, yet he had proven to be a loyal and supportive friend. He contemplated the possibility of trusting Ben in the same way he trusted Liam. Ethan wouldn't have hesitated to confide in Liam if he were present. However, the dilemma was whether he could extend the same trust to Ben. What if Ben reported him or inadvertently shared his secret with others?

Pushing aside these doubts, Ethan shook his head to clear the negative thoughts. Ben had stood by him through their pursuit of justice, proving his loyalty. Despite his own struggles, he had been a good friend. Moreover, Ethan's Code had no connection to Ben's parents' murder. Ben had enough on his plate already; he didn't need more worries in his life.

Ethan reached a resolution. He would trust Ben, just as Ben had trusted him. And in doing so, they might be able to navigate the complexities of their lives together.

"I need to change into my induction robes, but let's continue this conversation after the ceremony," Ethan decided, acknowledging the complexity of the situation. He would reserve his decision until after the induction ceremony, not wanting to drop such a weighty revelation on Ben without being sure he could handle it.

Ben observed Ethan, remaining silent. He understood that trust took time to build, especially after the months he had spent with Ethan's family. He was patient, willing to wait for Ethan to feel comfortable enough to confide in him. After all, Ethan had saved his life – that was proof enough of their bond. Ben put on a headset, immersing himself in music and games on his AICI.

***

Rayvena entered the lab, checking on the progress of the tests she needed. If they weren't ready, she made sure they would be prepared. As she moved further into the lab, she encountered Titus and Pike assembling explosives on a table. Leo and Nyla, shackled nearby, could only watch in concern, unable to warn anyone about the sinister plans of the Libertas group.

Leo couldn't help but voice his sarcasm, "I'm sorry. Why are we here watching this again?"

Rayvena turned her attention to them, wearing a sweet smile. "Hey, little ones. I thought you might want to join us in a little event today. It's your induction day, and we're going to turn it into a party. What do you think?"

Leo's response was laced with defiance, "I think you're a crazy... individual."

Nyla didn't hold back either, blurting out, "Bitch." Rayvena's façade cracked, revealing a stern glare aimed at her.

"I wouldn't jump to conclusions if I were you," Rayvena approached Nyla, her tone serious. She leaned in, her gaze intense. "We're not the villains here – the government is. They've manipulated us into believing we don't have the right to use our Codes. They fear our potential if they allow us to use our abilities freely."

Nyla met Rayvena's gaze fearlessly. She held no fear for her, seeing her as the enemy right in front of her eyes. She wasn't concerned about government manipulation or allegiances.

Leo chimed in with sarcasm, dismissing Rayvena's words. "You sound like a character from a cartoon. Someone filled your head with this nonsense, and you actually bought into it. You're truly as insane as Nyla said." His laughter echoed in the tense air.

Rayvena's attention shifted to the doctor, catching his fleeting expression before he hastily focused on his work. Leo's laughter irked her. She despised him, his demeanor, his words that seemed to mock her. She loathed being provoked.

Her expression darkened, and Leo's laughter faded as they locked eyes with mutual disdain. He thought if only he could break free from those chains, he would never give her another chance. He'd put her in her place. And this lab, he scanned his surroundings, he'd reduce it to ashes. He glared at her, his mind racing for an escape plan, a way to warn others. Sadly, the white chains kept him bound, restricting his every move. He sighed, his gaze shifting away from Rayvena.

Rayvena stormed over to where Titus and Pike were handling explosives. She expressed her frustration at Leo. "I wish you could see the future, Leo. Only then would you understand what we're fighting for. This isn't some amusement for us. We're fighting for a cause, for peace and freedom." Her demeanor shifted as if she were a teacher addressing a classroom, attempting to convince Leo and Nyla.

Leo's response was sharp, laden with skepticism. "And then what? Pangea crowns you as the new leaders?"

Rayvena's tone remained firm. "No, we coexist, sharing knowledge and resources while advancing our Codes, much like our ancestors did centuries ago."

Leo wasn't buying into her ideals. "You're living in a fantasy. We have to sustain the country; we don't have the luxury of indulging in pipe dreams."

Rayvena's persistence clashed with the unwavering skepticism of Leo and Nyla. Their beliefs and convictions were poles apart from her ideology, and there was no way they would ever align with her vision.

"Somebody's got to take the first step, Leo. Join us, and Libertas will shape a brighter tomorrow," Rayvena extended her arms as if to embrace her grand vision.

Leo and Nyla's laughter echoed in the lab. "Oh, sure. Let's all hop on the 'better tomorrow' train," Leo sarcastically quipped.

Rayvena's frustration flared, her patience dwindling. "Put them back in their cells," she ordered, her voice dripping with annoyance.

Leo couldn't resist another jab. "You mean the five-star accommodations over there? So grateful."

Her attention then turned to the doctor. "When you're done here, turn off the lights." Her command was firm and unwavering.

Rayvena couldn't comprehend how they found any of this amusing. As her frustration peaked, she abruptly turned and stormed out of the lab, leaving Leo and Nyla in their restraints.

***

Ethan, Ben, and Kira entered the cavernous hall, capable of seating 2500 people. They maneuvered their way through the rows of chairs, eventually finding an empty space to settle into.

A student showcased her talent on the stage, singing a melodious song that resonated through the hall, capturing everyone's attention. Her performance was met with enthusiastic applause and cheers from the audience.

The master of ceremonies seized the microphone, his voice booming through the hall. "I was searching for the bird that sang so beautifully in this vast hall, but I couldn't find it!" he exclaimed humorously, eliciting chuckles from the attendees.

Laughter filled the hall, the lightheartedness of the moment bringing an air of camaraderie. "Honestly, I thought we had a bird in here. Well, I'll have you know, I have a good voice too," the master of ceremonies proclaimed, raising his voice to sing and producing a sound reminiscent of a dying animal. The students erupted into fits of laughter at his comically awful attempt.

"Now that you've heard how bad my voice is, let's bring out our next speaker! I'd love to invite our principal to give us an opening speech," he announced, setting the stage for the next segment of the ceremony.

A wave of confusion swept through the audience, their puzzled glances exchanged with one another. Normally, it was the Sector Official who delivered the opening speech, not the principal.

Stepping away from the microphone, the master of ceremonies made way for Principal Fairday, who ascended the stage to the sound of light applause.

Ethan retrieved his AICI with the intention of recording the speech, but a tap on his shoulder from the student behind him brought a different perspective. The student informed him that recording wasn't necessary—AI drones were capturing the event, and the recording could be accessed through the school's portal. Ethan quietly stowed his device back on his wrist, deciding to listen instead.

As he surveyed the scene, Ethan noticed that every adult was adorned in sparkling robes, a departure from their everyday attire. He turned his attention to the Officials' section, searching for any sign of his parents. Yet, they remained conspicuously absent from the hall.

Principal Fairday took his place at the podium, standing before the assembly of Elites. "Unfortunately, it seems our Sector Official couldn't join us tonight due to an emergency," he announced, reading from his prompter. "But lucky for all of you, you have me to step in!" he quipped, injecting a touch of lightheartedness into his words.

The audience responded with a light chuckle, their mood shifting to one of attentiveness as Fairday continued. "Each and every one of you should be immensely proud of the dedication and effort you've put into reaching this point. Remember, donning your robe doesn't signify the end of your training," he emphasized, delivering his message with a sense of gravity.

Throughout the crowd, murmurs of agreement and acknowledgment resonated, the adults in attendance expressing their understanding of the ongoing journey ahead.

"And now, we shall recite the Classification mantra as you receive your new robes!" The beat of drums reverberated through the great hall, and the ceremonial music filled the air with an epic aura.

"Pulse Class, start us off!" Principal Fairday's voice boomed through the hall, directing attention to the Pulse Class students.

"See what others cannot!" The Pulse Class students rose to their feet, their voices united as they chanted while making their way down the rows. The mantra resonated through the hall as they collected their robes, donning the electric blue and yellow streaked garments. Jubilant cheers erupted as they proudly displayed their new attire.

"We are nature's right hand!" The Naturalist students followed suit, dancing gracefully down the center aisle. Their voices joined in unison as they chanted the mantra, and a sense of camaraderie filled the air. They eagerly grabbed their dark green and white streaked robes, celebrating with high-fives and cheers.

"Be bound by no space or time!" The Spatial Class students took their turns expressing their unity in their chant. Their gray and white streaked robes symbolized their dedication and prowess. Among the students, Ethan's gaze caught Austin's figure, devoid of the usual enthusiasm. His demeanor seemed distant and detached.

"The fastest pave the way!" The Sprite Class hurried to the center, the urgency of their chant matching their swift movements. They excitedly received their yellow and black-streaked robes, celebrating with a rush of energy.

"To know your enemy, know their mind!" The Psyche Class students descended gracefully, their elegant movements a reflection of their unique abilities. They took their time, each step exuding an air of sophistication. Their purple and gold-streaked robes represented their connection to the mind.

"Sketch the world!" The Sketch Class students clapped in rhythm, their excitement palpable. They proudly accepted their orange terracotta robes, ready to embrace the journey ahead.

Ethan watched as each class received their robes, feeling the energy and pride of the moment enveloping the hall. He couldn't help but reflect on the significance of his own impending induction, a moment he had eagerly anticipated.

Ben and Kira, having already progressed to their second year, watched the ceremony with beaming smiles, joining the cheers from the sidelines to show their support for their fellow students.

Amidst the excitement, Ethan stood up and raised his voice alongside his fellow Brutes, their collective chant ringing through the hall: "The strongest will overcome!" They marched proudly down the aisle, their footsteps echoing in rhythmic unison. Ethan's heart swelled with pride as he reached the center and collected his red velvet robe. The fabric felt more inviting than he had anticipated, symbolizing his journey and growth.

Surrounded by the sea of Elites and the dazzling lights, Ethan couldn't help but feel a mixture of awe and intimidation. However, the sense of community and shared accomplishment swept over him, making him embrace the moment's joy.

As he donned his robe, thoughts of Leo resurfaced in Ethan's mind. Determined to include his friend in the celebration, he grabbed an extra robe and began making his way back to his seat.

Principal Fairday returned to the podium, his tone taking a somber turn. "Amidst the excitement of today, let's pause to reflect on our societal journey," he addressed the audience. "It's a tale as old as time—a history filled with conflicts and strife. The Primordials, driven by their own ambitions, waged war among themselves, ultimately leading Earth to the brink of uninhabitability."

The weight of history hung in the air as Fairday's words reminded everyone of the past's struggles and the importance of their roles as Elites.

Ethan listened intently to Fairday's words, captivated by the unfolding history lesson. The story of their origins never lost its impact; it served as a stark reminder of the past's mistakes and the path they should avoid treading.

"Their relentless pursuit of power and progress compelled nations to accelerate their technological advancements," Fairday continued, his voice carrying the weight of history's lessons.

"And as you all know, a devastating plague emerged, claiming the lives of countless Primordials across the globe." A heavy silence blanketed the great hall, and Ethan's heartbeat seemed to echo in the quietude.

"Those who survived were left as a diminished version of what we now are—Elites. Eventually, the last remnants of the Primordials succumbed to the illness." "The salvation of Earth demanded the merging of its continents, giving rise to the Pangea we inhabit today." The audience erupted into applause and cheers, but Fairday's stern gesture quieted them.

"Primordials exemplified weakness and selfishness. Their choices left us with the lifelong responsibility of preserving Pangea's integrity," Fairday declared, his voice resonating with a mix of frustration and resolve.

"They prioritized personal agendas and greed over global welfare, forsaking unity for their own interests. Their actions were repugnant," he spat.

"But now, we know better! United as one nation, one people, we transcend the faults of our predecessors. We are the Elites!"

The hall roared with applause and cheers, a fervor that even Ethan couldn't resist feeling deep within himself.

"You've taken another step towards upholding our great nation," Fairday proclaimed, his words brimming with pride. "I implore you all to give your absolute best!" With a final bow, Principal Fairday concluded his speech, leaving an atmosphere charged with inspiration and determination among the assembled Elites.

The hall erupted into a standing ovation, and Ethan rose to his feet, joining the thunderous applause. As the applause gradually subsided, everyone settled back into their seats, fueled by a renewed sense of excitement and purpose.

Seated among his fellow Brutes, Ethan scanned the expansive crowd for any sign of Ben and Kira, but the sea of faces made it challenging to spot them with clarity.

However, the atmosphere took an unexpected turn as Principal Fairday continued speaking, veering away from the expected discourse. A hushed calm swept over the hall, and all attention was fixated on Fairday, his words resonating deeply within the listeners.

"I must confess, my aspirations extended beyond the role of a principal," he mused, capturing the audience's intrigue. Fairday had a magnetic quality to his speeches that compelled everyone to listen.

"We discuss the pursuit of improvement, but do we genuinely strive for it? Are we bound to our jobs, working until death, without the chance to aspire for something more? Is that equitable?" Fairday's words hung in the air, his thoughts an unexpected tangent from the ceremony's usual tone.

Confusion rippled through the crowd, uncertainty etched on their faces as they tried to decipher Fairday's sudden shift in focus.

"We are destined for greater horizons! Our students possess an untapped potential that we have barely begun to explore!" Fairday's voice swelled with passion, capturing the attention of everyone present.

"The Creator, from whom we received our divine Codes, deserves our gratitude for her blessings upon us. It is her wish that I strive to liberate our newly adorned students from the oppressive grip of our society." Fairday's gaze swept across the room, his words ringing with a sense of revelation.

"I apologize for the abrupt manner in which I've chosen to convey this," he added, his head bowed in what appeared to be a mixture of contrition and shame.

Professor Carson's eyes widened as realization dawned upon him. A wave of understanding swept through him—the phrase "the Creator" was a hallmark of the Libertas group's rhetoric. A sense of unease settled over the hall as they grappled with the implications of Fairday's cryptic words.

He sprang into action, shouting urgently, "We all need to leave now!" His words reverberated in the tense air, resonating like a clarion call to action. The abruptness of his demand jolted the attendees from their initial shock.

Before anyone could react, the imposing doors of the hall shattered, the forceful entry of the Libertas group ripping apart the veneer of normalcy. Unbeknownst to the assembly, Principal Fairday had been masquerading within the very group now infiltrating the ceremony.

Pandemonium erupted within the hall. Chaos reigned as students, parents, and even staff scrambled for the three available exits, driven by sheer panic. The members of Libertas streamed in, their purpose resolute and ominous. Amid the turmoil, students stumbled and fell, trampled by the frenzied stampede.

Ethan fought his way through the tumultuous mass, determined to reach the nearest exit. However, his steps faltered when he spotted Professor Carson amid the commotion. He reversed course, determination overriding self-preservation, and pushed back against the crowd, making his way toward the professor.

Despite the urgency of the situation, some students resentfully shoved past Ethan, irate at his perceived obstruction. Yet, he was resolute, unwavering in his mission to reach Professor Carson.

Meanwhile, the sinister members of Libertas unleashed their Code, rendering those they captured immobile with restraining breaker chains. With a surge of energy, they blinked out of sight, taking their captives along.

The professors raised their voices, rallying the students to heed their counsel. "Stay together! Do not engage! Evacuate now, or you'll fall into their grasp!" Their authoritative voices carried a sense of urgency that resonated even amidst the chaos.

The assembly, sensing the gravity of the situation, began to heed the professors' instructions. Students clung to their parents, weaving a cohesive stream toward the exits. Yet, the Libertas members, driven by a malevolent determination, pressed on, attempting to overpower the staff who stood between them and their objectives.

"Professor Carson!" Ethan's voice rang out above the cacophony, directed at the beleaguered teacher. His gaze was locked on the professor as he expertly navigated the chaotic fray, ignoring the clamor for escape that engulfed him.

Carson turned, locking eyes with the determined student who refused to abandon him. A fleeting expression of gratitude crossed his face, an acknowledgment that his sacrifice did not go unnoticed.

As Ethan's feet pounded against the floor, he was joined by Felix, who had decided to stand beside him in the face of adversity. A surge of camaraderie infused Ethan's resolve. "What do we do now? It seems like we're surrounded," Felix uttered, his voice laced with a mixture of anxiety and determination.

With a steely gaze, Ethan replied, "Every time I run from trouble, I end up facing even more of it. This time, I'm confronting my problems head-on."

Felix's lips curved into a sardonic smile. "How admirable," he quipped, a wry comment that masked his own determination to stand firm in the face of danger.

Amid the tense standoff, Professor Carson's voice cut through the chaos, an anchor of reason amidst the storm. "Using our Codes in this confined space could lead to unintended casualties. We must exercise caution," he shouted, his words carrying a sense of urgency.

Brute students, embodying their class's unwavering spirit, rallied around their professor, forming a defensive circle. On the opposing side, the Libertas members stood with Fairday, forming a stark divide within the hall.

Fairday's voice resounded, a haunting echo that briefly silenced the turmoil. His words, an offer of freedom tinged with a sinister allure, hung in the air, momentarily freezing the scene.

Then, from within the defiant crowd of Brutes, a student surged forward, their hands clapped together in a thunderous clap. The shockwave shattered the stillness, sending Fairday hurtling into a group of unsuspecting Libertas members. The impact was swift and chaotic, with bodies crashing into walls and cascading to the floor.

The great hall erupted with a cacophony of screams and cries as students scrambled to aid their fallen peers. The swift and brutal consequences of their actions became painfully clear – for each act of defiance, a swift and ruthless reprisal was exacted.

The sight of fellow students being restrained by the Libertas members struck a collective chord of fear. The prospect of using their Codes within this volatile environment, where even the slightest miscalculation could result in tragedy, weighed heavily on their minds. The balance between survival and harm had never been so precarious.

Compounding the dilemma was the uncertainty surrounding the consequences of their actions. The absence of established guidelines for such a situation added an additional layer of complexity. The taboo of Elites intentionally causing harm to each other loomed like a specter, a potential death sentence for those who defied it.

As the aftermath of the attack unfolded, the Libertas group reacted with heightened aggression. Provoked by the assault on Fairday, they surged forward, activating their Codes with swift precision. Once filled with the optimism of a joyous occasion, the hall was now consumed by the ominous dance of energy, the clash of powers leaving an indelible mark on this fateful day.

"Don't kill any of them! We're doing this peacefully!" Principal Fairday's plea reverberated through the hall, a desperate attempt to halt the violence that had erupted. The Libertas members heeded his words, immediately ceasing their use of Codes. Their intended approach shifted from aggression to capturing, from force to persuasion.

"Keep them alive and willing," one of the Libertas members murmured, lending a sense of eerie intention to their actions. Assisting Fairday to his feet, they began to withdraw, leaving a turbulent sea of panicked students in their wake. The realization that their lives were spared, though not their freedom, ignited a frenzied scramble toward the exit doors.

The chaos was palpable, a tangible force propelling Ethan and his fellow students forward. Gripping the spare robe in his hand, Ethan felt a renewed surge of determination. But amidst the chaos, a voice of reason emerged – Professor Carson. He valiantly faced the oncoming threat, using his Code to create space for his students to escape.

"Go, I'll hold them off!" Carson's command echoed above the fray. He dispatched several Libertas members with swift and calculated claps, creating a brief respite. Ethan hesitated, torn between his loyalty to his professor and the desperate need to flee. Carson propelled Ethan and the others forward with a final, urging shout, their path cleared by his selfless actions.

Despite the urgency, Ethan's gaze scanned the chaos, seeking his friend Ben. He spotted him in his orange robe, a beacon of familiarity in the tumult. Ben's wave signaled Ethan to join him, an offer of safety in the midst of uncertainty. A conflict raged within Ethan – the desire to stay and fight alongside his professor and the impulse to prioritize his own survival.

"Go now!" Carson's voice boomed, a mix of authority and urgency. It was a gut-wrenching decision, but the sight of his disabled professor incapacitated by the very enemies they were facing left Ethan with no choice. He pivoted on his heel, navigating the crowd with determination. The echoes of clashing Codes, panicked cries, and shoving bodies faded into the background as he focused on reaching Ben.

As he finally squeezed in next to Ben, Ethan felt a mixture of relief and guilt. He had left his professor behind, but survival now seemed paramount. The weight of their situation bore down on him as he glanced back once, his heart heavy with the image of Professor Carson battling valiantly against impossible odds.

Ben's firm grip on Ethan's wrist yanked him out of his momentary hesitation. Amidst the chaotic stream of panicked individuals, Ben's urgency propelled them forward through the tide of people desperately seeking safety.

Ethan's concern for Kira's well-being paused his steps. He glanced around, his heart pounding as he scanned the crowd for a glimpse of her. The pressing urgency to escape tugged at him, but his worry for their friend held him in place.

Ben tugged at his arm again, his voice raised in frustration, "Ethan, we can't help her now! We need to get out of here!" The urgency in Ben's voice penetrated Ethan's concern, snapping him back to the reality of their dire situation. With one final glance over his shoulder, Ethan allowed Ben to guide him through the chaotic sea of bodies.

***

Meanwhile, in the room where Leo and Nyla were imprisoned, Rayvena returned with a different demeanor – somber, almost regretful. Three men accompanied her as she entered the dimly lit space. Leo and Nyla, shackled by chains, stirred at the sound of her entrance.

As the lights flickered on, Rayvena spoke in a tone that seemed oddly detached, "My friends, I've made attempts to recruit you, but it seems that won't work out. You've been reassigned to the Gene Pool."

Nyla's curiosity prompted her to sit up, her chains clinking softly. Leo rubbed his eyes, adjusting to the sudden brightness as he tried to comprehend the situation. Pike, one of the men with Rayvena, turned on the lights, illuminating the space.

Leo's confusion gave way to anxiety, "Gene Pool? What's that supposed to mean? There's more to this place?" He squinted, trying to make sense of Rayvena's words.

Rayvena's violet hair cascaded as she approached, her expression carrying an air of resignation. "Not here, no," she began to explain. "But my role was to gather DNA samples, run tests, and assess potential recruits for Libertas. Yet, my efforts to convince you have been futile. The higher-ups have decided you're beyond my influence."

She raised her hands in a gesture of surrender as if distancing herself from their fate. Leo and Nyla pressed themselves against the wall, their chains clinking as they moved. Leo's anxiety escalated, prompting Nyla to intervene, her touch offering a grounding comfort.

Rayvena's tone turned almost mocking, "Cute, that fighting spirit of yours. I hope you keep it up."

Her gaze locked onto them as she delivered the final blow, "The Gene Pool is where the months of testing finally find their purpose."

Rayvena lowered herself, her eyes meeting Nyla and Leo's on the cold floor. "Needless to say, you're going to die there. So, this is farewell." Her words hung heavy in the dimly lit room, plunging Nyla's heart into darkness while deflating Leo's last flicker of hope.

Leo had been scheming, strategizing for an opportunity to escape, but learning that they were merely on the brink of a worse fate shattered his resolve. Months of enduring painful tests and experiments in this small lab room now felt like an exercise in futility. He chastised himself for not being more proactive, for failing to piece together the puzzle they were trapped in.

Chains clinking as they were reorganized around them, Nyla and Leo exchanged a final, pained glance, acknowledging the gravity of their predicament. Rayvena's intent gaze communicated a purpose that chilled them to the core, and soon, her command plunged them into an unnatural slumber.

Nyla and Leo's last conscious moments were filled with a sense of despair and resentment. They felt betrayed and abandoned by the world they once knew. Their fight against the unknown had taken a bitter turn, their courage standing powerless against the overwhelming force of their captors.

Rayvena turned her attention to the men accompanying her, her resolve unwavering. "You're really okay with doing this to kids?" Leo's voice, laced with bitterness, broke the silence.

Rayvena pivoted, her eyes locking onto Leo's defiant stare. Her response dripped with an unyielding determination, "If this gets me one step closer to avenging my father, then so be it."

A harsh chuckle escaped Leo's lips as he spat on the floor, his gaze never wavering from Rayvena's. She turned away, her attention shifting to Titus and Pike, her cold demeanor overshadowed by her drive.

"Prepare them and the others at this facility for transport," she ordered. The men nodded, moving forward to secure Nyla and Leo. Desperation fueled Leo's struggle as he kicked, spat, and fought against his restraints. Rayvena's eyes flared with a vibrant purple, and without delay, she unleashed her Code to immobilize him, casting a shroud of darkness over their fates.

"Go to sleep," Rayvena's command resonated in the dimly lit room.

Nyla and Leo's resistance faded as they slumped down onto the cold floor, their will to fight against the impending fate stifled by the tendrils of unconsciousness.

Despite her momentary pang of remorse, Rayvena swiftly brushed it aside. She didn't truly feel bad for them—sympathy was an emotion she had learned to suppress. And perhaps that was why, in a twisted way, she felt a modicum of satisfaction knowing that Nyla and Leo wouldn't be left to face their grim destiny alone.

Throughout the past few months, Rayvena had overseen various test groups isolated from one another. But Nyla and Leo were different; they had each other, forming a unique connection that Rayvena found intriguing. The boss had deemed each group an experiment with their own distinct purpose. Rayvena wasn't privy to the full scope of these experiments, but she knew the results were meant to contribute to the future betterment of Pangea.

When she had pledged her loyalty to the enigmatic Libertas, it hadn't taken long for her to ascend in rank. Her prowess with her Code set her apart, and she had become a prodigy in her own right. Despite her advancement, she harbored reservations about the true intentions of the group, often finding the spiritual aspect of Libertas convoluted.

Her motives weren't rooted in blind faith; rather, she was driven by personal goals and ambitions. Her alliance with Libertas was a means to an end, a pathway to freedom that resonated with her objectives. Ironically, this pursuit of freedom led her to lead one of the specialized test groups, sparing her from the confines of the group's sanctuary.

However, her position came with a condition—Kira was off-limits. A simple stipulation, Rayvena believed, but one that was complicated by Kira's friendship with Benjamin Valdez. The complexity of this situation wasn't lost on Rayvena, but her determination remained steadfast.

As events unfolded, Kira found an ally in Ethan, a fact that Rayvena couldn't dismiss. The dynamics were shifting, the pieces of a larger puzzle falling into place, and Rayvena found herself entangled in a web of allegiances and uncertainties.

Ethan Crambe. Rayvena couldn't help but chuckle to herself. In her estimation, he was perhaps the safest Elite to be around. Naive, foolishly poking his head into matters he had no understanding of. His involvement had amounted to nothing—no impact, no change to their intricate plans. He continued to meddle, oblivious to the grand scheme he was disrupting. If only he would accept that Leonitas was lost to them by now.

Rayvena surveyed the lab around her, a sense of purpose driving her actions. Phase One had been executed successfully; there would be no need to abduct more students for a while after this night. Perhaps Leo and Nyla would find camaraderie in their shared suffering. They could face the torment together, holding hands, united in their agony.

But Leonitas and Nyla had proven to be poor candidates for Libertas. They steadfastly refused to embrace the cause, a fact that vexed Rayvena to no end. Their stubbornness only intensified her animosity towards them. They had the audacity to complain about the pain she had inflicted upon them. Little did they know, their suffering was a mere shadow compared to what awaited them if they encountered her boss—the overseer of the Gene Pool.

The thought of speaking to him sent shivers down Rayvena's spine. He was an enigma, a figure both feared and revered within the organization. Perhaps, in the confines of the Gene Pool, Leonitas and Nyla would come to understand the gravity of their decisions. Perhaps they would realize the truth they had willfully ignored— that listening to Rayvena had been their only chance for salvation.

***

Ethan and Ben sprinted towards the school's entrance, a sea of chaos engulfing them. The air was thick with screams, a cacophony of panic and desperation. Fights broke out amidst the chaos as parents clung to their children, holding them tightly in fear.

Ethan wiped the sweat from his palms, his hand tightly gripped by Ben's. Together, they navigated the pandemonium, ensuring they wouldn't lose each other in the tumult. Ben's guidance was a lifeline in the swirling turmoil.

"Stay close, Ethan," Ben shouted over the clamor. "The stairs are just ahead."

They pushed through the surging crowd, navigating the maze of bodies, desperate to reach the safety of the staircase that would lead them away from this nightmare. The collective urgency drove them forward, an instinctual need to escape the clutches of those who sought to capture them.

Finally, Ethan and Ben reached the edge of the platform where the steps connected to the Academy. The scene was chaotic, with some individuals falling off the side in their desperate attempts to escape. Good Samaritans who tried to assist others often found themselves in precarious situations.

Ethan and Ben joined the throngs of students racing down the staircase, their urgency palpable. The staircase, appearing only when in use, lacked railings. This absence proved perilous as those unfortunate enough to be too close to the edge tumbled off, their screams mingling with the wind.

The precariousness of their position hit Ethan hard as he teetered on the edge. A sudden push sent him off balance, and he found himself on the verge of falling. Desperation fueled his arm as he reached out, his fingers brushing someone else's hand. It was a lifeline that pulled him back onto the steps, sparing him a terrifying fall.

"Now isn't the time for dying, Crambe!" Felix's voice was both stern and relieved, his grip firm. Ethan's gratitude was evident in his voice, "Thank you! I thought that was it for me." "Don't think I'd let you go that easily," Felix retorted with a hint of humor, trying to bring some levity to the dire situation. "Seriously, Felix, thank you," Ethan managed, bracing himself against the continuous push of the crowd. Ben rushed ahead, leading the way down the steps.

Ethan's heart finally settled back into his chest as they reached the bottom of the stairs. He regretted losing Leo's robe but was grateful for his own safety. Ben led the way, running further into a spreading valley of trees in the area.

"Where are you going? The safest option is to stick with the groups!" Felix pointed to the left.

Ethan had decided to follow Ben, no matter where he led. He was well aware that Libertas was likely on the hunt for him amid the chaos.

"We'll be fine! Go get help for the others!" Ethan shouted back to Felix, urging him to go. Felix shook his head, "Your choice! Just watch out!" With that, Felix turned and joined the flow of Elites heading toward the streets of Sector 71.

Ethan took a moment to assess their surroundings. They found themselves in a seemingly secure area near a lake, providing a momentary respite. Other students had fled to the streets seeking assistance, leaving Ethan and Ben alone for now.

A loud crack resonated through the air, and the staircase leading to the Academy began to flicker and vanish. In an instant, the steps disappeared completely, leaving those who had been on them falling several feet below. Without the staircase, those inside the Academy were now trapped, forced to navigate the chaos on their own. Students who had paused at the top of the stairs struggled to keep their footing, and some were pushed forward and off the edge.

"What the hell is going on? What are we supposed to do now?" Ethan's head was spinning, and he leaned against a tree for support. The situation was overwhelming—his parents' absence, the sudden revelation about their principal, and the current crisis.

Ben was also panting, catching his breath as he waved at Ethan. "We need to talk. Please, I can't go on like this."

Ethan, still catching his breath, gave Ben a puzzled look. "What do you mean, Ben?"

Ben's face grew serious, and he took a deep breath before continuing. "I'm not your Ben. You're not my friend, Ethan. So stop pretending you are!"

Ethan was taken aback, his confusion evident in his expression. He leaned off the tree, his tone serious. "Ben, we don't have time for games. Are you kidding me right now?"

Ben slid down a tree, settling onto the grass and gazing out at the tranquil, crystal-blue lake. He remained silent, closing his eyes as he focused on his breathing, attempting to regain his composure. After a moment, he opened his eyes and met Ethan's gaze.

"I'm sorry for yelling. Everything is just... so confusing," Ben said, his voice strained.

Ethan's concern deepened. "Are you hurt? Tell me what's going on, Ben." He kept a watchful eye on their surroundings, fully aware of the chaos still unfolding around them.

"I need to go back to my own timeline, Ethan," Ben exclaimed, a note of pain in his voice as he clutched his head.

Ethan turned his attention back to Ben, his expression a mix of disbelief and worry. He tried to process what he had just heard. "What did you just say?"

With his fingers pinching the bridge of his nose, Ben let out a pained sigh and massaged his temples. The distress on his face was evident as he continued, "I said I need to go back to my own timeline. To the future, specifically."

Chapter 31:
The World Summit

As the events unfolded at the Academy in Sector 71, every Sector Official had been summoned to a secret location through spatial portals. This location remained unknown to all within Pangea, including the Sector Officials themselves, as their duties required them to relinquish the knowledge of its secrets.

Impatiently, Quintella Crambe stepped out of her portal and entered an expansive jungle. The sight of the lush greenery stretching out seemingly endlessly was captivating, and she could spot her destination in the distance. While she had initially been supposed to attend her son's induction ceremony, an emergency meeting had been called, compelling her to miss the significant event. Skipping a summons was out of the question, regardless of the circumstances.

Surveying her surroundings, Quintella noticed towering structures made of silver and gold, along with castle-like buildings seamlessly integrated into the forest. The melodious chirping of birds echoed through the air, creating a harmonious symphony that surrounded her. The heat of the environment pressed against her purple robes, the fabric brushing against the dark, grassy soil as she walked with a sense of wonder towards the massive Citadel gate that lay ahead. A figure awaited her arrival.

"Welcome to the restricted sector, The Amazonian Citadel," the AI greeted, bowing respectfully.

Quintella glanced down at her AICI interface, which was glowing in red hues. "This doesn't resemble the restricted sector at all. I've been there before," she mused, her head tilting in curiosity. "Why have I been summoned here?"

The AI responded, gesturing towards the AICI on Quintella's wrist. "I advise against relying on that. In this sector, you're no longer within the bounds of Pangea. All communication, including your AI, Gallium, has been jammed."

The AI directed Quintella toward the entrance, and she walked through the gate. Alongside the AI, she proceeded along a white-bricked pathway that was adorned with shrubbery and teeming with wildlife. The environment felt like an entirely new world full of wonders. The area was a hive of construction activity, with AI drones whizzing around her, transporting machinery and equipment to various locations within the forest. The symphony of noises, including the chattering of monkeys, intrigued Quintella, adding to her sense of amusement.

As they walked, Quintella turned her attention to the AI. "I have a few questions if you don't mind," she began.

The AI responded with a static-filled voice and a red interface. Its design lacked humanoid features, and it seemed unfazed by her queries. "Perhaps one question won't cause any trouble," it replied.

Quintella's curiosity was insatiable, a common trait among the Psyche. She pressed on with her inquiries. "If this is our first time being summoned to the restricted sector, where exactly are we? This place is entirely unfamiliar to me."

The AI's response carried a hint of hesitation despite its otherwise composed demeanor. "The restricted sector cannot be accessed by conventional means. It's part of the land that has been kept secret and untouched on Earth, reserved for a specific purpose."

Quintella raised an eyebrow, slightly baffled. "But I've been to the restricted sector before, and this isn't it."

The AI's voice remained static, but its tone became more assertive. "I've answered one question, as promised."

Quintella huffed in response. "Technically, I never asked a second question," she retorted, her determination unwavering as they continued towards their destination.

They eventually entered a grand hall through the main door. Tan pillars adorned the hall, and a pattern of blue designs spread across the checkered marble floor. Above, golden chandeliers with diamond-studded candle holders cast a glimmering light upon the scene.

The grandeur of the surroundings was undeniable, but Quintella found herself puzzled by the opulence displayed in such a remote location.

As she followed the AI through the hall, she began to recognize familiar faces. Damien Caldwell from Sector 45, the Industrial Sector, caught her attention. He was deeply engrossed in tinkering with his AICI device, his Azure blue Pulse robes bearing oil stains— a common sight among inventive Pulse Class Elites.

Quintella contemplated stopping to talk to Damien as she had some questions for him. However, she decided against it, realizing he appeared to be preoccupied. Continuing her stroll, she noticed someone in her line of sight who stirred unpleasant emotions within her.

Zola, a representative from Sector 87—the Adult Entertainment Sector—was a figure that Quintella loathed. Despite being well into her sixties, Zola somehow managed to maintain a youthful appearance akin to someone in her twenties. This defied the common side effects of de-aging that most individuals experienced. Quintella acknowledged Zola with a curt nod, to which the woman responded with a dismissive huff before moving away. Quintella's envy was palpable as she absentmindedly ran her fingers through her own hair.

Suddenly, the AI came to a halt, interrupting Quintella's thoughts. "With you, everyone is now here," it stated before promptly depixelating.

Quintella looked around the room, spotting Richard among the crowd. Their eyes met, and he nodded in her direction. Clearly, he was fully engaged in work mode. It became apparent that all one hundred Sector Officials had been summoned to this enigmatic location.

The tolling of a bell reverberated through the Citadel, quelling the confusion that had filled the room. As the grand hall hushed, a door situated further in the back swung open, revealing seven fully-robed Elites with hoods. Each robe bore a distinct color representing their classification, and they marched forward in a disciplined line, advancing toward the gathering of Sector Officials. Their faces remained hidden beneath their hoods, yet their identities were well known to everyone present.

Beside Quintella, a fellow Sector Official muttered, "Oh no, we've never had to meet them in person." Quintella fixed her gaze ahead, her anxiety growing. This unexpected turn of events caught them all off guard. None of the Sector Officials had anticipated this meeting; they had merely assembled for what they believed was an emergency gathering.

The seven enigmatic figures continued their deliberate descent down the grand hall, the tolling bell resonating in the air and amplifying the weight of the moment.

Amidst the uncertainty, Quintella whispered frantically, "Is there a protocol for this? What are we supposed to do?"

Pierre Loveless, a particularly young Sector Official known for his prodigious intellect, took it upon himself to respond. At just twenty-five years old, his selection had raised eyebrows due to his age. However, he was determined not to be overshadowed by his more seasoned colleagues. Clearing his throat, he asserted, "I think we just kneel."

Doubtful murmurs rippled through the crowd. "Are you sure?" someone questioned.

Pierre's confidence remained unwavering. "I dunno, it's just what I heard."

Quintella's skepticism surfaced as she retorted, "Who would have told you that? We all know our memories are wiped at the end of our term."

A nearby voice chimed in, "If he's not certain either, why are you challenging him?"

Quintella shot a glare in the direction of the voice, but before she could respond, the seven robed Elites finally reached their destination. The incessant tolling of the bell finally ceased, plunging the hall into an expectant silence.

Quintella's realization struck like a bolt of lightning as the murmured word "kneel" rippled through the crowd, guiding them all into action. The leaders of each sector, herself included, promptly lowered themselves to the ground, assuming a posture of reverence with one knee touching the floor.

Seven figures, draped in hooded robes, stood before them—one for each classification. Each of the robed members nodded approvingly as the Sector officials knelt.

The Pulse Class Elite among them took the lead, his voice resonating through the grand hall. "We summoned you here today to discuss the future of Pangea," he declared with authority. "Unrest is brewing within our domain, courtesy of a cult known as Libertas. They aim to disrupt the very foundation upon which we've built our society."

With the signal to rise, the Sector officials returned to their feet while AI units provided chairs, and the officials began seating themselves, adjusting their glittering robes that signified their classifications. Amid the rustling and settling, a dissenting voice arose. "We're powerless against them if we don't even know who they are! Why are you intervening only now?"

Quintella had a strong inkling that it was the representative from Sector 10, known for his brashness. The Pulse hooded figure Axel raised his hand in response to the question, immediately silencing the room.

"We have much to discuss, and I trust I need not remind you that we could incapacitate you and have you replaced before your bodies even hit the floor." The chilling words hung in the air, casting an undeniable weight upon the gathering. "By the way, you may address me as Axel."

A shift in tone occurred as Axel continued. "Now, we've maintained a symbiotic relationship, haven't we? The World Government takes care of the everyday concerns of Pangea, while the Brain Trust observes and provides the necessary support for the citizens." The sweetness in his voice belied an underlying venomous edge. "It appears, however, that some of you may have momentarily overlooked the instructions that were given to you at the inception of your appointments."

Axel's calm demeanor only accentuated his passive-aggressive delivery, creating an atmosphere of unease among the assembled officials.

"We've devoted our efforts to creating, constructing, and ensuring that everything you require is readily available," Axel's voice carried through the hall. Although obscured by his hood, his gaze swept over each official present. "But let's not forget—we're the silent hand that ensures you all don't stumble. Think of us as a gentle nudge in the right direction." His tone retained its composure despite the underlying gravity of his words.

Tension tightened the air as everyone awaited the revelation of his next words. The weight of anticipation hung palpably in the atmosphere. "We've been observing—" He paused, casting a piercing look at each official in turn. "And quite frankly, we're underwhelmed." Though his voice remained even, a simmering anger surfaced beneath the surface.

Eyes darted toward the AI, suddenly recognizing that they still lingered among them. Axel's calm demeanor persisted, and he chuckled with satisfaction. "Ah, yes, the AI. But you should know that the AI on this island serves a different purpose than those on Pangea." His amusement seemed to grow. "While they're indeed designed to make your lives more convenient, their secondary role entails monitoring behavior on our behalf." He held the room's attention, his final words lingering with an eerie resonance.

Nervous glances were exchanged among the officials, realization dawning on them. The revelation of the AI's additional function was unsettling, and Quintella herself felt a tinge of discomfort. Had she ever mentioned her plan to Glade on her AICI? She struggled to recall.

One official mustered the courage to ask, "Sir, aren't AI meant to handle non-essential tasks so that we can focus on upholding our country?"

"Indeed," Axel affirmed, his enthusiasm apparent. "If we cease our labor, we're doomed. Hence, those who refuse to contribute must face the consequences. And that, my friends, leads me to my next point." The air grew heavier, his tone carrying a note of seriousness. "Over the past five months, six hundred and thirty Academic students have gone missing, while the Guardians have remained inactive." Axel's once steady tone now dripped with discontent.

Chaos erupted in the room as officials scrambled to present their explanations and defenses. Axel raised his hand again, quelling the tumult into silence. "If these disturbances aren't suppressed, the citizens might dare to think they possess a choice," he declared, his tone stern. "Should they halt their labor, our collective fate would be sealed. And thus, this so-called 'cult' is now our adversary."

"We recognize that our methods have earned your displeasure," Axel continued, a self-assured edge coloring his words. "However, rest assured, the execution of non-contributing citizens remains a crucial facet of our strategy. Every individual must fulfill their role."

As Axel strode closer to the assembly, the remaining six hooded figures remained stationary, a silent presence of authority.

"With this new edict," he went on, "we beseech you to return to your sectors. Any affiliation with this cult warrants instant execution upon identification." He folded his hands, satisfaction evident on his features.

At that moment, Richard Crambe stood up, his voice steady with resolve. "Pardon me, sir! Our predecessors, those who occupied this position before us, have upheld the principles of peace, stability, and prosperity—principles ingrained in our creed." He wiped his palms against his glittering red robes. "Or at least, that's the assumption, given our memories are erased."

"Yet our primary responsibilities encompass maintaining peace, enforcing laws with minimal violence, ensuring citizens work after their academy graduation, and fostering prosperity despite geographical constraints," Richard continued, his voice gaining strength.

Quintella observed in admiration as her husband confronted the leadership with unwavering determination. "Cut to the chase," Axel interjected impatiently.

Richard took a deep breath. "The course of action you're proposing would sow fear and turmoil among the populace. Are you suggesting we reveal the truth and rely on fear to control them? Such an approach contradicts the very essence of our mission." His voice echoed with conviction. "And can we truly justify the execution of our citizens based on their religious beliefs?" His last words were spoken more softly, laden with moral concern.

Another hooded figure, distinguishable by the orange Sketch robes, stepped forward, moving down the hall until he stood a few feet away from Richard. The darkness within his hood obscured his face from Richard's view.

"Richard Crambe, the Brute scientist," the Sketch-robed man addressed, his tone carrying a subtle intention to humiliate. The intended effect was achieved as Richard bowed and returned to his seat, his face turning crimson as he glared straight ahead—an unusual sight indeed. Axel retraced his steps, returning to his fellow members.

"No, we will not condone the execution of our citizens based on their beliefs, no matter how outdated those beliefs may be," the Sketch-robed individual declared, his voice intense yet tinged with a gentle edge. "However, we cannot afford to have them aligning themselves with a radical group of Elites who believe that overthrowing the government is the answer to their grievances."

The red-faced AI that had accompanied Quintella reappeared beside the Sketch-robed figure. "The Libertas group emerged during an Academy induction ceremony in Sector 71."

Quintella and Richard both stood up in alarm. "What happened?" they exclaimed in unison. Ethan's academy was located in Sector 71, and their anxiety spiked at the mention of the incident.

"It seems that nearly three hundred students were abducted, and the Academy itself was destroyed," the AI reported.

Quintella's breath caught in her throat, her heart racing. Richard responded with unwavering composure, "May I be excused to address this situation?"

"No. According to protocol, Sector 71's Chief Guardian will handle the matter. Our proceedings will continue here," the Sketch-robed figure replied.

Despite her personal concerns, Quintella knew her responsibility lay with the citizens of Pangea. She couldn't leave even if she wished to. She could only endure in silence as the meeting resumed.

***

Ethan and Ben stood at the tree line in the forest, their expressions reflecting disbelief. "It's impossible. I've been with you this whole time. I would've known if you weren't you," Ethan protested, struggling to accept what he was hearing—it was all too overwhelming.

Ben appeared drained, his exhaustion palpable. "I still exist here. In fact, I'm up there in the academy right now, likely with Kira."

"Wait a minute," Ethan interjected, piecing things together. "You were the one who brought me to Kira after I was attacked by Skylar at the academy entrance."

"But that's not why I'm telling you this."

Ben nodded, his eyes locking onto Ethan's. "I need you to understand that what I'm about to say is of utmost importance. Listen carefully, Ethan."

Ben appeared considerably tired and sickly, a fact that didn't escape Ethan's notice. "So time travel is possible? What are the risks involved?" Ethan inquired, his curiosity piqued.

Ben absentmindedly toyed with the grass beneath him. "Insanity... I now understand why it's such a challenging feat. I've been struggling to maintain control over my Code," he admitted. He lowered his voice, adding, "I'm starting to lose my grip on what's real and what isn't."

Pausing, Ben seemed to recall something important. "Two individuals can exist on the same timeline, but the longer you stay, the more strain it puts on your mind. It's like stretching a rubber band—it snaps eventually." His words seemed almost rehearsed, as though he was repeating information he had memorized.

Ethan's memory stirred a recollection from months ago surfacing. It could corroborate what Ben was saying, but right now, he had the perfect opportunity to ask the questions he had been wanting to ask. He knelt down to Ben's eye level, determination in his gaze. "Tell me. What's my next move? Where's Leo? Why did you come back?"

Tears welled in Ben's eyes. "I just wanted answers. I didn't anticipate making things worse," he confessed, his voice cracking. Ethan pressed for more, leaning in. Ben's whispered words entered his ear, causing Ethan to recoil involuntarily, falling backward.

"I can't comprehend this. It's all wrong! None of this should even be possible!" Ethan exclaimed, shaking his head in disbelief. He refused to fully acknowledge the truth, even though Ben had confirmed the memory Ethan had questioned. Glancing at Ben with a mix of pity and disappointment, Ethan demanded, "Why are you still here?"

Ben's eyes pleaded with Ethan, though he didn't speak aloud what he had shared. The implications were too overwhelming. "I don't know how to return. I've been trapped here all this time. I thought maybe you could help me," he admitted, his sobs flowing like a burst dam. Ethan stood up, observing Ben with a complex mixture of pity and slight disappointment.

"I've made a mess of things. My goal was to retrieve the necklace, but I arrived too late," Ben explained with a heavy sigh.

"Ben, I don't know if I can keep this secret. How could you have done this?" Ethan's voice held a mix of frustration and anguish.

Ben's breathing steadied as he gazed at Ethan, his eyes filled with pleading desperation. "Imagine the consequences if you revealed this to anyone. No one would believe you, and you'd risk execution just for mentioning it," he implored, wincing and coughing weakly.

"Ethan, please, it's difficult enough to think. Let me finish," Ben pleaded, sniffling and wiping his nose. "Leo is in a laboratory in Sector twenty-five. But you can't go, Ethan. The others don't know this yet, but I do. You're not a Brute Class Elite." Ethan's gaze dropped, his internal question answered by Ben's words.

"You never were... You're a Spatial Class Supernova user," Ben continued, sighing and closing his eyes. "You asked me about the mistake that brought me here. Well, I should've never allowed you to go to that laboratory."

Ethan couldn't help but interject, "If you didn't want me to go, why did you tell me?"

"Because when we went, you already knew where to go in my timeline. I assume it's because I told you at this moment," Ben groaned, his frustration evident. "I think your Code is the key for me to go home." The weight of each pause seemed to stretch into eternity for Ethan.

Ben pressed on, "And I also told you because you're exactly what Libertas is seeking to achieve their goal."

"What is Libertas' goal, Ben?" Ethan reached down and shook him gently. Ben stayed silent for a moment, then he gripped Ethan's wrists tightly, opening his eyes—orange eyes that indicated something was amiss.

"My head... it's pounding," Ben muttered, clutching at his forehead.

"Are you all right, Ben?" Ethan's concern was palpable.

"Enough talking, Ethan. I've given you the answers you wanted. Now, send me home!" Ben's eyes flashed with anger and distress. He swung a fist at Ethan, who stumbled backward to create some distance between them. Both of them stood back up, tension crackling between them.

"I tried everything. But if you can do it there, then you can do it here!" Ben's words were laced with desperation as Ethan took cover behind a nearby evergreen tree, trying to comprehend the situation unfolding before him.

Ben's punch struck a tree with immense force, causing it to snap and tumble aside. The atmosphere grew dense and oppressive, a palpable danger lingering in the air. Ethan struggled to grasp the implications of Ben's actions. As more trees fell, Ethan sought refuge behind another one, his mind racing to understand.

Ben cried out, nursing his gray-colored fist, his abilities showing signs of strain. Ethan glanced at his own hands, which remained unaffected. Perhaps this was a limitation of Ben's copied power. Ethan's attention then turned to his AICI, realizing it was broken, leaving him cut off from Gallium's assistance.

Ben's behavior grew more erratic as he started hitting his own head. His words were tinged with frustration and desperation. "Ethan, things have spiraled out of control. I've been stuck here for too long, and I've done things I can't even speak of to reach this point. But damn it, what's one more?" Ben's expression darkened, his fiery orange eyes appearing almost sinister. Ethan cautiously moved further back behind an evergreen tree, seeking shelter.

"Why did you have to lose your necklace, man? I could've left months ago!" Ben's voice echoed through the area, his frustration evident.

Ethan muttered to himself, "Why didn't you take it then?"

Ben surveyed the surroundings, taking in the peaceful sight of the floating academy above them, the reality of the hundreds of kidnapped students hidden from view. The crystal blue lake shimmered to the side, a stark contrast to the grim scene unfolding. Fireflies illuminated the area with their soft yellow glow, and a light mist of rain began to fall, Ethan wiping it from his face. The pine trees offered some scant cover, though there was no escaping the gravity of the situation. Ethan realized that he was on his own, left to confront this unsettling encounter by himself.

"What do you mean?" Ethan's voice trembled as he stepped back from behind the evergreen tree. Confusion and disbelief mingled in his expression. "Ben, we're friends. What are you suggesting?" He placed his hands against the rough bark, using the tree as his only shield. He cautiously peeked around to observe Ben's actions.

"You're not my friend Ethan. It's not like I actually need you...but if I kill you, would I finally be able to go home?" Ben's words were unsettling, carrying a mix of curiosity and desperation. He moved closer to the tree Ethan was hiding behind, pounding his chest and then his head.

"I just want to go home. I should have listened to Kira," Ben muttered, his tone laced with regret and frustration. His eyes darted around as if struggling to find a solution to his turmoil.

Ethan's heart sank as he observed the turmoil in Ben's demeanor. What could have led him to such a state? The Ben he knew wasn't cold or deranged. Ethan found himself torn between the incredibility of Ben's claims and the actions he was witnessing. It seemed that his friend was genuinely grappling with this twisted reality.

As Ben charged forward, his hand raised, Ethan felt a wave of crushing force descend upon him. The ground buckled and cracked under immense pressure, sending Ethan to his knees. The tree he had been using as cover groaned and snapped, tumbling aside as if bowing to the immense power.

"You haven't learned how to use your gravity yet," Ben's voice held a strange mix of relief and urgency. He stepped over the wreckage of broken branches and trees, his demeanor almost manic.

"If Supernovae are extinct, how did you copy it?" Ethan's voice was laced with frustration and desperation as he ducked behind another tree.

Ben peered around another tree, his expression filled with a strange mixture of exasperation and condescension. "Come on, Ethan, you're smarter than that. I obviously got it from you!" With a powerful gesture, he crushed the tree in front of him. The shockwave sent Ethan tumbling backward onto the ground, sharp branches cutting into his skin.

"Unfortunately, I haven't had much time to practice. Mistakes were certainly made." Ben's voice carried a hint of regret as he continued to manipulate the environment around them. Ethan took a deep breath, his eyes flickering to a shade of gray as he stood up once more, determination etched across his features.

Ben sprang into action, unleashing a barrage of gravitational forces aimed at Ethan. Each impact rocked the area, sending debris flying and the ground shaking. Ethan clenched his fists, his mind racing as he struggled to come up with a plan to counter Ben's overwhelming power.

A wave of dark black and white energy relentlessly pounded Ethan, forcing him back down onto the unforgiving ground. He gritted his teeth, determined to endure the relentless barrage of attacks. Each impact reverberated through his body, the sound reminiscent of creaking floorboards in an old house. But amidst the chaos, he knew he needed to grasp the essence of his Code. What had Professor Alice always taught them? There had to be some lesson, some technique he could use to counter Ben's overwhelming power. Ethan's life hung in the balance, and he couldn't afford to falter.

Straining against the onslaught, Ethan fought to lift his head, his vision blurred from the assault. The field of black and white energy continued to crush him down, threatening to snuff out his resistance. Through the chaos, he glimpsed Ben, relentless in his onslaught, his face a mixture of determination and desperation.

Summoning every ounce of his willpower, Ethan managed to turn his gaze skyward. There, beyond the swirling energies, he saw the night sky adorned with countless stars. The sight triggered a memory, a lesson from one of his recent classes. He clung to that memory, hoping it held the key to turning the tide of this battle.

***

In a classroom, Professor Alice stood before a mixed group of Brute and Spatial Class students, her gray robes a somber reflection of the topic at hand. Her eyes moved over each face, her expression grave.

"Today, I shall take you through a crucial chapter of our history—the Great Spatial Class War," she began, her tone carrying the weight of the past. The holographic display behind her projected images of war-ravaged landscapes – a stark reminder of the conflict's devastation.

Ethan sat in his seat, flanked by Cassidy and Felix. Across the room, Skylar and Austin's hostile stares bore into him, an unadorned reminder of the divisions that still lingered.

"This war was the most violent in our history, born from a dispute among the three subtypes of the Spatial Class," Professor Alice explained, her voice holding a mix of sorrow and determination. The holograms showed scenes of destruction, buildings reduced to rubble, and craters scarred into the Earth.

"The Supernova, who held authority over space exploration, rebelled against the existing order," Professor Alice continued. "They believed that we should abandon our planet in search of a new home. The other two subtypes, however, saw this differently."

Ethan leaned forward, engrossed in the history lesson. The idea that the Spatial Class had faced such internal strife was both surprising and unsettling.

"Supernova users possessed the ability to manipulate gravity and, in certain circumstances, even control sustainable black holes," Professor Alice revealed, her words drawing audible gasps from the class. "This power was a double-edged sword, capable of tremendous creation and destruction."

The class listened intently, the implications sinking in. Ethan's mind raced as he processed the information.

Could this forgotten knowledge be the key to facing Ben's overwhelming power?

"If they had succeeded in using that black hole to travel to another planet, it would have obliterated our own," Professor Alice explained, her words carrying a weight of historical significance. "Rumors suggest they came close to achieving their goal, but they had a critical vulnerability. Their power was weakest during the daytime when the stars weren't present."

Ever the provocateur, Skylar aimed a ball of paper at Ethan's head, sparking laughter from the class. Professor Alice swiftly intervened, reprimanding the class for their behavior and steering the lesson back on track.

"Their connection to the stars was unparalleled, which is why they were named Supernova," she continued, unaware of the undertones her words carried. "The decision to execute all Supernova users was a response to their attempt to alter the fate of our planet."

As she spoke, a subtle shift occurred in the room's atmosphere. The casual resentment towards Spatial Class Elites, already present in some students, seemed to deepen. It was a small moment, easily missed by the professor's well-intentioned teaching.

Professor Alice's voice turned nostalgic. "Despite the consequences, it's said that Supernova users experienced an unparalleled sense of freedom. They could simply feel the stars around them and let go. Flying among the stars must have been a breathtaking sensation."

Feel the stars around you and let go.

***

In the midst of his brutal confrontation with Ben, Ethan's body throbbed with pain. The onslaught of attacks seemed unending, and Ethan struggled to withstand the relentless force of his own Code being turned against him.

Drawing on his fragmented memory of Professor Alice's class, he closed his eyes and focused inward. He blocked out the sounds of battle and envisioned himself on his Hoverbike, soaring through the night sky surrounded by stars. The sensation of freedom, the wind against his face, and the vast expanse of the cosmos merged into a single, vivid image.

With a deep breath, Ethan opened his gray eyes and faced Ben. A cry of agony escaped Ben's lips, his gray hands trembling. He glanced down at his own hands as if they were the source of his suffering. Yet even in his pain, Ben persisted, sending waves of gravitational energy toward Ethan.

Ben knew that if Ethan managed to grasp the essence of his Code, there might be no stopping him in the darkness of night. It was a race against time, a battle of wills and abilities that would determine the outcome of this otherworldly clash.

Ethan extended his left hand toward Ben, his grip intent on immobilizing him. He noticed the color returning to his own hand. Drawing on his understanding of Supernova's gravitational abilities, he devised a plan to counter Ben's movements. If gravity was the key, then he had to find a way to control it against Ben.

His right hand touched the swirling black and white energy enveloping him, involuntarily absorbing it into his being. Ethan's perception of the world shifted as everything took on a surreal purple static hue. The spatial outlines of objects seemed to glow, and the stars blazed with an intensity he had never witnessed before.

With a newfound sense of power, Ethan imagined the force required to manipulate Ben's body size. Raising his arms and focusing his energy, he released a wave of black and white energy that ensnared Ben, freezing him in place. A sense of exhilaration washed over Ethan as he gazed at the energy emanating from his hands, realizing the depth of his abilities.

Ben's agonized howl cut through the air. "You're already this skilled at gravity manipulation?" His eyes flamed orange, reflecting his pain and frustration, yet he remained immobilized. "But it won't change a thing, Ethan. No matter how powerful you become, it won't alter who you are."

Ben's words grated on Ethan's nerves. "Shut up already!" he snapped.

Raising his hand, Ethan propelled Ben skyward with the surging energy, then sent him crashing back to the ground. He was beginning to grasp the intricate nuances of gravity manipulation, the power flowing through him like second nature.

The atmosphere felt different, as if Ethan's perception had expanded to encompass everything around him. He twisted his hand, creating a static-like force that brought Ben closer to him. As they stood face-to-face, the orange flames of hatred danced in Ben's eyes, mirroring the enmity Ethan had seen in other Elites.

Was this the same hatred he had faced before? Had he made a mistake? Why did Ben loathe him so intensely? Questions buzzed in Ethan's mind, his determination wavering. Clenching his teeth, he implored, "Ben, just tell me what I did wrong. Talk to me!" Ben writhed and struggled, his attempts to fight off Ethan's hold proving futile against the crushing pressure of the black static energy surrounding him.

"You're trapped, Ben. This is my domain now," Ethan taunted, his fist poised firmly in Ben's direction. He watched with satisfaction as Ben struggled against the invisible gravitational force that held him. "It's a choice between you and me, and I've made mine! They need me to return!"

Ethan's vision abruptly snapped back to its usual state, catching him off guard as Ben managed to break free from his gravitational grip. In an instant, Ben lunged forward, charging up Ethan's Code for a final desperate attack.

Ethan stood his ground, raising his fist to intercept Ben's assault. His voice echoed with urgency, a mixture of anger and concern. "Ben, stop this madness before it's too late! Don't do something you'll regret!"

But Ben's resolve was unyielding. "You arrogant bastard!" he retorted, his energy colliding with Ethan's in a blinding burst of black and white. The force unleashed obliterated the surrounding trees, tearing the ground asunder.

Amid the chaos, Ben winced as his arm shattered under the overwhelming pressure. The pain was excruciating, and he struggled to maintain his grip on the energy. Meanwhile, Ethan channeled all his power into his Code, pushing Ben back with the sheer strength of his attack. The impact sent shockwaves through Ben's body, leaving him battered and reeling.

Summoning his last ounces of strength, Ben launched himself through the air at Ethan, intent on delivering a final blow. Ethan readied himself, closing his fist to immobilize Ben once again. But this time, something was amiss. The energy he tried to command remained trapped within his hand, refusing to respond.

Realization dawned on Ethan too late as Ben hurtled towards him. Desperation gripped his heart, but he couldn't control his newfound power. With a gut-wrenching thud, Ethan's fist plunged into Ben's stomach, the force of the impact jolting them both.

Their eyes reverted to their normal states, shock and disbelief clouding their features. Ethan gasped as the gravity of what he had just done hit him. The choice was ripped from his hands, and he could only watch in horror as Ben looked down at his hands in resignation. The release of Ethan's grip allowed Ben to slump to the ground, clutching his stomach in agony.

"I'm sorry, I'm so sorry!" Ethan's voice trembled with fear and regret as he collapsed to his knees, his arms shielding his head from the unfathomable consequences of his actions.

Exhausted, Ethan sank to his knees, grappling with the weight of his actions. Would this have repercussions for his own Ben?

"I don't have time, Benjamin! Tell me, what is their goal? What do they want with me?" Ethan's voice trembled with desperation as he reached out his hand, only to recoil at the sight of Ben's blood. He lowered his trembling hand, unable to control the shaking.

Crawling away from Ben, Ethan turned his face away in horror. He attempted to wipe the blood off his hand on what little grass remained. "Why did you force me into this?" he muttered, anguish evident in his tone. Clutching his blood-stained hand to his chest, he slammed his fist onto the ground, his agony echoing in the air.

The situation was overwhelming. Nothing was adding up. Why was the school under attack? How did he possess an extinct Code ability? The Supernova Class had been eradicated by a civil war over a century ago, so how was this possible? Ethan's mind raced with unanswered questions, his desire for escape growing stronger.

Ben's labored breathing cut through the chaos. He stared at Ethan's back, appearing to have regained his composure. "Don't... go to that lab," he managed to utter.

Ethan turned back towards Ben, his face a portrait of torment. Dark particles swarmed over his arms, legs, and feet, dispersing into the wind. The ominous sight held an eerie familiarity.

"This again," Ben remarked, observing the particles with a solemn gaze.

Ethan averted his gaze from Ben, his tears mingling with the grass beneath him. He felt as if he couldn't face his friend, even if this version of Ben wasn't truly his friend.

"Stop crying, Ethan. Look at me. Hurry before I'm pulled back," Ben's strained voice urged.

Reluctantly, Ethan raised his head to meet Ben's gaze. Ben took a slow, steadying breath before continuing, "Imagine mentally going back in time but being physically trapped. That's what this is." His somber eyes locked onto Ethan's, filled with understanding. "I've been stuck here for months, but for me, it's only been a matter of seconds."

Ethan's confusion deepened. "What do you mean? I don't understand. What's happening to you right now?" His voice trembled, mirroring the uncertainty and fear that gnawed at his core.

"War, Ethan. A war is coming. I needed your necklace to help prevent it. That's why I'm here," Ben explained, his words punctuated by a cough.

"No, I mean physically. Kira said this was impossible. So how am I able to physically interact with you?" Ethan's voice quivered, a mixture of hope and trepidation in his eyes.

"My body is still physically there, right where I left," Ben explained, his tone carrying a note of urgency.

Ethan furrowed his brow, struggling to comprehend. "What do you mean?" His confusion only deepened, a swirl of thoughts and questions overwhelming his mind.

Ethan retraced the conversation in his head. Did Ben mention something about his necklace? And what was this impending war he spoke of? The influx of information left Ethan overwhelmed and struggling to process it all.

"It's actually quite simple—" Ben's voice trailed off as a massive explosion rocked the area. Heat surged through the air, and Ethan's head snapped around to locate the source of the chaos.

The once serene Academy campus had shattered into pieces. A chilling wave of horror swept over Ethan as he watched one large section hurtle downward, crashing toward the lake nearby. Another piece plummeted straight down, the screams of students and parents echoing within the collapsing structure.

Panic enveloped the scene as fragments of the academy splintered apart, scattering debris in every direction. Ethan's heart pounded in his chest as he stood frozen in disbelief, his mind struggling to process the devastation before him.

As chaos reigned, Ethan realized he was in imminent danger. His fear was palpable as he recognized that a portion of the school was hurtling straight toward him. Stumbling backward, he lost his balance and fell, his body overwhelmed by shock and fear.

In that heart-stopping moment, Ethan recalled that Ben was behind him. With a quick movement of his head, he looked back to see the last remnants of the dark particles fading into the wind. The future version of Benjamin had vanished, leaving behind a trail of unanswered questions and uncertainty.

The weight of it all crashed down on Ethan as he lay on the ground, the world around him in chaos. The sky was filled with debris, and the once-stately academy was now a shattered memory. As sirens wailed in the distance, Ethan could only watch, his mind whirling, his thoughts consumed by the enigmatic encounter he had just experienced.

About The Author

Jonathan grew up in Stroudsburg, PA, where, after spending his time reading fiction books in school, such as the Alex Rider series or The Mortal Instruments series, he discovered a passion for creating world-altering fiction stories himself.

This book, Code, is his debut in the dystopian fiction-writing world. Currently working on Glitch, the second book in the Elite Prodigies series, while making time to play with his Shiba Inu, Akamaru, and work.